WARNING

THE COMPLETE SERIES

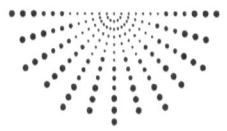

A. D. JUSTICE

Cover photo licensed by DepositPhoto

Cover design by Designs by Dana

Edited by Lisa A. Hollett with Silently Correcting Your Grammar

WARNING: PART ONE

Warning
Part One

Jillian Hart didn't belong in our world. She was an innocent, blinded to our ways and seduced by the charm of the mafia. I was a capo in the Marchetti Family, groomed to take control one day, and my father was the Boss, the Don. Damon Marchetti was a well-known name in the mafioso.

We never would've crossed paths if not for a fender bender with the wrong truck on the expressway. After escorting her to the emergency room as a precaution, I discovered she had business ties to a rival family. Simply being seen with me put her in jeopardy, so I kept her close for her own safety.

But one thing led to another, and she became more than my charge. I gave her one warning about my life. One chance to decide to stay or leave. She chose to stay.

Until all hell broke loose.

Then my ever-present alter ego took control, and I pushed too hard.

If she thought I gave up easily when the chips were down, she had another warning coming.

CHAPTER ONE

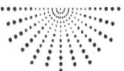

Damon

"Any last words?" With a quick click of the slide, a round was chambered, and the gun was ready to fire.

"Damon, I didn't betray you. Please don't do this," Milo begged from his position on his knees. He was an associate, not exactly part of the family, but someone we'd trusted to work for us. He broke that trust. So, I had to fucking break him. There was no going back once trust was broken. "You know I'm loyal to the Marchetti family."

Without further conversation, I put the gun against his forehead and pulled the trigger. Only cowards shoot a man in the back of the head. If a man deserved to die, he also deserved to be looked square in the eye so he had no doubt who pulled the trigger. In Milo's case, this low-level associate tipped off the firm's management about us dipping our fingers into the nurses' union benefit plan fund. I suspected this particular snitch worked for the Sanfratello family, our most active rival, and double-crossed us for them. But there were still a few loose ends to tie off before I could put a lid on that problem.

"Damon, we have a situation." Benny, my first level soldier and trusted driver, scraped a hand down his face while pocketing his phone with his other.

"What the fuck happened now?"

"Two of your guys were moving goods on the expressway and hit another car. The other driver insisted on calling the police. They're in the dump truck."

"What is it with this fucking day? Let's go see what those two idiots have done."

We left the dead snitch for the cleanup crew to dispose of his body while we maneuvered through traffic until we reached the crash site. Benny opened my door and I stepped out, quickly assessing the situation and sizing up the scene. Our dump truck sideswiped another car, leaving enough visible damage to negate any reasonable doubt.

Some petite brunette looker stepped into my line of sight, followed by an NYPD traffic cop. He looked up at me, and recognition lit in his eyes. With the traffic noises, I couldn't hear what they were saying, but I saw him pull her aside, leaving his partner alone to deal with my associates. One look from me and both of my guys knew I'd deal with them later, and those cops couldn't save them from what awaited them. After a couple of minutes, the brunette and the other cop joined us in mid-discussion about the damage.

The closer she got, the smaller she became. In four-inch heels, the top of the beauty's head barely reached my shoulder. The waves of her long brown hair framed her face, highlighting her emerald green eyes that gave away her every thought and feeling. Though petite, her legs were toned with feminine muscles.

"She can still drive the car. It doesn't even need a tow truck. It's fine," Luigi, my associate, argued.

"Look, I already told you. We got dispatched out here to work this wreck. The lady says she needs the police report, I gotta write the report. There's no way around it," Officer Ryan explained the procedure to my other associate, Paulie.

"I'm really sorry to do this," she offered. Though she was surrounded by big, burly men, she didn't shrink away. She stood her ground with a mixture of poise and respect. "I'm here for a few months on business, and this isn't my car—it's a company car. If I don't turn in the police report, I'll lose my job. I'd be more than willing to leave the insurance and police out of it if I could, but I can't afford to lose my job. I hope you understand."

Luigi spoke up. "Lady, all you had to say was you didn't know what happened. Someone in the parking garage must've hit it."

"There are security cameras in the parking garage. Besides, I'm not going to lie about it."

"Shit, lady," Luigi huffed.

"That's enough." I cut my eyes at him, and he immediately got the message. I took a step toward the beauty and purposely flashed her a reassuring smile. "I'm Damon Marchetti. And you are?"

"I'm Jillian Hart." She offered me her hand to shake, but I turned it and placed a soft kiss on her knuckles.

"Are you injured, Jillian? Anything hurt or sore?" I took a half step back and looked her up and down. For both my own pleasure and to inspect her for injuries.

"No, I'm fine. Just a little shaken up."

"I'll escort you to the emergency room and have you checked out to be sure. I insist."

She chanced a look at the cop she'd been talking to privately, and he gave a slight nod of approval. "It's really not necessary. I don't want to be any trouble."

"You're no trouble at all. Think nothing of it. I'll take care of everything. No need to worry." My gaze drifted to the two cops, who shifted nervously under my watch.

"Thank you for understanding. I really appreciate it." A warm, genuine smile I seldom saw in my line of work lit up her face. "Okay, then, should I just follow you to the hospital?"

"My mother would have my head if she found out I let you drive yourself to the hospital, in a damaged car no less. You can ride with me. Luigi will follow us in your car to ensure it's safe for you to drive later—after the doctor has cleared you."

"Such a gentleman," she said when I opened the back door of my car for her. After I slid in beside her, she continued. "Your mother must have raised you right."

"You're definitely not from around here, are you?" I found myself smiling at her in return, something I rarely did outside of the company of my immediate family.

"How'd you guess?" She laughed, her eyes twinkling with amusement.

"That accent gives you away. Louisiana, isn't it?"

"Exactly. New Orleans. Have you ever been?"

"No, unfortunately, New Orleans is one city that's never been on my itinerary. Seems I'll have to remedy that."

She dropped her head, her long hair falling forward to partially cover her face. Modest. Beautiful, but she didn't know it. Sexy, but she didn't flaunt it. Confident and professional, but not pretentious. Sweet and sassy, without being bitchy. This little beauty seemed to be the perfect package.

"You should really come down for Mardi Gras. The biggest party of the year."

"I'm not much of one for crowds or big parties," I replied and her smile faded. "Unless you'll be there."

Her dazzling smile returned. "I go every year. Usually with several girlfriends, but if you make the trip to NOLA, I'll give you the VIP tour."

"It's a date. You can count on it."

In my mind, I'd already claimed her as mine. The second I'd stepped out of the car and saw her standing there, I decided she'd be mine. The trip to the hospital was standard protocol in the family—leaving no stone unturned and no way for an injury to come back and bite us in the ass later. But when she got into my car, that was an intentional move. She'd be seen with me, and everyone would know to leave her alone or they'd face my wrath for messing with what was mine.

On their knees in an abandoned building with a gun pressed to their forehead.

On sight, everyone associated in any way with me, good or bad, would know I'd staked a claim on her. She was protected by a powerful family that took shit off no one.

But she was naïve to the ways of my world. She had no idea how our businesses operated, what our men were instructed to do to succeed, or what it would mean for her future when she agreed to join me. She would be warned and given one chance to walk away forever. But she had to get to know me first. That was the extent of my grand scheme—find a way to spend time with her, make her fall for me, then spring my occupation on her, and convince her to stay.

Piece of cake.

We walked through the emergency doors, my hand splayed across the small of her back. Possession is nine-tenths of the law, and I was leaving no doubts to the prying eyes that always lurked about. The nurse at the triage desk didn't even bother looking up at us when we approached.

"She's been in a vehicle accident. I need to have her checked out."

With a bored sigh and barely acknowledging us, the nurse picked up a clipboard and thrust it at me. "Fill these out, bring them back, have a seat, and we'll call you when we're ready for you."

"I don't think you understand me."

Her angry eyes flew up to meet mine, ready to fight, until she realized who I was. "I'm so sorry. I'll escort you to an exam room right now."

7

Jillian watched the exchange with a confused expression, then her gaze drifted around the waiting room full of patients who'd been there longer. The nurse jumped up from her seat, rushed around the counter, and opened the secure door to the bustling emergency room. The nurse settled Jillian into an exam room, and I waited outside the door until the doctor finished examining her. After several minutes, he reemerged to update me on her care.

"She's fine. No injuries, not even soft tissue. She seemed more nervous about explaining the damage to her company car than anything."

"Thanks, Doc. I'll take care of the car, and you know where to send the bill."

"Have a good one, Damon."

Jillian stepped into the hallway and glanced up at me shyly. "Dr. Falco said I'm fine and can go now. Is my car safe to drive?"

I could've made up any number of lies about her car and she'd have been none the wiser, but something in her trusting eyes wouldn't let me. "It is, but I have a guy who can fix the damage, and no one will ever know it was there. You'll have your police report if you ever need it, but I promise you won't."

She hesitated for a moment. "Does your friend own a car repair shop or something?"

"Yes, a body shop. He can make anything look brand-new again. Luigi can drop it off today, and it'll be ready for you in a couple of days max."

"All right, if you're sure. A couple of days of taking a cab to work won't hurt me."

She wrapped her fingers around my extended arm and walked through the hospital corridor close to my side. "No one said anything about you taking a cab back and forth every day. My driver will be at your disposal when I'm working. If I'm available, I'll be the one at your beck and call."

The reasons behind my offer weren't selfless. In my line of

work, trust was a rare commodity. Since I didn't know her or her family, I wasn't about to put blind faith in her that she'd keep her mouth shut. Whether I took her to work or my driver did, we'd know who she worked for, her whereabouts, and her daily patterns. Every piece of information could help in the future. Better to have the information and not need it than get caught with my dick in my hand and my pants around my ankles.

CHAPTER TWO

Damon

hen she rattled off her address, my suspicions were immediately aroused, and I knew I was right to keep her close. There was more to her story than she told, I was sure of it.

"Very nice building. Private garage, a doorman and concierge desk, a private gym with a swimming pool. Where do you work?" I watched her carefully for any signs of uneasiness.

"I'm a consultant with Morgan and Bartholomew out of New Orleans. I'm staying in one of their corporate apartments. Since I'm here for several months working with a client, it's more economical for me to live in their apartment than to put me up in a hotel. And it's more like home than a hotel room. It's a beautiful place—I *wish* I could afford it on my own."

Her self-deprecating laugh was genuine. And charming.

"What exactly does a consultant do?"

"For this client, I'm setting up process improvements for their entire Human Resources department, including their compensation and benefits systems. Sometimes they just need a fresh pair of eyes to evaluate their current protocols. Different clients have different needs, though most everything I'm involved with is process improvement."

"Interesting. Who's the client?" I kept pressing for information under the guise of conversation, but she didn't seem to mind.

"Blaine Financial Services." My expression gave away my thoughts for the first time since I was a kid and learned to keep my poker face intact. "What's wrong? Is there something I should know about them?"

"No, nothing like that. They're fine. I used to be friends with someone who worked there, and we didn't part on the best of terms. No need for you to worry about it though. That's old news."

The car stopped in front of her building, and my driver jumped out to open the door. I had the distinct impression she didn't want to part with my company just then, and I wasn't ready to let her go either.

"I've taken up so much of your time with my drama, and you've done so much for me. Not to seem forward, but would you like to come up? I'll make dinner, and we can eat in tonight. Unless you're married or have a girlfriend? Oh my God, I should've asked that first. You probably think I'm a terrible person."

Another genuine smile broke free across my face. "Take a breath, Jillian. I'm not married. No girlfriend. And I'd love to have dinner with you. But since it was one of my trucks that hit you and sent you to the hospital, I wouldn't feel right allowing you to cook for me."

"Your truck didn't send me to the hospital," she countered with a flirty smile. "*You* did. I'm perfectly fine, and I'd like to repay your kindness."

"Fair enough. By all means, lead the way." The company was one thing, but the open invitation into her private life was better than one I could've orchestrated.

Once we were inside, her apartment was much what I expected from this building. Large and spacious, two floors, and with all the deluxe amenities half the people in this city would kill to have. No one moves directly into a three-bedroom apartment on 79th Street in New York City without having powerful connections. My initial thought was either she came from money or she came here under an offer of a way to make a lot of money quickly. I'd have my people check out the corporation-owning-the-apartment explanation first thing in the morning.

"Can I get you something to drink?"

"Beer?"

She popped the top on a longneck bottle and handed it to me. "Make yourself at home while I start dinner."

A slow perusal through the furnished rooms revealed little of her life. The decorations were obviously already there when she moved in. None of her personal pictures were anywhere to be found. Any information I gleaned about her would have to be obtained the old-fashioned way—a combination of charm and spying. When I made it back around to the kitchen, I found her cooking and singing. She was naïvely oblivious to the dangers she'd subjected herself to by inviting a strange man into her apartment then turning her back on him.

Especially a man like me.

"Jillian, how long have you been here?"

"About two weeks now. I'm still trying to get my bearings of which way is uptown, downtown, midtown, side-town." She grinned broadly after the last, letting me know she was teasing. "Have you always lived here?"

"Yes, I have, so take this warning seriously. There are a lot of bad men who would love to do awful things to you. Inviting strange men up to your apartment and turning your back on them is a good way to become a negative statistic."

"Are you saying you're a bad man?" The expression on her face was both challenging and questioning.

"I have my moments."

"So, let me get this straight. You insisted I get checked out at the hospital after a minor fender bender, just to later murder me in my apartment while I'm cooking your dinner?" She quirked one eyebrow up at me. "That doesn't sound like a very smart plan, if you ask me."

"Why is that?"

"Because you've been seen with me by too many people. You're on security cameras at the hospital and walking into my building. There's no way you'd get away with it. So, it only makes sense that you're here for the food and the company." She crossed her arms over her chest, confident in her assessment.

She clearly had no idea how those of us who worked outside the confines of the law could make evidence disappear with a flash of green.

"Interesting theory. But don't put it to the test again. You don't know what men are capable of doing."

"Yes, sir." She saluted and turned back to the stove.

I had to adjust my cock at the sound of her sweet voice calling me sir. So many erotic scenes flooded my mind. I didn't trust her, but that didn't mean I wouldn't fuck her.

After eating, I played the grateful guest and helped her with the dishes. "I should go, but let me see your phone first." She handed it over without question, and I dialed my number. "Now you can reach me anytime." We agreed on a time for her morning transportation, and I left with the promise to see her the following day.

Jillian

The front desk called up to my apartment to let me know my ride had arrived. When I exited the building, I was surprised to find Damon leaned up against his car, waiting for me with a smug smile. The man was so damn sexy, without even trying to be.

When he first stepped out of his car on the expressway the day before, he stole my breath. The air around us changed, and every eye snapped toward him, watching his every move. His presence commanded attention before he spoke a single word. But when he spoke, he left no doubt about who dominated the scene. He had a hint of an Italian accent mingled with the classic New York style, giving the deep timbre of his voice a sexy edge to it. I was hesitant to get in his car for the ride to the hospital, but the slight nod from the cop reassured me.

That same cop had pulled me aside and warned me about the men who surrounded me, cautioning me to take care when dealing with them. Without revealing too much, he relayed they were not the type anyone should disrespect. Provided they were cordial to me, he said I should respond in kind. Then Damon was so nice to me and seemed genuinely concerned for my health, the cop's warning felt out of place and contradictory to Damon's personality.

That morning, he stood before me in his custom-tailored suit that fit his physique perfectly, dark brown hair with intermittent lighter strands, and those deep chocolate brown eyes that were both perceptive and engaging. The only warning I felt was the fluttering of excitement low in my belly.

"Good morning." His sultry voice beckoned me with a simple greeting. With my thirtieth birthday fast approaching, I shouldn't have been affected by him to that degree. I'd dated, been in long-term relationships, and had a couple of one-night stands along the way. But he made me feel completely inexperienced. "You are simply stunning. Maybe you should quit your job and come work for me instead. You'll give me extra incentive to go into the office every day."

"You are quite the charmer, Mr. Marchetti. What line of work are you in, by the way?"

"I own a commercial construction business. I handle the contracts and bids for jobs, while my crew of engineers and foremen oversee the worksites." He stepped to the side, opened the passenger door for me, then strode around to the driver's side. While watching him walk, I noticed a few other women stop in their tracks to stare at him the same way I did—with deep desire. The expressions on their faces were obvious—they hoped he'd glance in their direction. When he didn't, they moved on, disappointed but no less interested.

My smile remained in place when he slid behind the steering wheel and cranked the car. "What are you grinning about?" He finally cut his eyes at me over his shoulder, barely turning his head in my direction. "Don't think I didn't notice."

"You didn't notice the three women on the sidewalk who would kill for a just a glance from you. They were begging you to throw them a bone."

He threw his head back and laughed. "That's not entirely true. I noticed them watching me, working hard to get my attention. I just have no interest in giving any of them a bone of any kind."

"I kind of felt sorry for them. You didn't even flash them a smile."

One side of his mouth lifted in amusement. "Jillian, I'm afraid you're a little too soft-hearted to be in this city. You need to remember any one of those women would've killed *you* to sit where you're sitting right now."

"Does that mean you're dangerous to my safety and well-being?" I asked playfully. Maybe more than a little flirty.

That question garnered a wide smile. "That is a guarantee, doll." We stopped at a red light, and he looked straight into my eyes. "But you have nothing to worry about as long as you're with me. Anyone who's after you would have to go through me first, and that won't happen."

With our eyes connected, I felt something tangible pass between us. The flicker of desire was followed by a silent acknowledgment that we both felt it, and the knowledge we would give in to the craving. My days in the Big Apple were numbered. But at that moment, I wanted Damon to fill my nights.

"What about when I'm not with you? My car will be fixed in a couple of days, and then you won't have any reason to chauffeur me around. What if a strange man comes to my apartment for dinner, only to try to kill me?"

He pulled up to the curb in front of my temporary assignment and put the car in park. When he cut his eyes at me, I saw a flash of something feral and dangerous in them. And exciting. "We're adults, so let's be frank with each other. I know you want me as much as I want you. But you should know something else about me. I don't share what's mine, and I've already decided you belong to me. If I've read you wrong in any way, tell me now."

"No, you haven't read me wrong at all." I was surprised I could reply at all. His blunt confession stole my breath and scrambled my brain.

"I'm glad to hear you say that. So that we're clear, no strange men will be in your apartment. If I catch a man in there, he won't live long enough to regret it."

"We're crystal clear."

He reached up and threaded his fingers through my hair then stroked my cheek with his thumb. "You're so damn beautiful. Call me when you're ready for me to pick you up, and I'll be here."

3

CHAPTER THREE

Damon

"I just dropped her off. I want to know who she talks to and what she talks about. Tell me who she interacts with and how her demeanor is around the office. It's too much of a coincidence that she also works there." I hung up and allowed one of my most trusted soldiers to do his job. He was already on the inside, making matters much easier all around.

The one point I could always count on when dealing with broads was every single one was susceptible to flattery. Whisper a simple compliment, say it sincerely, and she became instant putty in my hands every time. Jillian was no exception to the rule. In fact, she even seemed a little easier to romance than the local women. Time would tell if that was because she was truly innocent, or if she was trying her best to play me first.

The day dragged by while I waited for information from Percy, my soldier in the trenches beside her. I tried to focus on my crews and the money they brought in from their jobs, but I found myself checking my phone far more frequently than usual. I had my own work to do, but my ability to concentrate was nowhere to be found. At the end of the day when Percy finally called, I was irritated and angry over everything and nothing at all.

"Boss, I've listened to her phone calls all day, eavesdropped on her meetings, and ran a thorough background check on her. This girl isn't part of the Sanfratello family. She's squeaky clean. I'll keep monitoring her to make sure I didn't miss anything, but right now I'd bet my life on it."

I released a sigh of relief. At least Percy settled that doubt in my mind.

"But there's something else you need to know," he continued.

"Tell me."

"They know she's with you, and they're already watching her very closely. One of their capos, Lorenzo, was in here earlier and met with her. He played it cool, pretended he was stopping by to welcome her to the team. But he started getting into personal questions about husbands or boyfriends, openly flirting with her and shit. When he left her office, he told his soldier to tail her when she gets off work to see if she meets you again."

"Thanks, Percy. Good work. I'll take it from here."

From Lorenzo's flirting and overt interest, I had no doubt the Sanfratellos were preparing to kill Jillian and remove her from the equation completely. If I picked her up after work, they would put out a hit on her, and their hitmen would most likely try to carry out the order before morning.

The problem was, she'd be in danger whether I showed or not. They'd approach her, coerce her to get close to me to gain valuable information, and use her as their informant. If she refused or was unable to help them, they'd kill her because they would've revealed too much of their plans to her.

Her company car was still in the body shop being repaired, but I could easily get out of chauffeuring her around. A quick phone call, a nonexistent excuse, and I'd be rid of the problem entirely.

Then I remembered her smile. Saw her face as plain as day.

"Motherfucker." I jumped up from my office chair and sent it flying across the floor in my wake. "I must be losing my fucking mind."

Minutes later, I maneuvered my car through the city streets. Block after block passed while I sped toward her. They'd know the moment I pulled up to the curb. There'd be no turning back if I didn't change my course right then. If she were with me when they made a move, it would ignite a war between the two families, and the casualties would be high.

But I didn't heed the warning blaring in my head.

"For fuck's sake. What the hell is wrong with me?"

Then I saw her standing on the sidewalk, waiting for me to whisk her away. When she saw my car, the same smile that captivated me the day before appeared. The dress she wore hugged her curves in all the right places, accentuating her best assets and drawing the eyes of every man who passed her. Desire and possession clashed inside me, followed by an uncertainty I hadn't felt before.

The desire was obvious. I'd wanted to fuck her until she was unable to stand on her shaky legs since the moment I saw her. Possession came easy—what was mine was mine. Period. But the possessiveness I felt when looking at her bordered on jealousy. I didn't like other men staring at her, thinking the same thoughts I had about her. They pictured her lips wrapped around their cock as she went down on them. They saw her on all fours when they fucked her from behind. They imagined her bent over, taking the punishing jabs that resulted in her screams of pleasure.

I knew exactly what their thoughts were, because I had the same thoughts about her.

When I brought my car to a halt, she slid into the passenger seat, and her sweet perfume wafted across the air, tempting me even more. "Hello, gorgeous. How was your day?"

"It was good but very busy. How was yours?"

"Fine. Except I couldn't get one beautiful Southern belle off my mind all day."

"You know, I'm kind of glad you had that problem."

"Are you now?" I quirked one eyebrow, throwing the flirting vibe back at her. "What kept you so busy today?"

"I started working on the retirement fund benefits, and I can already tell this part of the project will be a nightmare. From what I've seen, no one has actively managed the fund I'm assigned to in years."

"I'm sure you'll sort it out." I made a mental note to have Percy make sure she didn't unravel the trail. "I'm glad you had a good day."

"There was something strange that happened today, though." She scrunched up her face as she recalled what happened. "I've worked there for a couple of weeks now, but one of the senior directors came to my office today to personally welcome me to the team. I mean, I understand he's probably very busy, but I don't know why he decided to come to my office today and not when I first started."

"I couldn't even begin to guess," I lied. "Is that all he wanted? To welcome you to the team?"

"I guess. He asked about my life—if I was married, had a boyfriend, things like that. Then he left. Makes no sense."

"Maybe he saw you in the hallway and wanted to ask you out, so he was testing the waters with you."

She laughed and shook her head. "No, I doubt that. Men in high management positions like his would be too leery to proposition a subordinate. That could too easily set them up for a sexual harassment lawsuit, even if he asked respectfully."

I wanted to correct her. To tell her men like me didn't concern ourselves with petty threats of a lawsuit. To tell her the man she talked to wouldn't hesitate to fuck her then shoot her in the head while she slept in the same bed he'd just vacated. I wanted to warn her about these truths, but I couldn't without revealing myself too early.

The world was much different from her point of view than from mine.

"You're probably right. He's most likely just been busy and finally had a break in his schedule. You'll know soon enough if it's anything different." And I would know, too.

"Maybe. Anyway, thank you for picking me up. I feel like I'm such a burden—you have work to do too. I can take a cab back and forth tomorrow."

Why did it seem she was suddenly trying to get away from me?

"Already bored with my company, huh?"

"No, not at all. You've gone out of your way so much for me already. I feel guilty for taking advantage of your generosity."

"Doll, believe me, if I didn't want to be your chauffeur, I wouldn't be. I'm not afraid to say exactly what I think. And what I think is, I'm your driver again tomorrow."

"Okay. If you say so." She put her hand on my arm and gave it a light squeeze. "Thank you. I do appreciate what you're doing for me."

Checking the rearview mirror while driving was ingrained in me from my childhood. Our family members were taught to be extra vigilant about our surroundings at all times. After the same vehicle had followed me for several blocks, changing lanes and making rookie mistakes, I decided to test my paranoia. They tried to follow me on the first few turns I made, but I lost them when I doubled back on my route.

The game was afoot, however, and it wouldn't end anytime soon. Percy would have to find a reason to stick to Jillian like glue if she went back to work the next day. The rest of the night would determine that outcome. If they forced me to make an aggressive move, I'd have to tell her who I was sooner than I'd planned. If they were still in the recon phase, I'd hold out a while longer to see what I could find out about their end game.

Keeping the sexy woman at my side was a bonus, regardless of the reason.

"Where are we going? I know I've seen that same restaurant three times now."

"At first, I was driving you back to your apartment, but I decided to take you out to dinner instead. You cooked for me last night, so tonight is my treat." I hit the Bluetooth button and called Benny to arrange for him to meet us after dinner for the drive home.

As we walked into the exclusive restaurant in the Time Warner Center, she looked down at her attire and back up at me. "I'm not sure I'm dressed for this restaurant."

"You're perfect." With my hand on the small of her back, I guided her in, and we were seated immediately.

I ordered our wine and meals, and just as we engaged in conversation, a hush fell over the restaurant. When I looked up, I was surprised to see my father and his brother walking in. The Boss and Underboss of our family were known on sight by most people. The respect and fear they commanded were legendary. The goons that walked at their flanks and behind them were also unmistakable. When Dad saw me, he motioned for the soldiers to keep walking to their table.

I stood and greeted my father and uncle in the typical Italian family manner—a kiss on each cheek and a manly embrace. My father and my uncle were my mentors and were the two men I admired most in the world. "Father. Uncle Leo. It's good to see you both. Would you care to join us?"

My father, Vincenzo, smiled as he eyed Jillian. "I mean no disrespect by rejecting your offer, but I'd never interfere during your date with such a lovely young lady." He lifted Jillian's hand and softly kissed the back of her hand. "What is your name, pretty lady?"

"I'm Jillian Hart," she replied with a smile. "I can see where Damon gets his handsome looks."

"This one, you need to keep this one, Damon. I like her." Dad lifted one eyebrow when he spoke to me, issuing his unspoken command.

"Jillian, this is my uncle, Leo Marchetti."

Leo repeated my father's performance, pouring on the charm and making her face blush red with his compliments. The two men walked away to their table, leaving Jillian and me to chuckle over their blatant flirting.

"I love your dad and your uncle. They're so nice."

I almost choked on my sip of wine. No one had ever referred to them as *nice* before. Then again, I'd never witnessed them trying to be so good-natured with a stranger before her. She seemed to have a way with the Marchetti men. I made a mental note to keep her away from my brothers for as long as possible.

"Yeah, they're great. They seem especially impressed with you, too."

"Were you close to your father when you were a kid?"

"Our entire family has always been close. I have several brothers and one sister, so you can guess who got the special treatment." I laughed, recalling how my brothers and I harassed my sister when our parents were away. "She paid for it when they weren't around, though. We're still expected to show up for dinner every Saturday. We don't miss it without a good excuse. What about you? Brothers, sisters?"

She shook her head. "I'm an only child. My parents had me later in life, but I was very close to them both. My dad died two years ago. But I'm still close to my mom. We don't live too far apart, so I can check on her daily when I'm home."

"Must be hard on you both, losing your father."

"It was terrible. He seemed fine one minute, then a heart attack later, he was gone. My job is a challenge for both of us because I travel frequently. Mom's health has declined in recent years, and I actually thought I'd lose her before my dad. When I'm away, a home health nurse is with her during the day, and a sitter stays with her at night."

"That must be rough on you—shouldering all that responsibility alone."

She shrugged it off. "At least I still have my mom, and I can afford to hire the best caregivers. I have it better than a lot of people do."

We finished our dinners on lighter topics of conversation and rose to leave. My father and Uncle Leo were also finished, so Jillian and I walked out with them. Benny, my driver, had arrived and was talking to Joe, my father's driver, when we exited the building. The distinctive rumble of a car engine revving caught our attention just before Benny and Joe tackled us to the ground. Shots rang out, and bullets peppered the glass behind us, shattering it with a piercing clamor, before the car sped away.

When we began untangling arms and legs, I realized Benny had covered me, but I had instinctively covered Jillian. Cocooned in my arms, her whole body shook from distress and fright. "I've got you, Jillian. You're okay now."

She nodded but didn't speak, her teeth chattering from the adrenaline free-flowing through her veins. I stood and helped her up, my arms encircled her as she buried her face in my chest. My hands stroked up and down her back, soothing and assuring her she was safe.

My father met my livid gaze, his eyes burning with a mirrored vengeance. "Get her home. Leo and I will deal with this."

"Don't we have to give a statement too?" She stammered her question, though I knew she was looking for a way out of it. The last thing she wanted was to stay there.

"No, doll. My dad has a lot of friends in the police department. Once they have his and Uncle Leo's statements, they won't need ours." I walked her to the car and helped her into the back seat. "Stay here. I'll give my dad your number in case the police need to talk to you."

"Okay." The fear in her eyes was palpable, and she had a hard time releasing my hand.

"Benny, stand right here with her while I talk to my father."

Benny stepped into the open door and began talking to her about her job, trying to take her mind off the frightening event as best he could while he kept a constant vigil for her safety. I joined my father and Uncle Leo and explained everything that had happened up to that point, including the precarious position she'd be in at work the following day.

"Let her go to work. Percy will be there to protect her, if needed. We're not certain this attempt has anything to do with her yet, but we can't rule it out either. They've been making obvious moves, like they're taunting us. So, this could be related to something else. But if she changes her routine suddenly, they'll know, and then she *will* be in danger. We'll protect her for the time being, see if anyone makes another play. She should stay at your place tonight while we install extra security measures in her apartment."

"Yes, sir." I didn't argue with my father on business matters.

His word was final, and he was the Boss of our family for a reason. I'd learned that the hard way many years ago, when I was a punk teenager who thought I knew better than my old man. Taking Jillian to my home tonight definitely wasn't a hardship on me, though I wasn't sure how I'd convince her to spend the night with someone she'd just met the day before.

I slid into the back seat beside her and immediately recognized the signs of an imminent meltdown. Her bottom lip quivered, and her hands shook uncontrollably, even through the tight clasp she held them in. The shaking traveled throughout her whole body, from her arms and legs and through her torso. The warm and friendly smile that lit up her face was gone. Instead, her skin was pale, and her eyes were wide with fear, startling at the slightest sound. At the simple gesture of extending my arms out, she flew into my embrace.

"Damon?"

"Yeah, doll?"

27

"I can't stop shaking. Every time I close my eyes, I see the guns aiming at us all over again. Why would someone drive by and shoot at us like that?"

I gently pulled her away from me, but I kept my hands on her shoulders. With a heavy sigh, I leaned my forehead against hers. "Jillian, you deserve answers to set your mind at ease, but I can't give them. All I can do is ask you to trust me when I say my family won't rest until we find out who did this."

"I won't get a wink of sleep tonight. I can't even imagine how scared I'll be when I'm alone in that huge apartment." She stuttered her words through her chattering teeth, and I knew the opportunity I was looking for had just presented itself.

"You're coming home with me tonight. You won't be alone." I brushed my fingertips along her jaw.

"Are you sure you don't mind?" She didn't even hesitate to accept my offer. The fear that gripped her overrode any bout of modesty.

"Of course not."

"Am I sleeping with you? Or do you have a spare bedroom?"

"Doll, you're definitely sleeping with me, even though I have more than a few spare bedrooms."

"Don't tell your mom I asked that, though. Okay?"

I couldn't help but laugh over her request. "Okay, I won't tell my mom you asked to sleep with me. But can I tell her you forgot your pajamas and had to sleep naked?"

My attempt at humor helped, and she at least chuckled. "No, you can't tell her that either. She'll think I'm a terrible person."

"Doll, I'm a thirty-two-year-old grown man with older and younger brothers. My mother has no delusions that her sons are innocent little angels."

"That may be, but she's still your mother. She doesn't see you as a sexy, irresistible man."

"Irresistible, huh?" I looked down at her and wrapped my hand around the back of her neck. "Let's put that theory to the test."

4

CHAPTER FOUR

Jillian

When he slanted his mouth over mine, I was instantly lost in him. The panic that had taken up residence in my chest evaporated when his lips touched mine. The terrifying scenes of the drive-by shooting I just survived drifted to the back of my mind, while more invigorating visions took the forefront. His tongue swiped across the part in my lips, and I readily submitted control to him.

And he took it without hesitation.

I wanted nothing more than to forget everything that happened on that sidewalk and get lost in him. Was I using an unhealthy coping mechanism to avoid processing my true feelings? Definitely. Pretending I wasn't almost killed on the sidewalk of a busy street? Absolutely. My attempt to leave reality behind and let a handsome stranger take me home with him should've triggered a warning in my mind, but I was scared out of my wits, and he made me feel safe again.

Everything about the encounter was intoxicating. His scent. His tongue gliding along mine. His taste. The feel of his lips on mine. The way he held me in his arms. How he gripped my hair in his fist—possessive, dominant, daring. When he broke our kiss, my mind was hazy and my body was on fire. The way his hooded eyes darkened with desire when he looked at me obliterated any second thoughts I had.

"Take us by Miss Hart's apartment first, then we're going to Cooper Square, Benny."

I'd only met him the day before, but I had no intentions of applying the brakes. I felt the wind off those bullets when they buzzed past me. A hair's width difference and I would've been shot. A near-death experience gave me a new perspective on my career-driven life. I didn't want to die with a single regret, and if I passed up a night with Damon, regret would've been all I felt.

At that moment, I wanted nothing more than to surrender to his wishes, to give him all of me. After how he protected me during that terrifying incident and took care of me after they drove away, I thought maybe he was interested in more than a one-night stand. But if one night was all he gave me, I'd still happily take it. While I was in his arms, I hungrily accepted his kisses and caresses.

We separated when Benny pulled up outside my building and cleared his throat to get our attention. Damon extended his hand to help me out of the car, and we walked inside together. He entered my apartment first, keeping me behind him as he checked the rooms for intruders. When he was sure we were alone, I grabbed a small bag and threw everything I'd need for work the next day into it in record time.

We slid back into the back seat of his car, and our lips were again fused together after one heated look. When the car came to a stop again, Benny got out and opened the back door for us. I slid out behind Damon and looked up at the twelve-story brick building. I had no idea the unassuming outside would hold such opulence and luxury inside. We took a private elevator to the top of the building where Damon's condo encompassed three entire floors with expansive patios on each level.

As amazing as the entryway of the building was, it paled in comparison to the inside of his condo. Three floors of nothing but elegance and wealth, combined with the masculine air Damon projected naturally. The low lighting gave a stylish and romantic vibe. He removed his jacket and tie while I roamed around, taking in the enormous space.

Damon appeared behind me from nowhere. He wrapped his arms around my waist and pulled me tight against him, my back to his chest. He slid his arms up, crisscrossing over my chest while his lips left a scorching hot trail down the side of my neck. "You taste as good as you smell. I can't wait to taste you everywhere."

Chills ran down my spine and fanned out across my skin.

"I feel like I've waited a lifetime to get you alone."

His hands slid down to palm my breasts, kneading the swells and pinching my nipples between his thumb and forefinger. My head fell back to his chest, pushing them farther into his hands.

"Throughout dinner, all I could think about was how it'd feel to have your pussy wrapped around my cock."

A whimper escaped my throat.

"On the ride over here, it took all my willpower not to rip your panties off and fuck you in the back seat of my car, even though we weren't alone."

My breathing hitched. My arm reached up to the back of his neck. My hand cupped the back of his head. My fingers gripped his hair.

"Now that you're here, I'm about ten seconds away from wringing your body dry from repeated orgasms. So, tell me now, do you want me to stop?"

"No." My reply came out breathily, but it was all I could do to even speak. His words were my undoing, and his hands set my body on fire. His mouth on the sensitive skin of my neck removed any doubt lurking in the back of my mind. What he could do with that tongue in more intimate spots was just a heartbeat away.

His fingers grasped the hem of my dress and pulled it over my head. Standing in nothing but my lacy white bra and matching thong, I turned slowly until I faced him. His eyes roamed over my body, heating me from my core with a simple look. He pulled down the cups of my bra, revealing my breasts before covering one with his mouth. His hands snaked around behind me and unhooked my bra, letting it fall from my arms. Then his hands glided down my back until his thumbs hooked into my panties. He slid them down my legs, and I stepped out of them, leaving my high heels in place.

"I plan to fuck you all night long. Just when you think you've had enough, I'll be back for more."

I'd never in my life felt so desired as I did standing naked in front of him while he licked his lips and devoured me with his eyes. He walked me backward to the couch and sat me down on the cool leather. With my ass perched on the edge, he knelt before me and buried his face between my legs. My body responded fiercely as his tongue and fingers fucked my pussy. My inner muscles clenched and quivered forcefully with each movement of his onslaught. With a primal scream, I gripped his hair and called out his name with the first orgasm.

"You taste so fucking good, but I can't wait to be inside you. My cock will be so deep in you, you'll still feel me between your legs tomorrow."

"Yes." My voice was raspy and wanton.

His expensive clothes were quickly discarded and left in a heap on the floor, then he reclaimed his position kneeling in front of me. Sheathed and hard, he slid into my waiting sex. The walls of my pussy burned from the way he stretched me until my body acclimated to his size. I had no doubt I'd still feel his presence the following day. He grabbed the back of my head with one hand and pulled my face to meet his, then he pounded relentlessly into me.

His other hand played with my clit, circling, swirling, and pushing my hot button until I came apart again. And again. With the incredible sensations pulsing through my entire body, I couldn't even count how many times I came.

"Fuck yeah," he muttered, continuing his erotic barrage on my body. Then he suddenly stopped, walked me around to the back of the couch, and bent me over. "Hold on to something, doll."

Then *he* held on—to my long hair. He pulled it up in a ponytail in his hand and twisted the strands around his palm. As he pushed into me from behind, he pulled my hair then smacked my ass with the other hand. He rubbed the red out before he smacked it again. The pleasure and pain mixed, creating a vibrating sensation that ran through my veins and along every nerve ending. His occasional grunts and groans of pleasure only excited me more.

"That's it, doll. Soak me again. Your tight little cunt is driving me wild."

The more he talked dirty to me, the more turned on I became. A man I barely knew commanded my body better than any lover I'd known before. Whatever he ordered, my body obeyed without question or hesitation. His hold over me was all-consuming, and I didn't want it to end. I didn't want our night together to be a one-night stand. A meaningless fling. I wanted to get to know the man behind the curtain of control…the man I knew most people had never met.

"You feel too fucking good. I'm never letting you leave."

As if he read my mind.

"Now that I've felt you wrapped around my cock, no other man will ever touch you. I've claimed you…*all* of you." He ran his finger across the tight rim of muscle between my cheeks. "I can't wait to take this virgin ass. To know it's only mine. So fucking sexy."

The thought of anal sex had never appealed to me…before Damon. Before his words, his possessiveness, his desire to have all of me as his created a foreign but welcomed longing in me. As archaic as it sounded, the manly way he handled me, the dominating way he took what he wanted, and the thoughtful way he made sure I experienced more pleasure than I'd ever known made me feel more special than any declaration of love had in the past. No other lover compared to this man, in any way.

"Give me one more, baby. I can't hold out much fucking longer." He thrust harder, driving into me with a renewed ferocity until my screams of pleasure filled the room. I felt him pulsing inside me a moment later, followed by his growl of satisfaction. He helped me up then pulled me into a full-body embrace. "You are fucking amazing."

He knelt behind me, and I wondered what more he had in mind. His fingers gently wrapped around my ankle, and he tugged until I lifted it. One by one, he removed my shoes while his lips caressed the back of my thighs. When he rose, his mouth sought mine, his kisses more tender this time. We walked to the bathroom, naked and with our bodies still touching, until he moved one arm to start the shower.

I thought we'd have another raucous round in the shower, but he had other plans. The powerful and commanding man washed me with such a gentle touch, I wondered if he was the same man I'd been warned about. The way he pampered me was just as intimate as the amazing sex we'd had.

I wasn't naïve—I knew the words that fell from a man's mouth during vigorous sex weren't exactly the truth. While I melted a little more with his every word, I didn't believe we'd be together forever. But after the chaos of the night, the way he protected me, and then washed it all away, I wasn't so sure I could simply walk away without a scratch.

As I dried off, I heard drawers opening and closing from his bedroom. He appeared in the doorway, naked with beads of water still clinging to his skin. My eyes drank him in slowly—from the muscles that said he knew his way around a gym to the happy trail leading the way from his belly button all the way down. He purposely cleared his throat, drawing my attention and my line of sight back up to his eyes. With a smug grin that let me know he'd caught me looking, he handed me one of his T-shirts.

"I didn't see you grab any pajamas when you ransacked your bedroom. You can wear this for now. Let's have a glass of wine together on the balcony." He toweled off and slipped on a pair of shorts before we moved to the terrace that was as big as my entire apartment.

"Your condo is gorgeous, but this area is amazing." I turned slowly, taking in the numerous potted plants, top-of-the-line patio furniture, swaths of grass amid the paver stones, the outdoor kitchen, and the private lap pool. It was the perfect oasis in the middle of the concrete jungle.

As I leaned against the half wall surrounding the patio, gazing at the bright city lights below, the shooting replayed in my mind, and the fear began taking root in my chest again. My coping mechanisms were failing me, allowing the terrifying scene to repeat with alarming clarity. Damon seemed to sense my distress. His arms encircled me from behind. His chin rested on my shoulder, his cheek next to mine.

"You're shaking. Is the breeze up here too cool for you?" His tone was easy and soothing, but also knowing. He gave me an out, a way to avoid talking about my angst if I chose to take it.

But I needed his comfort. I needed to hear the words come from him. When he promised he'd take care of me, I believed him. "No, I just can't stop thinking about what happened earlier."

He turned me toward him and held my face in his hands. "I understand, but believe me when I say we have it covered. You don't have to worry now."

"That's all either of us can do, isn't it? Believe that the people responsible will be found and held accountable for their actions."

"I believe they will be. With all my heart and soul, I believe it."

CHAPTER FIVE

Damon

Though my gut insisted Jillian shouldn't go to work, I took her anyway. With Benny driving, I sat in the back with her and kept a vigilant watch the entire ride. She was more nervous the morning after the attempt on us than she was right after it happened. She said everything felt like a dream immediately after the shooting, but it all came rushing back when she had time to think about it—and it was suddenly all very real and scary to her.

"Will my car be ready today?" She fidgeted with her hands, wringing them and stretching them out on her thigh to stop herself.

I picked up one of her hands and brought it to my lips. She looked up at me, fear still evident in her expression. "Hey. Remember what I said?"

"You said not to worry because you'd protect me."

"I'm a man of my word, Jillian. I protect what's mine."

"And I'm yours?"

"You know you are."

She nodded and relaxed a little. "And my car?"

"It'll be ready this afternoon and waiting for you at your apartment." Her expression was a mixture of disappointment and relief.

I understood the feeling—I didn't want her to leave my side until I had a better grasp on what exactly was going down with the Sanfratello family. At least my dad's men had time to put extra security cameras in her apartment last night so we could keep an eye on her and any visitors—expected or unexpected. She'd be safe if she stayed in the building working, Percy would see to that. If she left during the day, my father's men would cover her, and she'd never know they were there.

"Something wrong?"

She dropped her chin and shook her head. "No, I'm fine."

I knew she was lying, but I also knew why, so I let it slide. She already thought she was imposing on me for the rides to work and back, so asking for anything more was out of the question in her mind. While I wouldn't mind if she spent the night in my bed occasionally, I wasn't ready for her to be a full-time resident.

Benny pulled alongside the curb and stopped. She inhaled a deep breath when I exited the car. I took her hand to help her stand then pulled her to me with my arm around her waist and my lips against her temple. "I'll be here when you get off work today."

When we drove off, I called Percy to tell him she was on her way up. Then I called my dad to find out what he and Uncle Leo had learned.

"Good morning, son. Your mother wants to know if you're bringing your friend to Saturday dinner." That was his greeting when he answered his phone, and the question from my mom wasn't a request or simple curiosity—it was an expectation.

"You ratted me out, Dad?" I chuckled, knowing even though he was the family Boss and his word was final in business, Mama's word was final on anything involving *her* family. My dad knew better than to cross her on any matters related to her children and their lives.

"She tells me every day how much she wants grandbabies, but none of her kids loves her enough to give her one after everything she sacrificed to make a happy home. You took a beautiful girl to dinner last night. She's hopeful."

"She's right beside you, isn't she?"

"Yes." I knew from the deep rumble of his laugh that she was already making plans for my wedding. It was what she did every time any of her sons had a date—she broke out the bridal magazines and started checking availability at wedding venues.

"Dad, I just met Jillian—and she works at Blaine Financial Services. I don't know what it all means yet. Make Mama stop before she sends out wedding invitations."

"Your mother and I only knew each other a week before I knew she was the one I'd marry."

I couldn't believe he was taking Mama's side. "But you were sixteen and lived in a small village in Italy. There probably weren't even any other women your age who weren't already family. It's different now. But that's not why I'm calling. What'd you find out last night?"

"First, there's no one better than your mother, regardless of where we lived. She wants to meet your girlfriend and decide for herself if this girl is a good match for you. Now, on to business. My guys tracked down the car and interrogated the driver. They're watching Jillian, but those bullets were meant for you. They think you're behind Milo's disappearance."

"Milo worked for the same company, managing the nurses' union retirement fund. I had good reason to believe he snitched on us to the Sanfratellos, tipping them off about our operations. He had to be taken out of play."

"Apparently, your girlfriend just happened to be assigned to the same fund after Milo abruptly left. That raised a lot of red flags, even though they should know we'd be more discreet. If we replaced him, it damn sure wouldn't be with your girlfriend. The Sanfratello family doesn't own Blaine Financial, but they have men in place to funnel money out the same as we do."

"Did you get rid of the driver?"

"No, but he's missing a few protruding body parts. I decided to send him back with a strong message to stay clear of you and Jillian. They stick to their business, we stick to ours. But if they so much as look at any of us wrong, we will finish them." His voice turned gruff and forceful, giving a glimpse of the man who terrified his opponents.

"If they're posturing and positioning for power, do you think they'll go for that?" I pictured Jillian in her office, unaware of the coming war, working beside Lorenzo. "Dad, Jillian knows nothing about this. They could tell her anything about us and she'd believe it."

"I think you need to give her more credit than that, Damon. Your Uncle Leo and I both saw how she looked at you last night. She likes you. A lot. As for the Sanfratellos, we'll know soon enough. We have people on the inside."

She deserved the benefit of a warning—about me, about Lorenzo, about what would be expected if she and I continued seeing each other. I had no problem with putting a bullet in the brain of anyone who crossed me, but she hadn't done anything wrong. I was the one who insisted on taking her to the hospital, and I couldn't have her innocent blood on my hands.

"Okay, Dad. I'm glad to hear it was me they were gunning for and not her. If they know what's good for them, they'll leave her out of it."

"I know that tone, Damon. If you threaten Lorenzo with mere words, you're just daring him to defy you. And then he will do it out of spite. Trust me, they heard my message loud and clear."

"You and Mama have always been able to read me like a fucking book."

"Of course. You're a Marchetti. As such, I expect you to bring her to the family dinner Saturday to meet your mother."

"Yes, sir."

We disconnected, and I turned the conversation to Benny, my longtime friend who knew my family almost as well as I did. "Benny, my mother wants Jillian there Saturday. How do you think it'll go?"

Benny met my gaze in the rearview mirror. "Jillian isn't Italian, Damon."

He didn't have to say more than that. I'd never hear the end of it from my mother. "You're right...it'll be painful."

I was too keyed up to sit in my office all day, so we made the rounds to my crew to collect money from their jobs, set up plans for new tasks, and gather any information they'd learned from the street. Word was the rival family was planning something big, moving their men around and shaking up their normal routines. But no one had any solid leads on what the final goal was. The top brass keeping the plans that close to the vest meant we had to be extra vigilant.

Back in the car, I glanced at my watch and realized it was well after lunch, but I hadn't eaten a single bite. The uneasy feeling hadn't left me all day, so I decided to ask my girl if she'd already eaten. She answered on the third ring.

"You must be a mind reader. I was just thinking about you," she said when she came on the line.

"Didn't I tell you? I can read your every thought. Maybe I should've mentioned that earlier, huh?"

"Oh yeah? What am I thinking right now, then?"

"You're thinking about how hungry you are, and you want me to take you out to lunch."

Her laugh filled the line, and my cock twitched from the sound. "You're amazing. That's exactly what I was thinking. Since you knew that, I expect you to be waiting for me downstairs."

"I'll be there by the time you step out the front door, so bring your sexy ass down to me."

"Yes, sir. I love it when you're so bossy like that."

She had no idea how her playful banter made my cock spring to life. "Doll, you haven't seen bossy yet. Just remember you asked for it when you get more than you bargained for later tonight."

"Tonight?" Her breathy single-word question revealed her excitement. "But I thought—I just assumed..."

She stepped out of the large glass door onto the sidewalk, her cell phone still pressed to her ear. I moved up beside her and murmured into her other ear. "You just assumed last night was a one-night stand?"

Her eyes shot up to mine, and a smile crept across her face. She shrugged one shoulder as she lowered her hand. "When you said my car would be waiting for me at my apartment and you'd take me back there this evening, I thought maybe you didn't want to see me anymore."

"Is that why you looked so sad this morning?"

"Part of why." Her voice trailed off, and a light pink flush covered her face.

"I guess I'll have to make a believer out of you, then. I say what I mean, and I mean what I say. If one night of that luscious pussy was all I wanted, you'd know it. I've told you more than a couple of times that I've claimed you, marked you as mine. But you still don't believe me. After tonight, you won't doubt me again."

"Okay." Her chest rose and fell in quick succession. Her lips parted, and her eyes flew open wider. My words struck a potent chord in her—one she couldn't deny she enjoyed.

"Lunch first." With my hand on her lower back, inching my fingers down toward her ass, I guided her to the car and opened the door. Seated beside her, I slid my hand between her thighs, and her breath hitched. One corner of my lips lifted, though I tried to hide my amusement. With a firm grip, I pulled her across the plush leather seat. "Don't you want to sit closer to me?"

"Yes, I do."

My finger stroked the sensitive skin of her inner thigh, causing goose bumps to pebble across her skin, then I pulled her knee over my leg. Her eyes never left mine as my fingers moved up her leg. When I reached the apex, I felt the strip of soft curls covering her pussy. Then it was my turn to be surprised.

"Why are you not wearing any panties at work?" I kept my voice low and my mouth close to her ear so Benny couldn't hear. The level of jealousy that bubbled up inside me was a first. I'd never had a problem attracting and keeping any woman, much less had a reason to feel jealousy over one. This woman tested me in all different ways.

"I forgot to grab a pair when we were at my apartment last night." Her breaths came faster, and her legs opened wider as my finger hovered over her entrance, teasing her with what was to come.

"You've been at work all day, with other men who want you the same way I do, without any panties on?" I thrust my middle finger into her wetness, and she bit back a whimper. With long, lazy strokes, I fingered her sweetness, wishing I could bury my face between her legs to taste her instead. The tighter she gripped my arm, the tighter her pussy gripped my finger. She held her breath and pulled her bottom lip between her teeth, trying to remain silent while her excitement increased. With a curl of my finger and a little more pressure, she came apart under my touch.

Her head fell back against the seat, and she closed her eyes for a moment. When she opened them, she watched me lick her juice off my finger. "Oh my God."

I pulled the silk handkerchief from my jacket pocket and wiped away the wetness between her legs. After I'd stuffed it into my front pocket, I turned my attention back to our conversation. "Are you going to answer my question now?"

"What did you ask?"

"Forget the question. Here's the answer. If you go commando

without me beside you again, your ass will be sore for a full week. Are we clear?" My eyes bored into hers. My tone drove the seriousness of my point home.

"We're clear." Her eyes darted back and forth between mine, taking in my determination. "You are one of a kind, Damon. Should I be flattered over your jealousy and possessiveness? Or concerned?"

She had me pegged, caught red-handed by my own words. My face softened because I couldn't deny the answer to the real question behind her words. "We're here. Let's eat."

CHAPTER SIX

Jillian

I saw the shift in his demeanor before he avoided answering my question, but I couldn't read him as well as he could read me. He took my hand as I got out of the car in front of a door I wouldn't have even noticed if I'd walked right by it. Inside, the restaurant was much more casual than where we'd had dinner the night before. The homey vibe was warm and welcoming, as was the older lady who greeted us with a smile.

"*Mio nipote!*" She pulled Damon into her arms and rocked from side to side. "It's been too long since the last time you came to see me. What, my nephew doesn't have time for his favorite aunt anymore?" She didn't give him time to answer before turning her attention to me. "Who is this pretty girl? Does your mother know about her?"

"Aunt Maria, this is Jillian Hart. Jillian, Maria is Uncle Leo's wife. She owns this restaurant and makes the best veal parmesan and spinach ravioli in the city."

She pinched his cheeks while wearing the brightest smile. "You only say that because your mama doesn't live in the city. You're a smart boy." Turning back to me, she continued speaking. "It's so nice to meet you, Jillian. Come, have a seat. Let me get you both something to eat. You're too thin—you need food."

She walked ahead of us and motioned to an empty table. "Have a seat. I'll bring your food out."

Damon recognized my confused expression. "Aunt Maria never lets me order from the menu. I eat whatever she wants me to eat."

He pulled out my chair, and we settled in for what smelled like a delicious home-cooked meal. "What did she mean when she asked if your mother knew about me?"

Damon smiled—that dazzling smile rendered me speechless every time—and appeared almost boyish for a second or two. "About that. After we saw my dad last night, he told my mother about you, naturally. I called him this morning, and I was given strict instructions to bring you to our family dinner this weekend."

If dying from hyperventilation were possible, I was sure my death was imminent. I'd met his father by coincidence, and that only lasted a couple of minutes. Dinner at his parents' house was a whole new ball game—in a completely different league. My mouth opened and closed several times to speak, like a fish gulping for air, but nothing came out. Damon reached across the table and took my hand.

"Breathe, doll, before you pass out."

Wouldn't *that* cause a spectacle in his aunt's restaurant?

"Damon, are you sure this is a good idea? I mean, we've moved fast as it is. But where I'm from, meeting the parents is a big deal. It's a major step in a relationship."

He sat back in his chair, his keen eyes assessing me and my words. "And?"

"And...when you tell her we only met a couple of days ago,

she'll hate me." My voice was panicky, anxiety making the pitch ratchet up higher and higher with every word.

His aunt Maria bustled through the swinging kitchen door, carrying two large plates in her hands. Another woman followed closely behind her with a tray of salads, bread, and drinks. Damon stood to help them place the food on the table and kissed his aunt on the cheek.

"Can we get some wine to go with this delicious meal?" His charm was fully intact, with no hint of the turmoil at our table not three seconds before.

"Of course, of course." Maria called to another employee to bring two glasses of Chianti to us. "Take a bite. I want to see your faces when you try it."

Despite how my stomach still rolled from the news of dinner with his parents, I cut a piece of the cheese-covered veal. The look of pure indulgence on my face pleased Maria if her beaming smile was any indication. "This is delicious, Maria. Pure heaven."

She looked at Damon. "I like her. And I love her accent. She's coming to dinner Saturday, no?"

My fork, loaded with fettuccine Alfredo, stalled halfway to my mouth. Damon nodded to answer her, but his gaze moved to mine.

"Will you be there, too?" I asked her.

"Of course. The whole family will be there, like always. It's tradition. You call me *Aunt* Maria, yes?"

Then she was gone. Apparently, questions were demands in his family. Damon sat, fork in hand to eat, but closely watched my reaction. "It'll be fine, Jillian. My mother wants to meet you. Now that Aunt Maria has met you, we don't have a choice but to go together. Mama's feelings will be hurt if she's left out."

"You're guilt-tripping me into meeting your mother."

That smile. Again. The mischievous glint in his eyes. "Absolutely."

I was beyond stuffed when we finished lunch, and Damon took me back to work. He walked me to the door, and when I thought he'd turn and leave, he pulled me into his arms and kissed me senseless instead.

"The only reason I'm letting you go back in with no panties is because I know you need your job to help your mother. Otherwise, you wouldn't leave my side the rest of the day."

I couldn't help but smile. His words were sexist and crass, but the inflection in his voice and the expression in his eyes told me so much more. Our relationship, if I could even call it that, was complex. The sex was off the charts hot. The connection between us was strong. But we hadn't had enough time to establish trust or even to get to know each other intimately, other than sexually.

"Damon, I know words only go so far, but I still want to tell you. I don't know where this is going between us, or if it's even going anywhere. But, as strongly as you feel about staking your claim on me, I feel the same about you. I'm not the least bit interested in any other man. I've never been one to date more than one guy at a time anyway, but I'd never disrespect you like that. Tell me now if you plan to see other women."

"Would you walk away from me if I did?"

His question felt like a kick to my stomach, but only forty-eight hours of close contact didn't give me much leverage. "Yes, I would."

"Good answer. Looks like you're stuck with me, doll." He sensed the change in me after that question, the doubt it brought to the forefront of my mind. The uneasiness that wasn't there before. "Jillian, I've never taken a woman home to meet my mother, much less to attend our family dinner. That's a big deal in my family. Everyone comes over—aunts, uncles, cousins—and our family is huge.

"I'm a man of my word, and I promise you'll be the only woman I see. Honestly, I just wanted to know that you'd stand up to me if I pushed. And you didn't let me down."

"Fortunately, I have a big set of balls, and I even know how to use them."

My smartass remark didn't faze him. In fact, I think his smirk and amusement increased. "Funny, I didn't find any balls when I thoroughly examined you with my tongue last night."

"Don't make me have to take them out of my purse."

He leaned his head back and roared with laughter. "So feisty. I like it." After another scorching hot kiss, he kept his arms around my waist and pulled his face back to look directly into my eyes. "I'll be back to pick you up and take you to your apartment—where I'll stay with you tonight."

"All right." I played it off like his declaration didn't affect me, but it did. He affected me in so many ways.

With my focus on what our night together would hold, I went back to work in my temporary office. Every time I walked into that space, I felt like I was intruding on someone else's life. Pictures of the man and his family still sat in frames on the credenza. His name was still displayed on the plaque on the door. His files and notes still sat on the corner of the desk. But Lisa, the woman in the next office, said he hadn't called in or shown up for work all week. She said he'd been a good employee and everyone was worried about him.

Milo Bianchi left several personal items and a lot of unfinished work behind if he just up and quit.

I pushed thoughts of him aside and dove back into the work waiting for me. The other area of Blaine Financial I'd worked in the first several weeks after I arrived was in much better shape. The retirement funds were a complete mess. Maybe that's why Milo quit without so much as a goodbye—making sense of the deposits, payments, accrued interest, and final balances was a nightmare.

A knock on my office door startled me, making me jerk my head up and release a slight yelp. Lisa chuckled, a warm smile covering her face, and pointed to her watch. "It's after five o'clock on a Friday afternoon, girl. Are you ready to quit for the day, or are you spending the night here?"

After a quick glance at the clock, I stood and stretched, stiff from sitting in one position for hours. "I'm definitely ready to quit, but I'm nowhere near figuring this out. I think I'll have to take this to my apartment and work on it more over the weekend."

I packed my laptop and files in my bag, grabbed my purse, and hurried outside to meet Damon. When I stepped through the door, Damon's angry glare stopped me in my tracks. "What's wrong?"

He pushed off the car and stalked toward me. If looks could kill, his fierce expression would've already murdered me. As he approached, I realized he wasn't looking at me—he was looking just over the top of my head. I turned to find Lorenzo close on my heels, his arm extending over me to hold the door open. I realized how my tardiness must appear. Lorenzo was a handsome man, close to Damon's age, tall and well-built. His expensive tailored suits accentuated his good looks and fit him perfectly.

"Nothing's wrong, doll." Damon pulled my body into his and pressed his lips against mine. My automatic response had me melting into his touch. His tongue swiped across my lips, and I immediately yielded.

When we came up for air, I remembered Lorenzo was standing behind me. I glanced over my shoulder and watched as the sneer aimed at Damon turned into a friendly smile when his eyes moved to meet mine. "Good night, Jillian. I'll see you Monday."

"Good night." A couple of seconds passed before I could reply, and my words came out stammered. He'd spoken to me only once before, but the familiar tone he used with me in front of Damon was different.

Damon's hand on my lower back gently pushed me toward his

car, so I decided to wait until we were inside to ask him about that heated, wordless exchange. He slid in beside me, with Benny behind the wheel, and closed the door. I stared at him for several long seconds, waiting for the muscle in his jaw to stop jumping,

"Something on your mind, doll?" His words were clipped, and his face held a hard edge, as if he barely held on to the little restraint he had.

"What was that all about?"

"What?"

"I'm a lot of things, Damon, but I'm not stupid. You know Lorenzo."

"I know him."

"Why didn't you say anything when I told you he came to my office?"

"Because your boss and I are not friends. Never have been, never will be, and I didn't want my personal dealings with him to cause you any discomfort at work."

"So that public display of affection was nothing more than showing you were happy to see me?"

He dropped his head toward his lap, and a small smile played on his lips. "It may have been a little more than that." His gaze lifted to meet mine, the small smile morphing into the full-blown irresistible one. "But, for the record, I am happy to see you."

"I think you know exactly what that smile does to me," I accused, narrowing my eyes at him while trying to hide my own grin.

His brown eyes darkened with hunger. "I didn't know my smile did anything to you, but I'd love to hear all about it."

The car stopped in front of my apartment building, and he jerked the door open, grabbing my laptop bag in one hand and my hand in the other. "Take the night off, Benny."

"Thanks, boss," Benny replied just before the door slammed shut.

Captivated by the desire in Damon's expression, I felt the tingling in my belly multiply after his next words. "Instead of telling me what my smile does to you, I'd rather you show me. When we're alone. And naked."

7

CHAPTER SEVEN

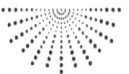

Damon

"M r. Marchetti, this was delivered for you earlier." The front desk security guard produced my small suitcase from behind the counter.

"Thank you." I grabbed the handle on my way past and keep walking toward the elevator.

I didn't miss the knowing smirk on Jillian's face. She knew the kiss served two purposes—I was glad to see her, but it was also meant to demonstrate I knew what the bastard was up to. Since I knew how he normally operated, I expected that pathetic attempt wouldn't be his last.

Fucking Lorenzo.

He showed me just how close he can get to Jillian, even with me standing directly in front of her. His arm was extended over her head. A flick of his wrist later, she could've been killed. He caught her totally unaware, and even after we left, she didn't realize how close of a brush with death she'd just had. Lorenzo tested the amount of discipline and self-control I had, because I wanted to level my 9mm squarely between his eyes more than I wanted my next breath.

The distrust he tried to create between Jillian and me only pissed me off even more. Her confused reaction after his pathetic move wasn't an act—she wore her feelings on her sleeve way too much. She thought I kissed her only to mark my territory, warning her boss that she was already taken. But that wasn't my reason, and Lorenzo knew it.

When she surrendered to me in front of him, she declared her allegiance to the Marchetti family. She announced her loyalty to me. With a heated public kiss, we warned Lorenzo not to attempt to come between us. If he had any doubts before, he knew she was mine afterward—in every sense of the claim.

The elevator doors opened, and we walked to her apartment.

"You are completely lost in thought. Have you heard anything I said?" Jillian put her hand on her hip and tilted her head at me, daring me to lie.

So I smiled and watched how her expression immediately softened. "I'm sorry, doll. I was just thinking about a couple of things I need to talk to my dad about—business stuff. I don't want to do it while we're having dinner with everyone, but I also don't want to give up any of my time alone with you."

I took the keys from her hand and unlocked her door, entering first as a precaution. That act was a Marchetti-man expectation, instilled in us from birth.

"Talk to your dad while I soak in the tub. I'll have dinner delivered so we'll have the entire night to ourselves." She dropped her purse on the entry table and kicked off her shoes.

"I don't know how you expect me to get any business done with visions of you all wet, naked, and alone in the tub." I soaked in her form, starting from her bare feet and making my way up to meet her gaze.

"We all have our burdens to bear, don't we?" Her sassy Louisiana accent matched the smile plastered across her beautiful face. "Actually, I use my tub-soaking time to call my mom. She likes to hear about my work, especially when I'm traveling. Picturing me talking to my mom should help while you finish your business with your dad."

"Now I have no choice but to create new visions of you naked in the tub. No offense to your mom, but I can't have that visual in my head for long." My expression was purposely blank to match my deadpan reply. My empty countenance only seemed to amuse her more, and within seconds, she was unable to hide her laughter.

She was so different from everyone else in my life. Naïve to the danger surrounding her. She wasn't jaded like I was—suspicious of everyone and every move they made, always looking for the ulterior motive that may give them the upper hand over me. She trusted me with her life—literally. She had no idea a cutthroat assassin roamed freely in her home, slept next to her in bed, and thoroughly satisfied her body. She didn't look at me with fear in her eyes. She didn't jump at my commands because she knew any sign of disrespect would be the last thing she ever did.

The hunger, respect, and affection her eyes held were for Damon, the man. Not Damon, the mafia capo. Not the ruthless killer. Not the son of the Marchetti Family Boss and nephew of the Underboss. Not the man groomed to take over once the Boss relinquished control. When she looked at me, I felt the difference to the point I craved it. In a city of over eight million people, she was the only one who saw past my steel outer shell.

"When we finish our phone calls, you just tell me how I can correct those visions for you. Maybe you can even join me so I can have my own fantasies about you."

"That fucking mouth." I shook my head at her antics, but the heat in the room rose ten degrees without warning.

"My mouth? It's all yours...don't take too long."

She walked toward the bathroom, her hips swaying with as much deadly intent and purpose as if she'd drawn a gun on me...

only her movements had a very different meaning and created a very different reaction. But business had to be handled before I joined her. After I heard the water running and the soft murmur of her voice greeting her mother, I walked into the kitchen and called my father's cell.

I explained the situation with Lorenzo and how I'd established my claim on Jillian in front of him. "It's time to tell her and give her the option to stay or leave, Dad. She's been loyal to me. I have no reason to believe she won't continue to be."

"No."

"Pardon?" I was sure he'd misunderstood me, but I knew better than to outright argue with him.

"Not until your mother meets and approves of her. If she gives her blessing, then you can tell Jillian. If not, then you can sever ties, and she'll be none the wiser."

"Understood. But what if she's in danger from Lorenzo? He would've taken her public display of affection as a pledge to our family."

"Not if she's working for him."

"Do you know something I don't know?" I'd considered that possibility at one time, but I had since dismissed it. Had I missed something?

"I know your mother hasn't approved of her yet. Bring her tomorrow. We'll know soon enough."

"Yes, sir."

We chatted for a few minutes longer about other business matters, but the conversation never returned to Jillian. My dad's elusive answers were intentional but not dismissive—if she were hiding anything, he'd find it. For him to insist she meet Mama, I knew he wasn't overly concerned with anything related to Jillian. We hung up, and I walked to her bedroom, my steps purposely silent as I approached her bathroom door.

The sound of her sweet giggles mixed with splashes of water caught my attention. The suspicious man in me said to eavesdrop, see if it was really her mother on the line. When I heard her describe me—my handsome face, sexy body, masculine air, and protective nature—a twinge of a feeling I hadn't felt in a long time bubbled to the surface. Guilt for doubting her squeezed my chest. I hung my head and absorbed the affection in her tone—affection for the man she *thought* I was.

"Mom, I really want you to meet him. Damon isn't like any man I've ever met in Abita Springs. Our little town of twenty-five-hundred people wouldn't know how to act around a man who's so dominant, refined, and doting all at the same time. Hopefully, I can convince him to make the trip down there. I've already suggested he should come to Mardi Gras with me, so we'll see. Keep your fingers crossed."

I rested my forehead against the door and closed my eyes, listening to her every word. My purpose was no longer to eavesdrop out of suspicion. No, I was listening out of admiration and fondness at that point. Her tone and inflection carried her love for her mother through the air, wrapping me in its natural warmth. Her Louisiana twang was more pronounced when speaking to her mother, and I couldn't help but smile to myself because of it.

A few minutes later, she promised to call back again the next day and disconnected after sending her love. The sound of water pouring from the tub faucet masked any other noise from inside the room. From her promise earlier, I presumed she was reheating the water for me to join her. Before she called my cell and caught me hovering outside the door, I rapped on it with my knuckles a couple of times before entering.

She flashed a seductive smile over her shoulder. "You're just in time, Mr. Marchetti."

My clothes dissolved into a pile on the floor in an instant. Jillian wet, naked, and waiting for me in the tub was all I needed to go from zero to full mast in under a second. I jumped into the tub, sending water sloshing over the sides, and caged her underneath me. Her bubble-bath-slicked skin was my siren call, one I was compelled to answer. She welcomed me without hesitation, without question. I swept my tongue across her lower lip, and she invited me in. My tongue slid against hers, devouring her sweetness and demanding more.

With a swipe of my knee, her legs parted, welcoming me to take my place between them. My engorged cock slid against the sensitive skin of her nether lips. I felt the heat from her pussy over and above the hot water surrounding us. The fiery desire in her eyes burned through me, and my relentless self-control disappeared. Only she could so easily disarm me, distract me, and consume my thoughts.

She thought I'd stand out in a town of twenty-five hundred.

But she stood out in a city of eight million.

She bent her knees, and I took full advantage of having unimpeded access to her sex. With a swift thrust, I buried myself inside her until my balls slapped against her ass. Her cries of pleasure mixed with my carnal grunt. Her velvety inner muscles squeezed around me as I slid in and out of her. Moans and screams filled the room so loudly I was surprised the neighbors weren't complaining. The pressure increased with every forward surge, and before long I had to grit my teeth to prolong the inevitable.

When her nails scored the skin on my back, I surrendered my control and melted into my own release. My lips immediately sought hers, instantly connecting on a deeper level when our mouths fused together. Drawing in a deep breath, I moved my lips along her cheek to her neck, leaving a trail of soft kisses on her heated skin.

Then I froze when reality hit me squarely between the fucking eyes. "Fuck, Jillian. I'm sorry, doll." I scraped my hand over my face, disbelief of what I'd done washing over me.

"What do you mean? Sorry for what?" Her trusting eyes implored me to explain.

"I walked in…you were wet and naked… I jumped into the tub without even thinking about protection. You're welcome to see my medical records—there's nothing to worry about. You can bet your sweet ass I've never made this mistake before. Losing control seems to be a recurring problem when I'm around you."

The flash of concern that passed over her features quickly vanished, but it was there nonetheless. "I'll offer the same to you, Damon. You're welcome to look at any of my medical records— I'm completely clean. In fact, my yearly exam results are saved in my phone. I have nothing to hide."

She couldn't fake the sincerity in her voice. Or the adoration in her eyes. Or the even tempo of her heartbeat. What could I say? I was a romantic, suspicious bastard. I watched her breathing and heart rate when she spoke, always looking for any sign of deception. Another first for me—I hadn't caught her in any sort of lie. Either she was especially good at lying, or she was the most honest person I'd ever met.

CHAPTER EIGHT

Jillian

eeting someone's parents shouldn't have been so nerve-racking, but I couldn't relax all day. Damon left my apartment midmorning with Benny in tow to handle some sort of incident one of his construction crews ran into. I stayed busy around my apartment as much as I could, but I stopped after I'd cleaned every room twice within an hour because of all of my pent-up nervous energy.

Though I wasn't sure I could focus, I broke down and took my laptop out of my bag. If Damon had to work most of the day, at least I'd have time to try to sort out the account that was tangled worse than cooked spaghetti noodles. I'd always loved solving puzzles, finding the missing piece that made everything else fall into place. Instead of focusing on my aggravation with the poor management of the fund, I focused on how satisfying it would feel to finish that assignment once and for all.

With every piece of paper from my files strewn across the table, I concentrated on matching all the numbers—deposits, withdrawals, interest accrued—until every cent was ticked and tied. Two names kept reappearing throughout the years of financial records, but I couldn't find any record of those names anywhere in the union's employee files. A sickening feeling settled deep in my gut, knowing the discrepancy wasn't an accidental omission. The transfers were too consistent and intentionally random, while still occurring late in the quarter. Without question, I had discovered a case of embezzlement.

The question was who was behind it, but that wasn't a question I was prepared to research. I was afraid to pry too much into the discrepancies—that was a job for the FBI, not me. Whoever was behind the elaborate scheme was obviously a professional and not someone I wanted to cross. The longer I stayed off the radar, the safer I was. By the time the bank fraud investigators collected all the evidence and made their move, I'd be long moved on to another assignment.

Hours passed as I tracked every discrepancy I found and reconciled the accounts as best I could, minus the embezzled funds. I listed every transfer date, name, and dollar amount I suspected was stolen in a separate document and saved both documents to my flash drive before putting it away. Since embezzlement was always an inside job, and I had no idea who to trust and who not to, I decided to take the information directly to the FBI. Anyone at Blaine Financial Services could be behind it.

The reminder I'd set on my phone chimed, alerting me it was time to dress for the Marchetti family dinner. And just like that, the dread from discovering the financial inaccuracies didn't compare to the terror gripping my chest from thinking about meeting Damon's mother. A hot shower later, I stood naked in my walk-in closet, staring at my clothes with no idea of what would be appropriate to wear.

"If that's what you're wearing today, we won't make it far past your bedroom door." The smooth, sexy voice startled me, but warmth flooded me the second I saw Damon.

"Help. I have no idea what to expect from your family get-together."

The corner of his lip lifted slightly in amusement before he moved behind me, wrapped his arms around me, and kissed my neck. "Relax, doll. You'll look beautiful no matter what you wear." He selected a navy blue wrap dress with white splotches and held it up in front of us. "I like this one."

"Decision made. Blue dress and brown summer sandals it is."

His big hands roamed across my skin, making it difficult to focus on getting dressed. His groan echoed the frustration I felt inside. "If you don't walk away from me right now, we'll be late, and I'll have to tell my mom it was because you distracted me."

"You wouldn't dare."

"I most certainly would. I'm not taking the rap for being late. She'll forgive you, but I'd never hear the end of it." His hand drifted lower, reaching the apex of my mound.

I swatted his hand away and stepped out of his hold, his dark chuckle filling the small space. With my eyes narrowed, I turned toward him and glared. "I can't believe you'd blame me for it."

I'd seen his sexy smile, his playful smile, and his mischievous smile. But he unhinged me with his sweet smile. He was no less dominant, no less powerful, but the air around us turned more intimate. That little voice in my head said this was much more than a passing fling, for me, at least.

"I can't even begin to tell you how refreshing being with you is. You're unlike anyone else I've ever known in my life."

Then he said *that*…and I knew I was a goner. I was hooked—without warning, without a second thought, and without a doubt. "Maybe then you won't forget me when I'm gone."

His smile faded, but his eyebrow arched slowly. "Where do you think you're going?"

"This is a temporary assignment. When I'm finished here, my employer will send me to the next place. It could be in our corporate office in New Orleans, or it could be somewhere else onsite like this one is. I won't know until I get the next assignment. But I'm still here for a while longer yet."

"I don't know that I'll let you leave, Jillian. You're already ruining me for any other woman. Maybe I'll just keep you here with me long after your assignment is finished."

His romantic declaration sounded a lot like a challenge...or maybe even a warning. I wasn't sure which he meant it as, though it could've been both. We didn't have a normal beginning as a couple—meet, date, increasing intimacy, *then* meet the parents. We seemed to have begun in the middle of a relationship and hit the ground running without a glance backward. But being with him felt so natural, so right, I couldn't question my blooming feelings.

"You'd get tired of me. Then what would I do?" I attempted to dismiss the heavy thoughts weighing in my mind with a little levity. "But for now, I have to get ready to meet not only your mother, but your entire extended family. No big deal...no pressure. Right?"

"Exactly." His demeanor was casual, but I felt his energy flowing out of him in waves. Power, intensity, authority—he possessed it all in spades. "No pressure at all."

An hour later, we arrived at his parents' palatial estate on the cliffs in Fort Lee, New Jersey. The enormous two-story European style home was big enough to hold my home in Abita Springs more than three times over. Add the professionally landscaped yard, Olympic-size pool, and tennis courts, and I felt completely out of my element.

Damon carefully watched my reaction when we pulled into the gated drive. One car after another lined the circular driveway in front of the house. His hand covered mine and squeezed, sharing his strength as best he could under the circumstances.

"Breathe, Jillian. You'll be fine."

I took his advice and inhaled a deep breath then slowly released it. "You grew up here?"

"Yes, my parents have lived here all my life."

"It's so beautiful. I can't wait to see inside."

"You'll get the presidential tour, then."

Benny pulled into one bay of the three-car garage and opened the back door for us to slide out. Once inside the house, the hand-carved moldings and coffered ceilings mixed with hardwood floors and dark wood accents forced an audible gasp from my mouth. "Oh, Damon, it's magnificent."

Loud voices filtered to us from what I assumed was the kitchen. What sounded to me like arguing in Italian didn't seem to deter Damon. He put his hand on my lower back and guided me through the house, mentioning names of the voices we heard. Cousins, aunts, wives of family members...they all blended together to my ears. Then one stood out above the others—a female voice with ample authority in her short bursts of directives. Language was no barrier when it came to picking up on a mother's voice doling out orders.

"That is my mother's voice," he muttered close to my ear. "Her name is Lina, and she's going to love you."

He stepped into the kitchen first, with me close on his heels. "Hi, Mama."

There was a sliver of silence before the room erupted into a round of "hello" from everyone. I stepped around to his side, a nervous smile plastered to my face, and the woman at the center of the kitchen stopped in her tracks. Her assessing gaze skimmed over me from head to toe then back up again. She held my attention without saying a word.

When her face brightened with a smile, I relaxed a little. She walked to me, held my arms, and kissed me on each cheek. "*Bellissima regazza,*" she began. "You are the prettiest girl!"

With her arm around me, we walked into the enormous formal dining room together. "Finally! My Damon brings a girl home to meet me. Isn't she beautiful?"

I glanced over at Damon, hoping he'd come to my rescue as a

room packed with strange faces stared at me with smiles of admiration. The experience was more than daunting for me, but Damon's cool veneer never cracked. He crossed his arms loosely over his chest and smiled along with his family. If I looked too hard, I'd swear that was a look of pride covering his face.

Before she handed me off to the family, she turned to me and said, "You can call me Mama Lina, yes? This is not disrespectful to your mother. It's a custom in the village where Vincenzo and I grew up."

Before she rushed back to the kitchen, she stopped to speak to Damon. I strained my ears to accidentally overhear what was said.

"She's your match, Damon. I see it in her eyes. She loves you, but she also has a strong spirit. Take good care of her."

Damon didn't answer her audibly, but from the corner of my eye, I saw him slightly incline his head. Before I could react to her words, Aunt Maria grabbed me into a big hug and escorted me around the massive table. Name after name was thrown at me, along with how he or she was related to Damon. How would I ever remember every name?

Many of the women were still in the kitchen, helping Mama Lina, so I ventured back there to ask if I could help with anything. I knew Damon had said she wouldn't let me, but I wasn't raised to sit idly by when there was work to be done. When I stepped into the kitchen, I heard Lina speaking English to another woman slightly older than me.

"Carrie, take this dish to the table for me."

"Of course, Mama." Carrie smiled at me as she passed with the dish hot from the oven.

"Can I help with anything?"

Lina shook her head. "No, *bella*. You're a guest in my home, so today you relax and enjoy. Can I get you anything?"

"No, ma'am, I'm fine. Thank you, though. My mom always taught me to help when someone cooked for me. It's considered rude where I'm from not to even offer to help."

She nodded, giving me an understanding look, and affectionately patted my cheek. "When your mom comes to visit me, I will explain. And I will tell her what a good girl she raised. She should be very proud."

I fought back tears from her kind words. My mom was all I had left of my family. If we'd had a huge family like the Marchettis, I couldn't help but think our lives would be much easier. "Thank you, Mama Lina. That's very sweet of you to say. My mom will be thrilled when I tell her about this."

She shooed me back to the table to eat appetizers and get to know the family. When I stepped back into the dining room, Vincenzo walked in from the door at the other end of the table. His eyes landed on me first, and a pleased smile covered his face. "Jillian, *cara*. I'm so glad you could join us today."

He opened his arms wide as he approached me, so I stood and walked directly into his embrace as if I belonged there. When his arms wrapped around me, I felt the familial bond that held the entire room together. I'd missed my dad so much in the two years he'd been gone, and I felt him in Vincenzo's hug. The familiar sense of a father who loved his family more than anything in the world surrounded me when I closed my eyes and pictured my dad. The hug was brief, just long enough to evoke enough memories of my father I was sure would revisit my dreams later that night. Vincenzo's big hands moved to my shoulders when he kissed me on both cheeks.

"Don't be shy here, *cara*. There's plenty of food to go around." He motioned toward my seat at the table and helped me with the chair. "Watch out for Uncle Leo, though. He tries to hide the garlic bread from everyone."

"I heard that, Vin. We both know Lina makes it all for me," Leo grumbled without looking up, then the two men laughed at the same time. They were obviously close and used to ribbing each other.

After several minutes of chatting with what felt like hundreds of Marchetti family members around the table, Damon took his seat beside me and casually put his arm over the back of my chair. He watched as I piled my plate full of food until I met his gaze with a challenging one of my own. "Why are you staring at me?"

"A couple of reasons. You're so beautiful I can't stand to look away from you. You're also unlike any woman I've ever met. Fifteen minutes with my family and you're already one of them. I've taken dates to expensive restaurants and they'd barely touch their food, but you're not shy about eating at all. I love how you enjoy it."

"Your dates didn't eat food you bought them?" My drawn brows showed my disapproval. "That was rude of them. It'd also be rude not to eat after your mom spent so much time making all this food. And it'd be a sin to let it go to waste—every morsel on this table is incredible!"

Strong but feminine hands grasped my cheeks from out of nowhere. "I heard what you said, *bellissima regazza*. Thank you. You just made an old woman's day!"

Lina scurried away as quickly as she'd appeared, leaving me dumbfounded. "What does *bellissima regazza* mean?"

"It means beautiful girl," Damon replied with a smile. "And *cara* means dear. My parents are quite taken with you."

"The feeling is mutual."

CHAPTER NINE

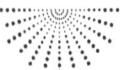

Damon

My perfect weekend with Jillian came to a screeching halt Monday when I walked into my office midmorning. Memories of her naked body writhing under my touch were still fresh in my mind when I strolled past Paulie toward the door that separated me from the storefront space. Her sounds of pleasure still reverberated in my ears. I was more than tempted to return to Blaine Financial and keep her as my hostage all day.

"Any problems with Roscoe this morning?" Paulie asked, pulling me from the instant replay of our early morning roll in the sheets.

"Nah. He'll think twice about holding out on us again, though." The office phone rang and Paulie picked it up. I kept walking and almost reached the door before he stopped me.

"Hey, boss, Luigi's on the phone. He's watching Jillian like you asked. He said she left the building, just running normal errands. But two Sanfratello guys are following her, too. He recognizes them—they're enforcers. Nasty ones."

"Tell him not to lose sight of her for one second and to text me their location. I'm on my way."

Benny and I flew out of the office while Luigi sent the address to our phones. My leg jumped with anticipation the entire ride as Benny weaved in and out of traffic as fast as he could. Enforcers on Jillian's tail could only mean one thing—Lorenzo was ready to make a move on her. He'd send his goons to pick her up, but he'd do the dirty work himself. I knew how his mind worked because I was also a capo.

My ties to the mafia were more than just a job. It distinguished me from the masses, made me who I was, and defined my future. Once you're in the family, you're in it for life. Lorenzo and his family were no different. The strict code had to be the same for the family to function. To be our rival, the Sanfratello family was every bit as organized and determined as my family.

When we finally reached Jillian, Benny came to a sudden stop in the street, and I jumped out to rush to her side. She was surprised to see me but also alarmed at the urgency in my steps when I sprinted to her.

"Damon." She startled. "What are you doing? What's wrong?"

"You have to come with me, Jillian. Right now."

"Get down, Damon!" Benny yelled as he ran down the side-walk toward us.

I didn't even need to look to know why his voice sounded panicked or why his heavy footfall revealed his husky frame had suddenly picked up speed. Jillian's eyes flew open wider, her bottom jaw dropped, and she struggled to find her breath and her voice. In that moment, my first instinct was to protect her, so I turned in the direction she was staring and pushed her behind me with one arm. A hot, searing pain tore through my chest, ramping up the adrenaline already coursing through my veins. My shirt became warm and wet before it stuck to me like glue.

Benny returned fire, hitting one of the Sanfratello goons and sending him to his knees, and continued his path to me. The second enforcer dragged his downed comrade to a nearby car and shoved him in the back seat. Jillian's shrill scream sounded from behind me, and I immediately turned to check her for wounds. Her face drained of color when she saw the front half of my shirt covered in blood, and she couldn't speak to answer me when I asked if she was hurt. I quickly ran my hand on my good side over her body while keeping my injured side as still as possible. Benny stood guard, watching the other car drive away in the opposite direction and ensuring another didn't take its place.

"D-Damon, you're shot!" Jillian at last could speak again.

"I know, doll. But are *you*?"

She shook her head violently from side to side. "I'm not hurt, but you're bleeding. You're shot, Damon! We have to get you to the hospital. *Immediately!*"

Sirens rang out, growing closer to our location, and I was in no shape to deal with the police at that moment. Besides, I knew Benny would get in touch with Uncle Leo, and he would take care of it.

"Calm down, doll. We're going right now," I reassured her.

Benny helped us to the car, and I slid into the back seat with extra care. Every movement hurt worse than the last. Each breath felt harder to inhale because of the intensity of the pain. My only consolation was I knew it wasn't a mortal wound, though that didn't make the bitch hurt any less. Had the bullet hit my brachial artery, I would've already known. Or passed out from blood loss.

Back at the emergency room Jillian and I visited the day we met, Dr. Falco waited for us in the ambulance bay to give us immediate access without questions from prying eyes.

"Fuck, Damon. It's only lunchtime. How the hell did this happen?" He helped me into an exam room and turned to Jillian and Benny. "Wait out here for a few. I'll let you know when you can come in."

Jillian nodded while Benny turned his back to the wall and stood guard outside my door. I gave her a reassuring smile to try to alleviate some of the worry etched on her beautiful face. "I'm okay, doll. Doc here will have me patched up in no time."

As the door closed, I saw her wipe the tears from her eyes, and that simple act hit me harder in the chest than the bullet had. Her worry for me was real. Her affection for me was genuine. In the chaos surrounding my family, those two facts were the only truths I was certain of beyond a shadow of a doubt.

Once I made it up on the table, he cut my shirt off to avoid moving my arm too much. "Jesus, Damon. Did you not even try to duck?"

I winced and sucked air through my clenched teeth while he poked and prodded around on my chest. "No. I was shielding Jillian."

He stopped and stared at me for a heartbeat, surprised and shocked speechless. "Well, I'll be damned."

"Don't make a big deal out of it. Just sew me up and send me home."

He shook his head. "Afraid I can't do that. The bullet is in your chest, and it needs to come out. Plus, it took part of your shirt with it, so the chance of infection is high. We have to see where that bullet is and get it out, then pump IV antibiotics through you for a couple of days."

"You're keeping me overnight?" I couldn't believe my ears.

"Absolutely. At least a couple of nights, in fact, after surgery. You think I want Uncle Vin mad at me over this? You're crazy as hell. I'll go check on an open operating room and have the nurses get you prepped. Do you want your friend to come in for a few minutes?"

"Yeah, send her in here with me. She's scared to death."

A minute later, Jillian walked in, pensive and red-eyed. "Come here," I commanded softly. She rushed to my uninjured side and dropped down into the chair beside my bed, her face resting on my bicep. With my arm bent, I threaded my fingers through her hair and held her to me.

"Dr. Falco said he's taking you to surgery," she said with a quivering voice.

"Don't worry about me, doll. I'll be fine. He's a great doctor. He's patched me up more times than I can count. I'll be out of here in no time."

She looked up, her gaze steeped in concern. "Why did you do that?"

"Do what?" No way was she asking what I thought she was asking.

"Put yourself in harm's way for me." A tear rolled down her cheek. "Don't ever do that again."

I chuckled, unable to withhold it after her demand. "Jillian. Remember when I said you're mine? That includes taking care of you—in whatever way you need me. I certainly wouldn't let someone shoot you."

"We need to talk about that, Damon. That's the second time someone has shot at me. I think it's time—"

"Mr. Marchetti?" the nurse asked from the doorway. "Dr. Falco has scheduled an OR for you. We've been instructed to get you prepped for surgery stat." She moved her eyes to Jillian. "You can go on up to the OR waiting room on the second floor now, and we'll update you when we get started."

Jillian nodded, wiped her tears, and leaned over to kiss me before she left. She lingered beside me for just a moment, the words she wanted to say on the tip of her tongue. But I knew the moment she swallowed them down, and she dropped her eyes to the floor as she left my room.

After I had blood drawn and X-rays taken, they wheeled me up to the operating room, and it was lights-out. I heard the nurse call the waiting room and ask for someone with the Marchetti family as I was going under anesthesia. My first thought wasn't of my mom or dad answering the phone...it was of Jillian.

· · ·

73

MURMURING VOICES PULLED ME FROM A DEEP SLEEP, THOUGH MY eyelids felt too heavy to open. I turned my head slightly in the direction of the voices, straining to understand the words. Then I heard her voice and felt her hand cover mine.

"Damon? You're out of surgery, and everything went fine. Your parents and Benny are here."

The soft skin of her fingers stroked my hand. She was close, I could feel her presence, but opening my eyes still took effort. I finally got one opened to glance around the room. All I could make out were dark figures around my bed, so I nodded and turned my hand to close my fingers around hers.

"Dr. Falco said you were lucky. The bullet was close to your brachial artery. Just an inch difference, and you would've bled to death before we got to the hospital." She stopped talking, inhaled deeply, and continued to update me on the injury. "You have to stay for a couple of days at least, mainly because he's concerned about an infection."

"I'm not staying in the hospital for two days," I mumbled.

"Yes, you are, or you will answer to me, Damon Marchetti." The stern tone of my mother's voice left no doubt my stay had already been discussed and decided. Usually, when my parents ganged up on me, I had little recourse.

"Hi, Mama," I replied sleepily.

"You heard your mother, son. End of discussion."

"Yes, sir." There was no point in arguing. Besides, I couldn't wake up enough to make an effective argument.

Jillian giggled beside me. She obviously had a part to play in the decision and had already learned how to use my parents to her advantage. That sort of made me proud of her spunk and pleased with how much she clearly cared about me. Not many women from my past would have taken the initiative she showed.

I turned my face toward her and slowly opened my eyes. Her beautiful green eyes stared back at me—still full of concern, but also a lot of love. She hadn't said the words, but I could tell. I could always tell.

"They won't always be around to protect you from me, you know?" My pathetic threat was betrayed by the smile on my face.

"That's where you're wrong," my mom replied, prompting Jillian to laugh out loud and shrug her shoulders.

"Mama Lina has spoken. Guess you have to listen to her." Jillian smiled broadly, her eyes sparkling with mischief.

Mama and Dad hung around until I was awake enough to have a full conversation. Benny had already briefed Dad, so we avoided talking too much about the details of the shooting. I knew Dad would check into the reasons behind it more. The Sanfratello family knew an attack on the Boss's son was a declaration of war, and our retaliation would be swift and devastating. What wasn't known was if I was collateral damage in an attempt on Jillian...or if they used her to lure me to a place where they could ambush me.

Either way, I knew I had a long lecture from my father waiting for the first moment we were alone.

CHAPTER TEN

Jillian

I stayed with Damon at the hospital. Even though I seldom missed work, I didn't think twice about going back in. The visual of his blood-soaked shirt wouldn't leave my mind. The terror of not knowing if I'd lose him on the way to the hospital was still fresh in my heart. I couldn't imagine not being beside him when he came out of surgery. Then when his parents left, I was apprehensive about leaving him alone.

"You can't be comfortable in that chair," he mumbled. His medication had kicked in, and he was feeling no pain.

"I'm not leaving you, Damon."

"If you're not going to sleep in your bed, you could at least sleep in mine." He opened one eye and arched his eyebrow at me. With care, he slid over in the twin-sized hospital bed and left a sliver of empty space for me.

I eagerly curled up beside him, my head resting on his good shoulder and my arm draped across his stomach. "You're sure I'm not hurting you?"

"Not at all. Go to sleep. We've had a long day."

Sometime during the night, the nurse made her rounds and began to chastise me for being in the bed with Damon. But with one word from him, she silenced her objections and went about her business. Her subsequent rounds were frequent but without incident. When the morning shift began, the new nurse didn't say a word about my place. I'd never mentioned that first hospital visit or how the cop had warned me about Damon and his men. While the officer didn't come out and say it, and Damon had never confirmed it, I had a good idea why his family commanded respect. Even in the hospital.

But I couldn't shake the feeling I was the intended target this time and he'd taken the bullet for me. I'd started to tell him in the emergency room, but the nurse interrupted us. Then by the time his parents left, he was too tired and needed his rest. I'd decided to tell him about the embezzlement I uncovered as soon as possible that morning. At least then he'd know what we were up against.

When his breakfast was brought in, I helped him sit up in the bed and arranged his food and drinks. "Do I need to feed you?"

The sensual look he gave me sent chills up and down my spine. Even shot, bandaged, and in a hospital bed, that man was deadly sexy. "We'll feed each other when I get out of here. For this, I think I can manage."

"Damon, there's something—"

"Good morning." Vincenzo's booming voice filled the room, followed by Uncle Leo's echoing greeting. "Jillian, sweetheart, I'm sorry to be so rude, but Leo and I need to speak with Damon privately. Would you mind stepping outside?"

"Dad."

"No, it's fine, Damon." I leaned over and kissed him. "I need to go to my apartment and shower. I'll be back in a couple of hours to stay with you again. If you need more time than that, just let me know."

"Thank you, *cara*." Vincenzo took my hand and kissed the back of it. "And thank you for staying with him last night. You don't know how much you relieved his mother."

"It's my pleasure."

"Is Benny here?" Damon asked.

"Right here, boss." Benny stepped into the doorway. "I'll make sure she gets there safely."

Damon nodded, but his eyes lingered on Benny's for a couple of seconds longer, conveying a hidden message. Benny nodded once, signaling his understanding, then we walked away together. I desperately wanted to question him about Damon and the rest of the family, but I knew better. Benny was loyal and would think my questions were too intrusive. If Damon wanted me to know something, he'd tell me himself.

When we arrived at my building, Benny escorted me up to my apartment and checked all the rooms. "I'm sorry I can't stay here with you. Joe is busy with an assignment, so Vincenzo and Leo don't have a driver. Call me when you're ready to go back to the hospital, and I'll swing by to pick you up. Do *not* call a cab." He handed me a business card with his number on it.

"Thank you, Benny. It'll be at least a couple of hours or so before I call you. I need to check in with work."

"Do not go to the office. In fact, don't go anywhere without me. Stay inside until I call and tell you I'm at the front door. We can't be too careful now."

"Okay." So many questions flew through my mind, but they'd have to be addressed to Damon. And I had plenty of topics to speak with him about, too.

I made sure the door was locked when Benny left, then headed straight for my bedroom. After a hot shower, I tied my wet hair up in a towel and called my manager, Ronnie, at the corporate office in Louisiana. I explained I needed a few days off for an emergency, without giving the details. His motto had always been family came first, and I didn't correct his assumption that the emergency was with my mother. Ronnie promised to call Blaine Financial and explain I'd be out the rest of the week.

After I'd finished drying my hair and getting dressed, I grabbed a suitcase and started packing a few things so I could stay with Damon. A knock on my door surprised me since the front desk hadn't called about a visitor. I moved silently toward the door and rose on my toes to look through the peephole.

What could Lorenzo want?

My cryptic emergency message must have alarmed him, but still, an unexpected drop-in at my apartment was hardly appropriate. I slowly opened the door and purposely gave him a quizzical look. "Lorenzo. What can I do for you?"

"I'm sorry to intrude. Ronnie called and said you were dealing with an emergency, but there is something urgent I need to speak to you about. It'll only take a few minutes, but I'm afraid it really can't wait."

"All right. Come in and have a seat." I stepped aside and extended my arm toward the couch.

I sat opposite of him on the love seat and waited for him to explain the urgent issue that couldn't wait until Monday. The one I knew I couldn't work on without my laptop from the office anyway.

"I'll get right to the point. I know what you found, Jillian."

I remained silent, not knowing if he was part of the embezzling scheme or if he'd been monitoring it himself.

"I really wish you hadn't stumbled across it. And I wish you hadn't been so damn determined to figure it out. We buried it so deeply in the transactions, it's amazing anyone short of an FBI forensic accountant found it."

He eyed me suspiciously, waiting for confirmation that would never come. I wasn't part of the FBI, but I had every intention of reporting the crime to them to handle. My suspicions of him being the one behind the recent events were at an all-time high, and I wasn't about to give anything away. I'd never been very good at lying, but I was sure as hell going to lie my way out of this situation.

"Are you an FBI agent, Jillian? Do you work for the government? Were you sent to my company to find evidence to use against me?"

"Of course not. Your company hired me to do a job. That's all I'm doing—my job. I've rotated through several departments in Blaine Financial without a hitch. I'm simply working the accounts I was assigned."

"I'm afraid I'll need more...reassurance...than just taking your word for it."

"What do you mean?" A cold chill ran up my spine, and a sick feeling sank low in my belly. The sneer that crossed his face was pure evil.

"If you're not with the FBI or some other government agency, I can only assume you work for the Marchetti family."

"This is ridiculous, Lorenzo. I work for Morgan and Bartholomew Consulting. In Louisiana. I'm only here for a short time on assignment. How could I possibly work for the Marchetti family? Do I look like a construction worker to you?"

A surprised expression took the place of the sneer before turning into a smile. "Do you really not know who you're fucking? This is priceless. Sweetheart, your boyfriend is a capo in the Marchetti mafia. His father is the Boss. When he's finished with you, you'll be somewhere at the bottom of the Hudson, fodder for the fish."

"I don't believe you."

I held my head high and the indignation in my voice was strong, but my insides were quivering with fear. Suspecting Damon was part of the mob was very different from having it verified. Discovering he was the Boss's son, and high up in the hierarchy of a mafia family, was disturbing. Hearing Lorenzo callously describe my fate with such pleasure covering his face was terrifying.

"You should. He's a dangerous man, and I know dangerous men very well." His pointed look hit its intended target in my chest when my breath seized. "Here's what you're going to do. First, you're going to give me all the information you've uncovered."

"I don't have it here. It's in the office."

He smiled, but it was condescending and didn't reach his eyes. "Jillian, I know you copied data on to a flash drive. You'll hand that over to me."

"I told you it's not here. It's in the office with the rest of my things. I didn't make it back yesterday to pick up my briefcase."

He nodded, accepting my excuse for the moment. "To prove you're not working for the Marchettis, you're going to kill Damon in his sleep."

"What?" I started shaking my head before the word came out. "No. I won't kill him. I won't do it."

"You will, or we'll kill her." He held up his phone and showed a picture of my mother. She was sitting on her front porch in her wheelchair. Her home health care nurse was beside her in the rocking chair. "I have a couple of men down in Abita Springs right now. Great beer down there, I hear. They're waiting for the word from me."

My tearful response was immediate. I just shook my head from side to side. None of this terrible mess could really be happening to me.

"Come now, Jillian. Don't get so upset. Your mom will be fine as long as you do exactly what I tell you."

"I'm not a murderer. I can't do it, Lorenzo."

"You can, and you will, or you'll be responsible for your mother's death. She doesn't seem to be in good health as it is. I imagine she'd have a hard time fighting back, no?"

My tears increased, turning from single droplets to flowing torrents.

"Here's how you'll do it. When he's discharged from the hospital, I'm sure you'll stay with him to play nurse while he heals. Wait until he's asleep, then slit his throat."

I gasped audibly then my hand flew over my mouth. My heart thumped against the inside of my chest, and my body trembled. Speech eluded me, and I was scared out of my wits. Kill Damon or they kill my mom? Cut Damon's throat in his sleep?

Could I simply tell Damon and let him help me out of the impossible scenario I faced?

"No wonder Marchetti picked you. I'm sure he can read your every thought like a book, too. Don't even think of running to him or his daddy with this. We're watching your mom, but we're watching you too. I'll know, Jillian. Do what I told you to do and your mom will be fine. You can move back to Louisiana with her, but you'd better never show your face here again."

He stood and walked to the door before turning to face me one last time. "You have twenty-four hours from the time Damon leaves the hospital. Tick-tock."

"Why? Why would you want Damon killed? I don't understand."

He tilted his head to the side and narrowed his eyes at me. "My men should've taken both you and Damon out on the street yesterday. But they underestimated how protective Damon is of you and how fast Benny is on his feet. With you taking care of the dirty work, my family can avoid an all-out war with the Marchetti family, while still taking out their top capo. They'll be busy mourning the loss of their son and leader while we finish seizing control of their considerable assets. You have easy access to him, and we have easy access to your mother. It all works out nicely in the end. Don't you think?"

He closed the door behind him, and I collapsed into a sobbing mess on the couch. An unimaginable choice was put on my shoulders. One that left me with no way out. No possible escape. No Plan B. How could I live with myself either way?

My mom was my world. She'd done everything for me. She'd

sacrificed so much to send me to college and give me a chance at a life better than she had.

And Damon. I had fallen for him in a big way. My heart connected with his. My body craved him. His family had become my family.

What could I do?

CHAPTER ELEVEN

Damon

𝓜y father surprised me with what I had thought would be a long and painful lecture about security and keeping myself safe. Instead, he praised me for the way I protected Jillian and didn't flinch when the shots rang out. He said he would've done no less for Mama, and that act was the only proof he needed to know I was in love with Jillian.

Love? Really?

After he'd left my room, his words made me examine her place in my life more closely. The mere thought of her returning to Louisiana for good greatly bothered me. Imagining her in the arms of another man created a great rage in me, from zero to a hundred in one second. She'd been away from my hospital room for a few hours, but I missed her terribly and watched the door like a hawk every time it opened.

Also, I had to face the fact that, I did, in fact, take a bullet for her. My safety didn't even cross my mind. But I couldn't bear the thought of her being hurt.

Fuck me. My father was right. I was in love with Jillian.

For the first time in my entire life, I was utterly and completely in love with a woman. Someone who didn't know exactly who I was, what I'd done, what I did on a daily basis. One who was as likely to turn me away when I told her as she was to assure me she loved me anyway. Another first for me was feeling apprehensive over revealing my true profession.

In my world, the strong survived. The stronger gained a reputation. The strongest were feared and revered for cruel and imaginative ways of keeping subordinates under their thumbs. But after admitting my true feelings, that wasn't how I wanted her to see me. She'd fallen in love with the man behind the silenced gun and cement shoes. I could only hope the light of love didn't diminish in her eyes when I told her the truth.

My plans for declaring my love for her were put on the back burner the second she walked through the door. She wheeled a small suitcase behind her and a large bag hung from her shoulder, but her eyes were covered with sunglasses and the smile on her beautiful face was forced.

"How's the patient feeling now? Any better?" She had her back to me, putting her things away in the small closet in the corner of the room.

"Some. Pain meds help. They tell me tomorrow will be the worst day of soreness. We'll see. How are you?"

She turned toward me and pushed her sunglasses up on top of her head, taking her hair with them and revealing more of her features. Her eyes were bloodshot, red-rimmed, and puffy. The end of her nose had a slight red tint to it, and her demeanor fell pitifully short of her normal cheerful self.

Without saying a word, she walked directly to my bed and slid in beside me. Her arm wrapped around my torso and squeezed lightly, holding on to me like she'd never let me go. She tried to hide the sniffles and soft sobs, though the evidence fell in big wet splashes onto my arm.

"Talk to me, doll," I prodded gently.

She shook her head but didn't look up at me. "Just so much has happened."

"Jillian, I know you're shaken up. You've been through a lot in a short time. There's something about me you don't know, so consider this your only warning, doll. My life isn't safe and secure. Shit like this happens frequently enough that I've accepted it. If you want to be with me, you have to understand that."

I began to reveal my true life to her slowly on purpose. If she decided the danger was too much to take, I'd let her go without disclosing the rest. If she walked away, it would hurt like hell. Of that, I had no doubt. But to protect her and the family, I would do it. But if her love for me outweighed her fear of the unknown...if she wanted to be with me despite the bullet wound in my upper chest...if she put her trust in me, she'd be treated like a queen. *My queen.*

"Damon, I'm pretty sure I know what you're telling me. In fact, I've known since the day I met you after the fender bender with one of your dump trucks. If you're trying to scare me off, I'm afraid it'll take more than this."

I knew she was the one.

"Then why the waterworks? What's going on in that beautiful head of yours?"

She raised her head to look at me. "I can't bear the thought of losing you, Damon."

"You won't lose me, sweetheart. I wasn't about to let those guys hurt you. My wound isn't as bad as you think it is.. But, if it makes you feel any better, my mom has already called Doc and told him to keep me an extra day." I rolled my eyes and shook my head, but I was resigned to my fate.

"Are you very sore?"

"Some, especially if someone touches it. But I've been moving my arm and shoulder so it doesn't get too stiff. It'll be as good as new by the time I'm discharged."

"I took off work the rest of the week. I'm not leaving your side for any length of time." She laid her head back down on my shoulder, claiming her place beside me.

"I'm glad to hear that, doll. Do me a favor and don't go back into the office to get anything."

"You don't have to worry about that, Damon. Work is the last thing I want to do right now."

At least I knew she wouldn't be anywhere near Lorenzo for the rest of the week. I'd already considered how to convince her to leave her position permanently. I was glad to hear I had several days and plenty of time to persuade her. The hospital room wasn't exactly the ideal setting to discuss the details of my family and the Sanfratello family. In a couple of days when we were back in my apartment and I knew we'd be uninterrupted, I planned to tell her everything. Once she understood what going back into that office meant, she'd quit working there on her own.

"You know, I'd love to strip you naked and give you a bed bath with my tongue."

Her shoulders started jumping before her laughter burst out. "I'm almost tempted to let you. But since your nurses visit your room three times more than they do any other patient, I'm positive we'd get caught."

"They do come in here a lot, don't they?" Jillian just confirmed my suspicions. With the pain meds fogging my brain most of the previous day and night, I wasn't sure my suspicions were valid.

"Yes. I got no sleep last night with that nurse coming in every few minutes. Has the day nurse been in as often?"

Before I could answer, my door opened and the current shift nurse walked in. She checked my IV, my vitals, and casually glanced around the room.

"Looking for something?" I asked pointedly.

She smiled, hiding her discomfort after being busted checking out my room. "No, just doing my job."

"Well, I feel fine. No need to come back in here until I call you." She met my gaze head on as I stared her down. Finally, she nodded once and left the room.

Jillian looked up at me with her eyebrows drawn down. "What was that all about?"

"I have a feeling my father had something to do with me getting extra visits from the nurses. That needs to stop because if they wake me up every few minutes tonight, I won't be a good patient at all. I'll call him in a few to put a stop to this."

Her warm body snuggled up to mine, combined with the pain killers I'd taken earlier, made it impossible to stay awake. When I recognized her breathing had evened out and her tensed muscles had relaxed, I leaned my cheek against her head and let sleep overtake me. My father's words from earlier echoed in my mind when the darkness shrouded my consciousness. With Jillian in my arms, I couldn't deny my feelings for her.

I loved her.

WHAT WAS MEANT TO BE A SHORT NAP TURNED INTO AN ENTIRE afternoon. My father's chuckle from the foot of my bed woke me. Jillian was still sleeping soundly. She apparently needed the rest after all the stressful events of the last thirty-six hours, on top of the constantly interrupted sleep from the night before.

"Hey, Dad. You checking up on me again?"

"You know I have to. Your mother makes me." He laughed as he took a seat beside the bed. "She looks comfortable there beside you."

"She didn't get any sleep last night. The nurses you paid extra to check on me more often have excelled at their jobs. But the one last night also woke Jillian every few minutes." I raised one eyebrow at him, daring him to deny he was behind it.

"Son, someone tried to kill you both yesterday. I couldn't take a chance that they'd come back and attempt to finish the job."

"Call off the bulldog nurses and put someone on the door. We need our sleep tonight."

"Consider it done. Joe found the guys who shot you. I have more information to relay to you. In private."

Two nurses appeared in the doorway carrying trays of food. Only none of it was hospital food. I cut my eyes to Dad. "Mama cooked."

One side of his mouth lifted. "Your mother's cooking can make anyone feel better."

I woke Jillian to eat, and she quickly sat up, acting as if we were teenagers caught by our parents. "Easy, doll. It's just time to eat. You hungry?"

"Starving. It smells so good." Jillian's hands went to her hair, and a panicked look overtook her face. "I'll be right back." She dashed off to the bathroom while the nurses set up our trays.

"Is the threat over?" I asked while Jillian was out of earshot.

"Not by a long shot, son. Eat up. We'll talk about it later. I'll fill you in on everything."

"I'm surprised Mama didn't deliver this herself."

"She wanted to. I got a tongue-lashing over keeping her away, but it's for her own safety. You'll have to come by and see her when they let you leave."

"Don't act like she didn't call my doctor and have him keep me an extra day. I know she was behind that."

Dad shrugged. "He's her nephew. You think he'll tell her no?"

Jillian emerged from the bathroom with her hair smoothed down and an embarrassed grin on her face. "The food smells delicious. There's no way that's hospital food."

"Mama cooked for us. Come sit down and eat." I motioned to the chair and bedside table the nurses arranged for her.

"How are you holding up, *cara*?" Dad asked.

"Honestly, I'm having a hard time with it, sir. All I can do is take it one anxiety attack at a time." She chuckled nervously as she took her seat.

"You're a strong little lady," Dad replied. "Don't lose heart just yet."

Jillian bit her bottom lip and nodded. "Be sure to thank Mama Lina for me, please. She really didn't have to send a plate for me, but I appreciate it very much."

"She's claimed you as her daughter now. You should expect her to treat you the same as she does Damon."

"Good and bad," I interjected, to my father's amusement.

Jillian smiled, and her eyes became glassy before she averted them. "Mothers are simultaneously one of a kind and all the same, aren't they?"

"Doll, you should call your mom soon. I know you miss her."

"I do miss her. I've been thinking about making a weekend trip back home to see her soon."

"Let's go. I'd love to meet her."

Jillian's eyes, filled with shock and surprise, flew up to meet mine. "You'd go with me?"

"Of course, doll."

"I'll leave you two to make your plans. Damon, we'll talk tomorrow night, yes?"

"Sounds good, Dad. Give Mama a kiss from Jillian and me. Tell her we said thank you."

Jillian was quiet during most of our meal, only giving short replies to my nonstop chatter. The weight of her stress must have been greater than I realized. A long weekend away on familiar turf would help calm her nerves. Seeing her mother after months apart would relieve the constant, nagging concern I knew plagued her. She was an only child, and her mother was in bad health. Jillian felt guilty for being away so much.

I'd have to find a way to bring her mother to New York because I had no intention of letting Jillian leave.

CHAPTER TWELVE

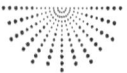

Jillian

*T*he past two nights flew by despite my attempts to stop time. I even tried to keep Damon in the hospital longer —even just one more night to give me time to figure out what to do. But other than a little soreness at the surgical site, there was no apparent indication he'd even been shot.

I thought he was bluffing a little though, being a tough guy for my benefit. There was no way his shoulder didn't bother him.

Benny waited at the curb and opened the door for us to get in. Damon wrapped his good arm around my shoulders and pulled me close to his side. Stir-crazy didn't come close to describing how he'd climbed the walls over the last twenty-four hours. Even so, I was in no hurry to leave. After he was given the all-clear by Dr. Falco, nothing could've wiped the smile off his face.

"I can't wait to get you back to my place. Alone. All to myself. I have so many plans for you. Don't plan on walking normal for a month."

His sexy voice in my ear made my temperature soar. His full lips against the shell of my ear sent chills pebbling across my skin.

His hand possessively gripping my shoulder erased my resolve to make him rest.

I'd already decided to tell him everything once we were in the safety of his apartment. The embezzlement. Lorenzo. My mother. I couldn't wait to unload everything I'd been holding inside. He'd know what to do and how to help me. I'd wanted to tell him what Lorenzo had threatened while he was in the hospital, but I couldn't take the chance of him leaving against medical advice then developing an infection. Damon would've walked out while wearing his hospital gown and headed straight for Lorenzo to settle it man-to-man.

I was a little nervous about telling him. I'd never seen Damon mad, and I wasn't sure how he'd react to my keeping something like that to myself. His sense of honor dictated he defend and protect his own. He'd told me many times he'd claimed me and I was part of his family. My only hope was he'd understand I'd never been in such a predicament before and wasn't certain how to handle it.

My mind was reeling with all those thoughts when his mouth found mine. Soft yet firm, he captured my lips with his, holding them as a willing hostage while I became a molten puddle of need and want. While the city blocks ticked by, everything except him disappeared. I was so lost in the man beside me, in his arms, in his kiss, in his entire being, I didn't care who was watching or listening.

My heart raced, and my breathing kicked up a notch. My hands shook and my insides quivered, but my mind stayed focused on the wicked pleasures he gave me.

His other hand reached up, his fingers gripping my hair, when I felt him flinch and immediately withdraw his hand. I pulled away, breaking our kiss, and gave him a knowing look. "I know that hurt you. Stop trying to hide it from me."

The sweet smile I'd only seen a couple of times made another appearance and completely wiped away my aggravation with him.

A good heart beat underneath his tough exterior, and I was a lucky woman to have experienced it.

"I'm all right, doll. Nothing to worry about. I can still take care of you."

"What if I want to take care of you?"

His eyes darkened with desire. "Oh, you can take care of me all you want. But don't think for a second that fine ass of yours isn't mine."

"Wouldn't dream of it."

The car stopped in front of Damon's building, and Benny opened the door for us. With a quick step through the lobby, we reached the door of his penthouse in record time. By the time we entered his enormous apartment, clothes were haphazardly flung wherever they landed in our quest to reach bare skin. He slowed only long enough to get his arm out of his shirt without injuring his wound.

He guided me as I walked backward to his bedroom. Our lips were fused together. Our hands were everywhere on each other's body, every bit as hungry to touch and feel as any other part of us. When the backs of my knees hit his bed, I broke our kiss and sat on the edge. He gently pushed my shoulders, telling me to slide back, but I slowly shook my head.

"My turn to take care of you."

I took his cock in my hand and began stroking him from base to tip. He grew harder and harder with each pass. My tongue circled around the head, skimming along the ridge before flattening across the top. He placed his hands on the sides of my head, and his fingers curled into fists and pulled my hair with them. When I took him deep into my mouth without warning, the low timbre of his growl rumbled through his chest. His hands gripped tighter in my hair, and his hips began to surge faintly.

My hand squeezed his girth, gliding up and down his cock in tandem with my mouth. The speed of his hips increased and perfectly matched my ministrations. He released a loud groan and held my head still in his grip.

"Are you sure?"

I smiled around his cock and continued toward my goal. He dropped his head back and every muscle in his body tensed in anticipation. "Fuck, Jillian." He moaned as he succumbed to his release, the hot, salty essence hitting the back of my throat in short bursts. With a quick glance up at his intense gaze with his cock still in my mouth, I swallowed every drop of him.

The next second, I found myself flat on my back with his face buried between my legs.

"It's been too long since I've tasted this sweet pussy. It's time for me to feast on you."

And he did. The room spun. I couldn't breathe between screams. My fingers gripped and pulled his hair. I begged him to stop when the intensity was too much...but he didn't. The more times I came, the more he was challenged to make another orgasm tear through me. It was the best torture I'd ever experienced.

When he moved to lie beside me on the bed, I straddled his lap and guided his cock to my wet entrance. His hands held my hips as I lowered myself onto him, taking him inside me to the hilt. I rolled my hips, gliding back and forth then up and down, riding him straight into another earth-shattering orgasm. He followed quickly behind me before I collapsed, resting my head on the uninjured side of his chest.

"You've earned a good meal and a nap. Then I expect to have round two later tonight," he murmured against my head.

"You're determined to kill me, I'm sure of it," I teased. "Do you have any groceries in the house? I'll cook something so you don't have to go back out."

"Mama cooked for us. Everything we could possibly want to eat is waiting in the refrigerator. Joe brought it all over first thing this morning."

"I love your mom *so much* right now."

We both rolled out of bed gingerly, but for very different reasons. He pulled on his lounge pants and tossed me one of his T-shirts to wear. After a quick trip to the bathroom to clean up, I told him to relax on the couch while I scoped out the dinner situation. He was exactly right—his mother had more than taken care of the food situation for the next few days. After making two heaping plates to replenish our energy, I joined him on the couch, and we ate in front of the TV like a couple who'd been together forever.

With my stomach stuffed and my heart full, I turned to face him and break the news. "Damon, there are a couple of important things I've been trying to tell you about, but we keep getting interrupted. The Saturday you were working, I stayed at my apartment and worked on my assigned account. It's been a mess from the start, and I fell into a rabbit hole trying to figure out what happened with the accounting."

He leaned back against the opposite armrest, listening intently to my every word. "Interesting. Go on."

My chin dropped to my chest, and my shoulders sagged when my phone pinged with the chime assigned to my mom's sitter. She would often text me if she had a question about Mom's care. "This couldn't have happened at a worse time. I'm sorry, Damon. Let me check that. It's about my mom."

"No problem, doll." Then his phone pinged with a text, and one side of his mouth curled up. "Guess we're popular, huh?"

He grabbed his phone out of his pants pocket while I dug in my purse for mine. "Doll, I have to call my dad. Go ahead and call your mom, then we'll finish that conversation. Sound good?"

"Perfect. I won't be long."

With my phone finally in hand, I unlocked it and opened the text.

And nearly dropped my phone.

It sounds like you're about to tell Damon everything and test me. I wouldn't advise it.

The picture that arrived next was another picture of my mom, in a different outfit…inside her house.

You won't win this game, sweetheart. Finish your job tonight or mommy dies.

My whole body shook, and I couldn't breathe. How did Lorenzo know about my conversation with Damon? Why did his text have the same tone I assigned Mom's sitter? Did he have someone there with my mom right then?

With shaking hands, I dialed Mom's number. Margie, her sitter, answered, and I finally let out a relieved breath. "Hello?"

"Margie, this is Jillian. Can I speak with Mom?"

"She's already asleep, Jillian. She's had a rough day today."

"What happened?"

"Oh, you know how she is. She tried to get up by herself and took a tumble. She's fine, but waiting in the doctor's office to make sure she didn't break anything wore her out."

"You or her nurse should've called me, Margie. Are you sure she's okay?"

"That's why I didn't call you. So you wouldn't worry when you're so far away."

I hung up with the promise of calling back early the next morning to talk to Mom and thanked Margie for taking such good care of her. Knowing I wasn't there when Mom fell made me feel even more guilty for leaving her. But after confirming she was okay, a much more terrible reality held my undivided attention.

I had to choose yet again between saving my mom by killing Damon…or telling Damon and killing my mom. I was right back where I started, only I'd learned Lorenzo was somehow listening to my conversations.

I wasn't a murderer. I wasn't a violent person.

What was I supposed to do?

"Is something wrong, doll?"

I nearly jumped out of my skin when Damon jarred me from my thoughts. When I looked at him, all I could see was myself standing over the lifeless body of the man I loved. Killed by my hand. The next flash was one of my mother, brutally murdered by strangers. The woman who raised me. Who sacrificed what she wanted so I could have what I wanted. Who trusted me to care for her in her twilight years.

"Jillian?"

"She fell today. Margie had to take her to the doctor to make sure nothing was broken. She's asleep, so I couldn't talk to her myself."

"I'm sorry to hear that. I know how much you love her."

"Do you think she knows?"

"Knows what, doll?"

"How much I love her." My chin quivered, and I held my breath to fight back the tears gathering in my eyes.

"I absolutely think she knows."

"I hope you're right. Guilt eats me alive sometimes." I stared at the floor, unable to look at him any longer.

"Are you ready to finish that conversation we were having?"

"Maybe later. The last thing I want to think about right now is work."

"I understand. How about that nap, then? We've had a long day."

"We have indeed. A nap sounds like a plan to me."

"I'm going to jump in the shower to wash the hospital off me then I'll join you in the bed."

He kissed me sweetly before walking off to his enormous bathroom. When I heard the water running, I grabbed the large kitchen knife off the magnetic strip and robotically moved to his bedroom. With the knife hidden under my pillow, I pulled his T-shirt over my head, laid it on the chair close to the bed, and slid between the silk sheets.

And waited.

CHAPTER THIRTEEN

Jillian

Seconds after the water turned off, Damon slid into bed behind me. His arm snaked over my waist and pulled me closer to him. I wanted to melt into him. I wanted to turn and wrap my arms around him. I wanted to tell him everything—in a whisper if I had to—but I just wanted him to know what I was facing so he could help me out of it.

But I couldn't take that chance.

I didn't know where Lorenzo had ears. Did he listen to us when we made love earlier? My heart broke at the thought. I closed my eyes, squeezing them tightly in anguish from the flood of memories flying through my mind. I didn't know how long I remained motionless, dying inside with each breath. Damon's evenly paced breaths and completely relaxed body drew my attention.

He was sound asleep. He was no doubt worn out from our earlier activities so soon after his hospital discharge. I was worn out from worry and stress and torment and sorrow. With no other choice and no time left, I carefully slid out of bed and took the knife under the pillow with me.

I crept around the bed to Damon's side.

Standing there not breathing, taking in his form and memorizing every detail about him, I raised my hand with the knife. And something in my mind snapped.

Damon

THE BED MOVED EVER SO SLIGHTLY, BUT I KNEW WHAT THE PLAY was. I kept my eyes closed, my breathing slow, and my ears tuned to Jillian's every move. She thought I was asleep, and she wanted to take full advantage of my incapacitation. She was careful, but I heard her every step as she moved around to my side of the bed.

And stopped.

I could hear her breathing—fast and shallow. Then she sniffled, and my heart broke along with the trust I'd instilled in her. Without opening my eyes or turning my head, I felt her move closer to me…hovering directly over me.

The blade of her knife hadn't yet touched my skin, but her intentions were clear. She planned to give me the Columbian necktie Lorenzo had demanded.

"Do it. Then go ahead and cut my heart out while you're at it."

She gasped loudly then a sob broke free. I grabbed her wrist and yanked her arm, pulling her over me and down onto the bed. With her small frame, she was as light as a feather. In seconds, she was underneath me, and the knife was safely secured in her hand pinned above her head.

"Slitting a man's throat isn't like what you see on TV, doll. It's not a simple slice then you're done. Killing a man like that takes a lot of practice to hone your skill. It takes a lot more pressure than you realize. You have to cut deep to get to the arteries. You need strength to hold him down because he'll fight like a wild animal when it's injured and cornered.

"You think it's just a slow trickle of blood, don't you? It's not. Arterial blood sprays everywhere...every time the heart pumps while he lies there, gargling, dying slowly while you watch. It's a very personal way of killing someone, because you have to be close to him. Maybe he lets you in because he trusts you. Maybe he doesn't believe you pose a threat. But once you've started, you have to *stay* close and make sure he dies.

"I think you've watched way too much TV, doll. There are a thousand and one ways you could've killed me and walked away without leaving a trace. Cutting my throat in my sleep isn't one of them. Only a skilled hitman can pull off that kind of hit—no one else who has a clue of what they're doing would even attempt it. Because they know they'd be the one who ended up dead."

I easily plucked the knife from her fingers and held it at her throat. Her eyes watered and her breathing halted. The fear in her eyes was real, but that wasn't the most prevalent feeling I read in them. Her heart was broken because she had betrayed me.

But I couldn't focus on how she felt. All I could think about was her betrayal and how she'd plotted to murder me in my sleep.

"Now, you're going to tell me everything I want to know. That skilled hitman I just described? I train them—teach them everything they know. The first time I even suspect you're lying, you'll find out exactly how ruthless I really am. Consider this your mercy warning. No one else has ever gotten one from me."

"I'll tell you everything. Anything. I promise, Damon. I wasn't going to go through with it. There's no way I could've hurt you."

"And yet, I opened my eyes to find you standing over me with a knife close to my throat. Was that your first lie?"

She shook her head briskly. "I'm not lying. I was trying to picture it and knew I couldn't go through with it. I was trying to figure out how to get out of this mess I'm in."

I knew killers—and she wasn't one. "I guess you'd better start from the beginning and tell me everything, then. Don't leave anything out."

Panic covered her face, and her eyes darted around the room. "Maybe we should go somewhere else and leave our cell phones here. In case someone is listening," she whispered.

"No one is listening, Jillian. That last text wasn't from Lorenzo."

Confusion turned to understanding as her reeling mind absorbed my words. I already knew more than I'd let on. She'd been tested and failed.

She described how she had to dig through financial documents to resolve an accounting discrepancy for her assigned account. In that analysis, she stumbled across evidence of an inside embezzlement job. She didn't recognize the names she gave me, but I did. One name belonged to one of my family's businesses. Money was being funneled from a Marchetti business, through Blaine Financial, and into a shell company set up by the Sanfratello family. The only name she recognized was the man who'd set up the scheme. The man whose vacancy she'd filled.

The man who'd betrayed me and I'd put a bullet in his brain the day I met her. Milo Bianchi.

The second name was an alias I knew Lorenzo used sometimes, but I didn't confirm that to her. She already knew he was involved somehow, but she didn't know to what extent. She continued spilling every detail of what she'd found, how she found it, and how she saved it all on a flash drive.

"Then Lorenzo showed up at my apartment and admitted his men shot you. They were trying to kill both of us. Since he couldn't make another attempt on you without starting a family war, he put it on me to finish. He said either I do it, or he will kill my mother."

I rolled off of her and sat up on the edge of the bed. With an aggravated huff, I ran my hand through my hair.

"I've tried to tell you several times over the last couple of days, but I never could finish. Then I was telling you tonight when I got that text. I thought he was listening somehow and knew what I'd planned. I wanted to tell you so you could help me figure out how to stop him."

I stood and paced back and forth, warring with my wounded pride and my feelings for the attempted-murderess in my bed.

And with the knowledge I already held.

"Jillian, are you really that naïve?"

"What do you mean?"

"Lorenzo specifically told you to slit my throat while I slept. He knew you weren't capable of doing that. He could've told you to poison me, shoot me, or even stab me in the heart. But slit my throat? Come on. He was setting you up to fail."

"But why? I don't understand. How was I supposed to know that? I've never killed anyone. I have no idea where to even start." Her voice climbed a few octaves as the panic rose in her throat.

I turned to face her, contemplating the words I'd say next. "You really have no idea who you're dealing with, do you? I'm very sorry to have to tell you this, Jillian. I really am."

Her hand flew to her mouth. She knew what I had to tell her.

"Your mother is already gone. Lorenzo's men killed her before my men could get to Louisiana. I'm truly very sorry."

Tears poured from her eyes, but she didn't respond. Both hands covered her mouth, and her eyes were fixed on mine. I didn't think she was even breathing at that moment. Shock and agony were vying for first place in her heart.

"When?" she asked meekly.

"They believe it happened yesterday."

"But I talked to her sitter tonight. She said Mom fell today and was asleep."

"Lorenzo's men have her. They knew you'd call. My men are looking for them now."

Heart-wrenching sobs racked her body as she came to grips with what had happened. Her wails carried through my condo, echoing off the walls and ricocheting back to us. My arms ached to hold and comfort her. My mind fought against the urge, reminding my stupid heart she wasn't trustworthy. If nothing else was real, her distress at that moment was definitely genuine.

After several long minutes, she rose from the bed and pulled my T-shirt over her naked body. Seeing her in my shirt stirred an unexpected possessive instinct I had to fight to tamp down. She stood facing me, but her eyes were fixed on the floor at my feet.

"What do you plan to do with me?"

Her tone was dull...flat...lifeless.

"I'm not going to do anything to you. I'm sure you know this, but I think you should return to Louisiana, pay your final respects, and don't come back here."

"Did you know she was dead before we left the hospital?"

"Yes. I did."

"But you didn't tell me until now?"

"I had to know what your choice would be. I had to know if I could trust you."

"I wonder, Damon...if the tables had been turned, and you had to choose between Lina and me...which one of us would you have chosen?"

With that verbal slap across my face, she walked out of my bedroom and left me standing in a mass of confusion. What *would* I have done if I'd been in her position?

A couple of minutes passed before I heard the door shut and the ding of the elevator. I walked into the living room and found my T-shirt laid neatly across the back of the couch. Her clothes, shoes, and purse were gone.

Jillian was gone.

My men would be there to watch over her in Louisiana until this war with the Sanfratello family was finished. They'd make sure nothing happened to her in the meantime.

I vowed to personally make Lorenzo pay. He'd played games with me and used the one I thought I loved against me. He

preyed on a woman with a good heart and an uncommon inno-
cence, then ruined her life. She'd forever blame herself for her
mother's death because she didn't tell me about the threat early
enough.

When we'd had the extra security measures installed in her
apartment, circumstances were much different. But they'd
remained in place all this time, and Joe had been monitoring
them, as he'd been instructed. Lorenzo anticipated the video
surveillance and had a signal jammer in his pocket. But he didn't
figure on the extra voice recording we put in place as a backup. It
picked up his every word, and Joe relayed the information to my
father, who then relayed it to me.

Only, we all received the information too late to stop them.

I didn't believe she'd do what he told her. I thought she'd come
to me and tell me about his ultimatum so I could take care of it for
her. It would've been so easy for me to handle the situation. But
then, I'd never told her about my skillset before that night.

She had several Blaine Financial employees listed as contacts
in her phone. I changed Lorenzo's number in her phone to
Benny's number after my father told me what had occurred. Then
I had Benny text her a picture of her mother I'd found in her
photos along with the threat. She fell right into the trap and
showed her true colors.

The rhetorical question she asked me before she walked out of
my life disturbed me. What would I have done if I were in her
shoes and forced to choose who would die? Could I allow my
mom to die to save Jillian? Could I let Jillian die to save my mom?
If I didn't possess the knowledge, resources, and skills I had,
would I have reacted any differently than she did?

I paced the length of my apartment repeatedly, going over
every detail of what she said, what my father said, and what
Lorenzo said.

I didn't expect to miss her the second she was out of sight.

I didn't expect to feel as if a piece of me were missing.

I didn't expect to be the pussy-whipped moron who wanted her to come back.

One way or another, I'd get Jillian Hart off my mind.

I'd forget about her and move on with my life.

I would've believed that too, if not for the warning in my head and my heart that said otherwise.

CHAPTER FOURTEEN

Jillian

Standing beside my mother's casket was surreal. Though I knew the nightmare I lived was real, everything about her funeral felt like a dream. Extended family and friends showed to say their farewells and tell me what a wonderful woman she was. Then they retreated to their lives and went on living as if my world hadn't just stopped turning. Nothing in my life would ever be the same again.

The state finally released her body after the investigation into her death. It was ruled as a homicide, but there were no leads on suspects. They wouldn't find any leads either. It would forever be an open case. After so long, it would become a cold case, and no one would care anymore.

Damon's men found Margie before it was too late. I was grateful for that, at least. Two deaths on my conscience would be too much. It was bad enough that I lost the man I loved because I'd contemplated killing him...only to find out my mother had already been murdered. Because I was between a rock and a hard place and I didn't know how to get out, I didn't speak up in time to change anything.

I was weak.

I'd never be weak again.

Mom's funeral was over two months ago and was mysteriously paid for by an anonymous mourner. I tried to settle back into a normal routine around Abita Springs. I worked out an arrangement with Morgan and Bartholomew to work at home and only drive into the office when needed. Dealing with the stress of everything I'd been through over those months took a toll on my health and sanity. What was important to me yesterday no longer seemed so important.

I watched the news and combed the internet for weeks looking for information on the Sanfratello family, but nothing indicated Lorenzo was missing or dead.

Damon hadn't tried to contact me in any way since the night I left his apartment. I also searched the internet for any glimpse of him for the first couple of weeks after I returned home. But if I'd seen him with another woman on his arm, I don't know what I would've done. So I stopped looking and tried to forget him.

Tried being the operative word.

I found it all but impossible.

"Jillian Hart?" the nurse called from the door.

"Yes, I'm here." I rose and walked through as she held it open.

"What brings you in to see the doctor today?"

I drew in a deep breath and released it slowly, trying to calm my racing heart. I couldn't believe I was about to say the words.

"My first prenatal visit."

"Congratulations," she smiled warmly. We went through the normal paces of checking vitals and answering medical history questions, then she set the paper gown and sheet out for me to change into before the exam.

After the exam, the doctor confirmed I was indeed pregnant and estimated I was around twelve weeks. The stress of losing my mother and Damon had affected my appetite, so I'd thought the nausea was also part of my near-breakdown. Finding out I was pregnant helped save me from falling into the deep chasm of depression. As much as my heart was broken over losing Damon and the way we parted, I couldn't deny how happy I was to be carrying his baby. Not that he'd ever know. Not that I'd ever tell him. Not that he'd even care at that point.

The nurse filled a bag with a plethora of prenatal supplies and information packets. I felt like a kid on Christmas morning peeking into the bag. I couldn't wait to get home and dive into everything. I scheduled my appointment for the following month and walked out of the office with the first genuine smile I'd had in too long.

I dug my keys out of my purse as I walked toward my car, and I stopped dead in my tracks when I finally looked up.

"You're looking well."

Damon was leaned against my car. His arms were folded over his chest. He was dressed casually, in formfitting faded jeans, a white Henley shirt that stretched tight across his chest, and a black blazer that still gave him a refined air. His blacked-out sunglasses shielded his eyes from me, but I still felt them piercing my soul. He had slight stubble across his jaw, like a perpetual five-o'clock shadow, that was sexy as hell. And he was there…in Abita Springs…in the parking lot of my gynecologist. One thing I learned the hard way about Damon, there were no coincidences.

"Damon. What are you doing here?"

"Is that any way to greet me after all this time?"

"You're right. That was inappropriate. Let me rephrase it."

He smiled and my heart dropped. But I was determined.

"Fuck off. And get the fuck off my car."

"Ooh, I don't know what to think about this new sassy mouth on you."

"You don't have to think anything about it. You kicked me out of your life. I've left you alone. I've left your name out of anything related to the investigation of my mother's death. Now you can turn around and go back to New York and do the same for me."

"Afraid I can't do that, doll."

"Why not? You had no trouble doing it three months ago. There's no reason for you to be here now."

"No reason, huh?"

"None at all."

"Maybe I'll stick around for a while, just in case."

"Suit yourself. Just stay away from me."

I pushed him aside—because he let me—so I could open my car door. His next words stopped my movement again.

"I thought we had a special bond, with you trying to kill me in my sleep and all. I'm disappointed you're not happy to see me."

"Damon, if I had actually tried to kill you, you'd know it. But I didn't. I was scared and felt completely alone. You helped push me to that point by having Benny send that text at the exact moment I was trying to tell you everything. When I turned to you for help, you pushed me away with your tricks. I didn't want to tell you while you were in the hospital because I was afraid you'd do something stupid and jeopardize yourself. I was trying to tell you, and you knew it. You knew what was happening the very second the text came in.

"You know, I questioned why *that* name had *that* specific tone assigned to it. I only used that tone for contacts involved with my mother. But I was so freaked out, I wasn't thinking straight to dig deeper and figure it out that night. I figured out you changed Lorenzo's number in my phone to Benny's, but you fucked up and changed the ringtone too. You made an impossible situation even harder for me. I hope you're proud of yourself for what you've done."

I slid into my car and drove away, leaving him standing in the parking lot. But I couldn't resist a quick glance in the rearview mirror. He watched me drive away, his hands on his hips and a determined set to his jaw. I hadn't seen the last of Damon Marchetti...that was for certain.

Inside my house, I settled in to get some work done and try to get Damon off my mind. But the lure of bag of pregnancy materials was too strong, and I couldn't wait any longer. I finally got up from the desk and dumped the contents out on my couch. Touching, reading, and looking at every gift, book, and pamphlet only made the excited flutters in my chest worse.

An unexpected knock on my door could only be one person. And he'd have to go away. I wasn't about to let him in just when I was learning to live without him. Only to have him rip my heart out when he left? No thank you. A second knock was ignored again...then he let himself into my house.

"What the hell, Damon?" I demanded as I jumped up from the couch.

He pushed the door closed behind him and walked across the room to where I stood. His eyes purposely landed on all the maternity paraphernalia strewn out on my sofa then slowly perused my body on their way back up to meet my angry gaze.

"Looks like I have a reason to stick around now."

More Damon and Jillian are coming soon in Warning, Part Two.

WARNING: PART TWO

Warning
Part Two

Jillian didn't heed my warning . . . but then, neither did I. She didn't know her life was still in danger or that her every move was being watched.

Convincing her that she needed my protection required all my resources. Even then, she didn't want me around.

Making her fall in love with me again would be nearly impossible.

But I'm Damon Marchetti, and I don't know how or when to quit.

1

CHAPTER ONE

Damon

Nearly three months ago, I walked into my parents' house on a Wednesday night, looking for comfort and solace after I was left reeling by Jillian's betrayal—and my complete idiocy. Dinner was already on the table, as I knew it would be, so I took my regular seat and began filling my plate full of food. Comfort food.

But before I could take the first bite, Mama swatted back of my head then took my plate away, holding it hostage just out of my reach. "Where is Jillian? What did you do to her?"

That was a rhetorical question, of course. Mama already knew exactly where Jillian was and why she'd left me. There were no secrets in this family when it came to her kids' love lives. I cut my eyes over to my father, the traitor who'd told on me. He smirked at me, taking Mama's side, as usual.

"Really, Dad?"

He shrugged, unaffected by my verbal jab. "You were wrong in what you did to Jillian, son. Your mother is right to be upset with you. And you made her curse, Damon. A lot. You know I don't like it when your mama curses."

Mama walked around the table, my full plate of food still in her hand, and sat down across from me. "You look me in the eye, son, when I ask you this question."

"Yes, ma'am."

"If you had to choose between killing me and killing Jillian, who would you choose?"

"Mama—"

"Don't Mama me! I asked you a direct question."

"I wouldn't choose. I'd take it myself first."

"That wasn't one of your options. Jillian didn't have that choice either. You should be ashamed of yourself. I am so disappointed in you, Damon. When I met her, I knew she was the one for you. I told you to be good to her, but you didn't listen to me. Now, you've disrespected her, and you've dishonored me with your actions. You've broken both of our hearts. You don't eat at this table until Jillian is back in my house again."

She stood and walked toward the kitchen with my plate in her hand. When she reached the doorway, she stopped and looked at me. "If you want to eat, your plate will be in here."

"There's no table in there. Or chairs."

"You can stand up and eat at the counter."

I looked at Dad for a little help, but he just shrugged before taking a big bite of his food. Right in front of me. As I stood in the kitchen, eating my meal at the counter while the rest of my immediate family ate together at the dining table, a twenty-pound sledgehammer hit me upside my head. The piece of the puzzle I had completely missed in my relationship with Jillian.

Mom and Dad were always on the same side. Always.

They stood shoulder-to-shoulder, figuratively speaking, and faced whatever problems were in front of them, together. They weren't separate units, testing each other's loyalty at every turn. There were plenty of times when Dad would shield Mama from his actions when he thought it was best, but never without her knowing exactly why whatever it was had to happen in the first place. Never without involving her in the important decisions he made or getting her advice when the possible outcomes of his choices were unclear.

They thoroughly believed two heads were better than one.

I should've used that approach with Jillian. But then, hindsight is always 20/20. Using the excuse that I didn't know for sure if I could trust her only helped ease my guilt slightly. My gut knew better. My instincts told me otherwise. My treacherous heart tried to warn my stupid head, but neither listened to reason. In the end, I betrayed myself every bit as much as, if not more than, Jillian did when she readied her knife at my throat.

Jillian and I were a long way from being my parents or having the trusting relationship they had, but the foundation was there. At least, it was before I fucked up in the most royal way.

But my parents raised me to work hard and fight harder for whatever I wanted most. In this case, I'd fight for *whom* I wanted most. The only one I wanted by my side. And when I got her back, I'd never let her go again. I didn't know how or when to quit.

"You look like a man who has a new mission," Dad said, pulling me from my thoughts. He wore a knowing smirk while watching me with his keen eyes. "A trip to Louisiana is in order, no?"

"An extended stay in Louisiana is definitely in order in the very near future. But we haven't found Lorenzo yet. He went underground after issuing the order to kill Jillian. Percy has had his ear to the ground on the street and has checked Lorenzo's emails at Morgan and Bartholomew, but so far he's come up empty."

"You don't think he's left the area?"

"No, not yet." I shook my head. "We've got eyes on his two first-level soldiers. They're still here, working to make alliances with one of the smaller families in the Tri-State area—the Rossi clan. We've already secured their cooperation and put one of our

119

men on the inside, though. Lorenzo is here, for now. When he figures out we've infiltrated the family he thinks will help overthrow us, he'll make a move on Jillian. I'm sure of it."

"In that case," Uncle Leo said from the doorway, "we need to find Lorenzo and shut the Sanfratello family down as soon as possible. Maybe we should call an emergency family meeting, Vincenzo."

Dad replied with a single nod, but his eyes never left mine. I sensed his concern for Jillian, knowing Lorenzo would never confront me head on. Lorenzo's modus operandi lacked the hallmarks of a real man. He'd go through my loved ones to get to me. Since Jillian failed her assignment, she'd be the first target. But I knew that motherfucker better than he thought I did. He'd bide his time, letting me think all had passed and was forgotten, then he'd make his move.

"I'll send a few of my guys down to cover Jillian. If they see any guys out of the ordinary lurking around, they won't hesitate to rush in and crush them."

"Good idea, Damon. Lorenzo's blatant move against you won't go unanswered. Trust me," Dad promised.

I'd hate to be in Geno Sanfratello's shoes after my father finished with him. Lorenzo sealed his own father's fate when he disappeared like a weakling.

"I'll gather the troops for a sit-down tonight." Uncle Leo turned to face me, his expression more serious than I'd ever seen on him. "You make amends for what you did to Jillian, Damon. Direct your loathing at the Sanfratellos for putting Jillian and you in this predicament in the first place, but you have to work this out with her.

"Your mother—she's not happy. Your aunt Maria—she said she's not speaking to you, so I had to smooth things over with her on your behalf. I promised her, Damon. I promised *my wife* you would fix this mess and bring Jillian back into the family. You know I don't make promises lightly, and I don't break them, especially when they're to my wife."

Uncle Leo gave me an out with Aunt Maria, putting most of the blame on Lorenzo, but that wouldn't work for me. I had no delusions of whose fault Jillian's leaving was. That was all on me. But Uncle Leo was right, I had to fix that little problem, at any cost.

My first order had to be protecting Jillian and putting an end to any threat Lorenzo posed against her. While my crew in New York and I searched every possible hiding hole, other family men would comb the area around Jillian's house, watching her every move to thwart any potential attack. Intrusive surveillance means would have to be put in place to protect her, and I'd catch hell when she found out, no doubt. But her safety was worth whatever tongue-lashing she had for me later.

I left my parents that night with a heavy weight on my chest. The maddening premonition that I wouldn't reach her in time lingered in my mind, making it damn near impossible to focus. When I took a mental step back and asked myself how I'd approach this if my heart weren't involved—a novel concept I'd never had to consider before—my path became clearer.

I'd burn the fucking city down until I got my man.

Flick my Bic...I was ready to start a wildfire.

"YOU HAVE NO REASON TO STICK AROUND," JILLIAN YELLED.

She placed her hands on my chest and tried to push me toward the door. But I didn't let her move me out of the way that time. She got away with it at the doctor's office simply because I allowed her to get in her car. But after I walked inside her house, there was no way I'd simply let her push me out of her life. Too much was at stake, and I had to make her see I understood that now. I knew where I fucked up, and I was willing to pay my penance in any way she wanted.

"No, doll." I wrapped my arms around her and pulled her against my chest. "You're not pushing me aside. Not this time. Not ever again. Even if you weren't pregnant with my baby, I'd have every reason to stay. Because I want to be right here with you."

She was torn between what she *should* do and what she *wanted* to do. Part of her craved my touch, urging her to relent and melt into my embrace. The strong, independent part of her needed to stand her ground, wanting the upper hand after the way we parted. I understood both sides of her personality all too well.

"Damon, what you did—keeping my mother's death from me when you knew how much she meant to me... I just can't forgive that."

"Doll, that night, I got a text from my dad at the same time you got the text. When he told me before I was discharged from the hospital, he asked me not to say anything to you until he was absolutely positive it was her. Just because they claimed to have gotten to your mom didn't mean it was true. Yes, we had reason to believe they were telling the truth, but we didn't know for certain. I couldn't take the chance of telling you what we thought but hadn't verified.

"Lorenzo was setting a trap for you—he *wanted* you to rush in and try to save the day. He'd planned to have you both killed that night. That's why her sitter was kept alive, so she could talk to you and tell you that story about your mom going to the doctor. They thought once you found out she'd fallen, you'd fly home right away no matter what the sitter said.

"I wasn't even supposed to tell you when I did, but I couldn't keep it from you any longer. Even after you tried to kill me in my sleep."

"I didn't try to kill you, and you weren't even asleep!"

I smiled, knowing that would be her response. But at least she was still talking to me. "I know, doll. What I'm trying to tell you is there are family rules that just aren't broken. No one simply ignores a direct order from my father without a damn good reason, and even then, there's no way to know how he'd react. I can count on one finger how many times I've gone against his wishes as an adult, and that one time was for you. I broke so many of my own rules for you, it's not even fucking funny. There's only one reason why I'd even think about defying him, and that's because I love you, Jillian."

She shook her head and dropped her eyes to my chest. Then she stepped out of my arms, and I knew the opposing feelings tore her apart inside like a civil war. "I can't, Damon. You hurt me so badly. The past three months without you have been pure hell, but I somehow survived. Day by day, I grew a little stronger, and so did my resolve to get over you. But now I have even more reason to protect myself from you—to protect my baby from you."

"You don't need to be protected from me any more than *our* baby does. I'm sorry for everything, Jillian. For hurting you, for not trusting you, for not listening to my gut when it screamed at me for doubting you in the first place. Most of all, I'm sorry I couldn't get to your mom in time to save her, and for not being able to tell you about our suspicions. Doll, I promise I'll never hurt you again. When a Marchetti makes a promise, it's for life. Especially if it's to the one we love. I hate that I've put this between us, but I'll prove how much I love you over time."

Jillian looked up at me, a sweet but slightly sad smile on her beautiful face. "That was a very moving speech, Damon. I'm sure you rehearsed it for a long time to get it just right. I'll bet that same declaration of love and promises would make any other woman drop to her knees and worship at your feet. Too bad it doesn't work on me.

"Now, you're trespassing in my house, and I've tolerated your intrusion far too long. Get. The. Fuck. Out. If you ever barge into my house uninvited again, I will have your ass arrested. I'm very good friends with the chief of police in this little town, and he'd be all too interested to hear everything I know about you."

"All right, doll. I'll go for now, but only because you're upset, and I don't want to make it even worse by staying longer. But I'm warning you, Jillian, don't think we are anywhere in the neighborhood of being over. I'll be back tomorrow so we can spend the day together. Until tomorrow, my love."

She opened the front door and shot me a look that dared me to defy her. Fuck me if I didn't walk out with a hard-on the size of the fucking Chrysler Building after the way she manhandled me. The things I'd love to do to that sassy Southern mouth of hers.

She may have kicked me out of her house, but I wasn't going anywhere. Nothing in New York held sway over me the way she did. And as long as she was out in the open, she was vulnerable to Lorenzo and his thirst for revenge and dominance in our world. And, as long as she wasn't by my side, he would wait in the wings for his chance at retribution.

Since the moment I learned she was pregnant, I hadn't been able to wipe the smile off my face. I knew I had my work cut out for me to convince her to forgive me, to remind her she loved me, and to show her how much I loved her, too. But giving up wasn't in the Marchetti DNA. Losing her wasn't an option. And allowing her to get rid of me wasn't in the cards.

Her warning still stood the same as the day I first issued it. Once she entered my world, there was no leaving it. That was one rule I'd willingly abide by…and also hold her to.

CHAPTER TWO

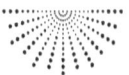

Jillian

*A*fter I locked the door behind him, I plopped down on the couch and stared blankly at the small soft-sided cooler designed to carry the baby bottles, part of my gift bag from the doctor's office. Realization hit me like a runaway Mack truck. My baby would be a Marchetti, and there was no way I could keep Damon's family from being involved in our lives. I hadn't even had time to process my condition before I had to face the fact that Damon would be a hands-on father.

Even if I never wanted to see him again, that wouldn't work in the grand scheme of parenting a child. I would keep the baby, no doubt about that. After losing my mother, being pregnant made me feel a strong connection to her again. My heart was shattered over knowing she wouldn't be there to answer all my questions, to help me after the baby was born, to tell me how to keep my sanity when I'd been up for seventy-three hours straight. But after having my mom and dad in my life every step of the way, I couldn't imagine locking Damon out of our baby's life.

The sacrifices parents made for their kids was already

becoming a reality for me. I had to rise above my intense dislike of Damon for the sake of my child. I reasoned with the conflict brewing inside me. I didn't have to like him to be cordial to him. I could pretend to be on a friendly level with him so my child would never be caught in the middle of our adult squabbles.

But I would never trust him with my heart again.

His carefully rehearsed speech was meant to thaw my heart and melt my panties. He was quite the charmer, I'd give him that. But I saw the real nature of the mafia man behind the façade, the man who'd known what predicament I was in and chose to add to my pain rather than help me. Seeing that side of him altered something in me—and not for the better.

My positive outlook on life changed and was replaced by cynicism and suspicion. I didn't want to be that person, but circumstances created the new me. I'd always wondered if people could really change or if that was just a hopeless romantic's wish. The answer came to me in a way I never wanted. People could change, but only under immense pain and pressure. At least, that was true in my case, and it made me question if I could be the Jillian my mom knew ever again.

"Three months!" I yelled, my hurt and anger bubbling over the surface the longer I thought about it. "Not one fucking word for three goddamn months. Then all of a sudden, he shows up here out of the blue. And declaring his love for me is supposed to fix everything? It's supposed to make it all go away, and we'll live happily ever after now? Fuck. No. Fuck him."

I stomped around my house, and the urge to throw something and break it into a million pieces was strong. But I stopped short of doing it, knowing I'd be the one who had to clean up the mess. I paused in my rant and leaned against the wall, closing my eyes and replaying the encounter again.

"What would he have to gain by telling me he loves me now? What's his game?" I asked myself aloud. "It's a little late to suddenly realize he loves me and can't live without me. He must have a different reason."

Three months ago, when I was in his bed and in his arms, I wouldn't have questioned it. Even though our relationship was still new and most everyone I knew would've considered it too fast, I would've run with it. But I was naïve and foolish, thinking he actually cared for me. I fell in love with him. I fell in love with his charm. I fell in love with his family. But he left me with nothing to show for it.

Well, not *nothing*. He left me with our baby...and a lifetime of being connected to a man who killed any hope I had of finding a lifelong love like my parents had.

I scooped up the cache on the couch and began putting the items away. Thoughts of decorating a nursery soon crowded out the thoughts of Damon and his unwelcome intrusion, and I started to feel happy again. With my laptop powered up, the first site I checked was Pinterest, where I could borrow from the creativity of others and still make it my own. Lost in the world of the interwebs, time slipped away faster than I realized, and soon it was past my bedtime.

When I slid between the covers, visions of Damon's face floated through my dreams. All night, my mind vacillated between reliving the most mind-blowing sex I'd ever known, to the greatest betrayal I'd ever felt. By the time the morning sun rose, I was even more tired than I'd been when I'd gone to bed. After a hot shower and a quick breakfast, I powered up my laptop and left my pathetic love life behind while I focused on work.

When the clock showed it was early afternoon, I took a break from creating a project plan for my new assignment so I could go through various sites for newborn nursery ideas. It was quickly becoming my new obsession. The need to create a happy, vibrant world for my baby was strong—one that was nothing like the real world I lived in.

The chimes from my doorbell stopped the creation of my

dream nursery board cold. With my body motionless, my eyes flitted up to the door, and my heart skipped a beat from knowing who stood on the other side.

"I am so stupid," I mumbled to myself. "Why would I even be excited to see him again?" Because I loved looking at the man, that was why. He was the most handsome man I'd ever seen anywhere —in person, on the screen, in a magazine. And, even after all we'd been through and despite how ridiculous it sounded, my stupid heart wanted to believe him. "I've been staring at pictures of gorgeous nurseries and the smiling faces of happy families way too long. I'm losing my damn mind."

I closed the lid of my laptop a little too forcefully as I stood then walked toward the front door. "Who is it?"

"It's Benny, Jillian. You can open the door—the coast is clear."

Damon wasn't the type of man who needed to send his right-hand man to speak for him, so I decided to let Benny in and find out what he wanted. When I opened the door, the aroma from the enormous bag of food he carried hit my senses all at once, and I nearly knocked him down when I tried to take it from his hands. Though he didn't let me. I was sure Damon gave Benny strict instructions not to allow me to carry my food to the kitchen myself.

Everything smelled so good. There was only one person I knew who could cook like that.

"Mama Lina is here too?" I asked Benny, stepping to the side to let him in. For the food.

"She is. She wants to see you so you two can talk in person, but she doesn't want to intrude if you don't want her here." Benny placed the food on the table and turned toward me, the unspoken question in his eyes.

"I see Damon is pulling out the big guns." I crossed my arms over my chest and arched one eyebrow at Benny.

He rubbed the back of his neck, cocked his head to the side, and an uncomfortable expression crossed his face. "Damon doesn't know she's here."

"What?" My arms dropped to my sides in my disbelief.

"Yeah. I'm between a rock and fucking hard place here, Jillian. On one hand, Damon will have my nutsac for keeping this from him, but I have strict orders from Vincenzo himself. Not to mention my orders from Lina. Maybe I need to take an early retirement when this assignment is over."

"How do you win in that scenario?"

He shrugged. "Just do my best to make sure nothing goes wrong and keep my mouth shut about everything I know. When things go right, there are fewer questions to answer, less of a chance I'll be put on the spot."

"But if you had to choose one person's orders to follow, whose would it be?"

"Vincenzo's. Hands down, sweetheart. He's the boss. I don't question the boss about anything. No one in the family does and lives to tell about it. You've seen how even his grown kids don't argue with him. They all know the drill. Damon wouldn't be happy about it at first, but he'd understand and support me in the end. He knows the family rules better than anyone."

My willpower waned, and I opened the bag, pulling out dish after dish of food Mama Lina sent over. Her generosity touched me, and I knew I had to speak with her. "Tell Mama Lina she's welcome to come over anytime. I'd love to see her."

"She's waiting out in the car. Is now a good time?"

I was surprised, though I really shouldn't have been. "Now's a good time. Tell her to come inside and have dinner with me."

Benny smiled, and I was fairly certain I'd just been played, then he rushed outside to escort her in. But no matter. I had questions that needed answers, and something told me Mama Lina was more likely than anyone else to shoot straight with me.

"My sweet girl, I've missed you. How are you? Have you been

eating? I was so heartbroken to hear about your mama. What can I do to make it better for you?" Mama Lina grabbed me in a tight hug and squeezed a little tighter with each question she rattled off.

"I'm glad you're here, Mama Lina. It's good to see you. Sit down, let me fix you a plate of this delicious food that was just dropped off at my house." I cut my eyes at her and laughed at her obviously proud smile.

After I grabbed the plates, silverware, and drinks, she jumped up from her seat and took over. "You sit, and I will take care of you. I enjoy being a mother. You will be a good mother too. I can tell."

Did she know? Had Damon already told her?

"I hope you're right. I feel a little lost now without my mother here to help me. It's scary, thinking about bringing a newborn home alone." I watched her closely and waited for my words to sink in.

She drove the fork deep into the dish of baked ziti with chicken to scoop out my helping, then froze. Her eyes met mine in an instant, then she stumbled trying to take the seat beside me. She reached out and placed the palm of her hand against my cheek, a myriad of emotions swimming in the same dark chocolate eyes her son had.

"Do you mean you're...pregnant...right now?" She stammered her words, just barely above a whisper but filled with so much hope.

"Yes, I just went to the doctor yesterday morning to confirm it. I thought that's why you were here—I thought Damon had already told you."

"Damon knows?" She straightened her spine and pushed her shoulders back. The tough, take-charge Mama Lina was back.

"Yes, he knows. He was waiting outside my doctor's office for me when I left, then he showed up here a little while later. You didn't come with him?"

"No, *bellissima regazza*. He must not have told you everything either."

"What do you mean?" I'd known the other shoe would drop soon. I just didn't expect it to be so soon.

"Damon has been here in Louisiana for almost three months now...to protect you, *cara*."

"I don't understand, Mama Lina. What are you saying?"

"Damon loves you, sweet girl. He's been worried sick that Lorenzo and his men would get to you before he could. He wasn't about to take another chance like what happened with your mother. He went against Vincenzo's wishes and left New York to be here for you—when you needed him. He's barely slept for keeping watch over your house at night. His men are here too, so you're protected at all times."

Tears sprang to my eyes and my hands covered my gaping mouth. The words were there on the tip of my tongue, but I couldn't speak them. My mind alternated between being confused and comforted by Damon's protectiveness. I chalked it up to prenatal hormones, but deep down, I knew there was more to my emotional response than that.

"My mother's funeral?"

"He was there, watching you from a distance. It killed him not to be able to tell you, to be the one you turned to for support. But he knew what he'd done was wrong. And it *was* wrong, Jillian. Don't think he didn't get an earful from me over it. And from Vincenzo and Leo and Maria. I raised my boys better than that, and his father and I expected more from him. Rest assured, he has learned his lesson.

"He knew you weren't ready to forgive him, it was much too soon. But if you ever did, it would only be because he had *earned* your love. What he should've done in the first place, yes?"

The donation that paid for my mother's funeral...that had to be from Damon.

"Mama Lina, I have to ask you about my mom's death. I have

to know what happened that night...why none of you told me... why you kept me in the dark. I mean, what if it had been Damon? Would you have forgiven Vincenzo for not telling you right away?"

She grabbed my hands in hers, and tears welled up in her eyes. "Jillian, I pray every single day that very scenario never happens and that I'm never faced with finding out exactly what I would do. Their work, it's dangerous, *cara*. They protect and provide for the family, and the family always comes first for our Marchetti men. But sometimes, to put family first, you have to protect the people *in* the family. Even from themselves.

"Let me explain. When Vincenzo gave the order to sit on the information until his men confirmed his suspicions, he did that out of love for you. I know it's hard to understand, because you weren't raised in this world. But he protected you, *cara*—that's all. He only wanted to protect you, because he'd already accepted you into the family.

"He knew how much you loved your mama and how you took such good care of her—even when you traveled for work. My husband, he knew you'd rush home and fight to the death to help her. He wanted to spare you from having to carry all that weight on your shoulders. We were just too late. The Sanfratellos were already there, waiting for you to walk in. You, your mother, and her sitter would all be dead...including your baby. Vincenzo is a good man, Jillian. He makes mistakes like any of us, but he would die for his family. You are part of our family now, and we both love you."

As the tears fell down her cheeks, so did mine. She pulled me into her arms, and I went willingly—immediately. For the first time in the months since I buried my mother, I released all my pent-up feelings at once, and I sobbed against Mama Lina. Crushed against the bosom of the only mother I had left in the world, I allowed her to provide the comfort only a mother knew how. She petted my back, stroked my hair, and murmured encouraging words in my ear. But, most of all, she didn't try to stop my cries. She stayed in the same position as long as it took—as long as I needed her—and just held me.

When the sobs subsided, and I had no tears left to cry, I raised my head and kissed her cheek. "Thank you, Mama Lina. I needed that, and I needed you. I'm going to wash my face—I'm sure I look a mess—then we'll reheat the food, if you still want to stay."

"Of course I want to stay. We have so much more to talk about, *bellissima regazza*. You go wash up, and I'll have your plate waiting for you when you return."

I couldn't deny how good it felt to have her there to take care of me...to mother me. One of the reasons I was still so angry with Damon was because he'd taken away the big family I thought I'd finally have. I lost not only him, but all of his extended family, at the same time I buried my mother. The loss was excruciating, but I realized while I sobbed into her chest I'd never fully dealt with the stress and pain of it all. How I'd held on to my sanity, I'd never know.

When I returned to the table, I purposely kept the conversation light to avoid another complete meltdown while we were eating. I had more questions, and she had the answers. But I'd push for those answers after dessert—because she brought the most scrumptious looking cheesecake I'd ever seen.

Great, food is already dictating my decisions. Is this normal pregnancy craving?

CHAPTER THREE

Damon

"What the fuck happened to the feed? I can't hear a damn thing inside her house. Mobilize the soldiers —*right now*. Lorenzo may be in there with another signal jammer. Fuck it, I'm going over there myself." If I found one hair harmed on Jillian's head, I'd become instantly worse than any serial killer in history. Jack the Ripper wouldn't have shit on me.

"Damon," Percy called sternly.

"What?" I barked back. "Are you fucking deaf?"

"You can't go over there, Damon."

"What the fuck do you mean I can't go over there? Of course I fucking can, and I fucking will. Right fucking now. Who the fuck do you think you are to tell me that?"

"I'm sorry, Damon. But we have orders."

Fuck. Me. He pulled rank on me with my own team.

"Dad called?" I put my hands on my hips and drew in a deep breath, trying to avoid losing my cool any more than I already had.

"Yeah, Damon. I'm sorry, man. He gave a direct order to keep you away from the house today for a while. He said you'd know when the time was right." Percy wasn't happy about relaying the message to me, and his angst showed in his rigid features.

"It's not your fault, Percy. Dad must have something else in play that he's keeping close to the vest. If he says I'll know when the time is right, then I'll know soon enough. He knows I'm not leaving here without Jillian."

"Does she know that?"

"Not yet. But she will."

"Think she'll move back to New York with you?"

I laughed, a short grunt with no humor behind it. "First, I have to get her to willingly walk across the street with me. I'm not even there yet. When I convince her to forgive me, maybe I can employ my entire family to help me get her to move to New York. With her mom gone, I don't know that she has anything else to keep her here."

With my plan of attack thwarted by my father, I planted myself on the couch in front of the television and tried to lose myself in something mind-numbing. It didn't work, though. My thoughts drifted back to what was happening at Jillian's house, and questions of why my father wouldn't have told me about it first.

"Fucking hell, Percy." I flew up off the couch and stomped across the room until I stood over him. All my fury burned in my eyes. "You know, don't you?"

"Know what, Damon?" His eyes were big and round, his pupils dilated, and his leg jumped from nervous energy.

"My mother is at Jillian's right now. Isn't she?"

"Damon, you know Vincenzo doesn't run his plans by me. He tells me what to do, and I do it."

"Answer the question, Percy." I grabbed his shirt and hoisted him up from his chair in front of the surveillance equipment.

"Yes. Lina is with Jillian right now. Vincenzo said we weren't allowed to listen to what they say."

"Son of a bitch! I knew it." I released him and started pacing the floor, running my hands through my hair and trying to figure out my next move.

"Come on, man. You just said you'd get your family to help sway her to our side. If anyone can do it, it's your mom. She has a way of making all of us do whatever she wants."

Then I did laugh, a real one. "That way she has about her is called Vincenzo Marchetti. If she doesn't get her way on one hand, he's always there to back her up and make sure she gets what she wants on the other hand. The man lives and breathes by her."

"Then you want your mom in your corner, right? This must've been her idea—to lock you out of the conversation so she can assure Jillian she's not lying to her. You need Jillian to trust *the family*, Damon. Let her start by trusting Lina."

"You're right, Percy. I know you are. Jillian hasn't had much reason to trust the family, especially me. You know, man, it'll just be hell admitting my mom had to talk my wife into marrying me."

"Whoa. You're already thinking marriage? You just met the girl."

"The girl is pregnant with my baby. And I love her. I don't need more time to know she's the one I want—the only one I want. Apparently, I just need more time to get her to realize that and want to be with me again."

Over three hours later, the sound in Jillian's house mysteriously kicked back on, but all I heard was dead bolts locking. We had cameras installed too, but those were only turned on when I was watching alone. If I had caught any of my men gawking at my girl, I would've ripped his eyeballs clean out of their sockets. I'd never been a jealous man until I met Jillian. Jealous was the wrong word...I was *possessive* of her. Not that I thought of her as anything I'd bought or owned, but I craved her. And I wanted her to crave me just as much.

Mama was right when she said I'd know when I met *the one*.

After telling Percy to take a break, I pulled the headphones over my ears and listened to every sound in her house. From the creak of wood floors to the faint squeak of closing doors, I pictured her every move. When I heard Percy's snores from the other room, I flipped the switch for the cameras and watched Jillian on the flat-screen monitor. She took my breath away, and just the thought of losing her could bring me to my knees.

I kept vigil in that spot for hours, watching her move from room to room. She'd pick up her laptop, scroll through a few pages, then walk back to the spare bedroom. She held the screen up to the wall and stood back as far as her arms would allow, trying to envision the decorations. Then she'd go back to her desk, scribble a few words, and add to the sketch in her notebook.

She was making so many plans and preparations for a tiny baby—and loving every minute of it.

Before long, she went into her en suite bathroom to get ready for bed, washing her face and brushing her teeth. Then she walked back into her bedroom and sat on the bed. She opened the top drawer of her nightstand, removed a gun, and placed it within reach beside her bed. Did she have a bad feeling? In the weeks upon weeks I'd watched her at night, she'd never done that before.

"Percy, get in here!"

He came rushing into the room. "What? What happened?"

"Something's off. She feels it. I feel it. You sit here and listen to everything. If you hear a limb scratch her window, you tell me. I don't care what it is. I'm going over there now, and I'll sit on her front porch all night if I have to. But I'm not staying here another second when she needs me there. Do not turn on that camera unless I say so."

"You got it, boss."

When I'd first moved to Louisiana to watch over her, I bought a house that was only two streets over from hers. Closer would've been preferable, but the one I found was already empty. We could've persuaded another owner to part with his home, but that would've aroused too many suspicions in her small town. The extra attention would've hurt more than helped.

Under the cover of night, I moved between the houses, following my route I established on day one. Avoiding dogs, fences, and security lights, I arrived in Jillian's backyard completely undetected. Percy was in my ear on a small two-way transmitter, feeding me information about what he thought she was doing from the sounds he heard.

Movement in the ornamental shrubbery caught my eye, and I crouched in the shadows to scope out the threat. When he moved again, my blood ran ice cold. An intruder, dressed in all black with a ski mask over his face, slowly reached up toward Jillian's window. Lorenzo had sent an assassin, but he had signed his own man's death warrant instead. When I got my hands on him, I wouldn't need a gun or cement shoes to finish him off. I wanted the pleasure of watching the life drain from his eyes.

I slid my gun out of the holster and attached the suppressor, silent and deadly just like I was trained to do. Then I moved closer behind him, keeping low to the ground, staying light on my feet, but picking up speed as I went. Before he knew I was behind him, I grabbed him in a headlock around the neck with one arm and placed the barrel of my gun against his head with the other.

"Don't. Fucking. Move."

He nodded, as much as he could with my choke hold secure around his throat.

"Are you here to kill Jillian?" I asked calmly. *Walk right into my trap, dickhead.*

His eyes darted around the yard, making me wonder if he had backup somewhere I hadn't yet seen. He tried to stall, not wanting to give me an answer. Not knowing which reply would get his brains blown out of his head.

"Answer me." I closed my arm tighter around his neck with a swift jerk.

He nodded again. "Yes," he croaked.

"That's too bad, fella. Do you know who I am?"

Another single nod.

"Then you know what I do to men who try to hurt my family." The unmistakable smell of ammonia filled the night air, causing my eyes to drift down to his crotch. "Excuse me, but did you just piss yourself? You're a hit man, for Chrissakes. Have some dignity. Fucking amateurs, crawling around at night, getting picked off by real hit men. It's embarrassing, really.

"Back to what I was saying. That's too bad—your being here to kill my girlfriend and all. That means I have to kill you now and get rid of your body tonight. I was looking forward to finally getting some sleep."

The big guy started flailing, trying to break free from my hold. His adrenaline spiked, and the fight-or-flight mechanism kicked in. He wanted to fight *and* flee, no doubt about that. He would disappear into the night if he could just break my stranglehold around his throat. In our scuffle, and my carefulness not to shoot myself with the angle I had the gun trained on his head, he managed to break free.

No matter, I could still do what I had to do to protect Jillian whether he was on his feet or on his knees.

"Lorenzo has a message for you," he taunted with a smug expression.

"Yeah? Let's hear it."

"He said to tell you her time is coming." He pointed toward the window to Jillian's bedroom. "But it won't be slow or easy or painless. He plans on having some fun with her first. Said he bets she's a real screamer in the sack, and he wants to hear her scream his name before she dies."

"I have a message for Lorenzo. You tell him I said he's not man enough to make her scream." Then I leveled my gun at him and shot him between the eyes. His body fell limp to the ground, and I stood over him, firing another round for good measure. "On second thought, I'll tell him myself."

"Cleanup crew is on the way, boss."

"Thanks, Percy. I'm going in to stay with Jillian now, whether she likes it or not."

"Good luck." Percy chuckled in my ear, and I couldn't help but smile along with him.

I knew exactly what he meant. She was just as likely to use her gun on me as she was to let me into her house. Maybe after I explained the very real danger she'd just narrowly escaped, she'd change her mind faster.

I raised my fist to knock on her door, but it swung open before I reached it. She had her gun drawn, aimed directly at my chest, so I jumped to the side and held her wrist in my hand. "Whoa, doll. It's just me."

"Damon, what the hell are you doing sneaking around my house in the middle of the night? Are you *trying* to get yourself killed?"

I released a loud, long sigh before I explained the reason behind my presence. And the man I'd just murdered in order to keep her safe. The blood drained from her face and her hand fell to her side, still tightly gripping the gun, but her finger was a little too close to the trigger for my comfort.

"Here, doll. Give me the gun, and let me help you sit down. You don't look so well all of a sudden." She released it into my grasp without argument, and I tucked it into the waistband of my pants. Then I scooped her up in arms, stepped inside with her glued to me, and locked the door behind us.

I had every intention of only taking her as far as the couch when she met me at the door. But I changed my mind the moment she wrapped her arms around my neck and plastered her body against mine. She shook all over and her teeth chattered—the fear that gripped her was all too real. Instead, I made my way down the hall and to her bedroom. After I deposited her on the bed, I double-checked the windows, closed the blinds, and drew the curtains together.

A. D. JUSTICE

Then I moved her to the guest bedroom, away from the windows on the back of the house that offered too much of an easy access to her. The only window in the spare room was smaller and higher off the ground. When she was tucked in, I lay down beside her on top of the covers and draped my arm over her.

"Rest now, doll. I'm not going anywhere tonight. I'm right here to protect you."

She buried her face in the crook of my neck and eventually drifted off into a fitful sleep. I, on the other hand, got zero sleep. With one man down, they'd come back with reinforcements. My men already knew the drill, but I wouldn't take any chances with Jillian's life by dozing off and getting caught unaware. Several times during the night, her whole body jerked, and she awoke with a stifled scream. From the few times she talked in her sleep, I knew she had nightmares about someone breaking in and getting to her.

Not on my watch, doll.

CHAPTER FOUR

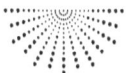

Damon

The last time she woke, the sun hadn't been up long, but she slid out of bed and headed for the shower.

"There's no window in there, so that's good. Just lock the door for protection, doll."

"Do you mean to protect me from *you* while I'm naked and wet?" A hint of a smile played on her lips. At least she was starting to joke around with me again.

"Doll, no door in the world could protect you from me under those circumstances." I winked and flashed her my best smile. "But after last night, I'm not taking any chances with your safety. We have to get you somewhere more secure before I can bust down the door and join you in the shower. Only then will you know what wet means."

"I'll shower first, then you can jump in while I stand guard. But, Damon, when you get out, we have to talk about last night. *All of it.* If I even think you're holding out on me this time, I will cut you out of my life completely."

"Is my sweet Louisiana belle becoming a ferocious tiger on me?"

She placed her hand on her stomach, instinctively protecting the precious life inside. "I'll be whatever I have to be for my baby. Even if that means I'll be a single parent."

The jab to my heart couldn't have hurt worse if she'd used a dagger and physically pierced it. Was she the type of person who would keep a child from its father? A father who wanted nothing more than to make the mother and his child his whole world? My stunned silence and pained expression told her all she needed to know, apparently. Her aggressive stance softened, and her gaze fell to the floor.

"We'll talk about everything after breakfast. I'm trying not to make any rash decisions about anything, Damon. But so much has hit me all at once, and I'm still trying to find my footing after confirming my pregnancy just yesterday. You may have to be a little more patient with me than normal."

"I can do that, doll. Jump in the shower. When you get out, I'll make breakfast, then we'll talk. My cards are face-up on the table, whatever you want to know."

"Thank you—for protecting me last night. And for this—for the way you're trying. I have to keep reminding myself your family doesn't usually operate this way with outsiders. I'm finding it hard to be understanding about some aspects of this myself, so I appreciate the effort you're giving."

She stepped into the bathroom and locked the door behind her as I'd asked. But I had to bite my tongue to keep from telling her she wasn't an outsider now. She was part of the family. And she always would be. Joining a mafia family was a lot like taking marriage vows, only there was no divorce that could dissolve the ties. She was married to the family the same as one day—soon—she'd marry me. And, like the family expectations, divorce wasn't a word in my vocabulary either.

But I knew my love better than she thought I did, and telling her those terms would only cause her feathers to ruffle. That would get us nowhere fast. But if she saw what it meant to be part of something as big and wonderful and mad and crazy as my family and all that came with it, I was certain I could persuade her to my line of thinking. And every step we took together until she reached that conclusion on her own would be another building block to cementing our future together.

One step at a time, doll, and you'll be mine forever.

"Damon, I'm out of the shower now," she called out about twenty minutes later.

I stepped into the doorway when she started combing her hair. "Thought you might enjoy this while I shower, then we can sit down and eat together."

"Mmm, that smells so good. What is it?"

"It's called Passion Tango, from Havana Tea. It's delicious."

"Where'd this come from? I don't have this in my kitchen."

"Percy brought it over when he brought me a change of clothes."

She took the steaming mug from me and sipped it carefully. "This is so good, Damon. Thank you."

When she started to leave the bathroom, I wrapped my hand around her elbow and stopped her gently. "I need you to stay in here with me, with the door closed and locked."

She cut her eyes up at me, a mixture of wariness and disbelief swirling in them. "And why would I need to do that?"

"One, because a man showed up here last night with intentions of taking you to Lorenzo."

Her eyes grew wide, and her lips parted on her gasp. She knew she couldn't defend herself against a man three times her size.

"Two, because if I hadn't shown up when I did, he would've crawled through your window and achieved his mission without my knowing where to even start looking for you."

She covered her heart with her hand and released a ragged breath. I knew she had the same thoughts I had—what Lorenzo and his goons would do to her, in a place where I couldn't find her to save her.

"And, last—but most important—three, because I'm about to get naked, and you know you want to watch."

She dropped her chin to her chest and released a hesitant laugh followed by a resigned sigh. "*Fine*, Damon. I will wait in here with the door locked while you shower. I'll just...sit on the commode and drink my delicious hot tea."

"By all means, my lady." I closed the lid and put a folded towel on top for cushioning. "Please have a seat and enjoy the show. Your face will be at the perfect level for viewing."

There's my sweet Southern belle and her scorching red face. So, she is still in there under that tough bravado.

She tried to avert her eyes, but I caught her looking. Several times. Because I took my time getting undressed directly in front of her. Unabashed. Unashamed. Blatantly offering everything I had for her taking. If the number of times she licked her lips was any indication, I thought we'd move on to the next phase of our reconciliation sooner rather than later.

We chatted while I showered, and she dried her hair and put on her makeup. She kept the conversation light, actively avoiding any topic that could be potentially volatile. But I was onto her game. She wanted to wait until I was dressed and we were on even footing again. With me naked and wet in the shower right beside her, she was more than a little distracted.

She was more than a little tempted.

To throw gasoline onto the flames, I purposely didn't towel off before I stepped out of the shower. In fact, I didn't have a towel in my hand at all.

"Sorry, doll. I must have forgotten to grab a towel before I came in here. Mind if I use yours?"

Her eyes followed the droplets of water as they ran down my torso and disappeared into my happy trail. Her lips parted, and her tongue darted out, swiping across her lips and making my dick jump in response. The rise and fall of her chest came in quicker bursts, and she was at a loss for words. I was just glad to have her somewhat under my spell again. From her small pants and lustful gazes, she remembered the pleasure I could give her.

"Is that a yes?"

She looked up at my face and caught a glimpse of my smirk. She shook her head and snatched the towel off the rod where it hung behind me. "Yes, that's a yes. Can we leave the bathroom now?" She thrust the towel at me, hitting me in the chest with it. I calmly took it from her hand and wiped down the front of my body.

"Let me check the room first. Sit tight." When I turned toward the door, I felt her eyes burning the skin of my ass as she stared at me. I looked over my shoulder at her, catching her in the act, and smiled. "Go ahead and look all you want. We both know you love my ass."

She rolled her eyes and pulled the corner of her bottom lip between her teeth in a poor attempt to hide her smile. It was there, though. Hope was there too—for my part. Hope that we could overcome the obstacles I'd put between us and get back to what we were good at. I grabbed my gun from the vanity counter and unlocked the door, stepping over the threshold ready to fire at anyone on the other side.

"You're still naked, Damon," Jillian said from behind me.

"Yeah, I can shoot just as well naked as I can with a suit on, doll. My clothes are out here on the bed. Come on out."

She watched me dress, and I couldn't help but notice the look of disappointment on her face when I pulled my shirt over my head and finished hiding my body from her view. But she knew I could read her like a book, so she kept her gaze anywhere except meeting mine.

"Can I go into my bedroom and get out of my nightgown now?"

"No need to wait until we're in your bedroom. You can get out of that gown right here, right now. I'll even help you."

"That's not what I meant."

"Ha. I think that's exactly what you meant. A little Freudian slip of the tongue. Say the word, doll, and I'll give you a slip of my tongue you won't ever forget."

Her skin flushed, her breathing hitched, and a slight tremor ran through, causing her hands to quiver. "I need to get my clothes on. Right now."

Fuck if she wasn't the most alluring woman I'd ever met. Just a few words of the right kind and she was more than ready for me.

"Come on, doll. I'll escort you to your bedroom." I slowly opened the door and checked the hall before taking her hand and leading her to her room.

Once inside, I locked the door behind us and kept watch on the windows while she stepped into her closet to dress. I heard soft sighs and muffled groans between the sounds of hangers sliding across the bar. She was still fighting her feelings for me, and I understood her hesitancy. People who gave me a reason to distrust them didn't get a second chance...or even a second breath.

Maybe she should've fallen into that category from the moment the knife in her hand was intended for me. But I knew, even at that very second, she couldn't go through with it. She wasn't the hardened type. She was soft and warm. Loving and giving. Feisty and full of life. Gorgeous and down to earth. And I knew, even before that fucked-up night, that I was in love with her. I just wasn't ready to face the truth that she was the only happily ever after for me.

I wasn't ready to put my full trust in someone and hand my heart over to her. No reservations and no holding back. No holds barred. But that changed when I lost her, and I realized what a fucking moron I was for doubting her in the first place. The shock to my system made me realize my heart was all in with her even if my mind wasn't ready for any of it.

"What now? I mean, I doubt your plan involves me staying here after someone tried to break in last night." She stepped out of her closet wearing a cotton dress that hit at mid-thigh, revealing her luscious legs and supple skin.

"You're exactly right. My men are watching, but it's still too dangerous for you to stay here. They wouldn't be able to stop a drive-by shooting or a Molotov cocktail lobbed through your front window."

She closed her eyes and pressed her fingers against her temples. "Don't say it, Damon."

"You've only had one prenatal visit. There are plenty of great doctors there. Wonderful hospitals. Top-notch care."

She kept shaking her head through my every word, fighting me every step of the way. But then, she wouldn't be Jillian if she didn't have that independent spirit.

"Mama and Aunt Maria are there. They can help us, give us advice, cook for us. My sister Carrie told me she wished you lived there so she could get to know you better. My whole family loves you, Jillian. Almost as much as I do."

"You know, Damon, you don't fight fair at all. You just used your mother, your aunt, and your sister against me, all at once. Then you mess with my head and tell me you love me."

"Jillian, I've never declared my love for anyone outside of my immediate family before in my life. Not one single woman can claim I've ever said those three little words to her. You are the only one for me. You always will be."

She whisked a tear from the corner of her eye before it had a chance to fall on her cheek. "You want to take me back to New York, huh? I just don't know, Damon. I've finally gotten settled back in here. I have a job to think of, health insurance, a routine I'm used to. Can I not just move somewhere else here?"

"Jillian, you know better than that. This only ends one way, doll." A thought occurred to me about her reluctance. She didn't want to leave the area where her mom was buried. "I'll bring you back to visit her grave as often as you want. All you have to do is tell me, and I'll make it happen for you."

"Really?" Her tone was so hopeful and so surprised.

"Of course. I'd do anything to make you happy, Jillian."

She nodded slowly, still deep in thought. "Let me think about it for a few minutes."

"Okay. You think while we eat. I still need to feed you and our baby. Come on, doll."

We walked to the kitchen, and I cooked a big breakfast for her, along with another piping hot cup of tea, and we ate together—enjoying each other's company. After we worked side by side on the dishes, I took her hand in mine and led her to the living room. She said she wanted to talk and she wanted all the details, and I had every intention of answering her questions.

But when we turned the corner, the hairs on the back of my neck stood on end. The SUV with the blacked-out windows creeping by her house caught my eye just in time to grab her and drop to the floor with my body completely covering hers. The bullets sprayed the front of the house, sending shards of the overly large picture window and all kinds of debris hurtling toward us. She tried to be brave and weather the storm of shrapnel zinging over our heads, but the terror of the moment won. I could barely hear her shrill screams over the noise of the rapid gunfire.

Shots rang out from a different direction, and I realized my men had flanked them, drawing fire away from the house. Still, there was no way I'd lift my head and risk moving from the relatively secluded spot where we fell. Shards of glass were stuck in my back and all down my side, but nothing I couldn't survive. Squealing tires and familiar voices yelling my name told me the coast was clear.

"Jillian, are you hurt?" I pushed up and sat back on my heels, checking her over for wounds. "Are you shot? Answer me, sweetheart!"

"N-n-no."

She sat up and wrapped her arms around me, her whole body shaking violently. Her arms scraped the ends of glass that stuck out of my skin, but I ignored the pain and ran my hands over her instead. Not feeling any obvious wounds, I wrapped my arms around her protectively and shouted orders to my men.

My only certainty was I had to get her out of that small town and under the protection of my family at a fortified safe house. That was the second attempt in as many days, and the force had increased exponentially. Their next move, if they couldn't snatch her, would be to bomb her house and obliterate it completely.

"Jilly, doll. We have to go right now. Do you understand?"

"Y-y-yes. T-take me with you."

CHAPTER FIVE

Jillian

*D*amon took care of everything.

He had someone pack all my clothes.

Someone else talked to the police and gave a full account of what had happened, leaving out key names and a few details here and there. A thick envelope exchanged hands, and I assumed everything was smoothed over with the reassurance we were leaving town.

Benny drove us to a small airstrip and we all boarded the private jet bound for New York.

I was silent every step of the way, other than the occasional one-word answers I gave Damon in my house and in the car on the way to the airport when he asked if I was all right.

Physically, I was fine, so that was how I answered.

I'm fine.

Mentally, I wasn't so sure how I felt.

Seeing his shirt and pants soaked in blood when I finally let go of him after the bullets stopped sent me into a new state of panic.

"It's just small cuts from glass, doll. Don't worry about me." He repeatedly reassured me while he changed clothes. But I saw all the cuts and the jagged splinters of glass sticking out of his skin when he changed into the clothes Benny gave him.

"We need to get those pieces of glass out of you, Damon."

"You can help with that on the plane. We have to get you out of here right now. Trust me, Jilly."

I noticed he had come up with a new pet name for me. Maybe it shouldn't have pleased me as much as it did. But I couldn't help but feel special because of the new term of endearment. He was trying to win me over. He was doing and saying all the right things. But I hadn't forgotten what he had done that he needed to make up for in the first place, or why I was so leery of letting him back in. I decided the wait and see approach was best. If he kept up the new and improved Damon after we were back on his turf for a while, then I could start to think about letting him in again. Trust was a completely separate issue. I wasn't sure I could ever trust him again.

The hail of gunfire that rained down on us was beyond terrifying, and my first thought when Damon used his body to shield mine was he would die, and I'd lose him forever. I'd already witnessed him get shot once on the streets of New York. That bullet was intended for me, too. And he saved me then, too.

Hence, my confusion. How could the same man who saved my life twice be the same one who set me up and crushed me? How could he make me feel protected yet guarded toward him? How could I feel so loved and so unloved by him at the same time?

My feelings about him and his actions were all over the board. I could chalk up the confusion to pregnancy hormones, but since I'd only found out I was pregnant a couple of days before, that was a bit of a stretch. The truth that I didn't want to face was I still loved him after everything we'd been through. Even though I didn't want to love him anymore. Even though I thought I'd gotten over him in the months we were apart. When I shouldn't have had any feelings for him except contempt. When I should have been focused on putting my world back together one piece at a time and moving forward without him in it.

But our connection was sealed for good...by the life growing inside me. Whether that meant we were a couple or not, I had to consider how my decisions would affect our baby in the long run, above how he affected me at that moment. During the ride to the airstrip, I'd make up my mind, then glance over at his side again, knowing he was in pain and needed medical attention.

He'd catch me staring at where his wounds were, and he'd squeeze my hand reassuringly, making me think maybe he was different, then I'd change my mind again.

The vicious circle of uncertainty felt impossible to break.

Then I remembered my stance on what made people change —*only under immense pain and pressure*. I didn't think anything Damon had experienced quite fit that bill. Perhaps he actually thought he'd changed—and it could have been that his demeanor wasn't entirely an act—but there was also a good chance he'd go back to his old ways once we fell back into a comfortable routine. Only time would tell, but until I had definitive proof the new and improved Damon wasn't a temporary fix, I vowed to keep my distance. Emotionally, at least.

By the time we finally boarded the plane, I couldn't stand the thought of his lacerations any longer.

"Take your clothes off."

"Doll, you have no idea how much I've wanted to hear you say those words to me. Now, there are a few more I'd like to hear, along with a few moans, followed by screams loud enough to shatter my eardrums."

"Very funny, Damon. That's not what I meant at all, and you know it. I assume you have a first aid kit on the plane? There's no telling what is buried in your skin and what kind of infection you'll get from all the debris. We have to get you cleaned up as much as we can."

"If that's what it takes to get your hands on me, I'll take it." He winked, one side of his mouth lifted in a smug smile, and he asked the flight attendant to bring the first aid kit to us.

When she returned with a full medical bag, my eyes bugged out of my head and my jaw dropped open. But, *of course*, he'd have a full range of supplies on board—occupational hazards and all.

"I'm not sure I'm qualified to use all of this—actually, most of this equipment. I'm not a flight surgeon, you know?" I chuckled to myself, though I wasn't sure if it was out of humor or the last step before a complete and total mental breakdown. Focusing on helping Damon allowed me to avoid processing the events for a short time. The nightmares to come would force the issue later.

"Not to worry, my love. We only need a few items out of there." He pulled out what looked like a skinny pair of scissors. "Hemostats. Here's the rubbing alcohol. A little peroxide to make things interesting. And some gauze. That should do it."

"No bandages? Magnifying glass?"

He rooted through the bag and found the magnifying glass, then handed me a box of various sized bandages. "Doubt we'll need them, but just in case. Where do you want me, Dr. Hart?"

"Is there a bed on this plane?" I looked around him, toward the closed door at the back of the plane.

"There sure is. Is this your subtle way of trying to get me into bed, Jillian?"

"I'm not being subtle about it all. Take your clothes off and go lie on the bed."

His dark laugh rumbled through his chest when he turned toward the bedroom. The pure masculine allure of it crashed into me like a tsunami, forcing me to fight the carnal urges trying to overtake my logical side. Being near that man was dangerous in so many ways—to my mind, body, life—and libido. We reached the bedroom and he stood to the side, extending his arm into the room.

"Ladies first." Then he closed and locked the door behind him.

Damon Marchetti would be the death of me one day, one way or another, I was sure of it.

With my pursed lips, arched eyebrow, and hand on my hip, my disbelief was written all over me. I didn't even have to ask the question—he knew instinctively what was on my mind.

"You can't blame a guy for hoping, doll."

I put the supplies on the bed and crossed my arms over my chest. My foot tapped lightly. *I'm waiting...*

His outburst of laughter didn't help. "All right, doll. I'm kidding with you. We still need to have that talk you wanted, because I'm ready to move past all this and get on with our lives together. Now we won't be disturbed, and we can kill two birds with one stone. Actually, we can kill three birds."

"What three would that be?"

"Having our talk, removing the glass from my skin, and having your hands all over my naked body. Winning combination if you ask me."

He simply refused to let me stay mad at him.

I closed my eyes and shook my head. "On the bed, Marchetti. On your good side."

He fully undressed, and I couldn't help but notice how careful his movements were when he removed his shirt and pants. The wounds hurt more than he showed; I already knew that, but seeing it all over again sent feelings of gratitude and empathy coursing through me. Just when he stretched out in the middle of the king-size bed, the captain came over the intercom to announce our impending takeoff. I sat behind Damon with the provisions at my side and began working on his injuries.

"I had a long talk with your mom yesterday afternoon." I waited for his reaction. Would he be surprised? Did he already know?

"Yeah, I heard about that after the fact. Seems she and my dad planned that visit behind my back. They didn't want me involved at all."

"Did that bother you when you found out? Being left out of the loop on important information?"

He waited a couple of extra seconds before he replied. "Yes, it bothered me a lot. At first, I felt betrayed by my own family and my men. I wanted to break everything in sight."

"But you had to deal with it because the order came from your father, right?"

"That's exactly right. As much as I wanted to, I couldn't go against his orders in front of my men. I have to show him the same respect they do because one day I'll take over the family from him. If my men saw me go against the head of the family, they'd go against me when I'm in his position."

"Your mom explained some of that to me during our visit. She said any sign of disobedience made the family look weak to your rivals, and a weak family wouldn't last long. If several smaller rivals banded together against a large but weak family, they could sway the allegiance of your men to get them to turn against you."

"Exactly. The balance has to be maintained so the family's strength and integrity remain intact. It's the cardinal rule of our world."

"But you broke it for me."

"I had to, with the way the events unfolded. It was my fault. I took responsibility for it with my father. Thankfully, only he and I knew what went down, so my actions didn't harm his reputation in the rank and file of the family. I was lucky in that. Even Benny doesn't know everything."

"What would've happened to you if the others had known?" I paused my work for a moment, genuinely curious about the inner workings of his family business.

"I would've been excommunicated from the family. Exiled to survive on my own."

"Cast you out to fend for yourself? Against Lorenzo and anyone else who had a grudge against you? Your parents would've done that to you?" My head reeled, and my heart pounded against my chest.

"To protect the family, yes. They wouldn't have had a choice." His tone was matter-of-fact, but I could feel the undertow of conflicting emotions in his tensed muscles. Facing that possibility wasn't as easy for him as it appeared.

"You risked that for me? I don't understand any of this, Damon." My frustration mixed with my anguish, making tears sting my eyes.

"What do you not understand, doll? Ask me whatever's on your mind. I'm an open book."

"Mama Lina explained your father's orders in detail, so even though I don't agree, I can understand why he didn't want you to tell me anything until he knew for sure. But what I don't understand is why you set me up the way you did.

"I needed you, Damon. I needed you more at that moment than I'd ever needed anyone in my life. And the words were on the tip of my tongue to tell you when that text came in. I had already chosen to turn to you and trust you with a situation I'd never even dreamed I'd have to face. You knew everything, but you betrayed me and stripped away any hope I had for a happy life. My heart will never be whole again. My mom died...without me by her side...at the hands of a monster. And I have to live with that now.

"Why didn't you tell me you knew Lorenzo had tried to force me to choose between your life and my mother's? Why didn't you immediately step in and *help* me instead of *hurting* me even more?"

He looked over his shoulder before he gingerly rolled onto his back, keeping his eyes trained on mine, then sat up to face me. Eye to eye, I saw his torment, felt his pain, knew he had deep regrets. But I needed an answer. I had to understand *why* he would do that to me. Was there any explanation I could even accept? Could anything he said change my mind?

159

"Jillian, I don't have a simple answer to your question. All I can do is explain a few things about my life and hope you understand, even if you don't fully agree. For the record, even I don't agree with what I did. I'm sure Mom told you that she and Dad don't either. They've given me the hell I deserve over it. For now, all I'm asking is for you to hear me out and consider my words. Okay?"

"All right."

"I was attracted to you from the moment I met you on the expressway. I didn't lie, it was standard protocol to have you checked out and cover your medical expenses so nothing came back to bite us in the ass. But I was so drawn to you, I may have pushed for you to ride with me to the hospital when you didn't have to. Then I stayed with you because I was under the spell of your beauty and charm. It's clichéd, but you were different from every other woman I'd ever met.

"Remember when we were in the car, and you said those three women were all trying to get my attention? You felt sorry for them because they couldn't even turn my head. Not to brag, but that's an everyday occurrence. People know my family. They want to be part of it. Women throw themselves at my brothers and me all the time—they want the exciting life, the money, the status. Not a single one of the women I've dated ever cared about me, the man behind the boss's son.

"At first, I didn't trust you at all, but that's par for the course in my world. We don't trust anyone until they've proven their mettle. When you said you worked as a consultant at Blaine Financial Services, all my red warning flags went off. I was faced with a difficult decision. There were two possible scenarios— either you were completely innocent and truly in the wrong place at the wrong time with that wreck. Or...you worked for the Sanfratello family and were sent to infiltrate the Marchetti family. It was my job to figure out which was true. Even after I knew the answer, I had to keep you close to protect you because I'd put you in danger just by being seen with me.

"The more time I spent with you, the more I lost my edge and my grip. You got under my skin to the point I was making decisions based on what was best for you instead of what was best for the family. You don't know how much putting the family first has been ingrained in me since birth. The stare down with Lorenzo at your office, taking a bullet for you on the sidewalk, letting you stay at my apartment before you'd been completely vetted—none of that had ever happened before. I wasn't Damon Marchetti, the crime family capo. When I was with you, I was just Damon.

"Your apartment was wired with audio and video equipment for a couple of reasons. We needed to monitor you as a potential threat, and we needed to protect you as a potential victim. When Lorenzo showed up, he had a signal jammer in his pocket to knock out our digital video, but the backup audio equipment was old-school analog, so it picked up the entire conversation.

"When you didn't tell me about it right away...when you didn't come to me for help after meeting my family and saying you understood the warning I gave you about staying with me...it stung bad, I admit. The thought crossed my mind that I'd been played, though nothing about you seemed to fit that type of person. When Dad told me his suspicions about your mom, not being able to tell you fucking killed me, Jillian. That was another first for me—secrets have never been difficult for me to keep. I doubted myself more than I doubted you.

"So, I arranged that stupid fucking test with Benny's help, thinking I'd prove two things. One, that I was still in control of myself, of the family, of my life. And two, that you were mine. That you'd come running to me and ask me to fix the problem you knew you couldn't. Then it all backfired on me—blew up right in my fucking face, and I took my frustrations out on you.

"I can't promise I'll never fuck up again in my life, because we both know that's not realistic. But I can and do promise my future fuck-ups will not be anywhere near that magnitude of stupid. I'll stick to the lower levels of fuck-ups, like forgetting to grab a gallon of milk on my way home because I'm too eager to see you.

"I love you, Jilly, and I'll do anything to make up for how I've hurt you. I promise you, on my honor as a Marchetti, I'll never give you a single reason to doubt my love again. I'll never give up trying to win you back."

6

CHAPTER SIX

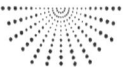

Jillian

*A*fter he finished his explanation, I gestured for him to lie back on the bed, and I began plucking pieces of glass, wood, and other unidentifiable fragments out of his side with the hemostats. Focused on my task at hand, I used the gauze to wipe away small rivulets of blood that trickled from some of the larger wounds.

"Does that hurt?" I asked softly.

"I'm okay, doll. Don't worry about me. I'm just enjoying all the attention you're giving me."

He hadn't yet given up on me, I had to give him credit for that. But I couldn't respond to his full confession. I felt so much—too much—until I simply shut down and felt nothing. "Comfortably Numb" by Pink Floyd instantly made sense to me. That's how I felt. Numb.

I considered the very real possibility that I was broken inside.

"Your mom said you've been in Abita Springs for the past three months. What took you so long to contact me?"

"Promise not to get mad at me?"

"No."

His body shook with laughter, and I couldn't help but smile. He didn't look back at me, so my own laugh was my little secret. "Fuck, I've missed that sexy, sassy mouth of yours. Fair enough. Yes, I was there that whole time, and I've watched you every day. All hours of the day and night. I knew Lorenzo would make his move on the one person who means the world to me, the one he could use to hurt me the most.

"I know him very well, Jillian. He's a coward in one sense, but he's also ruthless and cunning. He'd never have the guts to face me like a man. He'd send his goons to do all his dirty work. But he wouldn't hesitate to hurt you once he had you incapacitated. So, I watched and waited for him to make his move.

"The weeks leading up to yesterday were torture enough. We had tried to keep up pretenses that I was still in New York, hoping Lorenzo would grow a spine and step out of the shadows to approach you himself. When I guessed why you were going to see the doctor, I couldn't stand back and wait any longer. But when I revealed my presence, I think it prompted his men to act."

"So...they were waiting for you to show up at my house all this time? Watching me to see if I was meeting you out somewhere?"

"That's the theory. He was waiting to see if he could still use you to get to me, then take us both out at the same time. That's what I would do if I knew Lorenzo had a girlfriend and I wanted to take him out."

"Damon, I don't believe that for a minute."

"Why not?" He had the nerve to sound offended.

"You'd move in on her and force his hand right away. You'd have no patience for that."

I watched the smile cover his face. "You're probably right, doll. Maybe you know me better than I know myself."

"I wish that were true, Damon."

"You know I mean what I say, Jillian. You know I'm not afraid to say what's on my mind. My family means everything to me, and you're a part of that family. I'm stubborn and inflexible, except when it comes to you. I'll do anything and everything for you. I'm a hard-ass, no one fucks with me, and I'm always in charge. But you're my queen, and I'll bow at your feet. You know me like no one else does. You know me down to my soul, Jillian, because you're the other half of it."

He stole my breath with his words, and I didn't have a rebuttal. I couldn't argue with the points he made. I'd seen them with my own eyes. I'd been privy to a side of him few people outside of his family had experienced. Funny, protective, flirty, and teasing. He'd shielded me from harm and taken me to meet his family. I'd spent the night at his apartment and stayed in the hospital with him.

But could I live with being kept in the dark when my life was affected? Or my child's life? Or my husband's, if I stayed with Damon and eventually married him? Mama Lina explained to me how the family worked, the life she'd accepted with Vincenzo. Damon answered my questions with all the honesty I could expect. Even Benny confirmed what they'd both said without knowing how his words affected me. But those rules had never applied to me before meeting Damon. They had never been the guiding force in my life.

Until my mother's death.

Until we were pawns in the life-and-death game between the Sanfratello and the Marchetti families.

I wasn't sure I wanted that to become my life...my new norm.

Even if that meant I couldn't be with Damon.

Even if that meant one day I would have to see him happy with someone else.

I didn't take his warning seriously enough. I didn't give it enough consideration. My only thought was I'd be with him, and that would be enough for me. My naïveté regarding the finer intricacies of how a mob family worked would cost me dearly in the end. One decision would take the love of my life and the father of my baby away from me. The other decision would strip away all the freedoms I'd taken for granted all my life. But I had to wonder if my decision had already been made when I accepted his warning, when I accepted him for who he was.

I wondered if I'd ever be able to walk away from him.

I ran my hands over his back, side, and leg, feeling for any shards of glass or splinters of wood still embedded in his skin. "I think I got them all. Can you believe it? Maybe this fiasco won't require a night in the hospital, after all."

"Doll, I had no intentions of spending the night in the hospital. I'm not spending one more night away from you. The last few months without you have been the worst kind of hell, and I'm in no hurry to do that again."

I got up and discarded the used medical supplies but kept my eyes averted from his. When I didn't reply, he rolled off the bed and walked into the bathroom. While he showered and washed away the remnants of the day, I curled up on the bed and tried to wipe it from my memory. In the short time since I'd first met Damon, my life had been in danger more frequently than all my other years combined.

That was when the full realization of my predicament hit me.

With or without Damon, the danger would never go away while the Sanfratellos were still out there. The standing threats against my baby and me were real, with or without Damon in the picture. Only, without him, I didn't stand a chance of surviving. The drastically increased show of aggression we'd just survived was all the proof I needed. Lorenzo was determined to have me— dead or alive.

A strong, warm arm slid over my waist, quickly followed by a strong, warm body pressed against my back. "I love seeing you in my bed."

His sultry voice calmed my frayed nerves, and his commanding presence made me feel protected, but I wasn't ready to resume our relationship. My body was more than willing, responding to his every word and touch. But my mind refused to relax its constant guard over my heart. My arms drew tighter to my body, closing myself off to him and creating a symbolic protective barrier.

He slid his hand along my arm until he reached my fingers, then interlaced them with a light squeeze. "I know you're still having a difficult time with everything you've been hit with, doll. I also know it's not easy for you to trust me again. I'll have to work extra hard to earn that trust back. But I won't ever give up on you, Jillian. I'll never stop trying to earn your love again."

The vise around my heart gripped tighter. "What if I decide I can't live with the family rules? What if I decide I want out?"

I expected to hear a reiteration of the warning he originally gave me. At first, I didn't understand a lifetime member meant a shorter lifespan if I changed my mind, but that was the reply I waited to hear.

Instead, he took a moment to consider his words. Then he stunned me. "Once we've neutralized the threat, I'll let you go."

"Just like that?"

"If that's what you really want, Jillian. If that's what it takes to make you happy. It would kill me to do it, but I would for you."

"What would that mean for you? What would the family do if you let me go? What would your father do to you?"

"Don't worry about me, doll. You just concentrate on yourself and what you want. While you're making up your mind, I'll work on persuading you to stay with me."

Just my luck, when I relaxed in his arms, ready for sleep to take me away from reality, every muscle in my body began shaking involuntarily. The nervous energy I'd held at bay by focusing on Damon returned with a vengeance, flowing through me like wild rapids out of control. His arms and legs cocooned me in his protective hold. His mouth hovered over my ear, his lips grazed across the shell of my lobe, and he whispered loving, soothing reassurances until my teeth stopped chattering.

"That's my girl. Always so strong, so independent, so feisty. I love everything about you, Jillian. Even when you finally have to face the fact that you're not invincible. But, believe me, doll, you are very brave. You can relax now, I got you."

"How do you deal with it all, Damon? How do you stay so cool and collected when what's around you is scary crazy?"

"It's all I've ever known, doll. After watching my dad and my uncle handle business for as long as I can remember, nothing really surprises me anymore. The first time someone sprayed a hail of bullets at us scared the fuck out of me. But Dad and I had a long talk that night, and he stressed how I had to be strong enough to think clearly in the moment, so I could protect our loved ones. Like he protects Mama.

"I couldn't stand the thought of letting something bad happen to someone we love, of having the fault of that fall on my shoulders. That lit a fire inside me that burns to this day. What I do protects those I love, and I'm good at my job. I don't know another way to be, doll."

"If we're together, will you keep secrets from me? Will you keep me in the dark on where you are and what you're doing?"

"That's a hard question to answer, Jillian."

"It's really not, Damon. If I'm your wife, the mother of your child, and you have to go out on family business, will you keep it a secret from me? Will I be sitting at home with our baby, wondering if you're going to make it back alive? Dreading when the phone rings because I won't know if you're calling to say you're okay, or if some stranger is calling to tell me you're dead. If we're together, who comes first in your life, Damon?"

He sensed my question led to a deal breaker, I felt it in the way the muscles in his whole body stiffened. He didn't want to lie to me, but he didn't want to tell me the truth either.

"When we're married, I'll tell you where I'm going and what I'm doing. You will always come first with me, Jillian. Always. But —this is one warning I won't change for you so listen closely and understand my meaning—when we get married, there's no leaving. There's no such thing as divorce. There's no trial separation. We're a team. For life. Until death. That is nonnegotiable."

"When we're married. Not before? Not while we're working through this little problem you created in our relationship?"

"There's no leaving anytime. We're meant to be together."

"That's not what I meant, and you know it. You said when we're married, you'll tell me where you're going. You chose your words very carefully, Damon."

"I did say when we're married, because we will be—very soon. To answer your question, I meant exactly what I said. Marital communications have special privileges."

"Ah, I see. Marital privilege—I can't be compelled to testify against you. How romantic."

"It is, actually. That little clause ensures I get to come home to you every night and perform my husbandly duties. So, if you want to know all my secrets, you know what you have to do to get me to talk. Until then, I'll be glad to use my tongue for your pleasure in other ways."

CHAPTER SEVEN

Damon

*W*hen we stepped into my apartment, Jillian glanced around the large, open room and released a long sigh. She walked toward the master bedroom and stopped in the entryway, leaning against the doorframe. I watched as she stared at the king-size bed, memories of her last visit no doubt still fresh in her mind. Old wounds that hadn't yet healed. Doubts about how she'd handled the situation and if everything could've turned out differently still haunted her thoughts. Only, standing in my home made all her bad dreams very real all over again.

"Does looking at my bed bring back old memories—or give you all new ideas?" I stole up behind her and wrapped my arm around her waist, holding her tight against my body. She couldn't hide the shiver that ran through her body under my touch.

"Both." She tried to make her voice sound forceful, bold. But her breathing gave her true feelings away. "If you still have my favorite knife, we can create all new memories."

I smiled at the back of her head over her bravado, but only because I knew she couldn't see how proud I was of her spunk. If she wanted to push my buttons, I'd allow it. Without saying a word, I slowly slid my hand up the center of her body, across her perfect stomach, intentionally brushing across her breasts. Then when I'd almost reached her throat, she wasn't ready for my quick reflexes. With my hand securely wrapped around her neck, I spun her around to face me while pushing her body backward with my forward steps.

When her back bumped into the wall, her wide eyes searched mine, looking for clues to discern my state of mind. Had she angered the mad beast, or had she triggered the sexy, dominant side?

"Do you think I'll allow you to speak to me that way, Jillian? Do you think I'll tolerate disrespect in my own home?"

I hid my amazement as I watched her spine straighten, her eyes harden, and her jaw set firmly in raw determination. "If you think I care what you'll allow or what you'll tolerate, you're out of your damn mind. Whether I'm in your home, your mama's home, or out on the fucking sidewalk, I will always say whatever I want to say. And there's not a damn thing you can do about it."

My smirk broke free, regardless of how hard I tried to hide it. She visibly relaxed when she realized I wasn't being completely serious. "That fucking mouth of yours…the things I would love to do to it."

She returned my smirk with a provocative, confident one of her own. "You wouldn't dare try—"

Before she could finish her taunt, I crushed my lips to hers. Surprise stilled her movements for a moment, until I swiped my tongue across the part in her lips. She gasped with need, and I plunged deep into her mouth. With my hands on her face, I controlled her movements, tilting her head to deepen the kiss and keeping her locked in my grasp. I left my leg and used my knee to widen her stance.

The sweet sound of her panting filled the room when I ended our kiss. Our faces were just a breath away, my lips still hovering above hers in an erotic promise of more to come. Literally. "If I slipped my fingers into your panties, would I find your pussy wet for me, Jillian?"

I pressed my body against hers, without leaving enough room for even a hair to fall between us. With an upward surge of my hips, I thrust my hard cock against her clit. Even with all our clothes on, the sensation was enough to elicit a needful whimper from her.

"If I bent you over right here, with your fingers touching your toes, would you already be wet enough for me to fuck you until the most powerful orgasm you've ever had made your legs completely useless?"

"Oh my God, Damon." The breathy plea in her whisper stoked the fires of my desire.

"Tell me to stop and I will."

Her response was to lean up on her toes, closing the distance between us and locking our lips together in another sensual kiss. She linked her arms around my neck and pulled, lifting her feet off the floor. My hands slid under her bottom on instinct, pulling her up my body until she wrapped her legs around my waist. I ground my cock into her core, feeling her body come apart from the mere thought of what I could do to her.

"The last time we were in that bed...when I held you underneath me...I wanted nothing more than to fuck the stubbornness out of you...until your only thought was of me and what only I can do to your body." I confessed to my thoughts and desires between kisses, between licks, and between bites on her neck, leaving my mark on her soft skin. "The urge to do just that right now is overwhelming."

With a sudden jolt, she slid her hands down my chest until she found my erection pressing against my pants. Using both hands, she rubbed up and down my covered shaft before she quickly unbuttoned my pants and wrapped her silky smooth fingers around my cock. "Now, Damon. I want you to fuck me, right here."

I held her against the wall with one hand and shoved my pants down with the other, letting gravity finish the job. Reaching under her dress, I found she was already wet, her core hot with desire. I pushed her panties to the side and stroked her swollen clit before sliding my finger along her slit. She gripped her legs tighter around my waist and plunged her fingers into my hair, gripping the strands tightly in her fist.

"Damon, so help me God, do it now, or I'll find someone else who will."

"The fuck you will."

"I mean—" She started to argue, but my cock sliding into her wetness halted her words and released a loud scream of ecstasy.

Drawn together like never before, we held our position with our foreheads touching, our eyes locked in heated passion, and an invisible chain wrapped around us while I relentlessly drove deep inside her over and over. The connection I felt to her was stronger than anything I'd ever felt before. The warmth of her sex wrapped around my cock, like velvet hands pumping and squeezing me, was the most addictive drug I'd ever known. Even when my hair became slick with sweat and my legs threatened to give out, I couldn't stop. I wasn't ready to separate from the one person who could make me feel so much—too much—everything.

After one very long climax, when her body clenched around me with so much strength I couldn't hold back another second, I finally gave in and fell over the edge with her. My hips slowed to a purposeful grind as we both came down from the highest high of euphoria I'd ever experienced. My lips sought hers, leaving soft kisses everywhere they landed while I lowered her legs to the ground. Her face had the satisfied expression of a well-fucked woman, nearly boneless and unable to stand on her own.

Being the gentleman I was, I helped her to the bathroom and cleaned us both up, seeing to her every need first. We'd turned a major corner since I first made my presence in Abita Springs known, just a few days before. It definitely seemed longer than that. Three months without her had been hell, and it felt like a hell of a lot longer than it really was. The past few days were a drop in the bucket in comparison, but being with her while not *being with her* was hell in itself.

After that one hell of a reconciliation, I knew our paths had finally merged back into one, and everything else would work itself out. She'd protested, fought against her feelings for me one turn after the other, but I didn't mind a little cat-and-mouse game, chasing her to show my determination and commitment. I carefully watched her reactions after our impromptu wall-banging for any signs of remorse or shyness and was relieved to see none.

"I didn't hurt you, did I, doll?"

"No, not at all. That was your best work yet." The pleased smile on her face warmed my heart, gave me hope she was more than warming up to me again.

After everything that had happened between us in that room, I considered moving our master bedroom to the top level of my expansive apartment to give us both a fresh start. An alternative would be to completely redecorate the current room, giving it a new look, feel, and we could make all new memories in it. Which-ever option she chose was fine by me.

As it turned out, I didn't have to concern myself with either scenario. Not ten seconds after we'd dressed and walked out of the bedroom, Benny was at the door, escorting my dad and my sister into my apartment. And they shared a fucking wonderful idea.

"Hey, big bro." Carrie stepped into my apartment with a mischievous smile plastered across her face. "How's it going?"

"Little sis." I inclined my head in greeting but narrowed my eyes in suspicion. "Dad. What are you two doing here?"

"Heard you had a little trouble down in Louisiana. Abita

Springs, isn't it, Jillian?" Dad lifted her hand to his lips and placed a soft kiss on her knuckles. "I thought Damon said you lived in New Orleans."

"Probably because that's what I initially told him. It's the same area. Abita Springs is just across the lake from New Orleans but not quite as well known."

"Are you injured? Do you need anything, *cara?*"

"No, sir. I'm okay. Thank you for asking."

Dad felt the change in Jillian's reaction to him. I could read it on his face, and he was bothered by it. A lot. From the first moment they met, both Dad and Jillian seemed to be taken with each other—in a father-daughter way. Since she'd lost her father a couple of years before, I thought maybe Dad could help fill a void she had in her life. After their icy reunion, I wasn't so sure anymore.

I wasn't so sure what that meant for my chances of winning her back either. Despite the passion we'd just shared.

"Mama and Daddy thought Jillian might be more comfortable and safer if she stayed with me for a while instead of staying here with you." Carrie stepped to Jillian's side and linked their arms together. "And I agree. Besides, I've never had a sister, so this will be a treat for me."

"Hold on just a fucking minute." My temper flared, and I started toward my sister, pointing my finger at her. "Did you suggest this fucking lame idea, Carrie?"

"No," Dad interjected. "I did. Your mother and I talked about it, and we decided it was best, under the circumstances. Carrie is thrilled to invite Jillian into her home, but this was my decision."

"With all due respect, Dad, I disagree. Jillian is safer with me— I've already proven that at least twice now."

"No, what you did was get shot the first time and injured the second time. You could've been killed either way. Your judgment isn't sound where she's concerned, Damon. You've made mistakes, and neither you nor the family can afford more of the same mistakes in the future.

"Lorenzo is still on the lam. The Sanfratellos are waiting for us to stick our necks out in weakness so they can chop off our heads at the shoulders. My job is to protect the family, to do what's best to keep it intact. This is what's best for everyone."

CHAPTER EIGHT

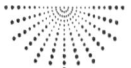

Damon

Dad and I stood toe to toe, our eyes locked in a battle of wills. I'd always done as he'd asked, as he demanded, except when it came to Jillian. I'd just managed to get her back on my home turf, in my apartment, in my arms. Getting her back into my life and back into my bed—not just the wall—*permanently* were next on my to-do list. Not necessarily in that order, but still one step at a time. My sister lived in Jersey—not too far from my parents, but not exactly convenient for me to drop in to see Jillian whenever I wanted. Or to seduce her in the shower.

Then Jillian spoke up and surprised us both.

"Maybe you should ask Jillian what she wants, since it affects her life, instead of talking about her like she's not in the room." Jillian placed her hands on her hips, her hard gaze darting back and forth between us.

"Jillian, *cara*, when it comes to the family—" Dad started to object.

"But I'm not part of *the family*. When Damon pulled his bullshit and kicked me out of his life, I did as he said and stayed away. *The family* brought me back to New York, but that doesn't make me a part of it.

"I'll stay with Carrie. We haven't been here long, so my clothes are still packed. It should be easy enough to move the only belongings I have left."

She knocked the air out of my lungs with her declaration. Even though we hadn't officially made up, I still didn't expect her to choose my sister over me after our intense reconnection. While I stood there staring at her with my bottom jaw hanging open like a fucking fool, she avoided making eye contact with me. When I finally collected my thoughts enough to close my mouth, it was to grind my teeth together so hard I couldn't speak even if she looked at me.

My sister, however, was thrilled.

Carrie's pleased smile was practically permanently inked on her face. At least she had the decency not to blatantly flaunt her victory in front of me, and I couldn't very well be mad at Carrie when her happiness was genuine. Still, how I'd ever overcome that hurdle and win Jillian back for good was unclear.

All I could see was her slipping even further away from me.

The big and little things in her pregnancy I'd miss out on—that I'd already missed.

Seeing her every day, spending time with her every night—everything I wanted for us suddenly became a pipe dream.

"I'm sorry, Damon, but I'm really excited to finally have a sister. I've been the only girl in a testosterone-dominated family for far too long." Carrie hugged Jillian around the neck. "And I hear I'm going to be an aunt soon. I can't wait!"

Jillian returned Carrie's smile, her radiant face driving that knife further into my chest.

Dad gave his men orders to take Jillian's suitcases down to his car before turning back to me. "This is for the best, son. Trust me."

With a firm set to my jaw, I answered with a single nod. There was nothing else I could say or do at that point without causing an unnecessary scene. Jillian had made her choice, and it wasn't me. I'd have to learn to live with the consequences of my actions, and not having her in my home was just one aspect of it. I had a sinking feeling I'd have a lot more restitution to repay before anything real changed between us.

When they walked to the door, I fell in line behind Jillian. So many words were on the tip of my tongue, but none came out. So many thoughts flew through my mind, but the only one I latched on to was how much I didn't want her to leave. But I had no choice but to let her go. She had to find her way back to me, and I had to earn her trust again. The only way out of this fucking fiasco was to prove to her that she wanted me as much as I wanted her.

Dad and Carrie walked on to the elevator, but Jillian stopped just outside my door. She turned and looked at me, her gaze finally meeting mine again. I could easily get lost in the emotions swirling in her emerald green eyes. She was conflicted and guarded, but concern for me was still buried in there.

"Thank you for saving me again this morning, and for getting me out of there in one piece. I wouldn't have made it out of my house if it weren't for you, much less out of the state."

"You don't have to leave here, Jillian. You can stay with me. What happened to the woman who was just in the other room with me? Where did she go?"

Her eyes flicked up to mine, a new warning shining in her emerald gleam. "It hurts, doesn't it? To believe you mean more to someone, only to find out you don't. Remember this feeling, Damon. Remember the confusion it brings, too. Maybe you'll feel a fraction of what I've felt."

"Ruthless. Cunning. Vindictive. Are you sure you're not already a Marchetti?" I crossed my arms over my chest and lifted one eyebrow in challenge. So, she wanted to inflict pain on me. Score one for Jilly.

"I can't stay here with you, Damon. Maybe I do still want you, but I'm not sure I even want to be around you right now. I'm definitely not ready to move in with you and have a permanent reminder of everything that's happened. You've been back in my life for a few short days, and in those few days, I've already had my house shot up and my life turned upside down. What happened in that room was only sex—we fulfilled a need we both had. Don't read more into it than it was."

She was lying. But the point was she wanted to hurt me. She wanted her revenge against me, and that was just one jab she could get in. The other was to leave my place and go to my sister's house, even though she was probably still scared of Lorenzo finding her. But she wanted to establish her independence, to show she didn't need me, to prove she could make it without me.

"Lorenzo has no idea who he's up against. If he did, he'd probably run the other way, afraid for his life."

"That's what you should do too. Run far away from me."

"Never going to happen, doll. I'll never give up on you. And don't think for a second Lorenzo will either. He won't stop until you're dead."

"I know he won't. Be careful out there, Damon. I don't want anything to happen to you. It would break your mother's heart."

"Don't worry about me, doll. I'll be fine. You're the one I'm worried about. I won't get any sleep tonight, wondering if you're okay. Call me if you need me for anything at all. It doesn't matter what time of day or night it is, I'll be there in half a second for you."

"Damon." Her whisper held so many meanings, so many words. So many feelings.

The elevator opened, and I watched her walk away, her steps slow and her head shaking from side to side. She joined Carrie and Dad before turning to face me as the doors closed. Then she was gone.

"What do you want to do now, boss?" Benny asked from behind me.

"I want to put an end to this. It's time to remind Lorenzo who he's fucking with once and for all."

Benny and I spent the following several hours preparing for a retaliatory strike that was beyond overdue. When two teams of my men were in place well after dark—one team outside Lorenzo's house in Brooklyn and the other at his every-once-in-a-while-girlfriend's house in Queens—we made our presence known.

"Everyone in place?" I whispered into our communicators.

One by one, my men replied.

"Now!"

On cue, we lobbed flaming Molotov cocktails through the windows on the first and second floors of Lorenzo's home. The fire raged, fueled by the furniture, curtains, and wind blowing through the broken panes of glass. Feet shuffled quickly inside, furniture slid across the wood floors, and the *whoosh* from fire extinguishers gave their positions away. Loud voices carried on the night air while we waited in silence, crouched in the shadows for cover. One distinct voice stood out over the others.

Lorenzo was inside the house.

The back door opened, and one of his men carefully leaned out, surveying the backyard. I let him have a moment of false security before issuing my next command.

"Blow the cars."

Flanked by his soldiers, Lorenzo emerged from his fire-ravaged home and started his sprint toward the detached garage. Before he could reach the safety of his bulletproof SUV, it exploded and took his garage out with it.

"Get Lorenzo outta here! Now!" The soldier in front took point, leveling his gun at everything and nothing in particular while his eyes frantically searched for the threat. He knew we were there, but he didn't have a clue where.

The other men shielded Lorenzo and ran across two of the

neighbors' backyards before veering between the houses, headed toward the street.

"Who has eyes on him?" I whisper-shouted into my communicator. "Do not let him get away!"

Shots rang out from the street before I could get there. Tires screeched, burning rubber squealed against the asphalt when they peeled away from the curb. Bullets pinged off the metal and bulletproof glass, but Lorenzo and a few of his men escaped. The ones with bullet holes in them still lay on the ground between the houses. The occupants wisely stayed inside, well away from the windows, and minded their own business for the time being. They'd wait until the shooting stopped before calling for help. The shrill sirens would cut through the city noise before long, though.

We grabbed the wounded men and shoved them into our vehicles.

"He's headed toward Queens." Benny flashed a rare smile toward me. "He's in for a surprise when he gets there."

"He won't stop. They'll see the commotion from more than a block away and change course at the last second. In hindsight, I should've waited until he got into his vehicle to blow it. A quick, sudden death is too good for him, though. I want my hands around his neck. I want to watch the life drain from his eyes. My smiling face will be the last thing he ever sees."

"Lorenzo's fuck buddy had a bad night too. Before the guys firebombed her house, they stole her car. When the place lit up like a Christmas tree, they sent her car careening through the yard and watched as it smashed into the front corner of her house. She ran outside in nothing but her flimsy nightgown, screaming and crying, causing a scene." Benny laughed as he relayed the word from the second team.

"Where are they now?"

"A few blocks down the street, waiting to see if Lorenzo shows up."

"Tell them not to kill him if they can avoid it. Bring him to me."

"You got it, boss. You know he won't show up, though. He knows we're gunning for him, and he's on the run. He'll get word of this long before he makes it to her house, and he'll head for safety."

"Still. Have them hold there for a while longer just in case. I don't want to miss another opportunity. We got lucky to find him at home tonight. I didn't expect him to be there, honestly."

"We have Carrie's place covered in case he grows a pair and shows up there. Don't worry about her or Jillian."

I nodded, grateful Benny could predict my next order. "Think he got my message?"

"He absolutely got it. He'll get the rest of it when we send his guys he left behind back to him in pieces."

"Abso-fucking-lutely."

9

CHAPTER NINE

Jillian

*L*iving with Carrie over the first few days I was there proved to be...interesting. Ar0und her family, she was quieter, respectful, and an obedient daughter. When we were alone, she was the complete opposite. The little sister I lived with was even more brazen than Damon. I also thought it was hilarious that almost no one in the family knew the real Carrie Marchetti.

"I love that you're pregnant with my niece or nephew, but I also kinda wish you weren't so I could take you out to the clubs." Carrie set a glass of water down in front of me while she tipped back a longneck beer bottle. "We'd have so much fun."

"Give me until a few months after the baby's born, then you have my permission to take me an all-night bar crawl." I laughed and took a sip of my water. "If we can sneak past your brother's innate radar, that is."

She smiled, holding the tip of the bottle close to her lips. "Damon's intense, I know. My whole fucking family is. The men are all macho tough guys, and the women are supposed to be damsels waiting for distress, so the men can save us. They forget I grew up in this fucking family too. I know exactly how shit goes down, and no one gives me credit for being able to take care of myself."

"Why is that? Why are the women treated with kid gloves?" I leaned forward, genuinely interested in her insight.

"That's the way it's always been, back from when my parents lived in the 'mother country.' We've heard the stories all our lives —about how strict the Italian mob families are, how they don't tolerate anyone thinking for themselves, how they enjoy living in the dark ages."

Carrie snickered, amused with her assessment of the old family life.

"The thing is, my dad taught me how to handle all kinds of guns. But he also taught me how to fight with my fists. He sent me to nine years of Krav Maga training. I can disarm the biggest brute with simple techniques, no brawn needed. But my parents try to keep me sheltered because they're afraid I'll get hurt. It's maddening."

"Why do I have a feeling they don't know half of what you do when they're not looking?"

"Because you're a very smart woman, that's why. I love my family, but they refuse to step into this century. They're adamant about always showing strength so our enemies can't exploit weaknesses, but that doesn't mean we can't have new and improved ways of doing business.

"Such as?"

"There's a big universe out there in the deep and dark webs. Small-time embezzlement schemes are a dime a dozen, and they leave a trail that'll get you caught in the end. World domination can't be achieved with in-person larceny. You have to think globally."

"You've started your own Marchetti business, haven't you? What are you doing? Hacking large businesses? Stealing identities? What are you up to, Carrie?"

"When I first started, that's along the lines where I dabbled. But I've expanded my business beyond that. Information is king now. Insider information for the stock market makes me millions of dollars, but all the other information they leave lying around on the deep web keeps them under my control. Blackmail is still a very effective business."

"You're scarier than Damon and Vincenzo put together, Carrie." I lifted my glass to toast her bravado. "I'm impressed."

"That's just the tip of the iceberg, sis. I'm building an invisible empire. Untraceable back to me in any shape or form. But every transaction eventually flows through my legitimate business, so every penny is accounted for on the up-and-up."

"Can I ask why you trust me enough to tell me all this? I mean, you've only known me for a short time. How do you know I'll keep your secrets?"

She threw her head back in laughter. "Jillian, I'm an excellent judge of character. Reading people is my forte. While Damon may be leery of everyone he meets, and even some people he's known all his life, I'm not suspicious of anyone who doesn't give me a reason first. But I also don't give anyone who crosses me a second chance to breathe either. Want to know what I saw the first time I met you?"

"Yes. Tell me."

"You were naïve, maybe a little too much, but a quick learner. Your family meant everything to you, and you wished you had a huge clan like ours. You wanted to belong somewhere, to fit as tightly as a jigsaw puzzle piece does in the picture on the cover of the box.

"I knew right away I could trust you because when you give your love, you give all of yourself with it. My brother royally fucked up when he doubted you, but I don't doubt your loyalty for one second, Jillian. You'll be my sister for life."

"You're right on the money—about all of it. And I will be your sister for life, even if I don't end up marrying your brother."

"I knew you needed a breather from him. Believe me, I can relate. You know Mama is already planning your wedding shower *and* baby shower, right?"

"Honestly, I figured as much." I shook my head and closed my eyes, picturing how she'd be hurt if I didn't let Damon back into my life.

"You really don't know if you want him back, do you?" She narrowed her eyes, daring me to lie to her.

"I don't have a clue what I want, Carrie. Right now, I'm so confused over everything—what I'm going to do, what I *want* to do, or even what I *should* do . Other than kill Lorenzo. That's the one and only thing I'm absolutely sure of at this point."

"As far as my family goes, you don't need to worry about how they'll react. Mama will be hurt, but she'll be fine. She'll still love you, and she'll spoil you and the baby."

"And Damon?"

"Damon will be crushed, but he'll survive. He's a big boy. It'll take him a few years to take the hint that you're, in fact, not marrying him, but only because he's dense and as tenacious as a bulldog. But in the end, this is your life, and you have every right to be happy. No matter what that means."

The problem was, I didn't know what it meant.

"You want Lorenzo dead, huh?" Carrie asked, her tone taking a serious tone. A deadly serious tone.

"Yes. Yes, I do."

"Do you want to do it yourself?"

I thought about her question for a moment. Could I do it myself? Could I look him in the eye and kill him? Could I commit premeditated murder?

Then I thought about my sweet mother and the intense fear she must've felt when Lorenzo's goons held her captive and she was too weak to even try to fight back. I thought about Lorenzo giving the orders to his men but not having the guts to do the deed himself. And I had my answer.

"Yes, I do. But I want him to suffer first. I want to steal everything he has, crush his spirit, and I want him to know it was me who beat him. Then I want to see the fear in his eyes before he dies."

"That's my girl. Are you sure you're not already a Marchetti?"

"Your brother is a bad influence. What can I say?"

"Do you have anything in particular in mind for destroying Lorenzo?"

"Let me think about it. I may have an idea or two I'm kicking around. I'm guessing he has a lot of family around here?"

"He does. You want to take them out first?"

"I want to reveal his secrets first—so that no one in his family ever looks at him the same again. I want to plaster all his dirty secrets and underhanded dealings across the headlines. Embarrass him, make him and his family look weak until he's shunned by everyone. Even alienate him from his men."

"I love how your devious little mind works. We will make this happen. Even if we have to make up shit and alter photos."

"Even better. The more he protests, the more people will believe it."

Over the following several days, Carrie stayed glued to her computer, sorting through file after file to collect as much dirt on Lorenzo and his businesses as she could. I could tell when she came across something really interesting—not embarrassing—because the evil glint in her eyes shone even brighter than usual. She kept all her plans and everything she found close to the vest, though. She definitely had one of the trademark Marchetti family traits down pat—the ability to keep secrets from everyone else.

Until.

"Hey, Jillian. Let me show you something." She gestured for me to follow her, so I jumped at the chance to get involved.

When we reached her secure computer room, I was amazed at her setup. Several monitors lined the wall, paired with multiple laptops and desktop computers. We moved in front of the screen she'd been working on, and she read what she'd found.

"Looks like my brother has been busy," she chuckled. "The night you came here, he went after Lorenzo and one of the women Lorenzo keeps on standby. Firebombed both of their houses before Lorenzo went deeper underground. Damon cast a wider net to get him, though. He put a contract out on Lorenzo's head, only he wants him delivered alive."

"Damon has a contract out on Lorenzo?" I felt like I was running to catch up. "How do you know it's Damon?"

"He sure does. And I know it's him because I know how and where he'd look for help. And I also know the specific terms he uses to identify himself as a Marchetti family member."

"How does this work? Do others bid on it? Is it first come, first served basis or what?"

"In this case, Damon offered a set amount of money for Lorenzo. So, anyone who captures him can answer in this secret virtual room to set up a meeting with Damon for the exchange of Lorenzo and the money."

"Would Damon know who he's talking to? Would he be able to trace you and find out if we replied to it?"

Carrie looked up at me, unfiltered excitement shone in her eyes. "He wouldn't have any idea it was me, and he'd have no way to trace the chat. I've thoroughly covered my tracks. You want to accept the contract on Lorenzo?"

"Yes, I do. We have to flush him out though, right? I mean, if Damon lost him after attacking his house, there's no telling where he's hiding."

"I can find him. Lorenzo isn't as smart as Damon. He's

sloppy. That's why his family isn't on top. They could've been had Lorenzo's father been more diligent about keeping up with his son. Lorenzo will mess up—he'll use a credit card under one of his aliases because he thinks no one knows the names but him."

"Do you know his aliases?"

"I sure do. Over the last couple of years, I've made it my business to know all about our enemies."

"Show me."

From her documents folder, she opened a file with several columns of names. At the top of each list was the name of one of the Sanfratello family members. She wasn't kidding—she'd been keeping tabs on them for quite a while. One name jumped off the page and grabbed me.

"Rafael Stanzoren."

"You know that name," Carrie stated, knowing she didn't have to ask. "How?"

"When I worked at Blaine Financial, I was assigned to a retirement account that was a mess. When I finally untangled everything, I realized money was being funneled out of a company called MadTrich, into the nurses' fund Blain Financial managed, then obviously into Lorenzo's pocket. One of the two names tied to the transactions was Rafael Stanzoren. I never found that name on any other document."

"What was the other name?"

"Milo Bianchi."

"Milo was one of our family's associates. He was secretly working for the Sanfratello family. MadTrich is also one of our family businesses, so Milo was using his status with us to help line Lorenzo's pockets with our money. I'm sure that helped Lorenzo convince our smaller rivals to join forces with the Sanfratello family at first. But those allegiances dissolved when Lorenzo couldn't deliver on his promises."

"Let's be the first ones to find Lorenzo. Imagine Damon's face when the two of us show up with Lorenzo in hand to cash in on his contract."

"He'll be pissed as hell, Jillian. That's the expression you'll see on his face—like a cartoon character with steam coming out of his ears and his eyes bulging out of their sockets."

"Maybe then we'll be even."

10

CHAPTER TEN

Damon

"*L*orenzo is quite the snake, isn't he? Slithering underground and hiding until he thinks the danger has passed." Benny walked beside me toward the car.

"He knows he's dead. It's only a matter of time. Every hit man within a hundred-mile radius will be after Lorenzo now."

"Are you sure going to Carrie's at this time of night is such a good idea? She's more likely to shoot us than Lorenzo is."

I had to laugh at that comment. Not because Benny was wrong, but because he was right on the mark. Carrie wasn't the innocent little angel the rest of the family thought she was. Our father acted as though she were fragile and would break in two. He put her up on a pedestal and kept her away from anything that could harm her. Or, I should say, he tried to—she wouldn't have it, though. On the surface, she let him believe he had all the control. In reality, she was a force to be reckoned with, and word had spread about those who learned that lesson the hard way.

"My sister better not shoot me. That would absolutely ruin my night."

195

I had plans to spend quality time with Jillian. I hadn't seen her in five days, and I'd reached my limit of waiting. The few texts we'd exchanged weren't nearly enough to satisfy the need for her burning deep inside me. She resisted my attempts to get her to sext with me. She flat out denied my request to send naked pictures of herself. When I suggested we chat by video, so I could watch her satisfy herself, she said she'd turn her phone off if I even tried it.

She was slipping away from me. Minute by minute. Hour by hour. Day by day. I was losing her.

Even more so than when we spent three months apart.

I had to convince her we were good together, that we were meant to be together.

Outside Carrie's house, I slipped through the yard, around the house, and stopped outside Jillian's window. With my luck of late, Carrie's alarm system would already be armed, sounding the bells and whistles the second I tapped on the window.

"What the fuck do you think you're doing?" My eyes were blinded by a bright flashlight, held by my sister. "Do you know how close you just came to having your head blown off?"

"I'm here to see Jillian."

"Does my front door not work?" She dropped the light from my eyes, leaving huge black spots dancing in my vision. I could make out the silhouette of her bent arm with her hand on her hip and her head cocked to the side. It didn't take any imagination to know she wore an annoyed expression on her face.

"Carrie," I started, my voice lowered and my tone sincere. "I can't lose her. Not again."

"I'm not sure that decision is up to you, big brother. But I won't stand in the way of your attempts to win her over. If she says you have to leave, don't you dare argue with her, though. She's a guest in my home, and you won't make her feel unsafe here."

"I wouldn't do that. One major fuck-up is more than enough. All I want now is to show her how much I love her."

"You really do love her. Don't you, Damon?"

I nodded. "I do. More than you can imagine."

"All right. I'll try to put a good word in for you now and then when the opportunity arises. Don't hurt her again, or you'll deal with me long before Mama or Daddy can reach you. She's pregnant with my niece or nephew, and I plan on being the favorite aunt for a very long time."

I smiled, appreciating how protective my sister was of Jillian. "She's pregnant with my daughter or son, Carrie. I plan on being the best father and husband for the rest of my life."

With my vision cleared after the earlier blinding from her flashlight, I saw her face soften. "Go win back your baby mama, Romeo. Just try not to scare the shit out of her by crawling through her window unannounced."

"Does that mean I can follow you through the front door unannounced?"

"Come on," she called over her shoulder and shook her head.

I hustled to cover the ground between us and walked through the front door. She pointed down the hall toward one of the guest bedrooms then left me to work out my new plan on my own. To earn Jillian's trust again, I thought the straightforward approach would be the best.

I didn't just happen to be in the neighborhood...an hour away from my apartment.

I didn't have an obscure reason for visiting my sister.

I didn't have anything of hers I needed to drop off.

The simple truth was I missed her, and I wanted to see her again.

When I reached her closed door, I rapped on it lightly with my knuckles a couple of times. Then I heard her sweet voice call out.

"Come on in."

With the door slowly swinging open, I leaned against the

frame and waited for her to come into my line of sight. She sat on the bed in a spaghetti strap camisole top and pajama shorts. She was propped up on pillows against the headboard and held a *New Mother* magazine in her hands. Surprise lit her face for a moment since she was clearly expecting Carrie to be on the other side of the door rather than me. Then a small smirk replaced the shock, and I knew she'd expected me to show up sooner or later.

"Hello, doll."

"Hi, Damon. Let me guess—you were in the neighborhood and thought you'd drop by to say hello."

I shook my head, keeping our gazes locked. "Nope. I've missed you and wanted to see you. So I drove all the way out here solely for you."

She tilted her head to the side, surprised at my honesty—and maybe also a little pleased with it. "Really? Did you have any other plans once you saw me?"

"Not really. Although now that I'm here, I could easily come up with one or two things. You just say the word. Give me a nod. A wink. Fuck, I'd even take an eye twitch right about now."

My stab at self-deprecating humor at least earned a genuine laugh from Jillian. With a smile that brightened her face in place, she stared at me thoughtfully for several heartbeats. "Who is this handsome devil standing in front of me, and where is my cocky devil hiding?"

"Your cocky devil is pushing against the teeth of my zipper, waiting for you to find your way back to him. Your handsome devil is the same man he's always been—all yours, doll."

Her face flushed, the pink tinge giving way to full-out red, but she didn't look away. There was a new boldness behind her stare. A new confidence I hadn't seen before. It was sexy as hell on her.

"You have me at a disadvantage, Damon."

"How's that?"

"You know your dirty mouth has always turned me on. But it

seems my pregnancy hormones have amplified my libido...especially where you and your mouth are concerned."

If the flames soaring through my veins escaped, the entire fucking room would incinerate.

"I've told you, and shown you, many times—my mouth is more than willing to do whatever your body needs. My tongue is all yours, and it fucking loves how you taste. My cock is as hard as steel right now, ready to relieve your body of every orgasm it has pent-up inside. Twitch your eye in my direction, doll. That's all it'll take."

The ball was in her court, and the decision was entirely hers to make.

"I'm not saying yes, but you have no idea how much I want your tongue between my legs right now."

I stepped into the room and closed the door behind me.

"Believe me, doll. If it's even a fraction of how much I want my tongue between your legs right now, it's a hell of a fucking lot."

"Only your tongue? You don't want anything else?"

"I want what you want. If that's all you're game for tonight, it won't hurt my feelings at all."

"But what about you? I'd feel like I left you hanging."

"I'll be fine, doll. Don't worry about me. Just let me take care of your needs. As long as you're satisfied, I'll be satisfied."

She laid the magazine on the bedside table, the heat flashed in her eyes, and her tongue darted out, wetting her lips. She wanted me, no doubt, but she wouldn't get me or my tongue until she spoke the words. In no way was I a patient man, except when it came to meeting her needs. For that, I'd wait all fucking night.

With my back against the door, I crossed my arms over my chest and waited. Her brows furrowed in confusion for a second, a hint of doubt appeared in her eyes, then understanding took over. I lifted one brow slightly, letting her decide how she'd answer the question on her own.

"Damon, I need you to come over here and give me a tongue

lashing." She stood, pulled her camisole tank top over her head and let it drop to the floor at her feet. Then she slid the shorts down her legs, never averting her gaze from mine.

I crossed the room in two strides, my dick pushing so hard against my zipper I was sure it left an imprint of the metal teeth. She stood before me again in her au naturel beauty, a sight I hadn't been able to fully appreciate in way too fucking long. She wanted a tongue-lashing. My tongue was ready to worship every inch of her.

I watched without breathing as she lifted my hand and placed it on her breast. When our eyes met again, she whispered to me. "Touch me, Damon. I've missed you. So much more than I even realized."

If she wanted my touch, I was more than happy to oblige her. I lifted my other hand to her exposed breast, covering it before massaging them both. Vigorously. Every pass of my fingers across her skin became more forceful out of sheer desire. The rougher I became, the more she leaned into me, asking for more My thumb and forefinger circled one of her nipples before squeezing with a slight twist. A seductive moan as her back arched, pushing her breast farther into my hand, had me nearly busting out of my pants.

I dipped my head and covered the other nipple with my mouth, pulling it between my teeth while teasing it with my tongue. The taste of her skin was intoxicating and addictive. Every hit created an intense need for my next fix. Working my way up her body, I licked and sucked on the soft skin of her neck. Her muscles relaxed under my touch, her body melding into mine when I wrapped one arm around her waist and pulled her closer.

With a mind of its own and knowing exactly what to do, my other hand slid down her body, my fingers grazing the supple skin of her side and stomach before reaching her heated core. I skimmed my fingertip along her slit, barely touching her but setting off fireworks inside her just the same. She curled her fingers into my shirt, her nails scraping against my skin through the fabric as she gripped tightly. She widened her stance, a not so subtle hint that she wanted more.

"Tell me what you want, Jillian. I want to hear you say the words." My lips hovered over the shell of her ear. The low murmurs sent goose bumps across her skin, and her nails dug deeper into my skin.

"I want your fingers inside me, Damon. Don't stop." Her ragged breaths and hooded eyes were sexy as fuck, but hearing her admit what she wanted thoroughly lit my fuse.

"I thought you'd never ask."

With one swift thrust, I buried two fingers deep inside her pussy. Her wetness coated my hand and nearly brought me to my knees. She never could hide her reactions to me, how much she wanted me, and knowing that only made me want her more. The thought of dropping to my knees held a definite appeal.

She watched me slide down her body. As I knelt in front of her, we kept our eyes locked. The anticipation of what was to come and the thrill of keeping a heated promise spurred me on. Her bottom lip was pulled between her teeth, her lips were slightly parted, and her eyes burned with desire.

"Fuck, Jillian, I can't wait to taste you again." I leaned closer and flicked my tongue against her clit. Just for a second. Just enough to tease her and build the excitement.

But she had other plans.

Her fingers dug into my scalp, gripping my hair with a new ferocity I'd never seen in her. She jerked my head against her pussy, shameless and eager.

"I said, don't stop."

"Yes, you did. Just remember you asked for this."

In one abrupt move, I turned her back to the bed and hoisted her onto it with my free arm. My fingers still pumped in and out of her as I ground the pad of my thumb into her sensitive clit. Her moans filled the room, my fingers filled her pussy, and then my mouth devoured her clit. Like a starving man, I couldn't get enough. I tried to start out being easy, circling and sucking on her clit to make her crazy for me.

But I was the one who turned into a madman.

One taste wasn't enough. Gentle was never our thing. Waiting was for other people who had more time. While continuing the barrage with my fingers, I added a full-fledged assault with my tongue. Up. Down. Inside. Around. Side to side. Every fucking orgasm she possessed was mine, and I was hell-bent to claim them. Every scratch of her nails, every squeeze of her thighs, and every scream that echoed off the walls was worth it. By the time I finished with her, she was reduced to a quivering pile of beautiful skin...with a gorgeous, thoroughly satisfied expression.

"Will that hold you over until next time, doll?"

"Mmm." As she moved into a full-body stretch, a huge smile split her face in two. "That felt so good, Damon. All my stress just disappeared. Now I'm a useless mess, can't feel a single bone in my body."

"Don't worry, doll. Next time, you'll feel a bone all right. You'll feel a very hard bone *all night*. Don't you doubt it for a second."

While she lay sprawled out on the bed, high on our own ecstasy, I covered her body with mine and purposely slid the bulge in my pants across her extra-sensitive clit. Her eyes flew open, and her breath halted as she waited for my next move. So, I dipped my head and captured a sensual kiss.

"Are you ready to come stay with me now? You can have this every night."

"Aw, Damon, I think it's so sweet that you're trying so hard. I thought you understood after the last time we were together, though. I'm only using you for sex. If you're uncomfortable with that, I completely understand. Just tell me, and I'll find someone else who's okay with it."

"I'm not uncomfortable with it at all. You can still use me for sex while living with me. In fact, you're welcome to use me for a good fucking every day of the week. But if you're looking for some strange maybe I should too."

I knew she was trying to bust my balls. She wasn't as slick as she liked to think. She expected a very different reaction out of me—like a possessive, caveman, flying off the handle, ranting madman—and under normal circumstances, that was exactly what she would've seen out of me. Her crestfallen expression when I turned her own game against her instead was almost comical. But I had to fight fire with fire, make her work as hard to stay away from me as I worked to get to her back. I hated the verbal seesaw, back and forth without any real resolution, but she still wasn't ready to tap out, and I was nowhere near ready to throw in the towel.

We were two of a kind, whether she'd admit it or not.

"You had three months without me. I'm sure you had your fair share of *strange* anyway."

"I don't usually kiss and tell, doll. But I seem to break a lot of rules for you." I paused, intentionally, and she perked up, suddenly very interested in what I had to say. "There hasn't been anyone else for me since the day I met you. You didn't take my warning to heart. I told you quite a while ago, if you stayed, you and I were in this forever."

"How can you be such an asshole one minute, and so sweet and romantic the next?"

"I'm just talented that way, I guess. Tell me, would you rather I just give up on you? Leave you alone so you can get on with your life without me?"

"Do you really want to know the answer to that?" A hint of her bluster was in her tone, testing me again.

"Yes, I do. An honest one."

"I don't know, Damon. I honestly don't know what I want anymore. Every time I think I've figured it out and made a decision, I get lost inside my head and doubt myself again."

"Get out of your head and follow your heart. It knows what to do, whether that brings you to me or not." I lowered my face to hers. "Good night, doll," I murmured against her lips. Then I poured all my love into my kiss, letting her feel everything I felt.

"Good night, Damon."

Minutes later, I slid into the car where Benny was waiting. I glanced over at him and raised my eyebrows. "Everything go okay?"

"Yeah. It was just like you said it'd be. Carrie was in a hurry to see who was sneaking around her house, so she didn't lock her computer before she stepped away from it. I installed the keystroke logger program without a hitch, and I saved it in a system folder she wouldn't naturally think to look in. And I've already confirmed we have remote access into her servers, so we can access any computer she has on her network. The programs are hidden, but we just have to hope she doesn't run a full system scan and accidentally find them."

"I don't think she'll give them a second glance even if she does find them. Not with the way we named them. They just look like regular system files. I know those two are up to something. Carrie was too adamant for Jillian to stay with her for them not to be. We just have to figure out what."

CHAPTER ELEVEN

Jillian

"You look way too happy. Should I be afraid to ask what you've done?" I slid into the chair across the table from Carrie with a cup of hot tea.

Carrie was already at the kitchen table when I got up, a steaming coffee mug in hand and a beaming smile on her face. Her eyes were glued to her laptop screen. Knowing what she was capable of made me more than a little leery to ask why, but curiosity got the better of me. Plus, if it had anything to do with Lorenzo, I definitely wanted in.

"I've been thinking about how to coax the rat out of his hole. Then it just came to me. Everyone hates rats."

"Okay." Admittedly, I didn't get where she was going at first. Then it hit me. "You're a genius. How do we make him look like a rat?"

"I concocted a fake news story with enough real information even his family and his men will question his allegiance. Then I submitted it to all the local news stations and papers. His family name is well-known, so they'll run with it."

"What's the story?"

Her grin widened.

"I've written two, actually. The first one puts our game in motion, then the second one seals his fate. The one that'll become breaking news any minute now is about the money missing from the nurse's fund at Blaine Financial.

"I did a little more digging after we talked about his embezzlement scheme. It's actually worse than that. He used that money to establish a Ponzi scheme. He paid his first investors a hefty dividend, so they invested more. That also made others want to get in on the action, so they invested heavily in his scheme. When his allies find out what he's done, they'll be gunning for him. But since he's a made man, they can't kill him without his family retaliating against them."

"Okay, so that's the part that's true. How will that bring him out of hiding if he knows everyone wants to kill him?"

"Because the second story will leak soon after, revealing he met with the FBI—as if he's a rat who turned on his family and allies. Right now, the Sanfratello family is hiding and protecting him. With the first story being true and out there for the world to know their business, they'll be suspicious enough of him to cut him out. The FBI's only response will be they can't comment on what is or isn't an open investigation.

"I don't think his father would allow a hit on him without irrefutable proof, but Geno Sanfratello has to protect his whole family first—not just his loose-cannon son. Until Geno has proof Lorenzo *didn't* go to the FBI, Lorenzo will be exiled from the family safe houses. He'll also be more likely to agree to a meeting if we dangle a carrot in front of him with the promise to help clear his name."

"But he won't know it's us he's meeting, right?"

"Exactly. We'll make him think it's an associate or a family friend. I know a few names of the men who are in their circle of trust, but they don't live in the immediate area. We'll pick one of those wise guys to come to his aid after I do a little work to ensure the plan can't backfire on us."

"How would it backfire on us?"

"If the one I pick has moved back to the area and has already been in touch with Lorenzo, or if he's already dead and the family knows that, things like that. I need to get into Lorenzo's phone and email accounts to see who he's talked to already, then go from there."

"What can I do to help? You've done all the work for my revenge against him."

"This is mostly for you, but Lorenzo has screwed my family over too. Once you're part of the Marchetti family, you don't have to face anything alone. We all have your back. When he fucked with one of us, he fucked with all of us. All you need to do is prepare yourself for the meeting with him. I'm still not convinced you should do it—especially being pregnant. It's not like we can arrange a sit-down meeting in a public place if you're going to kill him."

"No, I guess not. He'd expect somewhere private and off the beaten path if his former partners want to kill him, wouldn't he?"

"Absolutely. His family owns a garbage transfer station in Brooklyn. He wouldn't suspect a meeting there as much as he would other places since it's Sanfratello property. I'd be okay with leaving Geno a little present on the doorstep of his office."

"Carrie, what happens to the Marchetti family after I do this?"

She shrugged and gave me a dismissive wave of her hand. "It'll be an all-out war. But don't feel bad about that. A war has been brewing since the day they shot Damon, whether they know it or not. They tried to make it look like they were after you from the start, but we know better. Daddy and Uncle Leo plan every detail of their revenge, and they don't tell anyone until they're ready to make a move. They prefer to wait so their enemies let their guards down, and Daddy uses the element of surprise to his advantage."

When I lifted my mug for a sip of tea, Carrie's phone pinged with a news alert. She threw her head back and roared with laughter. "Step one is in play, Jillian. The first news station just released the story."

She opened the article and read it aloud to me, exuding pride with her every word. She was right—the article was incredibly damaging to Lorenzo. The details were much too specific and far too knowledgeable about the inner workings of Blaine Financial and the Sanfratello family to be fabricated. Everyone involved in Lorenzo's scheme, from the ones who helped create the elaborate ruse to the people who were cheated out of millions of dollars, would be furious.

"Can't you just hear the collective growls from the Sanfratellos everywhere? They know what this means. Their empire is crumbling around them." Carrie closed her laptop and stood. "It's going to be a great day, I can just feel it."

She walked to the sink behind me to rinse her cup. I heard her open and close cabinet doors and drawers, but my mind was a million miles away.

It would be a great day when I was able to put everything behind me and only look forward to the future. I'd never been one to plot an elaborate revenge on anyone, regardless of how I'd been hurt. I'd certainly never even contemplated premeditated murder —I'd never even had a reason to consider it. Before Damon, that was. Since meeting Damon, I'd not only planned it, I almost attempted it.

With the news article going viral, there was no turning back. I'd face Lorenzo soon enough...and I'd have to face myself in the mirror. One way or another.

Could I let my mother's killer live while she was in the ground?

Could I live with myself after taking a mother's son away from her?

How long would the vengeance continue to destroy these two families?

Would my baby become a casualty of the Marchetti-Sanfratello war?

"Carrie." I turned as I called her name, and I found her standing beside me with a bowl of cut fresh fruit. She passed the food to me with an empathetic expression then took her seat across from me with her breakfast.

"Jillian, let me explain this to you as best I can. Lorenzo will die, one way or another. When he ordered the hit on Damon, you, and your mother, he knew he'd just signed his own death warrant. Even if he'd been successful, he still knew what would come. We're flexible when it comes to bending and breaking man's laws. But there are family laws that aren't broken—they just *aren't*—but he broke them.

"You don't have to be the one to do it, though. If you want to out of respect for your mother, I want to give you the opportunity. If you can't or don't want to, I don't expect you to do it. No one does. But make no mistake, it will be done. Your mother, you, and Damon will be avenged. He will pay for what he's done."

My decision changed from one minute to the next, alternating back and forth between the person I never wanted to be and the person I might have to be for my mom's memory. The problem was, I didn't know if I could live with being either one.

"What are the unbreakable family laws?"

"Don't disrespect the Boss in any way—undermining him, disobeying him, embarrassing him. Don't kill any made man without approval from the Boss or Underboss. Don't rat out your family—you must be loyal to a fault."

"Lorenzo broke all of those, didn't he?"

"Yes, he did. The hit orders disrespected and embarrassed his father. The Ponzi scheme proved he wasn't loyal to his extended family—he was stealing money from people who trusted him with their lives. He isn't an honorable man. Look at the Marchetti men in comparison. Everything they do is for the family, for the people they love. Damon threw himself in front of a bullet for you. He even openly defied Daddy—somewhat, anyway. Had others seen that behavior, you may not have ever seen him again. But Mama was on Damon's side in that argument, so Daddy didn't stand a chance. Still, Damon loves you, and he'll do anything and everything just to protect you."

Funny, just a few short months ago, I had a completely different definition of an honorable man. A self-professed hit man wouldn't have been anywhere near the list. Her words made me reconsider how I saw Damon, though.

"He did take a bullet for me. Then when he was in my house, he shielded me from what felt like machine gun fire blasting through the front windows. He had glass and wood all down his side...because he covered me with his body.

"Carrie, I have to ask you about something that's been on my mind. I'm sorry to put you on the spot, but my thoughts and feelings are all over the place. I've never been so confused about what I should or shouldn't do before."

"Ask me anything. One thing you'll find out about me is I never lie. Lying is for people who are afraid, and I'm not afraid of anyone."

"Is this how my life will always be, whether I'm with Damon or not? Will I always have to watch over my shoulder for the next person who wants to use me to get to Damon? Or use my baby to get to him? Am I looking at a lifetime of being shot at when I walk down the street and having to shoot back at the people who are trying to kill me?"

She flashed a small smile, and I knew she understood exactly how I felt. "You walked into this scenario at a terrible time, Jillian. Milo, our associate who helped Lorenzo steal from us, had just been relieved of his duties. You showed up at the hospital with Damon the same day, then rotated into Milo's role in Blaine Financial. Talk about bad timing and circumstantial evidence—but that's all Lorenzo had to go on. What are the odds that Damon

Marchetti's lover worked for our rival family, in the same role a double-crossing rat had just left?

"After we settle the score, everything will calm down again. Lorenzo went rogue on his family and ours. That doesn't happen often. If you marry my brother, you'll be protected your entire life. Knowing Damon, you'll be protected the rest of your life even if you don't marry him. He'll never stop loving you."

We finished our fresh fruit with lighter conversations and a few laughs, sharing stories from our childhoods and growing closer to being the sisters we'd both always dreamed of having. Having someone to talk to who didn't try to sway me one way or another was refreshing. Her words stayed with me throughout the morning while she wreaked digital havoc in her home computer lab.

"I'm heading out to my first appointment with the obstetrician up here in a few minutes." I leaned against the doorframe to her office. "Thanks for getting me in so soon."

She turned to look at me over her shoulder, a hint of a smile playing on her lips. "How are you getting there?"

"I'll call a cab. It's not that far, and I know you're busy."

"First, I'm never too busy to take you anywhere you need to go. Second, you really don't need to go anywhere alone right now —even to the doctor. And third…Damon is waiting for you outside. He's driving you."

"I knew you were hiding something from me! Your smirk gave you away. Did you tell him to come drive me?"

"No, he called about thirty minutes ago to remind me you needed a good doctor, like I'd forget or something. Anyway, I told him you already had one and had an appointment. Fell right into his trap, because then he threatened me with all kinds of things until I told him when. I'm trying to respect your privacy, but my brother is impossible. I'm sorry about that."

"It's fine, Carrie. Really. He can go to the doctor with me every time I go for all I care. I'd never cut him out of anything he wants to experience, especially with his first child."

When I stepped outside, Damon was in his normal stance, leaning against the car, his hands in his pockets, his eyes constantly scanning the area for any threats. Then his gaze locked on to me, and I felt my body heat from the inside out. The flutters in my stomach expanded to include my chest as my heart raced, thumping against my ribcage.

Would I ever get used to seeing his handsome face and sexy physique?

He pushed off the car and walked to meet me. Goose bumps immediately spread across my body, washing down my arms in waves and leaving no doubt of how much he affected me without even trying.

"Hello, doll. Is it wrong that I love how much you still want me? Gives me a little hope for us." He leaned down and placed a soft kiss on my lips. Without hesitation, or even a single second thought, I reciprocated. Maybe a little too enthusiastically. In mid-kiss, he broke out into a broad smile. "You just keep punishing me until you think I've had enough. Because when I get you back, I'm going to punish you until I think you've had enough. And believe me, doll, I can dish it out even better than I can take it."

HE STEPPED TO MY SIDE, HIS HAND SETTLING ON MY LOWER BACK and his leg brushing against mine with each step toward his car. The fluttering became firebombs detonating inside me, setting off every nerve and fueling the fire of my desire for him.

Would I ever become immune to his charm and the feel of his touch?

"I'm all yours, completely at your beck and call today. If there's anything you need or want, I'm your man. It's my pleasure to give you anything and everything you could ever want or need."

The low murmurs of his deep voice close to my ear sent shivers down my spine. The thinly veiled sexual innuendo made me bite the inside of my cheek to stop the whimper from escaping. After our last tryst, I didn't want him to stop. I didn't want him to leave. He showed much more restraint than I felt.

And there he was again, hinting at giving me the most intense pleasure I'd ever felt. If he just came out and asked me, I wouldn't say no.

I was sure he already knew that, though.

CHAPTER TWELVE

Damon

"You look beautiful today, as usual." I opened the door and waited for Jillian to settle into the front seat of my car. Then I leaned in and stole another long, sensual kiss from her succulent lips.

Her hooded eyes told me everything she felt. With the right word, she'd be my rag doll to bend and twist however I wanted all night long. At the moment, anyway. She'd been hot and cold. Willing and distant. Sure and unsure. I knew all too well she could change her mind again at any second. She hadn't made any commitments to me since she'd returned.

So I decided to adopt a new tactic with my Southern belle.

She had to come to me—on her own, telling me and showing me what she wanted from me. One word from her was all I needed to rock her world and relieve all her pent-up sexual frustration. One word, and she'd move in to my apartment to be with me every day and every night. One word, and she'd know first-hand what it meant to be treated like my queen.

Until she said that word, I'd keep applying the subtle pressure.

I'd remind her what she was missing out on, while still spending as much time with her as she'd allow. But my approach would be more subdued. My offers would be fewer and farther between. I'd stay my same, charming self, but after our last discussion, I sensed she was leaning more toward her independence. The warning in my heart told me to prepare to be sorely disappointed.

"Thank you." She sounded slightly out of breath, just enough to be sexy and seductive. It was going to be a long fucking afternoon if she didn't step up and admit her feelings real damn soon.

With a wink and a slight smirk, I closed her door and moved to the driver's side. Since we were going to see the doctor about our baby, I told Benny to stay at the office and cover for me. I wanted to be alone with Jillian, so she would see us as a couple, soon to be a family. Telling her wouldn't work—I had to show her.

She had to see it for herself and want it without my coercion.

That was probably the hardest fucking thing for me to do. Persuasive tactics were my specialty, whether that was by force, by threats, or by smooth negotiation. But that wasn't the type of life I wanted with her or for her. She was bold and beautiful and bright—and I wouldn't change a single thing about her.

"How's life with my sister?" I asked as I slid behind the wheel.

"It's been very entertaining and enlightening. I love her. She's like the sister I've always wanted but never had."

"There were plenty of times while we were growing up my brothers and I would've gladly given her to you. But I suppose I'm glad we kept her instead."

She laughed, catching my jest. "I've seen a lot of Marchetti in her, and she told me a few stories from when you two were kids. I can imagine she was a handful."

"Was? She still is. What are you talking about?" I reached over and took her hand in mine, lacing our fingers together. She didn't pull away, to my shock and amazement. I admit I held on to a little hope for us to pull through this none the worse for wear.

"Okay, you've got me there. She's very smart and a whiz on the computers. I wish I knew half of what she's forgotten about them."

"I'm glad you two are getting along so well. She feels the same about you, in case you were wondering."

"Thanks for telling me. It's nice to hear my admiration is returned."

I'd never been known for my ability to make small talk. With the recent events, I was in no mood to even try.

"Did you happen to catch the news today? There was an interesting update that flashed up on my phone. I had to open the article on my laptop and read it a second time on the big screen." I cut my eyes over to her, watching her reaction for any deception.

"Oh?"

My sweet, mostly innocent Jillian was still in there. At least my sneaky sister hadn't changed that yet.

"Yeah. You didn't see it?"

"Um. Well. I'm not sure which news article you saw. Why don't you tell me about it?"

"It was all about Lorenzo, Blaine Financial, and how he was running an underhanded scheme to cheat his family and partners out of a shitload of money. You didn't see that?"

"Oh, that one. Yes, I heard about it today. Um, Carrie read part of the article to me, but I didn't read it myself. I think she must've had the same alert you did. I remember hearing her phone chime, and I thought it was text message at first. But it wasn't a text. It was just the app on her phone telling her there was a breaking news story."

Guilty. She was so, so fucking guilty. I had to physically stop myself from laughing out loud.

Fuck, I loved her so much. On top of everything that made Jillian special, she was such a good-hearted person she couldn't even pull off a poker face over something so simple.

"It was a breaking story, all right. It'll break Lorenzo for sure. I doubt he lives to see the morning."

"Why do you say that?"

"Because he disobeyed a direct order from the boss of his family. Even though that's his dad, Lorenzo isn't above correction. He's caused Geno trouble before, and Geno gave him one last warning. That's part of why the Sanfratello family is considered weaker than ours. Geno doesn't have enough of a backbone to do what needs to be done when it comes to his kids. This latest fuck-up will be Lorenzo's last. Mark my words."

"Geno would put out an order to kill his own son?"

"He won't have a choice. The consigliere will advise him to do it, and their underboss will carry it out. It'll probably break Geno, too. Their whole family is likely to fold."

"Where do you think he's hiding?"

"I don't have a clue where he is now. He ran after we took out his house and his old girlfriend's house, just in case he tried to run to her place for cover. His family has been keeping him off the grid. That'll change now with his fugly mug on the cover of every newspaper and on every news station. Geno will do damage control with the rest of the family and their allies, so that means Lorenzo will be on his own for a while."

Jillian remained silent a little too long after her sudden initial interest in Lorenzo and where he could be, silently contemplating the information I'd given her. Her brows were drawn down, and her thumbnail was securely held between her teeth. One of two things had to be going on in that beautiful head of hers. Either she was *afraid* he was a loose cannon, gunning for her from every direction...or, she *hoped* he was a loose cannon and would show his face soon. Neither scenario sat well with me.

She had every reason and right to want revenge against him after what he took from her. But then again, she had every right and reason to exact her own choice of revenge against me, too. Since Jillian hadn't been back to my parents' house with me, Mama still hadn't let me eat at the table with the rest of the family. I remained in exile, banished to the kitchen counter, forced to stand during my meals. Looking at Jillian sitting beside me, having her near me again, I realized I'd stand in the fucking corner for the rest of my life if she just forgave me.

"Do you think he'll come after me again to try to regain good standing with his family?"

I felt the weight of her stare on me, analyzing my reaction and waiting to assess my reply. To what end was my question, one I'd have to carefully gauge without outright asking her. My suspicions were high, but that was nothing new for me. I'd never fully trusted anyone outside of my immediate family—and a couple of them had even given me reason to doubt their word at one time or another. The thing was, I hated being suspicious of Jillian. Though it ran counter to my natural instincts, I found myself wanting to trust her, wanting to push the doubts aside and kick caution to the sideline.

"It's very possible, Jillian. I won't lie to you about it. I'd rather you watch over your shoulder for a while than have a false sense of security. You know as long as I'm still breathing, I'll never let anyone hurt you."

"You're not always around, Damon. You may not have a say-so in the matter."

"All the more reason why you should be living with me instead of my sister."

"But I'm not living with you. I'm living with Carrie, at least for the time being. Until this clusterfuck with Lorenzo is over and I can find my own place."

That sucker punch to the gut fucking hurt.

With a quick glance at her face, I realized she wasn't saying it to hurt me. She wasn't smirking. There was no sense of satisfaction in her expression after driving that metaphorical dagger deep into my heart. She simply made a statement about her future, and I didn't appear to be in her vision of it. When she said she was confused and couldn't make up her mind, she meant it. It seemed she'd made a decision and was sticking to it.

The life I'd envisioned for us was no longer in question. It was over and done.

"Well, once Lorenzo is out of the picture, you won't need around-the-clock protection. You may not need protection at all by then. Let's just get through one day at a time without incident."

My monotone reply couldn't be helped. At one time in our relationship, I'd warned her I'd never let her go, but that turned out to be not so true. As much as I wanted to rail against it, to shake some sense into her, I finally had to face the reality that she didn't want to be with me. That my family may be irreparably damaged. That there would never be more than what we were at that moment.

Parents of an unborn baby who weren't destined to be together.

I loved her enough to want her to be happy, regardless of what that meant for me. That didn't mean I had to be happy about it. And I wasn't. I just fucking wasn't.

"What? No clever warning of how I belong to you and I'll realize that all too soon?" The teasing tone of her voice conveyed the coy smile that brightened her face, but I kept my eyes on the road.

"No, Jillian. Not today."

The sobering thought of another man eventually taking up residence with the woman I loved and the child growing inside her hit me at full force. The last thing I felt like doing was smiling or laughing. The worst fucking part was I only had myself to blame for it.

"Damon." She said my name on a soft whisper, a hint of an apology lingering in the air.

But I wasn't ready to hear those words from her. I couldn't sit there and listen to her tell me she tried to move past it, how she wanted to love me again but just couldn't bring herself to actually do it. Even though I could see it in her actions, hear it in her voice, and feel it in the air, hearing the actual words would be my undoing.

"Here we are. Let me check our surroundings first. I'll get the door for you when it's safe to get out of the car."

Never had I faced anything like what I felt in that moment. I could've been in a foreign country, with no friends and no understanding of the native language, for as much as I knew about the next steps I should take. The only me I knew would've coerced her in some way until she gave in—bribes, threats, kidnapping—whatever it took. The new me, the man I didn't even recognize—still wanted her to choose to be with me, to want to be mine. But he was preparing to let her go for good...to admit, after exhausting all means, he was defeated and there was nothing left to fight for, no matter how much it fucking killed him.

For the sake of Jillian's happiness, I finally understood I had to let her go, regardless of how much I loved her. Holding on to her, trying to keep hope alive, and trying to elbow my way back into her heart hadn't done either of us any favors up to that point. My choices pushed us to the breaking point, and I'd been a selfish asshole long enough.

Strange how a few minutes and a short conversation could change everything I thought I knew, who I thought I was.

The idea of getting advice from my old man crossed my mind, but as far as I knew, he and Mama never had a single doubt they'd be together forever. Because of that, I wasn't convinced taking advice from him on the matter was the best course of action. Maybe inaction was the only course I had left. Don't do anything. Don't try anything. Don't force anything.

Just let it be whatever it was.

When everything was said and done with Lorenzo, I'd check out of Jillian's life. I'd be the best father any kid ever had, but I'd do it without her by my side.

Every ounce of me revolted against that decision. Every fiber of my being said to man up and be a fucking Marchetti. Take control. Don't back down. See it through until the bitter end, just like I'd done my whole damn life. If some fucker tried to move in on her, he'd wish he'd never been born.

But that would only hurt her more. And if I'd vowed to never let anyone hurt her, that promise had to include me.

After a thorough scan of the cars and people in our immediate area, I opened the car door to help her out. The rueful gleam in her eye when she stood and faced me only strengthened my resolve. I wouldn't accept pity from any-fucking-body. Not even her.

"Let's get you inside while I'm reasonably sure the coast is clear. We don't want to push our luck more than we absolutely have to right now."

With my hand on her lower back, I steered her away from the parking lot, toward the front door of the two-story doctor's office building. She cast several sidelong glances at me as we walked the short distance down the sidewalk, but my refusal to acknowledge them coupled with my hypervigilant surveillance around us prevented her from speaking. Once inside the building, I relaxed somewhat and removed my hand from her back, knowing Lorenzo would never attack inside the doctor's office that many wives of made men used. He wouldn't make it ten feet outside the door before every faction in the Tri-State area had mowed him down.

We sat quietly while she filled out the new patient paperwork, then only made small talk now and then when something inter-esting flashed on the television. The invisible wall between us went up one brick at a time, but we both felt it.

"Jillian Hart," the nurse called from the doorway.

Jillian stood, but I remained planted in my seat. She looked down at me, confusion, shock, and maybe a small wave of pain crossing her face. "Are you not coming back with me?"

"If you want me to come back with you, I will. If not, I'll stay here and give you some privacy."

"Damon, I'd like for you to be there with me. It's important to me."

"In that case, I'll be right beside you."

Inside the exam room, I moved from poster to poster to study the stages of fetal development while Jillian changed into the hospital gown. Memorizing every detail from conception to birth, I pictured how big our baby was at nearly four months. Only six inches long…less than the length from the tip of my middle finger to my wrist. By the time I'd started to make my second round, anything to delay the inevitable conversation, the doctor rushed through the door with her chart in hand.

"Hello. How are Mom and Dad doing today?" He was an older man, closer to my father's age, balding with white hair wrapping around the lower part of his head. He extended his hand to shake mine first. "Daryl Bowers. Good to meet you."

"We're fine," Jillian answered with a smile.

He took her hand in both of his and gave her a warm welcome. "According to your records from your doctor down in Louisiana, you're around four months now. Does that sound right?"

"Yes, it does."

"Perfect time to see if we can hear the baby's heartbeat on the Doppler. Just lie back there, and let's see if the baby wants to cooperate with us today."

With a blob of gel on her exposed belly, he began to move the wand across her skin, seemingly ignoring all the sounds from the speaker that I thought were important. Then he stopped and homed in on a specific area when he apparently recognized what he'd been searching for.

"Hear that?" he asked, smiling at Jillian. All I heard was something that sounded like horses galloping…but underwater. "That's your baby's heartbeat."

He turned up the volume, the fast beat of my baby's heart filled the room, and the haze in my brain cleared. The unmistakable sound of a rapid heartbeat permeated my soul. Fast. Strong. Beautiful. When it began to fade, he moved the wand to find the right spot again. Then his brows drew downward, and he cocked his head to the side, listening intently.

He turned to his nurse. "Chelle, I'd like to get her to the ultrasound room. Can you go make sure Pat is ready for us?"

Dr. Bowers slipped the Doppler into his coat pocket then extended his hand to Jillian, helping her sit up on the exam table. "Let's go in the ultrasound room and let Pat, our sonogram technician, take a look at the baby."

"Is something wrong? What's going on with our baby?" I stepped closer to Jillian and took her hand in mine as she stood.

"Come with me. I'll be able to explain everything in just a minute."

We followed him to a smaller room. An exam table sat at the far end, against the wall. Beside it was the ultrasound machine and a large monitor where the sonogram technician waited for us. After Jillian was comfortable on the table and more gel had been spread across her stomach, Pat moved the larger wand into place low on Jillian's abdomen.

Then she looked up at the doctor... and they smiled at each other.

"Well, Jillian, congratulations. You're having twins."

13

CHAPTER THIRTEEN

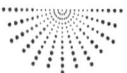

Jillian

"What? What did you just say?"

There was no way I heard him correctly.

Pat chuckled, no doubt that wasn't the first time she'd heard disbelief and sheer panic at the same time. "There are two distinct fetuses. Two distinct hearts. Two of everything. Congratulations!"

In my stunned state, I couldn't reply. I looked back and forth from Dr. Bowers to Pat several times, waiting for them to laugh and say they were only kidding. But they didn't. Then I turned my gaze to the flat screen that had captured Damon's attention and stared at the grainy black-and-white images for several seconds. I began to make out the shapes. Though they were small, there were definitely two separate bodies moving inside me.

Tears sprang to my eyes—tears of joy, elation, confusion, terror. Sheer and utter happiness. My only regret was that my mother wasn't there to experience the miracle with me.

Damon moved closer to Pat, completely oblivious to anyone else in the small room, and lifted his hand to the screen. His fingers traced the clear outlines of both our babies with an expression of complete awe and wonder on his face. His lips moved, but I didn't hear any audible words. He was talking to our babies, making his silent oath to them. He stood rooted to his spot for several seconds after he dropped his hand at his side. Then he nodded, his silent decree set in Marchetti stone.

When he turned to face me, the determined man I first met had returned in full force. Any doubts or second thoughts I'd sensed on the ride over were gone. The cool, steely exterior of the deadly hit man inside him was back. His eyes dropped from mine to my stomach, and I knew his primary focus had shifted from me to the twins I carried. The Marchetti bloodline lived inside me, and Damon would uphold the code of family honor that had driven him his entire life by protecting them at any cost.

"Do you have a history of twins in your family?" Damon stepped closer to me, his eyes sliding up my body until they locked on to mine.

"No, none. This is the first set of twins on my side."

"There's always a first for everything," Dr. Bowers interjected. "Family history isn't always a clear indicator."

The trepidation in my eyes must have been painfully obvious. Damon ran his fingers along my jawline then gently held my chin between his thumb and forefinger. "Don't be scared, doll. Our babies will be perfect, just like you."

Dr. Bowers chatted with Pat for a few minutes as she printed out multiple sonogram pictures. I couldn't stop staring at the monitor, watching the tiny, active babies inside me.

"When will I start to feel them moving?"

"You'll begin to feel it anytime now. It's usually around the sixteen-week mark. It'll feel like little flutters low in your abdomen," Dr. Bowers said. "Then before you know it, you'll feel kicks and full somersaults."

The doctor and technician finished printing pictures and left the room so I could get dressed in private. Chelle waited outside the door until we emerged and escorted us to Dr. Bowers's office.

We sat in shocked silence and waited for him to join us. Actually, I was stunned silent, but I could see the wheels in Damon's mind turning at lightning speed. Whatever plan he was formulating had his full attention.

When Dr. Bowers joined us, he handed me a thick book on what I could expect from being pregnant with twins and an envelope with copies of the sonogram pictures. While I would've loved for my mother to be the first person other than Damon and me to see them, I couldn't wait to show Mama Lina. Though I could barely focus on the doctor's words, I wanted to share everything he said about my care going forward and ask Mama Lina to help Damon and me navigate through the rest of my pregnancy.

If I thought having one newborn was scary, the thought of having two at once was absolutely terrifying.

Somehow, I managed to fumble my way through the rest of the appointment, gathering all the information I could about twin pregnancies and how it would be different. When Damon opened the car door for me, I stopped shy of sliding into the seat and lifted my eyes to his.

He'd avoided that connection for most of the ride and nearly all of the visit. But as we stood in the parking lot, his gaze didn't falter.

"What are you thinking, Damon? What's going on up here?" I lightly tapped his temple, then rested my palm against his cheek. Disappointment filled me when he didn't lean into my touch, not even slightly.

"I'm just trying to process everything you and the babies will need to be safe and comfortable. A nice gated house instead of an apartment in the city so we can install extra security measures. Hopefully, you'll find something you like close to my parents and my sister, so they can help out at a moment's notice until I can get there. Finding the right full-time nanny who can be ready to start as soon as they're born so you can get plenty of rest."

"Where will you be?"

"Never too far away."

With that, he motioned for me to get into the car. I obeyed robotically, visions of the finest material things money could buy surrounding me, but no husband coming home to our children and me every night. No father in-house to help with midnight feedings and two a.m. diaper changes. No Damon in the bed beside me to hold me and help keep me safe through whatever storms came our way.

Suddenly, that house he suggested felt somewhat empty and alone without him there to share it with me. Joint custody meant one of us would miss a lot of important milestones in the babies' lives, even something as simple as learning to roll over or sit up alone. In the short time it took him to walk around the car and slide behind the wheel, I'd already felt the loss of so many wonderful firsts we should experience together.

Weighed against the grudge I tried to hold on to, my personal vendetta to make him feel the pain I'd felt over the past four months began to feel petty and small. When I considered how my choices could impact our children their entire lives, guilt began to consume me.

My father was a huge part of my childhood. As a young child, I remembered looking forward to the time I spent with him every day. After he died, rushing to meet my father as he arrived home from work every day were some of the most bittersweet memories I had.

If Damon and I continued on our current path, our children would never experience the anticipation of waiting for their dad to return home at the end of the day. They'd miss out on so many nights of him rocking them to sleep, safe and secure in his strong arms. There would be times when they would want him instead of me—learning to ride a bike, dealing with bullies at school, advice on dating. My whole life seemed to flash before my eyes, and the huge, gaping hole in it was the void only Damon could fill.

How important was my anger if I had no one to love and no one to love me?

The driver's door opened, and the masculine scents of bergamot, cinnamon, and leather filled the car. His signature cologne set my senses ablaze and left my body burning with need for his touch. While he started the car and maneuvered it into traffic, I studied his strong profile. His thick black hair, those chocolate brown eyes, the sexy eternal five-o'clock shadow faded beard. Damon was still the sexiest man I'd ever seen. He was dangerous but affectionate. He was calculating yet generous. He was cruel and somehow sweet.

The warning in my head wasn't loud enough to overcome the yearning in my heart. Giving him another chance was dangerous to my heart and mind. Mentally and physically, he could crush me into oblivion if he betrayed me again. But something told me he wouldn't. His family code. The way the Marchetti clan had adopted me as one of their own. Even the space and time he gave me after I returned to New York with him told me he wanted what was best for me, regardless of what it did to him.

But being kept in the dark about the plans and information he and his father discussed openly was a deal-breaker for me. If they trusted me to be part of the family, then I wanted to be a full-fledged member. Not a stepchild they merely tolerated and placated.

To be truly considered one of them, I'd have to prove my mettle. And I only knew of one way to do that.

If Carrie and I could pull off our cockamamie plan and somehow incapacitate Lorenzo until Damon met us, we would both be viewed in a different light. We'd be trusted and respected —at least more so than our current situation. And maybe, just maybe, I could move past the helplessness I felt over being unable to save my mother when she needed me. Maybe it would renew my sense of empowerment and independence.

Or maybe I was grasping at straws and it would all go horribly wrong.

I was never good at guessing odds, though I figured they were much less than fifty-fifty. Probably more like seventy-thirty...and not in my favor. The only ace in the hole I had was Carrie—her time in the family, her training, and her underground activities she'd managed to successfully accomplish without any help at all.

After a couple of glances in my direction, Damon finally turned and stared at me straight on, lifting one brow in question with an amused expression on his handsome face. "Something I can do for you, doll?"

I answered him with a candid smile. One that reached my eyes and covered my face from ear to ear. "That's a loaded question to ask a woman who just found out you impregnated her with twins, Damon."

A salacious grin spread slowly across his face. His bedroom eyes twinkled with mischief, and his voice dropped to a low timbre when he spoke. "I'm more than willing to try to do it again. And again. And again. However many times it takes to hit the jackpot a second time, doll."

Ah, my cocky, sexy hit man was back.

"That would be hard to accomplish since I'm already pregnant right now."

He shrugged one shoulder, and one side of his lips lifted slightly. "Practice makes perfect."

"You wouldn't know what to do if I suddenly agreed to your requests for sexual favors."

He laughed out loud. "See, doll, that's where you couldn't be more wrong. I'd know *exactly* what to do, and I think we both know it."

I did know that about him—all too well.

When we arrived back at Carrie's house, I was more than ready to start pushing the timing of our plan. My life and heart had been in limbo long enough. And Lorenzo had gotten away with his bullshit long enough. He needed to pay for what he did, and I needed to be the one to do it, so I could close that horrible chapter and move on. Carrie had been working behind the scenes for hours on end, developing the news articles and setting up the smoke and mirrors.

Damon opened my door then took my hand to help me stand. He pulled me up, my chest sliding against his, and I thought the heat from the friction would set my clothes on fire. Or, maybe I hoped it would, so they'd burn off me and I wouldn't have an excuse to turn him down again.

"When this is over with Lorenzo, I'll schedule some time with a Realtor who knows what to look for in a piece of property for our family. She can take you house-hunting in the safest areas. When you find one you can't live without, all you have to do is tell her. I'll take care of the rest. You won't have to worry about a thing except what color you want to paint the walls. Mama would love to take you shopping for furniture—she lives for that shit."

"Is that what you think is best?" My bottom lip started to quiver, so I pulled it between my teeth, trying to control it along with my emotions.

"I do. You're right. You'll want to stretch out in your own place well before the babies are born. You'll want to decorate the nurseries and have everything just perfect before they come home. Baby showers—my whole family will fill the house with gifts. I know you don't want to store all that at Carrie's."

He wasn't kidding, but he wasn't being mean either.

He was simply being practical, matter-of-fact.

Just like that, what I thought I wanted changed again. I'd wanted to hurt him, to push him away, to make him leave me alone. I'd done my best to guard my heart and keep him out of it. Though he had been in my thoughts every single day since we parted, I'd fought against what that really meant.

And now...

He was giving me what I thought I wanted—a life without his

interference. He was leaving me alone while still providing for his children. I'd accomplished pushing him away and hurting him time after time with my trivial jabs, while he'd tried several times to make amends. He'd broken the Boss's rules and chanced being exiled from his family—for me. That could've meant death for him.

He walked me to the door to make sure I got safely inside. I had to admit, I did love the extra care and attention Damon gave me. With the exception of one awful night, he'd always made me feel safe and protected. I suddenly wanted nothing more than for him to stay, but I had to have distraction-free time with Carrie.

"Do you want to take a few of these sonogram pictures with you to show your mother?"

"I'd love to show my mother, but I want you with me when I do. Why don't you come to family dinner with Carrie this Saturday? We'll show her together then."

"Okay, I'll be there Saturday, then. Thank you again for driving me today."

"Always my pleasure, doll."

I stood just inside the foyer and watched him drive away with my heart heavy, and uncertainty settled in my gut again. Had I lost him? Was it too late to carry out my plan for vengeance? Would it make any difference if I killed Lorenzo or not? I turned away from the window and went to join Carrie in her secret command center.

"Carrie, I'm ready. Let's draw him out and get this over with."

"Thought you'd never ask." She pressed a key on her laptop. A series of command prompts ran through several lines of code sequences, then a satisfied smirk covered her face. "And, article number two has just been delivered. By morning, Lorenzo Sanfratello will be wanted by every member of his family, along with anyone else who has ever had a kind word for his family."

"What's in this one?"

"A very elaborate story detailing how Lorenzo has agreed to

work with the FBI in exchange for immunity and some very convincing pictures of him and an FBI agent meeting in secret. I added a few of their real embezzlement methods to make it as convincing as possible."

"Then tomorrow, we set our trap to catch a rat."

CHAPTER FOURTEEN

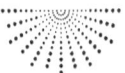

Damon

"Boss, those two girls have been busy. Very busy. Your soldiers are on standby to move in at any moment."

Benny's call woke me from a dead sleep, right in the middle of the best fucking dream I'd had in a long time.

"Tell me." I glanced over at the clock and scrubbed my hand across my face. Two thirty in the fucking morning.

"They've arranged a meeting with Lorenzo in about thirty minutes. They convinced him they're a friend of the family who's willing to take him in and help him clear his name. After the shit hit the fan with that news article, I'm not surprised he jumped at their offer to help him. He has to be desperate right about now."

"You've got to be fucking kidding me. They're meeting him alone?" My voice echoed off the walls. I was wide fucking awake all of a sudden. Throwing my feet over the side of the mattress, I propelled myself out of the bed. With my phone help between my cheek and my shoulder, I threw my clothes on in the dark in a rush. "Where?"

"Geno's garbage distribution station in Queens."

"Pretty smart move, I have to give them that. Doesn't mean I'm not going to throttle them both when I get there. Get over there, and have the men surround the building now—and I mean they better be *close*. I'm on my way."

"Figured you'd say that. We have the block surrounded, just waiting for our special guests to show up."

Benny and I disconnected as I rushed out to my car. I knew something more was up than their internet stalking of Lorenzo. Both Jillian and Carrie had acted very strangely over the last few days. Stranger than usual, that is. I'd dropped by to see Jillian a few times, to ask if she needed anything and see how she felt, and she did her best to get rid of me as soon as possible every fucking time. Had I not known they were already targeting him, I would've sworn she had another man sneaking in her bedroom window at night.

One or two nights of sitting outside Carrie's house all night, watching said window like a fucking hawk, convinced me otherwise. While I had faced the fate of our relationship, I wanted to be the first to know if she'd moved on. I didn't want to find out from anyone else.

But tracking Carrie's keystrokes on the dark web had been harder than we thought it would be. We had the words she used, but finding where she used them was pure hell. In a virtual world that was designed to preserve anonymity, we searched everywhere and anywhere we could imagine she'd frequent. We found a few spots and were able to piece enough together to make an educated guess that she'd found Lorenzo.

Thank God Benny stayed on it until he found all the bread crumbs Carrie had left in various online private rooms. He must have been at it all night since he followed them to the empty building in the middle of the night.

For the entire drive, I wrestled with my anger over the situation. Carrie was slightly better able to handle herself against Lorenzo than Jillian was, but not by much. She way overestimated her abilities while far underestimating her opponent. Jillian had no business what-so-fucking-ever being there, especially at four months pregnant. Had she told me she wanted to execute her revenge against Lorenzo herself, I would've arranged it for her. I would've walked her through every step. I would've ensured her safety while ensuring his demise.

But she didn't come to me.

She trusted my sister's lead instead of mine.

She was about to walk into a situation she couldn't just turn and walk away from. Once Lorenzo saw her face, he wouldn't stop until she was dead. Even the two of them together couldn't control him—not physically and not mentally. He'd prepared for his role his entire life. Every action was second nature to him. Where Carrie and Jillian wouldn't be able to read the situation at a glance, Lorenzo could. They wouldn't be prepared to face any backup he may bring with him, or for the very real possibility that he'd gain the upper hand and use one of them against the other.

They'd stand and fall together, not leaving the other behind to call for help. And that very weakness would end up getting them both killed.

My sister liked to play mobster, but she had no real-world experience in man-handling a six-foot, two-hundred-plus-pound man made of muscle. She thought she could easily best them because she'd had years of a military-style defensive combat training. But she didn't understand these men wouldn't give her the chance to get that close to them. They'd put a bullet between her eyes at first glance. She was a known Marchetti, a natural enemy.

I wanted to whip her ass and Jillian's ass for even thinking they'd have the upper hand in this bullshit scheme. There was no way we'd all walk away unscathed. That knowledge alone jacked my blood pressure through the roof.

I finally spotted Benny's car, parked in the complete blackness in a side alley, and turned off my lights as I parked behind him.

After I made sure my interior lights were off, I silently exited my car and crept up to Benny's open window.

"What's the story?" I kept my voice low and my eyes trained on the darkened building across the street.

"Carrie and Jillian just went in about ten minutes ago. Lorenzo made a few passes around the block, I'm sure looking for a trap and a way out, but he parked on the other side of the building. He stopped and checked out my car. The hood was cold, though, so he didn't bother to check inside. He's sloppy, Damon, but that doesn't mean he isn't dangerous. Tony has eyes on him. Said Lorenzo's smoking a cigarette and pacing in front of his car. He's not convinced he's safe yet."

"Of course not. The building is still dark. That's a sure sign the person waiting inside isn't friendly. What the fuck were they thinking?"

Rookie mistakes. Telltale signs. No one whom Lorenzo would trust would make the kind of mistakes they made. Lorenzo was desperate for a friend—someone who would protect him and hide him from the rest of the world. But desperation made him even more dangerous, because he knew he had nothing else to lose.

"Think you should try getting in the back door and help them out?" Benny cut his eyes over at me, though he already knew my answer.

"If we don't all get killed tonight, I'm going to beat both of their asses when I get them home." I swore under my breath and took the black ski mask from Benny's outstretched hand. Then I slid my black leather gloves on my hands and made my silent trek through the shadows.

My decision to enter the building was risky—for many reasons. The majority of Lorenzo's family and soldiers had turned on him, but there was always the possibility a few remained loyal —or at least helpful. There was a fine line where family was concerned. If he were reinstated as a capo later, he'd retaliate against those who blatantly shunned him in his time of need.

Eventually, anyway, though not openly. Several of the men would have unexplainable accidents.

There was no way Carrie went inside the building unarmed, and I was sure she had Jillian armed to the teeth. Either of them could shoot me, not knowing I was the one sneaking in the back door instead of Lorenzo. The slightest noise could set them off, shooting first and asking questions later. Fear coupled with a spike of adrenaline would either make them freeze up completely or empty their magazines into me.

Then there was Lorenzo himself. I had no way of communicating with my men, so I had no way of knowing if Lorenzo had taken another stroll around the block for a second or third pass. Crossing paths with him would definitely lead to an altercation, though I'd rather run into him face-to-face, outside in the darkened alley and away from the girls. But if he entered from the front around the time I entered from the back, the girls would be caught in the cross fire between us.

The entire scenario had too many variables and too many dependencies for me to feel the least bit comfortable with what I had to do. But there was no fucking way I could leave them in there alone. Not my sister...and not the mother of my unborn children. Risking my life was worth their safety a million times over. And, if I was being honest with myself, maybe I also hoped my actions would help redeem my past behavior in Jillian's eyes.

Maybe she wouldn't want that big house all to herself anymore.

Maybe we could have our own family.

You know, if she didn't shoot me first.

My eyes scanned the area as I approached the fence surrounding the building, putting me out in the open and vulnerable to being seen. After making sure it wasn't electrified, I picked the lock on the gate and hurried inside. The pitch-black night gave me cover inside the privacy fence, but every little sound caught my attention as I approached the huge metal door. Rats scurried around the enormous garbage bins, squeaking and clawing at the metal. Their noises would help cover mine, but they also covered for anyone coming up behind me while I picked yet another lock.

When I felt the tumblers in the lock give way, I sensed the moment of truth had arrived. Opening the large metal door would reveal my presence—there was no way around it. The concrete at my feet showed wide, arcing marks from where the door had previously scraped against it. The rusted metal hinges would creak loudly from the weight of the swinging door.

With my hand firmly gripping the lever door handle, I pushed it down and jerked the door open in one swift motion. I stepped inside the building, closed the door behind me, and then took a few long strides into the room. The silence in the large office was deafening. Years of experience told me I had guns trained on my chest, ready to blast holes in me at any second. Tension filled the air, even though they held their breath.

"Doll, it's just me. Don't shoot." I pulled the ski mask off and let it fall to the floor.

"Damon?" Shock filled Jillian's voice, the quiver her voice revealing her underlying fear.

"What are you doing here, Damon?" Carrie hissed at me with the same fear, plus anger, in her tone.

"Keeping you two from getting yourselves killed. Lorenzo's outside right now. He's here to meet a *friend*—not someone he doesn't know. Don't you think a friend would have a light on inside, so he'd know it was safe to come in? You two need to get out of here *right now* and let me handle this."

My eyes adjusted to the total darkness of the room, and I was finally able to make out the outlines of their shapes.

"No." Jillian's voice was firm and sure, with no hint of lingering anxiety. "I need to do this, Damon. For my mother."

"And I will let you do whatever you want to do to him, doll. I won't try to stop you. Just let me make sure he can't touch you first. Please, Jillian."

That was the first time I'd ever begged anyone. But she was more than worth it to me. My pride meant nothing if she and our babies were gone.

She was silent, weighing my request and her options.

"Jilly, listen to me. If anything happened to you and our babies, I could *not* handle it. Do you hear what I'm saying?"

"I hear you, Damon."

From her softened tone, I knew she understood the entire meaning behind my words. Losing her would result in more than sorrow, more than depression. I'd have no reason to go on.

"Where do you want us to wait?" Carrie asked.

"Go out the back door, through the gate, and to the end of the alley across the street. Benny is waiting in the car there. I'll come out and signal when it's safe for you both to come back."

"Okay. As long as I have your word that he's mine soon." Jillian moved to stand directly in front of me. "Swear it, Damon."

"You have my word, on my honor as a Marchetti capo. He's all yours as soon as it's safe. Please go now, doll." I placed my hands on her face and pulled her lips to meet mine. "I love you, Jillian."

Her jaw dropped open and a quick gasp followed. She brought her hands up to mine, her smaller fingers covering mine. "Damon, I lo—"

"Now this is just too fucking sweet." Bright, fluorescent light filled the room, temporarily blinding me when my involuntary reaction kicked in and made my eyes squint from the sudden harshness. "And how fortuitous that I'd find the Marchetti family in my father's business establishment. I mean, I really couldn't ask for a better setup, could I?"

Fucking Lorenzo Sanfratello.

I snatched my Glock 19 from the waistband of my jeans with one hand and began to move Jillian out of his line of sight with my other arm. My aim stayed trained on Lorenzo as I stared down the sights of my barrel.

And that was when all hell broke loose.

Doors opened and closed from every direction. The shouting of angry voices echoed off the cinderblock walls, creating more confusion and chaos. Multiple feet shuffled and scraped across the concrete floor, making it impossible to keep up with who was where. The loud crash of office furniture breaking after being overturned or knocked out of the way came from every direction all around me. There was no way I could shield Jillian or Carrie. We were completely exposed from every angle.

The earsplitting *bang* of multiple shots fired in close quarters sent my adrenaline through the roof. The loud cries of pain just before the sickening thud of bodies hitting the floor filled my ears. Though I'd heard it many times before, knowing the love of my life and my sister were unprotected made my gut churn.

Then the urgent scream of my name quickly became a muffled whimper.

And my blood ran cold.

More Damon and Jillian are coming in Warning, Part Three...

WARNING: PART THREE

Just when I thought I had everything figured out, life blew up in my face without warning. The missing pieces of the puzzle weren't clear, and the stakes were too high to merely hope for the best.

Absolute facts I'd believed my entire life turned out to be lies and the truth was harder to accept than the family ever realized. Protecting my loved ones was my only priority. Any threat had to be eliminated—no matter the consequences.

How deep did the treachery go? Only one way to find out.

CHAPTER ONE

Damon

𝓗ow could time simultaneously stand still and rush by? I had no fucking idea how, but it did.

One second, my sights were set squarely between Lorenzo's eyes. My breaths were controlled as I started to squeeze the trigger, despite my promise to let Jillian take out her revenge out on him. He made his presence known before I could get Jillian and Carrie out of the building. Out of pure protective instinct, I was going to kill him where he stood.

Then everything went to shit.

Doors leading to the various other areas of the business opened, revealing several armed Sanfratello soldiers. Closets, bathrooms, private offices, and the distribution bay—the soldiers emerged with their guns drawn and murder in their eyes.

"Did you really think I was all alone? My men would never abandon me, and they know I'd never abandon them. They also know I'd never turn traitor against them. But that picture of me with the FBI was very convincing, for those who don't know better. Bravo." Lorenzo took a step closer, and his gaze shifted from me to Jillian.

"But you did betray them. They have no idea you're pocketing the money from your embezzlement scheme and making it look like Damon took it instead." Jillian's revelation made many of the men pause, their eyes searching Lorenzo's face for clues to the truth.

"Nice try, Jillian, but I'm afraid your lies won't work."

"Lies? No, Lorenzo, I have no reason to lie about it. But I do have proof of it. I wonder how loyal they'll be when they see you've taken all the pension money and created a Ponzi scheme that they're funding."

Eyes all around the room shifted from Jillian to Lorenzo, their expressions changing from intrigued to suspicious. Unsure of who was lying and who was telling the truth, several men momentarily lowered their guns. Lorenzo glanced around at them, his face shrouded in a mixture of disbelief and fear, before he began bellowing orders.

"Why would you listen to Damon's whore on the side instead of a man you've known your whole lives?"

"How else would she know about the pension money, Lorenzo?" One of Lorenzo's soldiers spoke up, his voice accusatory and his stance aggressive.

I watched in slow motion as his index finger slid toward the trigger, his barrel pointing at Lorenzo. The worst-case scenario was about to go down, and there was nothing I could do to stop it. The time to get Jillian and Carrie out of harm's way had passed. When the first shot was fired, all hell would break loose.

"You motherfucker. I trusted you. I stood up for you to your entire crew, and now you've made me look like a fucking idiot." His finger wrapped around the trigger, his eyes narrowed, and his face contorted into a nasty snarl.

Just when I was convinced Jillian, Carrie, and I would be caught in the cross fire between Lorenzo's men, the exterior doors burst open with a resounding bang when a dozen of my men kicked them in. With their guns drawn and ready to do battle, they began shouting orders at Lorenzo's men to drop their weapons. The element of surprise rendered our enemies immobile long enough for me to turn to Jillian and Carrie and yell over the raucous noises.

"Run!"

I don't know who fired the first shot, but that one blast from a gun was all it took to fill the room with flying bullets within a nanosecond. The wind off one nearly parted my hair as it whizzed by me. With my knees bent, I crouched in a defensive position and aimed, knocking one of the Sanfratello soldiers to the floor.

One of my guys turned a heavy oak desk over and crouched behind it, using it as cover to pick off more of them. Others quickly did the same, using desks, bookcases, and filing cabinets— whatever wasn't bolted to the floor was knocked over as a makeshift barrier.

It felt like hours, but in reality, it had only been mere seconds since the first round was fired. In no time, casings littered the floor around my feet as I emptied my magazine into the men behind the guns pointed at me. With my path temporarily cleared, it was time to nab Lorenzo. If I had to, I'd kill him myself, but I only wanted to wound him so Jillian could finally have closure after her mother's death.

I wanted to give her that, at least.

The noise level inside that room was off the charts, the decibels loud enough nearly to deafen me as I quickly glanced around the overturned furniture to locate the bastard. But my sixth sense was on high alert, and somehow, I heard one word over everything else.

My name, carried on the air in a terror-filled scream.

I whirled around, doing a complete one-eighty, to find Lorenzo holding Jillian in front of him as a human shield. Her hair was gripped tightly in his fist, and he used his hold to move her where he wanted with a violent jerk. The barrel of his gun was pressed against her temple. His ugly sneer mocked me. She was teary-eyed, and her terrified expression chilled my blood.

Then Benny rushed Lorenzo from the side, his stocky build slamming into the two of them like a locomotive and taking all three of them to the ground. When they fell as a single unit, Lorenzo's gun discharged.

Jillian's shrill scream was reduced to a pained whimper.

My heart stopped beating. My lungs stopped doing their job, not a molecule of oxygen moved through them. Time stopped ticking. The world stopped turning.

I saw red...dark red blood pooling on the floor under her.

My own blood ran cold. Like ice flowing through my veins.

Out of the corner of my eye, I saw a couple of Lorenzo's men rush out the back door, quickly followed by my men. Only my immediate team was left standing inside the building. The Sanfratello soldiers littered the floor, their bodies riddled with holes.

My feet moved without conscious thought, knowing I had to get to her. I had to save her. Lorenzo's eyes flew open wide when he met my murderous gaze. Benny had tackled them to the floor, his thick body covering both Jillian and Lorenzo. Jillian landed on top of Lorenzo, also trapping him in place. He tried to scramble out of the tangle of limbs, but I was much faster and on a mission.

My fingers gripped the back of Benny's shirt, and I flung him off Jillian like he weighed no more than a feather. Blood covered her shirt, soaking her and the floor under them. With Benny's weight lifted, Lorenzo was able to scoot back and almost reach a sitting position before I stopped him.

My gun was still in my hand, ready for action with a fresh magazine. I thrust the muzzle into his mouth as far as it would go. His entire body shook with fear, knowing a trigger-happy finger would relieve him of the majority of the back of his head.

"I fucking dare you to move. I dare you to even breathe. Try me, you fucking piece of shit."

No way would I give him a chance to finish the job. I had to get Jillian out of there. I had to get her to the hospital.

"Jillian, talk to me, baby. Where are you hit?" I ran my free hand over her, pulling her shirt up to locate her wound. Blood was everywhere, but I couldn't find the source. The more time I spent searching, the faster the blood would pour out of her body until she had none left to lose.

She turned her head, her brows drawn down and the skin around her eyes crinkled in pain. The guttural noises she made sounded like a wounded animal bleating. My heart leaped in my chest—she was still alive. But not for long if I couldn't locate her injury, stop the bleeding, and get help.

"Jillian! Come on, doll, tell me where you're hurt. Help me out here."

She opened her eyes and finally spoke in a broken staccato. "Not. Shot. Winded." Then she realized Lorenzo was still behind her, and she slid across the floor away from him.

"Whose blood is this, then?" My eyes flew over to where Benny still lay, where I dropped him in my rush to get to Jillian. The front of his shirt was stuck to his skin, soaking wet with his blood. The pallor of his skin was ghostly white.

Carrie dropped to his side. "Hold on, Benny. Help is on the way. Just hold on." She covered the wound in his chest with her hands, applying pressure to slow the bleeding as much as she could.

"Jillian, are you okay, doll?"

"Yeah, I'm fine now. Benny's shoulder hit me in the ribs when he took us down, knocked the breath out of me. I felt the gun go off between us, but the shock waves from the bullet were so close, I couldn't tell which one of us it hit for a minute there."

"Can you hold this while I help Carrie with Benny?" I inclined my head toward the barrel of my gun still securely rammed down Lorenzo's throat.

"I'd love to." She wrapped her fingers around the handle then shoved it a little farther into his mouth. "It'd be a shame if my trigger finger slipped, wouldn't it?"

I jerked my shirt over my head and covered Carrie's hands with it. She slipped them out from under the fabric, bunching it up over the wound, and pressed down again. Her worried eyes met mine. "I called our family doctor. He's on the way, but I'm not sure Benny will last that long."

"We brought help," another voice called from the front door of the building.

I jerked my head in that direction and found the Consigliere and the Underboss of the Sanfratello family approaching, their muscled goons at their flanks. Behind them, two men in medical uniforms rushed toward us with a gurney in tow. They knelt beside Benny, assessing his wounds and grabbing medical supplies from the oversized container they brought in. Within seconds, they loaded him onto the stretcher and rushed out the door with him. The siren pierced the early morning hours as the ambulance sped away with my best friend.

The Sanfratello leaders stopped, and I pushed up to my feet to meet them. Whatever end they had in mind, I'd take it standing up like a man.

"Do what you want with me. Just let the ladies leave unharmed."

"We're here to collect the confused men who mistakenly followed Lorenzo," the Underboss said. "Geno has plans for them, if they repent. We're not interested in you or the ladies. This time."

More teams of paramedics rushed in, helping the wounded and working quickly to move them out of the office until everyone who was still breathing had been evacuated. When the bosses were satisfied the job was finished, they turned to leave with their goons completely covering their backs.

Lorenzo wasn't able to speak with my gun shoved halfway down his throat, so he reacted to their departure with loud, pleading noises. The Underboss stopped in the doorway and turned to look at us over his shoulder.

"Lorenzo, you made your bed. Now you have to lie in it. I'm not going to rescue you. Damon knows what will happen if he kills you. But you're the one who started this. It was your scheme to steal money from the very men who protected you. We don't tolerate disrespect in this family. As the Boss's son, you should know that better than anyone."

He gave me a pointed look before closing the door behind him, leaving us alone in Geno Sanfratello's business. With Geno's son left in a precarious state. I knew what message he wanted to send me. Killing a bona fide member of the Sanfratello family, even one as shitty as Lorenzo, would have consequences.

Killing him would be worth whatever they threw at us later.

"Today is just not your day, is it, Lorenzo?" I grabbed the front of his shirt and hauled him to his feet.

Jillian stood with us and withdrew the gun from his mouth when she saw Carrie righting an overturned chair. I pushed him into it, causing him to lose his balance and stumble ungracefully as he plopped down on his ass. After locating a broken lamp on the floor, I pulled out the cord and tied his hands to the legs of the chair behind his back.

"He's all yours, doll."

2

CHAPTER TWO

Jillian

inally. Lorenzo was at my mercy, tied to a chair in an all but destroyed office building that belonged to his father. It was almost poetic justice—killing him in his father's place of business, leaving his bullet-riddled body as a macabre gift for the first unlucky person to walk through the door.

Damon stood beside me, silently giving his support while also acting as my personal bodyguard. The air surrounding him held complete confidence. Nothing about our situation gave him even a moment of hesitation. Carrying out family business came as easily to him as breathing. Had I asked him, he would've put a bullet between Lorenzo's eyes without blinking. We would've already been on our way back home—wherever that would be for the day—and we'd never have to speak of it again.

But I wouldn't ask him to finish what I'd started.

Carrie and I planned to turn Lorenzo's dead body over to Damon to collect the reward offered on the dark web; that was originally why we set up the whole rouse. She wanted to prove herself to the family, and I did as well, but in my own way. She once asked me if I was sure I wanted to kill Lorenzo, but small, telltale signs after we had that conversation told me she didn't believe I would see it through. The more we talked about it, the more she changed the plan from our original idea. The closer we got to actually executing the plan, the more she pushed the idea of trapping Lorenzo, giving him to Damon, and cashing in on the bounty instead executing him ourselves.

But I didn't care about the money. When we talked about what we'd do, I didn't push my agenda on her once I realized her hesitation with it. My plans were my own, and I kept my cards well hidden. She could get whatever money she wanted out of Damon, but Lorenzo's life was mine. It had been since the day he murdered my mother, even if he didn't know. Even if everyone in my life thought I was too weak to actually carry out the dirty deed.

Maybe I was at one time.

But I promised myself I'd never be weak again. I promised my mother her killer would pay for what he'd done as I stood over her grave the day I buried her, the tears pouring out of my eyes and mixing with the raindrops from the torrential storm that raged around me.

Without saying a word, I passed Damon's gun back to him. He gave me a perplexed look, questioning my intentions, but I had other plans before I outright killed Lorenzo. Carrie wasn't kidding when she said she'd trained for years to fight. She had a small arsenal of weapons, so I helped myself to her brass knuckles. They were illegal, but she didn't let that little inconvenience stop her from owning several pairs. The ones I chose for Lorenzo were actually made out of cast iron, perfect for inflicting more damage and adding extra pain to my punch.

Lorenzo watched as I slipped them over my knuckles and squeezed the palm grip. His gaze drifted up to mine, and for a moment, I could've sworn I saw a hint of admiration in his eyes.

"You know, when tough guys use those in movies, they make it look so easy. But the reality is very different. You'll break your fingers if you try to throw a straight-on punch with them on." Lorenzo spoke calmly, but I sensed a hint of sadness in him. I didn't get the feeling that was because of what I was about to do to him, though.

"You don't speak to her." Damon grabbed Lorenzo's face, squeezing and shaking Lorenzo's jaw as he spoke through gritted teeth. "I will rip your fucking throat out if you utter one wrong word."

Damon released him with a violent snap of his wrist, making Lorenzo's head jerk to the side. When Lorenzo turned his gaze back to Damon's, there was no anger or hatred in it. But his confident mask had dissolved, revealing his vulnerability.

Lorenzo nodded at Damon. "You don't have to do this, you know. There's a better way to handle this problem, Damon."

"Better than blowing your head off? This, I've got to hear."

Lorenzo drew in a deep breath, straightening his back as he inhaled. "We could work together."

"Why the fuck would I ever work with you on anything?" I stepped forward, piercing him with the daggers flying from my eyes. "Why do you think you deserve to live after you murdered my mother?"

He looked to Damon and lifted one eyebrow. Damon nodded, giving Lorenzo permission to speak to me. "Choose your words wisely. If you upset her, you'll lose your fucking tongue."

"Jillian, I didn't kill your mother."

"You ordered your men to do it because you didn't have the balls to do it yourself. But I do have the balls to kill you for issuing the order, though."

"I also didn't order my men to kill her. My father did, no matter how hard I fought against his decision."

"You'd better start from the beginning and explain exactly what you mean. Tell me everything, or I swear to God, you'll wish you were dead before I finish with you. You're the one who gave me the ultimatum to kill Damon or you'd kill my mother."

"Yes, I did do that, but just hear me out. My father has been trying to start an all-out war for some time now. He wants huge shootouts in the street between our families. He wants a show of brute force that resonates through every borough and daily media coverage of our battles. The bigger, the better. When he positions the Sanfratello family just right, he has a plan to annihilate all of the Marchetti family.

"One step in that plan was to take Damon out of the picture, one way or another. You were a convenient target that day my father's men shot at you two on the street. They were *supposed* to hit Damon, but make it look like they were after you. That way, Damon getting hit in the cross fire could be explained away.

"My threat to you was supposed to make you run back to Louisiana to be with your mother, knowing Damon would follow you. He assumed responsibility for your safety the first time you were seen with him, and my father knew that. Dad said Damon would go after you, at least long enough to set his Sanfratello takeover plans in motion. That's what Dad told me, anyway. I found out too late to do anything about his plans to kill you and your mother when you arrived. That order never came from me, Jillian."

"Why should I believe you?"

"The Underboss and Consigliere of my family just walked out, leaving me here to die. They want you to kill me for several reasons. First, it'll validate the war they're going to wage against the Marchettis anyway. But it'll ensure the smaller factions side with them.

"There are very few laws we follow outside of our own code of honor. Killing a made man is one of those laws we just don't break. A Marchetti-sanctioned hit on me would guarantee other families would align with my father because they wouldn't trust the Marchetti name anymore."

"And the second reason?"

"Second, they already knew I was running that scam, taking money from our own men and our allies. Do you really think my father cares about that? He only used it as leverage against me because it fits his cause. I've been saving that money for the past year, squirreling away as much as possible, because I've been planning my getaway. That money was my ticket out of this life. They're using it as a flimsy excuse to leave me here with you—like they don't take money from everyone they know."

Lorenzo dropped his eyes to the floor, and I stood there staring at him, my mind reeling from all he'd shared. How could I doubt what he was telling me? He knew I was hell-bent on killing him. He had nothing to lose by telling me the truth now. But then, on the other hand, how could I believe him? He could very well try to play me by feeding me lies and half-truths until I let him walk away.

He looked lost. He looked as if his best friend had died. He looked as if he'd just experienced the ultimate betrayal in his life.

If what he said was the truth, then I supposed he had also felt the bitter sting of betrayal. His own father sacrificed him for a chance to be the area's mafia king. Geno was ruled by blind ambition and ruthless intentions. Even his own son wasn't given advance warning or the least bit of protection.

How could I possibly know fact from fiction? How could I know with absolute certainty he had told me the truth? How could I let him live with even the slightest possibility that he was the one responsible for murdering my mother?

I cut my eyes to Damon to gauge his reaction to the overload of information. His expression was passive, giving nothing away about his inner thoughts. Whether he believed Lorenzo wasn't part of the equation. In his mind, Lorenzo was a Sanfratello, and all Sanfratellos were the enemy.

That wasn't good enough for me.

Then I looked at Carrie, hoping she'd be an easier book to read than her older brother was. How I'd ever missed the signs before that moment was beyond me. Maybe my own path to vengeance had blinded me to everything else. Maybe keeping my secret plans for the meeting with Lorenzo had prevented me from seeing she had her own secrets.

The one and only fact I was certain of was that Damon had no clue whatsoever.

Everyone had so many fucking secrets. Their world seemed to create them out of the blue.

"And reason number three why they want you dead is because they found out you're secretly in love with a Marchetti, right? They knew part of your escape plan included taking her with you —and that would hurt the Sanfratellos more than it would the Marchettis. With your father making a bid for top dog, his son running off with a member of the rival family would cast a lot of doubt on his ability to manage his family."

Dead silence filled the room.

"I'm right, aren't I, Carrie?"

She wouldn't look at me.

Lorenzo wouldn't look at me.

Damon *couldn't* look at me. He couldn't stop his eyes from darting back and forth between Carrie's and Lorenzo's faces, waiting for one of them to crack.

Pieces of the puzzle that never fully made sense began to fall into place. Carrie's change of heart over trapping Lorenzo with the intent to kill him was the main one. She said she wanted to make Damon pay us the fee he'd posted on the dark web, but she had plenty of her own money. She ran her own illegal schemes and had stolen more than enough money through insider trading and blackmail. She didn't need the chump change Damon offered in comparison.

"Did you think the two of you would run away together when we came here tonight, Carrie? Was that your plan all along?"

Lorenzo looked at Carrie, hope brimming in his eyes and anticipation covering his features. "Is she right, Carrie?"

"Hold up just a fucking minute!" Damon bellowed, running his fingers through his hair with one hand and pointing his gun at Lorenzo with the other. "Just wait a goddamn minute. Are you saying this is true? You've been sleeping with my sister?"

"Put the gun down, Damon." Carrie stepped between Damon and Lorenzo, her hands on her hips and a stern expression on her face.

"Yes, Damon, put the gun down. You know better than to point it at your sister." The deep, commanding voice bellowed from the entryway, causing all four of our heads to jerk in that direction.

Vincenzo and Uncle Leo had joined our spontaneous gathering. While Damon's, Carrie's, and Lorenzo's eyes were glued to the Boss and Underboss of the family, I turned my attention back to Lorenzo. He wasn't breathing at all. He'd completely frozen in place, as if instantly changing into a statue would save him from the Marchetti family members who quickly surrounded him. The intense fear radiating from him was palpable because he knew his life was over. He had a chance of talking his way out of the situation by appealing to Damon and me. But not Vincenzo.

"Daddy." Carrie's one-word plea escaped on a whisper, but Vincenzo didn't miss it.

"Carrie, what exactly did you think would come of this relationship? Did you think I'd give you two my blessing?" Vincenzo leveled his penetrating gaze on his daughter, expecting her to give an answer.

"No, sir. I never thought you'd give us your blessing." The daring, confident woman I'd grown to know transformed into a fearful child, afraid she'd disappointed her father beyond repair.

"No, you knew better, didn't you? So, what was your plan, then? To run away with him, leave your family behind, break your mother's heart?"

"I didn't think of it that way, to be honest. All I wanted was to be happy."

Vincenzo appeared taken aback by her admission. He hadn't expected that response. The doting father in him wanted his daughter to be happy. The rigid boss in him didn't want her to be happy with a Sanfratello. The man in him was conflicted about which of his sides should win the argument playing out in his mind.

"You're my niece, Carrie, and you know I've loved you like one of my own kids since the day you were born. So believe me when I say, you'll be happy. Just not with him. Get up, Lorenzo. You're coming with us." Leo stepped toward Lorenzo, ready to use excessive force if necessary to make Lorenzo leave with him.

I could almost hear Carrie's heart break as the tears ran down her cheeks, but she stood motionless in place. Damon was conflicted—he was visibly upset over his sister's broken heart, and he wanted to protect her. But his position in the family wouldn't allow him to act on his feelings.

Vincenzo. Damon. Carrie. All three wished for a different outcome, another way to handle the conflict before us, but none was willing to break the shackles of their family laws that held them prisoner.

Then I felt it—the flutter in my lower abdomen. My babies, warm and secure inside me, perfectly happy in their own little world.

CHAPTER THREE

Damon

*N*ever in a million fucking years would I had believed I'd be caught in the middle of such a shitstorm. My sister had always been impetuous and pulled a lot of harebrained schemes in the past, but fucking the son of the Sanfratello Family Boss took the damn cake. Apparently, it was the night for getting caught with my dick in my hand and unprepared for visitors since Dad and Uncle Leo walked in during that hell of a revelation.

Then my strong, independent, fearless sister started crying.

Fuck if that didn't tear me apart inside. She never cried—not even when all of us boys would gang up on her when she was little. She'd stand toe-to-toe with any of us and put us in our fucking places. But she wouldn't disrespect our father, especially not in front of Jillian and Lorenzo. Her hard veneer cracked because she knew what would happen to the man she loved when Dad and Uncle Leo left with him. And she blamed herself for it.

Then I put myself in her shoes, thinking about what I'd do if the situation was different and they forbade me from being with

Jillian. But before I could speak up to stop Uncle Leo from his mission, Jillian beat me to it.

"No!" She stepped between Leo and Lorenzo. The brass knuckles were gone, and her gun was held flat against her stomach in an aggressive move. "You're not taking him anywhere. This was my plan, my sting operation—you have no right to step in and try to take control of the situation."

"Jillian, that's not how this works, *cara*." My father's patience in business was nonexistent, but he at least attempted to use a soothing tone with her.

"That is exactly how this works, Mr. Marchetti. You interrupted me, not the other way around. I'm calling the shots here. If you want to get to Lorenzo right now, you'll have to go through me. I *will not* just step aside, and I *will not* back down. If you think you can hurt the mother of your grandchildren and get away with it, by all means, give it your best shot."

Uncle Leo glanced at Dad, then extended his arm with a quick reflex and pushed Jillian aside, bulldozing past her. When she fell to the hard concrete floor, all I saw was red. The next thing I knew, my father was yelling at me.

"Damon, let him up! Let go of him, son! Right now!"

I didn't remember any of the details regarding how, but when I came back to myself, my hand was firmly wrapped around Leo's neck. His face was a deep red, his eyes were bugged out, and his mouth opened and closed, gasping for air. Both of his hands clawed at my hand, scraping my skin off in his feeble attempts to break my death grip on him.

I leaned down, my face barely an inch from his to make sure he got my full message. "You don't fucking touch her—ever. Being the underboss doesn't give you the right to push the mother of my children. If you ever pull that shit again, they'll find Hoffa before they find the first piece of you."

When I pushed off of Leo, he sat up, holding his throat and struggling to inhale enough oxygen to replenish his burning lungs. Dad helped him stand but didn't attempt to hide his anger at Leo. "Go wait in the car," Dad growled.

Leo glanced around the room at the rest of us, contemplating what he should do next versus what he wanted to do. I embarrassed him in front of too many others. That wouldn't and couldn't go unanswered. No matter what they planned for me, I wouldn't change a single thing about my response. No fucking way would he get away with putting his hands on Jillian in anger. He was lucky he was still able to breathe on his own.

When his angry gaze landed on Jillian, it lingered there a second too long. He was clearly laying the blame for the shift in family dynamics squarely on her shoulders. I moved to stand directly in front of her, hiding her small frame with my large one, and stared him down.

"Careful, old man. You won't be so lucky a second time."

"Leo. Outside. Now." Dad's thinning patience was obvious in the gruff tone of his commands. Once Leo was out of earshot, Dad turned his ire on me. "Do you have any idea what you have done, Damon?"

"What *I've* done? Really, Dad? You just watched him knock Jillian to the ground. She's four months pregnant with my babies, for fuck's sake. And you're just okay with him doing that?"

"No, but that was for me to handle. Not you."

"Yeah? Maybe he'll walk into your house and knock Mom to the floor next. Are you just going to sit there and watch, let him get away with it because of who he is? Have a little talk with him later to explain why that's wrong? Do you really expect me or any of your other sons to just sit there and not do anything?"

The mere mention of anyone doing that to Mom was enough to jar him. I immediately detected the fury that flashed across his face before he reined it back under control.

"That's what I thought. Don't expect me to just fucking accept it any more than you would."

"You know every broken rule has a consequence, Damon. Leo

has his own for what he did. It wasn't your place to dole out the punishment for it—it was mine. You overstepped your bounds, you'll have to face the consequences for that. Jillian disrespected Leo and me, she'll have to face the consequences for her actions. You know this is how the family works."

"I'm actually seeing a lot of shit I never thought I'd see in *the family,* Dad. But now that I know your immediate family is at the bottom of your importance list, it makes my decision a little easier to make."

"What decision is that?"

"It's past time for me to start my own family and leave your definition of family behind. I've given enough of myself to further your cause. That's all I've done for my entire life—put you and the family first. Then Leo disrespected Jillian and me in that manner, and you think I'm not entitled as a man, as a father, to protect what's mine. I'm not living like that. It's not in me. That isn't how I was raised."

"You know what happens once you leave the family, Damon." Sadness and dread infused his tone.

"Take care, Dad. Your family is disappearing before your very eyes. Next time you look around, you may be standing all alone."

After cutting Lorenzo's bonds, I hoisted him up out of his chair with one hand while guiding a stunned Jillian toward the back door with the other. Carrie wiped the tears from her face and met Dad's uncertain stare.

"Goodbye, Daddy." Her voice broke on his name, echoing the sound of her heart shattering in her chest.

Dad remained in his same spot, watching with a stoic expression as the four of us walked out the back door. I cast one last glance over my shoulder when I said my goodbyes.

"Give Mom our love. Tell her we'll miss her."

The scrape and creak of the big metal door closing marked the ending of one era in my life and the beginning of another. The new one would be without my parents and my extended family, but Jillian and our children would be front and center in my life.

"Jilly, are you okay? Did he hurt you?"

"I'm fine, Damon. But what have you done? Go back in there and make up with your father while you still can." Jillian put her hand on my arm, squeezing tighter with each word.

"Damon was right in his decision, Jillian. Uncle Leo never should've touched you. Dad shouldn't have allowed it, and he shouldn't have called Damon down. That scenario couldn't have played out any other way." Carrie drew in a deep breath, trying to calm her own frayed nerves.

"I'm parked over in that alley. Let's get out of here while we can. I have to get to the hospital and check on Benny."

"How can you both be so calm after what just happened in there?" Jillian gaped at us, dumbfounded by our lack of emotion. "We're talking about your father—the only one you'll ever have. Do you know what I'd give to have one more day with my dad? You can't just walk away like this."

"Can I speak to her, Damon?" Lorenzo asked. I'd almost forgotten he was with us.

Jillian glanced at me, then turned her attention to Lorenzo. "Yes, you can."

"Having *family first* pushed on you your whole life has a way of making you realize your place, whether you want to face it or not. The family always comes first—not the individual. None of us expected Damon's father to put his kids first. They may have hoped he would, but deep down, both Damon and Carrie knew that would never happen." Lorenzo spoke from experience, knowing as well as my sister and I did where we ranked overall.

Jillian eyed him with skepticism, still unsure if she should believe his narrative of her mother's death. But I believed his story. He had every reason to put the blame on his father in an attempt save his own hide, but I trusted my gut instincts. They'd never steered me wrong. Reading the signs, watching his body language, and knowing what I did about his family, I had no doubt he'd told us the truth.

"You can believe him, Jillian. On all accounts. Lorenzo knows I'd kill him if I ever found out he lied to us, whether he's with Carrie or not."

"It doesn't help anything now, but I never meant to shoot Benny. And I wasn't going to shoot Jillian. I knew you wouldn't risk hitting her, but I didn't expect Benny to take all three of us to the ground. He tried to jerk my gun out of my hand when he tackled me. The trigger is light, and my finger grazed across it just enough to make it fire." Lorenzo's demeanor showed his regret in his downtrodden expression and his slightly slumped shoulders. He wasn't cut out for this lifestyle, no matter how hard he tried to make it work for his old man's sake.

"Thanks for saying that, Lorenzo. I do appreciate your honesty."

A car screeched to a halt in front of us, and I stepped in front of Jillian, ready to shield and protect her from whoever waited inside. When the door opened, I slid my gun into the holster and extended my hand to Matteo Falco.

"Doc, I can't tell you how glad I am to see you. Sorry to drag you out here at this time of night."

"I'm an emergency physician, Damon. I'm used to these hours by now. I'm just sorry I couldn't get here sooner. What can I do?"

"Can you check Jillian over? She got knocked down pretty hard a couple of times. She insists she's okay, but she's pregnant, so I don't want to take any chances."

"I'll do what I can for her, but I'll give my standard advice of following up with her obstetrician for the baby. I don't carry that kind of equipment around with me." Matteo walked Jillian around to the passenger side of his car. He helped her recline in the luxurious leather seat while he knelt down on the ground beside her.

I listened intently while he asked questions about how she fell, where she hit, and if she was hurt or sore anywhere. Then he asked about her pregnancy, how far along she was, and if she'd had any concerns to date. Then he grabbed his stethoscope from his bag and checked her over, listening in all the routine spots.

"Can you hear a fetal heartbeat with that?" I asked.

"Not yet—not until she's at least twenty weeks along. But from her account of what happened and the way she fell, I can assure you there's no cause for alarm. The baby is well protected in there."

"Babies," I corrected.

Matt looked up at me, surprise registering in his face. "Twins, Damon?"

"Yeah. Can you believe it?"

He laughed good-naturedly. "Actually, I can. You always did have to try to show everyone else up."

"*Try*, my ass." It felt good to laugh again for a second. Then I recounted the last conversation I'd had with my father, filling him in on the recent split from the family.

"Look, Damon, I'm not one to judge you. Everyone knows I'm here to patch up the holes when they get shot, but that's the extent of my involvement with the family business. I didn't spend all that time in medical school to be sent to prison, lose my license to practice medicine, or get shot in some dark alley over a stupid turf war.

"If you're ready to get out of all this, you know I'll support your decision. And I don't blame you for putting Uncle Leo in his place. He had no right doing what he did to Jillian. Had he used his usual tactics, he really would've hurt her."

Jillian's eyes grew bigger at Matteo's revelation about Uncle Leo. She'd never witnessed Leo's aptitude for savagery. From the day she met him, she'd only seen his charming side, the part of him she found warm and charismatic. When he knocked her aside, he showed restraint in his actions, though she didn't see it. Leo was a cold, cruel bastard when he wanted to be.

Like his brother, my father.

Like my father's son.

"Thank you, Matteo. I appreciate your support."

He turned his attention to Carrie and Lorenzo, a small smile playing on his lips. "You two always were competitive, trying to one-up the other. I don't know which of you won this round. Damon and Jillian having twins, or a Marchetti and a Sanfratello falling in love. Maybe we should call it a tie now before this goes any further. If you two have kids, which family should we expect them to support?"

Matteo's words were spoken in jest, something the rest of us would expect from anyone who understood how the family worked. Jillian's gaze moved to meet mine, and I watched her expression change as she processed the true gravity of what he'd said. Her smile over Matteo's playful jabs at Carrie and me slowly faded. Then his words began to sink in, and she couldn't hide the unease in her eyes. All roads would only bring her to one conclusion, though, and I knew she'd hit that dead end before she'd even realized it.

"Well, Jillian, you seem to be perfectly fine. You may be a little sore tomorrow when all the adrenaline of the night's excitement wears off. Have you felt the babies move yet?"

"Actually, yes, I felt them move for the first time during this unbelievable clusterfuck of a family reunion."

"Unfortunately, you didn't catch us at our best tonight. Have you felt them move since you've been resting here?"

"Yes, I have a couple of times."

"That's a good sign. I'm not concerned, but it's still a good idea to follow up with your doctor since he has the proper equipment. Is there anything else I can do for you, Jillian?"

"No, Dr. Falco, I'm okay. But thank you anyway."

We said our goodbyes and watched Matteo drive away, each of us temporarily lost in our thoughts.

"What happens now?" Jillian asked, looking to me for direction.

"We get you somewhere you can rest and relax until the doctor's office opens, and I go to the hospital to check on Benny's status."

"Don't do that, Damon."

"Do what?"

"Treat me like I'll break, so you have to hide everything from me. I'm fine and so are the babies. But I'm concerned about Benny too. He was shot trying to save me, so I want to go to the hospital with you."

"You two go ahead to the hospital, Damon. My car is parked only a couple of blocks away. Besides, Lorenzo and I apparently have a lot to discuss now." Carrie wrapped her arms around my neck to hug me goodbye and whispered as she squeezed, "Watch your back, big brother."

"You be careful, little girl." I hadn't called her that in years. Using that moniker seemed fitting given the circumstances.

She stepped back, a sad smile crossing her face. "Thank you, Damon. For everything you did tonight. You've never let me down."

"And I never will, Carrie." My eyes shifted to Lorenzo. "Don't let anything happen to her. I'll be in touch with you two later."

Lorenzo nodded in agreement and wrapped his arm around Carrie before they began walking toward Carrie's car. We didn't have long before the Marchetti council convened an emergency meeting to decide our collective fates. A hit on two of their own family members, on top of a capo in a rival family, wasn't a decision that would be made lightly.

But it would be made.

"We should get going too." Jillian put her hand on my arm, pulling me out of my thoughts about our impending doom.

"Looks like I get you all to myself again, doll."

CHAPTER FOUR

Jillian

*D*amon was quiet on the way to the hospital, lost in his own thoughts as he drove. He held such a tight grip on the steering wheel, his knuckles were white the entire ride. His eyes remained glued to the road as we flew through every red light at the early morning hour. Damon's best friend was barely clinging to life when he was whisked away by the paramedics. He was understandably preoccupied with thoughts of what we'd find when we arrived.

Nothing about the night had gone as Carrie and I planned. We thought we'd covered every possible scenario and planned for every conceivable turn our plan could take, but we were wrong... about *everything*. At that point, I couldn't even fall back on the excuse that our intentions were good, because they weren't. I went there with the sole objective of killing a man. I wanted to watch him die. Instead, another man's life was in danger. A man who didn't hesitate to intervene for my protection.

If Benny died, his death would be my fault. If we lost him, it would be because I wanted to be taken seriously in a world where

I didn't even belong. Where I had no place, no history, and no future. That realization slapped me across the face when Matteo was performing his exam on me. His innocent jest about Carrie and Lorenzo having kids struck me—hard. Their kids would be forced to choose a side...to pledge their allegiance...to be part of the family. But they couldn't win, because the opposing family would find a way to take their vengeance. It was a never-ending cycle of death and destruction.

That meant the same, and more, would be expected of my children. As hard as I tried to picture strong young men like Damon or fearless young women like Carrie, I couldn't shake the fear that gripped my heart. The knowledge that, one day, my children would be in Benny's present situation, and I'd be on the receiving end of a phone call to relay the horrible news.

During that moment, I realized I couldn't live in Damon's world, no matter how much I loved him. My children wouldn't live in his world. I wouldn't allow it, because if I did, the burden of burying my children would fall on my shoulders. That was too much to ask, too much to bear. Knowing how well Damon could read my thoughts, I didn't even question if he knew I'd made up my mind.

He knew.

That particular fight with Damon would have to wait. After we knew Benny would be okay, I'd broach the subject and try to explain my reasoning. Once everything calmed down, his father would be back to reconcile. Mama Lina would make sure of that. I wasn't under any delusions that Damon and I would have any future together, that he'd leave his family business and join me in suburbia. But I wholeheartedly believed he'd put our babies first. He'd do what was best for them no matter what it cost him.

In the meantime, I wanted him to know he wasn't alone. He wouldn't face the mess Carrie and I dropped at his feet solo. For as long as I was able, I'd stand by his side and give him the strength he needed to face whatever happened. Losing Benny would be a significant blow on top of his exile from the family, however long that lasted. I reached over, placing my hand on his shoulder, and waited for him to glance my way.

"I'm here for you, Damon. Whatever I can do to help, to take any of the burden off your shoulders. This is all my fault, and I'm sorry you have to clean up the mess I've made. But I promise, I won't leave you to do it alone. I'll be beside you every step of the way until your family is whole again."

He pulled my hand from his shoulder and laced our fingers together, resting them in his lap. "As much as I appreciate your offer and would love to milk it for all the amazing guilt-sex I can get out of you, I can't let you take the blame for what happened with my father. He knows how much I've given in my life to this family. And he knows Uncle Leo was completely wrong in what he did to you. That doesn't happen, Jillian. It's part of that mandatory respect rule we have—that also extends to you, to a degree. Even if they didn't recognize you as mine, I still wouldn't let him get away with shit like that."

"What's going to happen now? Will your dad change his mind and take up for you?"

"I really don't know what he'll do, doll. This has never happened before, so your guess is as good as mine. I wouldn't count on it though. I'm sure the rumors of my actions have rippled through the ranks by now. There's no scenario I can see that allows both Leo and me to live and return to the same dynamics as before."

"You would kill your uncle? Or he would kill you?" I couldn't believe my ears. Damon was so matter-of-fact about the whole situation, while I couldn't imagine how the family could ever be the same after.

"No need to worry about any of that right now, Jilly. Tomorrow will bring trouble soon enough. I'll deal with it when I have to."

His stony expression turned thoughtful, and I knew exactly

what he was thinking before he asked the question. "What was on your mind when Doc was teasing Carrie and Lorenzo about having kids?"

"Now really isn't the time to talk about that."

"No time like the present, doll. It may be all we have."

My heart raced because he already knew the answer—he'd read my thoughts from the expression on my face. "I was thinking I'd never allow that scenario to play out with my children. As much as I love you, and I do, I don't know that I can stay with you if you're in this lifestyle. If they'll be expected to follow in your footsteps. If you put *the family* ahead of your immediate family the way your father and uncle do."

He nodded slowly as he considered my words, but he wasn't surprised in the least. We both knew his question was a test of sorts. He already knew the answer and wanted to see if I'd tell him the truth. I'd planned to anyway, but not while rushing to the hospital to check on his critically wounded friend.

An ambulance pulled into the emergency room bay just as we arrived, so we followed the paramedics through the restricted entrance. We frantically searched the exam rooms but didn't find Benny. Damon stopped one of the doctors, who obviously recognized him on sight, and asked about his friend.

"He was taken to emergency surgery, Mr. Marchetti."

The doctor gave us directions to the surgical waiting room where the nurse in the operating room could reach us for status updates, but he explained Benny would be taken straight to the trauma ICU floor after surgery. We wouldn't be able to see him until the first designated visiting time later in the morning.

"How'd he look, Doc?" Damon asked. His voice was even. The ticking in his tight jaw was the only outward indication of his unease.

The doctor hesitated for a second, understanding what Damon was really asking. "He was in bad shape when he came in, Damon.

You both should hope for the best but prepare yourselves for the worst."

The only other person in the waiting room with us was asleep in the far corner, oblivious to our presence. Damon moved the phone from the front desk to a small table beside a few chairs, stretching the cord as far as it would reach. Then he rearranged the chairs until he'd created a makeshift bed. When we finally took our seats, the fatigue I'd held off all night hit me with full force.

"Stretch your legs out on that chair and lay your head in my lap so you can get some sleep. I'll wait up for the call about Benny."

Without waiting for me to move, Damon wrapped his arm around my shoulder and gently pulled me toward him. Swiveling in my seat, I lifted my feet up onto the extra chair as my face lowered to meet his leg. I vaguely remembered his hand brushing my hair off my cheek before I closed my eyes. Then I went out like a light.

A sudden loud noise startled me in my deep sleep, making my whole body jolt at once. Then it stopped, and I settled back into the warmth Damon naturally provided and allowed a peaceful slumber to overtake me once again. Somewhere in the back of my mind, the low murmur of Damon's voice registered, though, so I fought against the fog clouding my thoughts until I was awake enough to comprehend his words.

"No, I don't have any other questions. Thank you for...everything."

Then he placed the phone receiver back into the cradle. But he didn't move or try to wake me. I forced my eyes to open, though they revolted against me with what felt like a thousand pinpricks, and I pushed up until I could see his face.

"Oh my God. Damon, no! Please don't tell me he's..." I bolted up from my reclining position and faced him. But I couldn't say the word. I couldn't finish my thought.

Damon nodded. "They did all they could to save him, but the point-blank shot did too much internal damage. The surgeon was surprised he even lived long enough for the ambulance to get him here, much less into surgery. But he refused to bow out easily. Benny was a fighter till the very end."

"Damon, I'm so sorry." My voice broke, and tears sprang to my eyes then steadily flowed down my cheeks. There was no point in trying to wipe them away. The constant stream wouldn't stop anytime soon anyway. "This is all my fault. If I hadn't been so stupid, so set on doing everything my way, none of this would've happened. Your family. Your best friend. You've lost everything because of me. I'm so ashamed. And, this sounds so hollow, but I'm so fucking *sorry*, Damon. I'm so sorry."

At that moment, I wasn't looking for his sympathy. I didn't want his assurances that everything would be okay, that we'd somehow work it all out. My guilt and shame were such a heavy burden, I couldn't even lift my eyes to look into his. But I knew it paled in comparison to the burdens Damon carried on a daily basis.

All I wanted was to take responsibility for what had happened and to show I'd face whatever the consequences of my actions were. If I could've gone back in time and changed everything, I would have. But there was a reason why they say hindsight is 20/20. There was a reason why the road to hell is paved with good intentions. There was a reason why saying *I'm sorry* doesn't automatically make everything right again.

"What can I do? Can I talk to your parents? Can I try to help them understand what happened, and why, so they'll forgive you? Tell me what will help you, Damon, and I'll do it."

"You really want to know what will help me, Jillian?"

Summoning all the courage I had left inside me, I raised my chin from my chest and looked directly into his sad eyes. The sexy chocolate brown shade in them had lost some of its luster to weariness and bereavement, driving the dagger further into my chest. Regardless of the pain, I had to face it because my indecision and lack of foresight had cost us both dearly.

"Yes, I do. Tell me, and I'll make it happen for you."

"No matter what it is?"

"No matter what it is."

He studied me for a minute, his eyes moving back and forth between mine before roaming over my face. The sincerity I saw in them would've moved me to tears had I not already been crying. "Marry me."

My bottom jaw dropped in surprise. That wasn't at all what I expected him to say. "What?" My shocked reply came out as a whisper. "Damon, I'm serious. What will fix this rift in your family so you can be happy again?"

"The only family rift I care about fixing is the one between us, Jillian. The only people I need in my life to be happy are you and our babies you're carrying. This room is far from the romantic setting where I wanted to propose to you, to ask you to be my wife and spend the rest of your life with me. But considering just a few hours ago I thought your life would end right before my eyes, I'm just thankful you're sitting here with me right now.

"We're adults, so let's be frank with each other. I know you want me as much as I want you. But you should know something else about me by now. I don't share what's mine, and I've already decided you belong to me. Now, say you'll marry me as soon as possible, because I've been as patient as I'm capable of being."

Something feral and dangerous flashed in his eyes, reminding me of the Damon Marchetti I first met. The man with the confident swagger, the commanding presence, and the exciting air of intrigue surrounding him. As much as Benny's death hurt me, and no doubt hurt Damon, I realized then that Damon had lost many other friends in his lifetime. His grief over Benny was no less important, but maybe the frequency of his losses had dulled the sting of death over time.

But, in his heart, I was different from everyone else in his life.

He'd told me he couldn't handle losing me. The man who sat beside me with a cool, collected exterior moments after losing his best friend would've crumbled had that stray bullet taken my life instead. I believed him when he said he only needed me to be happy.

"Yes, I will marry you, Damon. Because you're all I need to be happy, too."

His smile returned a little of the mischievous gleam to his eyes, but I didn't miss the underlying threat they still held. An animal is more dangerous when it's wounded. But Damon was more lethal when he was afraid. And the only thing he feared was that someone would hurt me.

When he kissed me, my nerves all lit at once, as if I'd touched a live wire. Life with him would never be dull, that was for damn sure.

"Thank you for not forcing me to take extreme measures to get that answer out of you. Let's go back to my place, feed you, and try to get some sleep." He linked our fingers together and stood, helping me up as he went.

"Will we be safe there, Damon? Will your family come after us?"

"Don't worry, doll. I'll keep you safe."

He meant for his dismissal of my fears to make me feel better by not giving them credence, but I couldn't shake the feeling that everything would soon come to a head. Like a shaken soda bottle would explode in someone's face when opened, the bombshell news of Benny's death would ripple throughout the family and blow up in all of our faces.

"Damon, Lorenzo killed Benny. Even though his gun accidentally went off, your uncle will not see it that way. And he won't care. When he finds out we didn't kill Lorenzo, he'll be furious and could come after you."

"Maybe." Damon shrugged, giving no sign he was concerned in the least. "Time will tell."

An hour later, the sun was high and glimmered against the high-rise buildings of Manhattan as we pulled into Damon's security-controlled garage underneath his building. We took the express elevator to the penthouse apartment he owned, and he locked it when we exited. Then he made sure the stairwell was locked and called the concierge desk with strict instructions for no visitors, regardless of who it was.

When his phone rang a few minutes later, my stomach dropped to my feet, knowing it was the beginning of the end. But his shoulders seemed to carry a little less weight when he hung up. "Now that that's done, let's get you something to eat."

"Now that what's done? Who was that? What's going on?"

"Just a few of my guys who heard the whole story, beginning to end, and have pledged to remain loyal to me. Nothing to worry about, doll."

"No, there's nothing to see here. No coming mafia family war. No World War Three scenario playing out in front of us. Just another normal day on the farm."

He chuckled, that dark laugh that rumbled in his chest and shot an arrow straight into my libido. "Omelets with spinach and bacon, it is. You can jump in the shower while I cook if you want."

"I'm not turning that offer down."

Damon's shower was amazing. The multiple heads spraying from different directions felt like fingers massaging away the tension while washing away the grime from the night. I lathered up with his body wash despite the masculine scent it left on my skin. At least I would fall asleep wrapped in all things that made me think of Damon.

After we finished eating, I slid between the sheets while Damon showered. I pushed back the memories of the last time we were in that exact position, minus the knife missing from underneath my pillow. Within a few minutes, I felt the dip in the mattress when Damon eased into bed with me. I opened my eyes, taking in his shirtless torso, the peaks and valleys of his muscles, the way he moved with the agility of a finely tuned athlete.

He settled into bed facing me, unable to hide the exhaustion in his eyes, or his love. Through everything, I still saw his love for me in them.

"Is there anywhere you've always dreamed of getting married? I'll take you there, and we'll make it official immediately."

I loved these conversations with Damon when he wasn't the Marchetti family capo. He was just Damon, the man. My man.

"My dream place is a little too far for a quick trip, I'm afraid."

"Yeah? Where's that?"

"Hawaii."

He stroked my cheek with his thumb. "How about I take you to Maui for an extended honeymoon soon, but first we jet off to the Bahamas for a nice, warm, toes-in-the-sand beach wedding?"

"That sounds like heaven, Damon."

5

CHAPTER FIVE

Damon

$\mathcal{L}$ate afternoon had set in when I woke up. If I was exhausted, Jillian must have been nearly dead on her feet. She was still in such a deep sleep, she didn't move in the least when I got up. After I dressed, I left her to rest while I went into the den to assess our situation. Before I joined Jillian for a long nap, I'd silenced my phone so we wouldn't be disturbed. But the moment of truth had arrived—the time had come to check my phone for any messages or attempted contacts.

"Now or never, Marchetti." I unlocked my phone and stared at the lack of phone calls or text messages from my family. Seemed I had my answer.

Since I hadn't heard from my mother after the showdown at the garbage distribution center, the odds that she'd chosen my side were slim to none. On that note, the council members undoubtedly would've met and voted on my standing within the family. Because my sister had fraternized with the enemy, her fate was also in question. Having no word from her was slightly concerning, but then, she'd be lying low for a while, the same as I was. Radio silence wasn't unusual given our extraordinary circumstances.

The direct line from my building's security desk rang, making my heart rate jack up and putting me on high alert. They knew better than to disturb me when I specifically told them not to, unless they had a damn good reason. The only time my order had been disobeyed in the past was because Vincenzo Marchetti showed up in the lobby unannounced.

"Yes?" I snatched the cordless receiver from the base then immediately moved to my hidden closet that held my arsenal of weapons.

"I'm sorry to disturb you, Mr. Marchetti, but Marco is here to see you, and he says it's an emergency." The guard's apprehension was obvious.

On one hand, he had to face disturbing me when I'd given strict instructions otherwise. On the other hand, he was standing in front of my brother Marco who was every bit as intimidating as he was big.

"Put him on." I walked through the first level of my apartment, checking every possible entryway someone could use while Marco distracted me on the phone.

"You can stop checking the windows, brother. I'm here alone."

"Come on, Marco. You know better than that. Why would I take your word for it?"

"Damon." When he paused, I did too, knowing I wouldn't like what he had to say next. "They have Carrie."

"Who has Carrie, exactly?"

"A couple of Leo's goons picked up both Carrie and Lorenzo about an hour ago on *Uncle Leo's* orders. They were taken to Leo's house outside of Fort Lee. Let me come up. We have plans to make."

"All right, Marco. But I'm warning you—if this is some kind of trick to nab me, it won't end well for you."

"You've never trusted anyone, little brother. Where has that gotten you?"

"That is precisely what has kept me alive. Put the security guard back on the phone."

When Marco handed the phone off, I gave my approval to allow him to come up and re-engaged my secure elevator. Then I hurried to wake Jillian, just in case my brother was sent as a mercenary on behalf of the council. I was relieved to find her exiting the bathroom, dressed and ready to face company. When I gave her the same gun from earlier that morning, shock registered on her face before concern took over.

"What's happened?"

I quickly filled her in, adding one of my brothers was on his way up. "You have to be ready to shoot him at any moment, Jillian. He's part of the family—he knows how it works. They'd send him here to get close to me. They'd use Carrie's predicament as a cover story to make me put my guard down. But they obviously don't know me well enough because it only makes me more suspicious."

"Just don't shoot your brother before we find out for sure. If Leo does have Carrie, we have to save her."

That "we" would be a problem because there was no way in hell I'd let my pregnant fiancée go anywhere near Leo's fenced fortress. I'd only convinced Jillian to marry me a few hours before, so I wasn't about to risk losing her again. And that's exactly what would happen if she stepped into Leo's line of sight. After the confrontation I'd had with him, blood wouldn't mean shit. In fact, if he was truly holding Carrie, his plan was to draw me in then kill us all.

The question remained—who in our family had chosen Leo's side and who had chosen mine? Father against son. Mother against daughter. Brother against brother. We all knew what had been drilled into our heads for years. But when push came to shove, would my immediate family actually turn on me?

When Marco knocked on the door, I motioned for Jillian to

stay out of sight. Until I knew what his true intentions were, I'd assume he was my enemy. Marco and I had been close while growing up. Less than two years apart, we were the closest in age and in personality. Our take-no-shit attitudes came naturally and developed well before either of us realized what our family business really entailed. That personality trait had suited us well in our individual business ventures but not so well in personal relationships.

My ambition only slightly exceeded his. That was why I was next in line to be the Boss over my older brother. I'd taken the streets by storm and by force faster and more ruthlessly than he had, earning a name for myself as I went. In all honesty, Marco and I were equally as bullheaded as we were cunning. He and I were an explosive combination when we were together. Whether that was good or bad in the current instance remained to be seen.

I opened the door, keeping my right hand out of sight, holding my gun and my finger close to the trigger. With my poker face intact to hide my thoughts, I met Marco's intense stare with my own. "Marco."

"I'm sorry to hear about Benny, Damon. That really fucking sucks."

"Yes, it really fucking does."

"You look like shit, by the way."

"What do you want, Marco?"

"Put the gun away, little brother. You don't need it. I told you why I'm here." He walked past me, and I pushed the door closed before dropping my gun hand to my side. "Where's Jillian? Is she waiting in the wings to shoot me?"

"Only if you make her."

"You don't trust your own brother?" He had the nerve to appear insulted.

"My brother happens to be a capo in a large organized-crime syndicate. He's been trained to put *the family* first, not his brother or his sister. So you'll have to forgive me if I'm not fully convinced your objective in coming here is benevolent."

One side of his mouth quirked upward slightly at first before morphing into a full-on smile in an uncharacteristic display of amusement. "My objectives are never fully benevolent, Damon. Except when it comes to you and Carrie. You and I have always been close, and you know I've always been protective of our little sister. No one else fucks with her—*no one*. Leo crossed a line he never should've even thought about, regardless of who she's dating."

"You knew, didn't you? You already knew she was dating Lorenzo."

He shrugged, seemingly unconcerned. "I'd heard rumors. Whether it was true or not didn't mean shit to me. She's grown and it's her life—she's entitled to live it however she wants. I'd only get involved if someone tried to hurt her, which is why I'm here now."

He turned his back to me, walked into the den, and made himself comfortable on the couch. "Damon, bring Jillian in here and let's come up with our plan. You can both keep your guns pointed at me the whole time if that makes you feel better. All I care about is getting Carrie out of Leo's house in one piece."

Jillian stepped into the hallway and looked at me for a cue on how to proceed. With her hand in mine, I led her to the opposite side of the room, and we sat together facing Marco. She placed her gun in her lap then laid her hand over it. She wasn't pointing it at him, but he got her point nonetheless. Marco grinned at her boldness and nodded slowly, admiration obvious in his expression.

"It's good to see you again, Jillian. I'm glad Damon convinced you to come back with him. He was hell to be around after he lost you."

"After my house was shot to pieces, I didn't really have much choice but to come with him. But I'm here now, and I have no intentions of leaving again. Tell us about what's happened to Carrie."

"Right to business. I like it. From what I've pieced together, Carrie and Lorenzo had just arrived at her house together when a couple of Leo's goons busted the door down and grabbed them. A neighbor heard the ruckus and called the police. One of my guys was monitoring the police band and heard the dispatch to Carrie's address. They gave the license plate and description of the car, and I tied it to Leo.

"When I called him, he ignored my calls. So I drove straight to his house, and his enforcers were manning the gate. They refused to let me in, and not so subtly threatened to shoot me in the back of the head if I pushed my luck. By then, I was so fucking pissed off I couldn't see straight. When I called Dad to get him involved, Mama answered his phone and said he couldn't talk. She was crying, Damon."

"What? Mama answered his phone...and said Dad couldn't talk?"

I couldn't believe my ears. To my knowledge, that had never happened before. The significance of that small act was huge in our family. Not that Dad was always available. But that he wasn't taking calls when the family was coming apart at the seams.

"It's completely off, right? I tried to push Mama for information, but I couldn't get much out of her. I have a very bad feeling this isn't going to end well at all." Marco scrubbed his hand over his face.

"Vincenzo and Leo are brothers, but Leo kidnapped Vincenzo's daughter? Won't your dad defend his daughter against his brother?" Jillian's eyes darted between Marco and me, waiting for one of us to assure her our father would come to his daughter's rescue.

"We don't know, Jillian. We don't know what Dad will do in this situation. This is all new territory for us." I covered her hand with mine, knowing she was as worried about Carrie as I was.

"What do you think we should do, Damon?" Marco looked at me for guidance because I should be the next in line for the Boss position. But that was before I attacked the Underboss.

"Did you not hear what happened this morning?"

"Of course I heard. You almost killed Leo for knocking Jillian to the floor. I don't blame you. Old fucker should've known better. He has crossed the line with too many of our guys' wives, only none of them have balls the size of basketballs like you do. They're all fucking proud of you, man." Marco's smile lit up his face despite the dire circumstances. "I only wish I could've been there to see it happen."

"Why have I never heard this before? None of my men have ever said anything like that about Leo."

Marco shrugged one shoulder. "Because of your status, man. They can't complain to you about Leo when you'll take Dad's place soon. That's a surefire way for them to end up on the Boss's bad side. They just keep their heads down and do their jobs."

"Does Dad know?"

Marco stared at me a few seconds too long before answering. There was more to that story than he wanted to say in present company. "He knows."

"I'm sorry, but your whole damn family is insane." Jillian jumped up from her seat, her voice rising with every word. "We can't just wait and see what Leo decides to do with Carrie and Lorenzo. We need to go talk to your parents—we have to talk some sense into them! If you two are afraid to do it, I'll be glad to tell them both exactly what I think about the entire fucked-up mess."

Marco's mouth gaped open at Jillian's outburst. He'd never witnessed that feisty spitfire side of her. Then he cut his eyes to me and roared with laughter. "All right, then. By all means, show us how it's done. I wouldn't miss this for the world."

"Jillian, doll, I really don't want you involved in this any more than you already have been. This still isn't a safe situation for you. Maybe not even for me."

If looks could kill...

"Marco, has the council met?" I needed to know what they'd decided about our fate before we made any move.

"Not officially, because Dad and Leo weren't there to cast their votes. The other council members are ready to boot Leo out and put you in his spot, though."

That wasn't the outcome I'd expected. Jillian turned her gaze to me, her leery expression wordlessly questioning me. What would I choose—being the underboss of the crime family, or being the provider for my family with her? Putting *the* family first, or putting *my* family first?

"Good to know I don't have a sanctioned hit out on me, at least. Same goes for Jillian, I assume?"

"Absolutely. Dad hasn't exactly hidden the fact that he loves Jillian like she's his daughter."

"What?" Jillian's jaw dropped open, shocked to hear the words spoken aloud.

She and Dad had a special bond from the first time they met... until Dad withheld information about her mother's death. Since then, she'd only given him an icy greeting when she saw him. She'd lost her father just over two years ago. Even though my dad was only a temporary replacement, losing him opened an old wound.

"You didn't know that?" Marco asked, tilting his head to the side while he studied her reaction.

"No, not really. I thought we were fond of each other at first, but then..."

"I heard what happened with your mother, and I'm sorry about that. But believe me, Jillian—that was Dad's way of protecting you. If he didn't care about you, he would've let you return to Louisiana and deal with that situation on your own."

"You can tell me more about this later. Right now, we can't let

Carrie face this alone. Let's go to your parents' house and talk to them first. If they won't listen to reason, then we'll figure out our plan of attack." Jillian walked toward the door without waiting for either of us to reply.

"Will she leave without us?" Marco stood and watched as Jillian left the den.

"She will. Without a second thought, brother."

"Are you sure she's not already a Marchetti? Seems you've found your match in stubbornness."

"You have no idea."

When we arrived at my parents' house, the gate enclosing the driveway was closed. No cars were parked out in the open, and all the garage doors were down. I still would've placed odds on Mama being home, safely locked away in their mansion that appeared vacated for a reason. The gates swung open when I keyed in the code, and I pulled into the garage. We waited for the door to finish closing behind us before we exited the car.

Inside the house, I heard the murmur of low voices coming from the dining room. No doubt they were plotting and scheming on their own, trying to figure out the best way to storm the well-secured fortress to save Carrie. The voices stopped as we approached the doorway, making me pause momentarily before stepping into the room.

My parents sat at the table, Mama trying to pretend she was unaffected by everything happening around her. But her red-rimmed, puffy eyes gave her secret away. When I got closer, the streaks of bloodshot in them were impossible to miss. She wanted to appear strong for all of us, but she was falling to pieces inside.

I moved to her side and held out my hand. She looked up at me, unsure of my actions, but she finally put her hand in mine. With a soft tug, I helped her to stand then wrapped my arms around her. In an instant, she gripped me tightly, buried her face in my chest, and sobbed.

6

CHAPTER SIX

Jillian

$\mathcal{W}$atching Mama Lina break down in Damon's arms was almost more than I could bear. She loved her children, that was clear. All of them held a special place in her heart, and she couldn't choose one over the other no more than she could move the moon and stars. Though, for her family, she would die trying to do just that if it would help them.

One glance at Vincenzo told me he wasn't holding up much better than Mama Lina was. He was only a little more adept at hiding his feelings after years of practice. That was when I realized he reminded me of my dad when we lost my grandmother. Daddy was so brokenhearted over losing his mother, but he put up such a strong front while he comforted me.

That was what Vincenzo was doing for his wife. Comforting her while his heart was breaking inside.

Vincenzo's eyes were fixed on a single spot on the table. His throat muscles were working overtime, trying to swallow down the ball of emotion stuck in his throat. Had he looked up at Mama Lina and Damon, he would've joined her in an all-out sob fest. I moved around the table until I stood behind him then I wrapped my arms around his neck.

"We're here to help. We'll get Carrie back, safe and sound."

His big hands wrapped around my arms, a squeeze his only reply. But he said more with that simple gesture than his words could've conveyed. For the first time in months, I felt hope that we could be the big happy family I'd always dreamed of having.

Marco rubbed his mom's back before taking a seat across from Vincenzo. Mama Lina stepped out of Damon's embrace, kissed his cheek, then took her seat again. Damon's gaze landed on me, still hugging his dad, and I saw one side of his mouth lift ever so slightly before his poker face was back in place. Then he looked directly at his dad.

"Are we good, Dad?"

I released my hold on him and took the seat next to him.

Vincenzo nodded. "Of course we are, son. Your mother and I were just going over everything that's happened and what our next steps should be. In one way, I was right to take up for Leo since he is the Underboss. What he did to our Jillian wasn't right, and I planned to handle that with him in private. But after talking to your mother about it, I realize I was wrong. It is your place to protect her, to defend her, and to exact revenge when someone mistreats her."

"I wonder, did you come to this realization before or after your brother kidnapped your daughter?" Damon was barely containing his rage. I could feel it simmering just under his surface.

"Fair question. I questioned my actions before he took your sister, but not soon enough to prevent it."

"Why is he doing this at all, Dad? He's always had a cruel side, but never toward his own family like this." Damon felt the sting of his uncle's betrayal. The confusion it caused, and the resulting pain, were driving him on.

"He's jealous of you, Damon. Apparently, I've been blind, and he's been hiding what he truly wants. While we've been grooming you to take over as the Boss so he and I can both retire, he's been planning to overthrow you and take the Boss role for himself." Vincenzo leaned back, drawing in a deep breath to calm his anger. "My own brother betrayed my son right under my nose, and I never knew. Now he's holding my only daughter, I presume, as insurance to get what he wants and still keep his head intact."

"You presume? You don't know for sure what he wants?" Damon's brows drew downward as the wheels in his head turned at a breakneck speed. He attempted to put the pieces together himself, but crucial information was obviously still missing.

"Leo won't answer his phone. Your mother talked to Maria for only a minute before the line went dead. Maria was crying, saying how sorry she was and that she didn't know what was going on. Apparently, he's been hiding his deceit from his wife too."

"What happens now? How do we get Carrie and Lorenzo out of there alive?" I glanced around the table, noting the concerned expressions and hesitant replies.

"*Cara*, I can't allow you to be part of this. Even if you weren't pregnant, it's much too dangerous for you to be there. If Leo captured you, he'd use you for more bargaining power against Damon. Or, one of his men could shoot you on sight—and they would, without thinking twice about it." Vincenzo patted my hand, in a gesture of both reassurance and appreciation. "I can't let him have Carrie *and* you."

"Absolutely not, doll. It's bad enough he has my sister, but I would become completely unhinged if you were hurt. I just lost Benny. Don't make me face that with you and our babies, too." The tone of Damon's voice wasn't one of a command, but more of a plea. One that pulled at my heart more than anything he'd said to me before.

"I just feel so responsible. If Carrie and I hadn't set that trap for Lorenzo, maybe none of this would've happened."

"All of this was in the works no matter what you two planned,

Jillian. Leo must've been working to undermine Dad and Damon for some time. Maybe he made his move because Carrie and Lorenzo were together and that just made it much more convenient. But make no mistake, the outcome would've been the same regardless. You don't own the blame for this." Marco held my gaze deliberately, getting his point across that the family didn't hold me responsible for anything.

"Then what can I do to help, short of storming the keep and rescuing her myself?"

"You can stay here and help me watch Leo's security cameras. We've accessed the feed to their security system. You and I will be the eyes and ears for our men. That's how we can help protect all of them." Mama Lina dried her eyes and straightened her spine, finding a new purpose to focus on instead of worrying about her daughter.

"Whatever will help, I'm willing to do it."

Damon, Marco, and Vincenzo left to gather the rest of their loyal men together and begin staging their assault. Car after car packed with brawny and scary men arrived, their serious expressions and piercing eyes daring anyone to fuck with them. They filed into the house then disappeared into the basement. Every time the door to the lower floor opened, I overheard Damon issuing assignments to the various teams. Every sliver of information that filtered up the stairs only increased my urge to join them, despite knowing I shouldn't.

"Jillian, come with me, *cara*. There's something else we can do while they're still working downstairs."

I followed Mama Lina into a large room that reminded me a lot of Carrie's setup. Several iMacs lined the desks along three walls of the room. Large flat-screen TVs hung on the walls, the images on them changing every few seconds with the feed from the security cameras outside Leo's house.

"Are there cameras inside his house too?"

"There are, but they're on a closed loop, so we can't access them. Yet." A familiar masculine voice replied from behind me. I whirled around to find Matteo had joined us.

"Matteo, thank you for doing all of this. You know you're my favorite nephew." Mama Lina kissed him on both cheeks then drew him into a tight embrace. When he smiled, his love for his aunt shone in his eyes.

"So, on top of being an emergency physician, you're also a tech guru? Very impressive."

He chuckled as Mama Lina released him and waved his hand dismissively at my compliment. "It's nothing. I took a few coding language and ethical hacking classes. Now I'm just putting them to good use to help my favorite aunt. If you need me for anything, I'll be over here in the corner, getting ready to connect to the interior cameras as soon as our guys attach the transmitter on-site."

"Thank you, Matteo." Mama Lina took my hand in hers and led me to another computer. "Jillian, let's make Benny's funeral arrangements so we can pay our final respects. Damon will appreciate us taking the lead on it. One less thing he has to worry about in the middle of this mess. I know it bothers him, putting off Benny's funeral while he saves his sister."

I noticed she didn't say "while he *tries* to save his sister." Either she knew Damon wouldn't have it any other way, or she couldn't face the possibility of any other outcome. I understood how she felt, though. I also understood that the probability of Carrie not walking out of Leo's house alive was higher than any of us would like. Even thinking about Damon not making it back in one piece was enough to induce a panic attack in me. That was when I looked at Mama Lina with new eyes.

The lives of her husband, daughter, sons, nephews, and friends were all on the line. Her entire world could be wiped out with the pull of a trigger. She was staying busy because idle time allowed her mind to wander too much. It forced her to face the stark reality that people had to die in order for her immediate family to live. Whether it was her brother-in-law, her sister-in-law, or

Leo's loyal soldiers, blood would be spilled and lives would be lost.

Either way the coup went, Mama Lina's life would be forever changed.

She and I sat down together and made the call to begin arrangements. Since the funeral director, Charles, was a family friend, he agreed to go into the city immediately to transport Benny's body to the local funeral home.

"What about Benny's family? Have you already notified them?"

Mama Lina gave me a small, sad smile. "He didn't have any other family but us, that we know of. We took him in when he was a young teenager. He was a runaway, living on the streets, eating out of garbage cans. But he was tough—he didn't let anyone push him around. And when he came here to live with us, he insisted on earning his keep. He refused to take a handout. So, Vin took Benny under his wing, taught him the family business, and he kept his promise to remain loyal to us until his death."

I wiped the tears from my eyes, my heart breaking for a man I barely knew. "Lorenzo didn't mean to shoot him. Benny tackled us and tried to pull the gun from Lorenzo's hand, and it went off. He was trying to save me, though. I know he did it for Damon more than for me, but still…"

"Damon's the one who insisted we take Benny in. Vin and I weren't too keen on bringing a strange boy into the house, especially with Carrie being younger. It'd be one thing if he robbed us blind while we slept, but if he had touched our daughter, nothing on earth would've saved him.

"But Damon vouched for him, guaranteed nothing bad would happen, and wouldn't take no for an answer. Damon received the worst punishment of his life for defying Vincenzo over Benny. Turned out, Damon was right about him all along, and we had nothing to worry about. Damon still says Benny was worth the beating he took for arguing with his father."

"Damon once mentioned learning his lesson about going against Vincenzo when he was a teenager. That must've been it."

"That was the one and only time. It was very bad, Jillian. That kind of punishment wasn't uncommon in our small village back in Italy. The mob ruled with an iron fist, and you learned your place very quickly, so seeing other boys after they'd been beaten didn't faze me after a while. But when I first held my newborn baby, I couldn't imagine allowing anyone to hurt him like that. When Vincenzo finished with him, Damon was black and blue all over, and I didn't speak to Vincenzo for two solid weeks."

"Damon said he'd only defied Vincenzo once as an adult, and that was for me. Well, one time before yesterday, that is."

"That's right. That's also part of why Vincenzo didn't punish Damon over it. Vin knows his son doesn't take such a bold stance for just anyone. The person who earns Damon's trust has to be very special and possess traits Damon is willing to fight for, to risk everything over."

People could change, but only under immense pain and pressure.

Damon risked facing Vincenzo's wrath again—the physical pain of it, the pressure to play his part in the family, the real possibility of being exiled or killed—to be with me, to protect me, to make both of us whole again. He had experienced immense pain and loss, and he lived under constant pressure. Damon had changed—for me.

"Mama, Jillian, we're leaving now. We'll be back when we have Carrie and Lorenzo." Damon stood in the doorway dressed in jeans and a thick black sweatshirt. He wore a shoulder harness with gun holsters on each side. Around his waist, he wore multiple knives sheathed in leather sleeves.

I had just found my way back to him. There was no way I could stand losing him again. In one swift motion, I flew out of my seat and into his arms. As if he had anticipated my move, he instantly pulled me off my feet and crushed me against him.

"Promise me you'll come back to me. Promise me you won't

get hurt. I want to hear you say the words, Damon." My insistence had a purpose. Damon was a man of his word, and if he made me a promise, he'd move heaven and earth to keep it. "We have a wedding to plan, a life to live, and a family to raise. You can't leave me here alone. Promise me. Now."

He squeezed me tighter. "I promise I'm coming home to you. There isn't a man alive who can stop me. You're never getting rid of me, doll."

"I love you, Damon."

"I love you too, Jillian."

He pressed his lips against mine, and I eagerly returned the kiss. When I felt his tongue swipe across my lip, I willingly gave him full access. With thorough and intentional movements, he made love to me with his kiss. His tongue repeatedly slid across mine, sending waves of goose bumps across my skin. With his full, firm lips, he lit a fire inside me that burned only for him.

Then he lowered me back to the ground, placed one last kiss on my lips, and left with the others. As I stood there with my chin quivering and tears trying to pool in my eyes, I realized his sweatshirt wasn't as thick as I originally thought it was. He was wearing a bulletproof vest underneath.

That wasn't as comforting as I thought it would be.

CHAPTER SEVEN

Jilllian

ama Lina and I watched with bated breath when our men arrived at Leo's house. When they first left us, I had no idea how they'd even get inside since Leo's men were guarding the gate. More armed guards had to be inside too, waiting for Vincenzo to make a move against them. My advice to Leo, had I talked to him, would be if he planned to screw his family over, make sure he was the smartest member.

The enormous home was inside a brick fence that lined the entire property. But Leo never considered his family was even more versed in the fence's strengths and weaknesses than the owner. The estate had once been a horse farm, covering several acres of lush green grass and clumps of trees for shade. The brick fence along the back of the property was built to allow the water from a small stream to flow freely into the man-made pond. Instead of making a grand show of force at the front door, Damon and his men parked a half-mile away from the back fence line, removed the steel grate, and waded in the water until they were well inside the perimeter.

From there, they sprinted in small groups from one point to the next, checking their surroundings and taking new cover with every move. Silent and meticulous, like a group of trained Special Forces warriors on the prowl, they advanced with precision and determination. Damon gave his mom and me a play-by-play through his Bluetooth earpiece. The low murmur of his voice coming over the speakerphone in the family's command center was reassuring until they were within range of the cameras around the exterior of the house.

Damon remained silent while Mama Lina and I relayed where Leo's enforcers were every time the screen from the security feed changed. I watched, detached from all feelings, while limp bodies from both sides of the battle fell to the ground as they advanced. Damon was safe and he was on a mission to save his sister, so I convinced myself that her safety was all that mattered. Had I been capable of doing the same to save my mother, I'd like to think I would have done whatever it took without giving the evil deed a second thought.

"Matteo, I'm at the house now. Walk me through how to install this transmitter so Mama and Jillian can see what's going on inside." Damon's hushed voice came across the speaker without a trace of the exertion I'd just watched him expend.

Matteo was just as good with computer hacking as he was with emergency medicine. He talked Damon through the process of connecting the transmitter to the security system, allowing the signal to broadcast the interior camera feed across the airwaves. Once we confirmed we had unimpeded access to the cameras inside, Matteo decided it was time for him to leave.

"They're safe from anyone watching the monitors inside. I set it so the security feed monitor inside the house is on a continuous loop to give Damon an advantage. I'm not staying for the rest of this—I've done enough as it is. Leo and Maria are my aunt and uncle too. But I left my number on the desk for you if you need me. I'm due at the hospital soon, and I have a feeling I'll be treating at least a few of these guys tonight."

"Thank you for helping with this, Matteo. I know you try to stay out of taking sides on anything to do with family squabbles, but I can't imagine not being able to see Damon while this is going down. That would drive me crazy." I rose from my seat to hug him goodbye.

"Try not to get too involved with any of this, Jillian. You'll get sucked in before you know what's happening. This life will change you in ways you'd never believe." Matteo kissed me on the cheek before he left, leaving me reeling with his almost prophetic warning.

Seated back in front of the monitors, I focused on my task of keeping Damon alive and unharmed while he entered the lion's den. There were too many men in that house who would want to be the one to take out the next Boss. The notoriety from that act alone certainly would be enough to set someone up for life in Leo's eyes.

"Damon, there's a huge man just inside the door in front of you. He doesn't seem to know you're there yet." Even though no one around him could hear me, I found myself whispering into the speakerphone anyway.

I held my breath when Damon turned the knob, slowly and silently, and stole up behind the enormous goon waiting inside. Damon motioned to his men to keep going before he put the other man in a choke hold from behind, but the plan to subdue his opponent didn't work. Damon's hold was broken, and the two men faced each other, watching and waiting for the next move.

If I expected the big guy to go down easy, I'd never been so wrong.

"Damon Marchetti. I knew you'd be stupid enough to show up here. I'll be sure to send flowers for your funeral."

"Raul, there will be a lot of funerals after today, but mine won't be one of them."

The two men dove at each other, their fists flying and making contact with the other. They rolled around on the floor, taking turns being on top and beating the shit out of each other. On one flip, Raul jumped to his feet and began backing away. But Damon was undeterred and quickly followed him in hot pursuit. His arm jutted out, making contact with Raul's battered face again.

The thud of fists pounding against flesh echoed through the office, making Mama Lina reach over and grab my hand in hers. We both squeezed as we watched helplessly. Blood streamed out of Damon's mouth from Raul's jab. Damon wiped it away and his eyes hardened. I saw the cold-blooded killer inside him emerge on the vibrant screen in front of me.

After an uppercut to Raul's chin that stunned him, Damon drew his gun from the holster, leveled it at Raul, and pulled the trigger. In no more than a full second, Damon made the decision to kill the man rather than continue fighting him. He showed no sign of hesitation—or regret. When Raul's knees buckled beneath him and his large body crumpled lifelessly to the floor, Damon stepped over him and continued walking without a backward glance.

"Do you see Carrie and Lorenzo on the feed?"

Damon's calm voice felt odd after watching him murder someone up close. The other men outside who were shot were farther away from the cameras. In my mind, I could rationalize it away by pretending I was watching a realistic movie and compartmentalizing my thoughts and feelings. Then the distinctive sound of gunfire in distant rooms rang out in the room, stealing my breath from my lungs.

"Jillian?" His voice hinted at his inward aggravation from having to ask twice in that situation. But I still couldn't speak.

"Damon, they're in the media room downstairs." Mama Lina pressed her lips together and inclined her head toward me. Understanding of what I was trying to come to grips with shone in her eyes. She hit the mute button while Damon made his way through the enormous house, his men having cleared the way ahead of him. "It's okay, Jillian. Let's just help them get through this, and we'll talk about what's happened, yes?"

"Okay." I inhaled the deepest breath I could and released it slowly, calming my frayed nerves and refocusing my attention on the people we were helping keep alive.

Damon wound his way through the mansion, through doorways and hallways, until he approached the door to the basement. I quickly flipped through the interior camera views, watching his every move, until the stairway down to the basement filled the screen. In the split second I saw his hand touch the doorknob on one screen, something on the other screen caught my eye. It was small, barely visible in the lower corner of the screen.

"Damon, wait!"

But I was too late to stop him.

Even through the speakerphone, the blast was so loud we both winced in pain. The bright flash of light blinded our view through the cameras momentarily. When the light dissipated, my heart skipped a beat before it started racing, pounding in my chest so hard I could feel my shirt moving over my heart. Damon was knocked to the floor by the blast. He tried to stand up, only to fall over and hit the floor repeatedly. Several times in a row, he held his arms out in front of him, feeling for his surroundings, while trying to right himself again.

I hit the mute button so Damon wouldn't hear the fear in my voice.

"Mama Lina, is he…is he *blind?*"

When she didn't answer, I quickly glanced over at her. She shook her head back and forth, tears streamed down her face, and her hand covered her gaping mouth. Not wanting Damon to feel alone, I hit the button again and tried to calmly talk to him through my panic.

"Damon, talk to me. What's happening?"

No reply.

"Damon!" I yelled, panic rising in my chest.

"He won't be able to hear you for a while, *bella*. That must have been a concussion grenade. I remember Vin and Leo talking about using them. His vision should start returning any second now, but he won't be able to hear anything for several more minutes at least. He'll be disoriented and unsteady on his feet for quite a while."

"So…he's helpless. Inside Leo's house."

"Yes." Her voice broke on the simple, one-syllable reply.

Then we heard loud voices and angry shouts coming from the stairwell in front of Damon. Several men came rushing out, and I recognized Leo, standing in the middle of them. They flanked him, covering him on all sides. The sneer of disgust on his face as he neared Damon made my stomach turn. When Leo reached Damon, he swung his leg back and kicked Damon in the stomach with all his might.

I watched, helplessly and with tears streaming down my face, as he repeatedly kicked and stomped Damon all over his body. Damon's sight returned and he tried to dodge the blows, but after being disoriented by the grenade, he couldn't move fast enough. His body suffered damaging jolt after jolt, until he completely passed out. Witnessing that brutality triggered something in me. I'd never felt so helpless, so heartbroken, or so furious before in my life.

Watching him made me realize something I'd never wanted to face. Had I known what was happening with my mom and rushed in to try to save her, I wouldn't have been able to handle the brutality. I wouldn't have been strong enough to stop them. I wouldn't have had the mental capacity to handle seeing anything they did to her in person. I was barely functioning watching the scene with Damon play out on a monitor in front of me.

Witnessing men like Leo hurt my frail mother would've been too much.

I wanted to believe I was an inner badass, but too many mirrors had been shoved in front of my face since the first day I entered Damon's world.

More shots were fired and more masculine voices called out, out of view from the camera I had trained on Damon. Part of me wanted to change the view, to see who approached them, but I couldn't stand the thought of losing sight of him. His chest was still moving, although slowly, but at least he was still breathing. That screen was the only string of hope I had to hold on to.

"It's Vincenzo and Marco! Thank God they made it through the front gate." Mama Lina jumped up, pacing back and forth behind our chairs but keeping her eyes glued to her unconscious son.

Vincenzo's men surrounded Leo and his guys before disarming them. Marco looked down at his brother's battered body, and the same murderous rage I saw in Damon's expression blanketed Marco's eyes. Just as Marco lunged at Leo, Vincenzo grabbed Marco's arm and held him back.

"Not yet." Vincenzo spoke to Marco, but his stare never veered from Leo. "Help your brother first."

Marco knelt beside Damon. "Hold on, bro. We're going to get you fixed up. Jillian, if you can hear me, call Doc and tell him we're on our way so he'll be ready for us."

With shaking fingers, I dialed Matteo's cell and waited impatiently for the call to connect. When I heard his voice on the other end, I barely gave him time to say hello before I started pouring out the details at him.

"Calm down, Jillian. The trauma team will be on standby in thirty seconds. Just get him here."

Marco called Mama Lina after he'd loaded Damon in the car. They wouldn't wait around at Leo's for the police or ambulance to show up. She and I flew out of the house, heading straight for the emergency room where Matteo worked.

To say I was waiting on pins and needles for Marco to arrive at the hospital with Damon was a gross understatement. Every tick of the second hand on the clock was more excruciating than the last. The screeching tires outside the emergency room could only signal the arrival of one person.

8

CHAPTER EIGHT

Damon

"*I* said I'm *fine*. I'm not staying here."

My busted lip and swollen jaw somewhat muffled my words, but I still got my point across. I'd been in the ER for hours already. I'd been poked, prodded, evaluated, scanned, X-rayed, and otherwise violated in every medical fashion I could imagine. If anything life-threatening were wrong with me, they would've found it by then. Since I was able to sit up on the hard gurney, going home only made sense to me.

But if Matteo saw how much it hurt to move any muscle in my body, he'd call Dad and I'd lose the argument before it even began. As long as I held my breath and didn't flinch, I was certain I could convince him not to admit me.

"Damon. You look like you've gone twelve rounds with Mike Tyson while your hands were tied behind your back. Come on, man. You don't want to miss what goes down next, I get it, but you really need to stay for a couple of days." Matteo stared at me, refusing to be the one to back down.

"I'll be fine. Jillian will take good care of me. Won't you, doll?"

"No." She crossed her arms over her chest and glared at me. "I thought they killed you, Damon. You need to look in a mirror, then you wouldn't be so impatient to leave. There are cuts, bruises, sprains, and broken bones all over you."

"Plus a concussion—from the grenade *and* from the beating you took afterward. This kind of shit doesn't happen to just anyone, Damon." Matteo shook his head, exasperated with me.

"I feel much better now. Finish patching me up and send me home, Doc."

"Just so we're clear, Damon, I am *not* agreeing to this. If you leave, you'll be leaving against medical advice, not with my consent."

"Understood. You've done enough for me. I'll sign whatever you need me to sign so it covers your ass."

"You'll have a hard time signing anything with broken fingers." Jillian gestured toward the cast on my right hand. My fiancée was sorely displeased with me.

"I'll hold the pen with my teeth. It'll be fine." I winked at her and immediately regretted it.

She saw the bolt of pain run through me from the simple movement, and her mouth dropped open in shock and anger. The swelling around my eye rendered the X-rays inconclusive, but I couldn't deny the area hurt enough to say my occipital bone was at least cracked. Though they didn't know for sure, the ophthalmologist on call insisted we treat it as though it were broken. Extra precautions, extra medications, extra time to heal. All of that could be done at home, though.

"Are you always going to be this stubborn?" Both her eyes and the tone of her voice challenged me, daring me to give her anything but the truth. Any other time, her feisty, fiery side would've been a complete fucking turn-on.

"Yes, you know I will be, doll. Almost as much as you."

"Jillian, come with me. I need to go over the medical protocol with you for each of his multiple injuries. If you see any of the warning signs, call an ambulance immediately. Don't wait for Damon to agree. You hear me, cuz?"

"I hear you, Doc. If it comes to that, Jillian will have the final say. I won't argue with her."

"You have a significant concussion, Damon. You may not even realize you're being combative with her if it gets to that point." Matteo arched his eyebrow, asking me one last time to stay in the hospital. But I couldn't. Bad timing was an understatement.

"We'll stay at my parents' house for a while so we'll both have help. Send a home health nurse with me—a big, burly man if you think that's best. I can't stay here any longer, though."

Understanding, despite his hesitancy, dawned in his eyes. I wasn't *only* being stubborn, that time anyway. There were legitimate reasons that prevented me from kicking back in an uncomfortable hospital bed and watching TV all day while I waited to be discharged with a clean bill of health. Family business that was still unfinished. Business that couldn't—*wouldn't*—wait for a few days while I recuperated. With any luck, I'd have time to recover when all the craziness settled down.

"You wait here until I get home health care arranged. I won't negotiate with you on that. If you force my hand, I'll call Uncle Vin, and this argument will be over."

"I'll wait right here." I had to learn to pick and choose my battles. That was one fight I'd gladly concede to Matteo. When he and Jillian left the room, I turned my attention to Mama. "How's Carrie doing?"

"She says she's okay, but I just don't know. She's still shaken, and they roughed her up some, but I suppose she'll be all right. When Marco called, he said Lorenzo looks more like you—so they called a doctor to check him over. Maybe Leo's goons used him as a punching bag to intimidate Carrie and make her talk. Or maybe they were just toying with both Carrie and Lorenzo while they waited for Vincenzo or you to show up. I don't know." She very seldom rambled like that.

Mama was usually a take-charge woman, doling out the assignments and barking out orders like a drill sergeant. The worry and apprehension that gripped her mind all day were manifesting outwardly, through the repeated wringing of her hands and scattered speech. There wouldn't be many questions Leo would ask Carrie since he already knew everything there was to know about the business.

"Mama." I waited for her eyes to meet mine. "Carrie is stronger than you know. I'm sure she was scared for a while, but she's a fighter. She'll be fine. You'll see."

"How could Vincenzo's brother turn on him like this? I just don't understand. They've had their differences, but they've been close for several years now."

"I don't know yet, Mama. But that's what I intend to find out—as soon as I get out of here. Where did Dad take Leo?"

"They're all still at Leo's house. When Marco knew you were okay, he left here and went straight back over there. Paulie took Carrie and Lorenzo to my house."

"Did Paulie stay there with them?"

"I'm not sure, but I would think so. Why do you ask?"

"Mama, I need my phone. Where is it?" When I moved with the intention to stand, she jumped up from her seat and stopped me.

"I'll get it. Don't try to get up. I'm afraid you'll fall and injure yourself more."

She grabbed the plastic bag containing my clothes and set it on the bed beside me. While she removed each piece of clothing, looking for my phone, I eased the hospital gown off and started dressing to leave, thankful they'd left my boxers on when I arrived. When I stood to pull my pants up, she shook her head disapprovingly but didn't argue.

"Uh, Mama, your son needs a little help here."

She put my shoes on the floor at my feet then faced me. When I gestured at the button on my jeans, she let out an amused chuckle. "You mean *the* Damon Marchetti is admitting he can't do everything?"

"I can do most things. But I can't button my pants with broken fingers in a cast." Smiling hurt like fuck, but to show her I was okay, I lifted my lips on one side in a confident smirk.

"Sit down. I'll help with your socks and shoes while you make your calls." She handed my cell phone to me, and I gingerly took my seat back on the gurney.

I hit the button for Paulie and willed him to answer the phone immediately.

"Hey, Boss. I didn't expect to hear from you. Everything okay?

"I'm okay, Paulie. Are you still at the house with Carrie and Lorenzo?"

"No, Carrie told me to go back and help make sure Vincenzo is safe. I'm at Leo's with him. What's going on, Boss?"

"I'm not sure, Paulie, but I have a bad feeling. Grab Luigi and a couple of the other experienced guys and get back to Carrie right now. I'll be there as soon as I can. Tell Dad I said so, will ya?"

"You got it, Damon."

We disconnected, and I had to consciously focus on not shaking my leg in my impatience. For one, the jarring motion wasn't good for my condition. But more than that, I didn't want to worry my mom unnecessarily. I had a gut feeling another surprise waited in the wings for us. I just wasn't sure what it could be, and I didn't want Carrie left unprotected again.

A nurse walked into my room to check on me and realized I'd turned off the machine taking my vitals. Had I physically been able to remove my IV, that also would've been out of my arm. But as it was, my button-down shirt was draped over my shoulders since my cast wouldn't fit in the sleeve, and the IV was still stuck in my good arm.

"Mr. Marchetti, I know you're ready to leave, but Dr. Falco is still making your home health care arrangements. As long as you're a patient, I still have a job to do and that includes monitoring your vital signs until you sign your discharge papers. You have to wear the blood pressure cuff and the oxygen monitor while you're in this room. And, with your head injury, you need to lie back on the gurney so you won't fall on the floor if you suddenly become dizzy."

"Is your last name Ratched, first name Nurse?" I quipped before obeying her direction. When I was settled against the raised back of the gurney, she hooked everything back up and turned on the machine.

"No, my last name is In-Charge, first name Head-Bitch. Don't forget it."

My consequent laugh really fucking hurt with my broken ribs, busted lip, and swollen face. But damn if I didn't need it. She waited for the machine to finish the first cycle and seemed pleased with the results. Before she left the exam room, she checked on Mama, asking if she needed anything. Then she pointed two fingers at her eyes and flipped her hand around to point one finger at me.

Well played, HBIC. Well played.

She paused in the doorway and turned off the overhead light. "Try to get some rest while you're waiting. You look like somebody beat you up."

I had to give her credit. Her snarky comments lifted my spirits. When I received a text from Paulie that said he and the others were back at the house with Carrie and all was quiet, I finally allowed myself to rest. A few minutes later, Jillian came back into the room, but by then I struggled to keep my eyes open. The events of the day on top of the hours I'd spent in the emergency room definitely took a heavy toll on me. A toll I would've rather slept away than faced, but I still had too many unanswered questions.

The sting of Uncle Leo's betrayal was very sharp, pricking my skin like knives. Someone had to make me understand how the fuck he could do this to his own family. As much as I hated what had happened, I knew Dad must have felt ten times worse. He must have been reeling from the conflict inside him—his brother versus his daughter and son. The penalty for that level of betrayal was definitely death, but I wondered if my dad would be able to carry out the sentence against his own brother.

"Okay, your home health care is all set, but I can't get anyone out there until their office opens in a few hours. Jillian and Aunt Lina will have to be your nurses for what's left of tonight. Your full-time care will be at your mom's house as soon as possible this morning. I've covered every possible acute medical scenario I can with Jillian. If anything appears out of the ordinary, she'll call the ambulance and have you transported back. Once you're back in my ER, I'll declare you as an altered mental status patient, and you won't have any choice but to stay. We clear?"

"Loud and clear, Doc. I may even enjoy the vacation." I rose from the gurney and settled into the wheelchair after the nurse removed all my external paraphernalia.

"Here, you can't leave the hospital without a shirt. Take these scrubs. I cut the sleeve on the shirt so your cast will fit through it." Jillian took the shirt from Matteo and helped me ease into it. "Remember what we talked about, Jillian. Call me if there's anything I can do."

With that, Matteo left the room, and Jillian signed my discharge papers. The nurse walked behind me, pushing my wheelchair while the three of us remained silent. Regardless of how that part of our story ended that night, our family would never be the same again. There forever would be an empty chair at the table along with an empty hole in our hearts where the man we thought we knew once resided.

"It's been a long day and night. I'm so ready to go home." Mama sat in the back seat with me while Jillian drove.

"We'll drop you off and let you get some sleep, Mama. Jillian will take me on to Leo's house so I can check in with Dad on what's going on."

"Damon, your father has everything under control. If he needed you, he would've called you by now." Mama couldn't help but worry; it was what she did. But I knew she was also worried about Dad because she hadn't heard from him either.

"We won't be long. Jillian needs her sleep too. We'll be fine."

No sooner had I gotten the words out, and my phone rang.

"Marco. Tell me."

He gave me the rundown of everything that happened in my absence. Leo's interrogation and obstinate behavior. Dad's aggravation and increasing brutality. But he wanted answers, so he wouldn't kill Leo until he had at least some of them. He'd torture him within an inch of his life, but Dad would make sure Leo held on just a little longer.

Then Marco began relaying one of their conversations, and his words left me speechless.

"Marco, don't let your guard down. Jillian, step on it!"

CHAPTER NINE

Jillian

*D*amon's sudden agitation sent warning shock waves through my nerves. The deadly game we'd been caught in was far from being over, that much was clear. My every sense fired on overdrive, my mind reeling from running through a list of everything that possibly could've gone wrong. The list was too long and every option was too daunting, but that didn't stop my endless parade of assumptions. With my foot slammed down against the gas pedal, I maneuvered through the early morning traffic which was steadily increasing as we approached rush hour.

"Damon, what is it?" Mama Lina asked.

As I drove, I continuously scanned the area in front and behind us. When I checked the rearview mirror, I adjusted my position until I could see them both. Mama Lina's worried expression was expected, but his wasn't. Had I ever seen my cool, calm, and collected hit man with a hint of fear in his expression before? Concern for the safety of those he loved, yes. But true fear? Never.

"Later, Mama. Let me check a few things first."

315

She didn't argue. She didn't push or try to question him further. She just accepted he couldn't tell her what he knew or what he suspected. Then his gaze met mine, and I could tell from the change in his expression he knew exactly what I was thinking.

That could never be me.

What we would do about that little dilemma was still to be seen. I wouldn't yield, and I wasn't sure he'd bend. But one of us would have to...if we were going to stay together.

"Jillian, when we get to Mama's, you stay there with her. I'll drive myself over to Leo's house."

"The hell you will!" I blurted out the words before I even thought about them. "There's absolutely no way I'll let you drive, Damon. You have pain medications in your system. You just got out of the hospital. You have a concussion. You'd be lucky to even make it over there alive."

"Why do you need to go to Leo's?" Mama Lina's stern tone was back. "You're not going alone. Jillian is right. You're certainly not driving."

"Fine." Damon's lips disappeared into a thin line, his aggravation not quite hidden. "Jillian can drive me over there and drop me off. I'll catch a ride back with Marco or Dad."

He thought his idea was the best solution, but he should've known me better than to think I'd go along with that plan. He was in no shape to be alone, much less to rush into another dangerous situation. The man was beyond hardheaded. He was reckless with his own safety while being overprotective of everyone else. None of it should've surprised me, but then he shouldn't be surprised by what I planned to do either.

"Son, do you really think that's a good idea? Matteo arranged for a nurse to take care of you. He didn't even really agree to let you leave the hospital—you forced his hand. You shouldn't be doing anything but resting and recuperating."

"I know, Mama, but I have to do this. There's no way around

me being there for it. Dad and Marco are still there—they have everything under control."

Neither Mama Lina nor I were stupid enough to buy that line of bullshit. If there was no danger, he wouldn't object to either of us going with him. Instead, he couldn't wait to get rid of us while he faced whatever was happening alone. And already severely injured.

We reached Mama Lina's house and were immediately greeted by a handful of the biggest men I've ever seen in real life. They surrounded the car, checking inside, in the trunk, and underneath the vehicle before allowing us to enter. Never mind that the homeowner was in the car, or that the next Boss was sitting beside her. Apparently, they had strict orders to check everyone, and they weren't too keen on being the ones to allow a breach.

"Damon." Mama Lina stopped as she was getting out of the car. She was hesitant to finish, but she couldn't let it go. "Find out about your aunt Maria. Was she part of this? Where is she?"

"Maria didn't know anything about it, Mama. Leo kept it from her. She was taken to a safe place until we've finished. Then we all have decisions to make."

She couldn't hide the inner pain and conflict over her sister-in-law. She loved Maria, that much was clear. She couldn't bear to think of anything happening to the woman who was like her own sister. That was when another family truth hit me.

Every member of the family had lost so much in their lives. Friends, family—people they loved—had been stripped away from them far too soon and much too often. Accepting their inevitable death didn't make it any easier to swallow when the time came. Maria's ultimate fate weighed heavily on Mama Lina's shoulders as she walked into the house, and it broke my heart that I couldn't help her.

"Pay attention to the directions I give you so you can get back to Mama's okay," Damon said from the back seat.

"Don't worry. I have my phone with me if I need it. My GPS works just fine."

His hand covered his forehead. His fingers gingerly rubbed back and forth. "Yeah, right. My mind is on something else. I didn't even think about that."

"You've had a long day."

His hand dropped from his face, and his eyes narrowed in suspicion. I saw his expression in the rearview mirror, but only in my peripheral vision. The man had an uncanny ability to read my thoughts and anticipate my every move. For my plan to work, I had to master the poker face that came naturally to him.

"So have you…and the babies. All three of you need rest."

That was a trap—one I recognized instantly.

"The babies are fine. We got a little rest while you were in the ER. I've felt them moving around, being as active as ever. I'm a little tired, but nothing to be worried about. I'll sleep when I get back to your mom's. Honestly, I'm more worried about you. Your mom had a good point when she said Matteo wasn't even going to let you leave the hospital. Your full-time nurse will be at the house in a matter of hours now. It'll be awkward if you're not there too."

"Don't worry about me, doll. You just get home and stay inside with the doors and gates locked at all times until I get back."

"All right. Whatever you say, Damon."

Damn it. My lack of argument was way too obvious. He placed his hand loosely over his mouth and stared at me with those piercing eyes.

"Just know you're going to pay for this in some unsuspecting and unpleasant way in the very near future. Don't think for one second I'm letting you off the hook. I've just decided I want a little more time to plan my revenge on you." I slowly lifted my eyes to the rearview mirror and met his gaze straight on. Mustering the best resting bitch face I had, I stared at him, quirked one eyebrow to finish off my pointedly unhappy expression, and dared him to push my buttons.

"Is it weird that I'm really fucking turned on right now?"

"Yes. It is weird. I think someone crossed the wires in your brain during one of your CT scans tonight," I deadpanned.

His dark chuckle rumbled through the car as we sped toward Leo's house, the morning sunlight barely breaking the line of the horizon. He gave me turn-by-turn directions until we reached Leo's street, but my mind wasn't on memorizing the turns and street names. My focus was on what I'd do after he got out of the car. When I looked back at him again, his head was leaned against the back of the seat, his eyes were closed, and his knuckles were white from gripping the seat belt. He was in so much pain. The parts of him that weren't in a cast or bandaged were black and blue. In that shape, he was far less capable of defending himself than he'd admit.

He'd already given me the house number, so I knew exactly which driveway to turn into. When I shifted the car into park, he opened his eyes and looked around, weariness etched in every line of his gorgeous face. He didn't want to go inside any more than I wanted him to, but his commitment to the family ran deep.

Something was off, but I couldn't put my finger on it. Something didn't feel right about the entire situation. Nothing visible had spooked me, but I couldn't shake the intuition inside me.

"Straight back to Mama's, Jillian. Wait for me there."

"Do you need help getting inside, Damon? You look like you're about to fall down, and you haven't even stood up yet."

"I appreciate the offer, but I don't want you inside that house, doll. Don't worry about me. This will all be over soon."

That's what I'm afraid of, Damon. You just don't realize it.

He slid out of the car, taking extra care with every move he made, and stood between the door and the car for a moment to steady himself. I watched him walk slowly toward the house, knowing every step sent jolts of pain through his battered body. But he'd never allow others to see that weakness. Regardless of how much the effort drained his energy, he'd maintain the image he'd worked all his life to curate.

To keep up my own appearances, I put the car into gear and pulled around the circular drive, heading through the front gate toward the main street. When he closed the front door behind him, I jerked the wheel to the side road and parked along the tall brick fence. With the car completely hidden from anyone inside the house, I jogged back to the front gate and slipped through before the panels completely closed.

The gun Damon always kept under the front seat was tucked securely in the band of my jeans. He had a bad feeling about what was happening, but he wasn't as slick as he liked to think he was. I saw him slide a pistol under his extra-large scrubs shirt while I was driving. Whatever Marco said to him, it was bad enough to knowingly risk his life over. But the ominous feeling I had was a warning that it was more than a risk—it was a certainty.

When I reached the front door, I pressed my ear against it, listening for anything inside. Voices near the door. Shouting. Feet shuffling. Guns shooting.

But there was nothing at all.

Before opening the door, I took one last look around the exterior—and that was when I realized what was off about the entire scene.

Vincenzo's car was gone.

As softly as I could, I opened the door and slipped inside, leaving it barely cracked in case I needed to make a quick exit. Standing in the foyer, I strained my ears to locate any noise that would lead me to Damon. Not hearing anything in the house, I recalled how far the basement was from the front door.

That was where I had to go—I could feel it in my gut. I withdrew the gun from my waistband and chambered a round, hoping the magazine was full and kicking myself for not checking it first. I followed the path I'd watched Damon take only hours before, until I stood in the ornate great room, staring at the spot where Leo and his men tried to beat Damon to death.

The door leading downstairs was blown off the hinges, pieces of it barely clinging to the screws. Splatters of his blood had dried on the wood floor, bringing the visions back to life in my mind again. Then I heard a muffled voice. A man's voice. With my gun ready, I began my descent down the steps, treading lightly in case the creak of wood gave away my presence.

The basement was huge—matching everything else in the enormous house. The long stairway led to a long hallway, with seven doors that were all closed. I crept through the mostly dark area with only a handful of night-lights to guide me. Stopping at each door, I pressed my ear against it and lingered only a second or two before moving on to the next one.

"Leo, you're our uncle. How could you do this to us? We're your blood!" Marco's angry voice echoed down the hall, revealing their location. "Look at Damon—you almost killed him, when either of us would've died for you."

"I can't really expect you to understand right now, Marco. You would have, though, had your brother became the boss of the family over you. If you had to take orders from him every fucking day. If you had to watch him promote his son ahead of you at every turn. Lucky for you, you'll never have to face any of that."

"How? How the fuck did you pull all this off? And right under Dad's nose."

"Haven't you figured it out yet, Marco?" Damon asked, and I felt my heart jump through my chest. "He partnered with Geno."

"What?" Marco's stunned reply matched my own reaction.

"Good job, Leo. I give credit where credit is due. You played this game to perfection. Killing Jillian's mother was a nice touch, knowing we'd place the blame squarely on Lorenzo and annihilate him because of it. Brilliant plan to eliminate all the competition along the way."

I covered my mouth with my open hand, controlling the

screams building inside my chest. More answers were coming, and I didn't want to do anything to stop their discussion. Damon wasn't finished, I could tell by the way he spoke—slow and meticulous, spelling out the plans of Leo's betrayal. Leo hadn't answered—I wanted to hear his confirmation that Damon's accusations were true.

"Not everything went according to plan," Leo began, his smugness oozing off him and filtering into my ears. "You and Jillian were supposed to die on the street—both times. Those fucking idiots couldn't hit the broad side of a building. They had every opportunity to finish the job on all occasions. Jillian was supposed to run off to save her mother, and you were supposed to chase Jillian to save her, then you'd all three die together. But you fucked that up too, so her mother had to die alone.

"But you know what they say...if you want something done right, you have to do it yourself. So, it's up to me to take you two out of the equation, and then I'll move on to Vincenzo and Lina, right after he tells me where he hid Maria."

"You had a disabled woman killed, Leo?" Marco was still in shock, trying to catch up with the conversation. I knew exactly how he felt.

"When those idiots fucked up and only injured Damon, I went to the hospital that day to prevent any suspicions. I had to play the doting uncle, after all. Geno originally issued the order, but I decided to make a move while you were laid up in the hospital. So I flew to New Orleans, drove to a little town called Abita Springs, and found one Annemarie Hart. We drove her to the outskirts of Manchac Swamp, and I shot her in the back of the head. We only kept the sitter alive to lure Jillian back home. She was going to die too, but you sent your men down instead of showing up yourself, even after I'd made sure word was sent back to Vincenzo. No matter, though. It's been a long time coming, but your time has come, Damon. Say goodbye to your brother."

I heard Leo rack the slide of his pistol.

I pictured him taking my mother into the swamp. Her wheel-chair couldn't have been easy to push through the mud and the muck, bouncing over uneven earth and sinking into the soggy ground. She most likely knew what was happening to her...she must have been scared out of her mind. Then he killed her out there—where no one would ever find any evidence to link him to her murder.

A contradiction of emotions I didn't understand overcame me —a raging storm of vengeance and a peaceful notion of closure.

Without giving my plan conscious thought, I twisted the knob and pushed the door open. Damon and Marco were each tied to their chairs, and Leo stood on their left side with his gun at the ready. Shock from my intrusion registered on all their faces, but only one of them concerned me at that moment.

Leo threw his head back, roaring with laughter. "This day literally couldn't get any better. You walked right into my hands."

"You killed my mother."

"Yes, I fucking did. Now put that fucking gun down. You don't scare me, little girl. You don't have the balls to shoot me."

"Maybe you're right, Leo. Maybe I don't have it in me to kill a man in cold blood."

His sardonic chortle was meant to be a snide sneer at me. His last hateful jab to tell me how much he disapproved of me and my weakness.

But I wasn't weak.

I vowed never to be weak again.

"But I'll never know for sure until I try."

His surprised reaction only lasted for a millisecond before my finger squeezed the trigger.

Then he wasn't laughing anymore.

The one act I thought I was incapable of committing had come so easily. Watching his lifeless body fall to the floor wasn't what shocked me. Knowing I'd just killed a man wasn't what rendered me speechless. Thinking about the repercussions of what I'd done wasn't what scared me.

I'd just killed the man who murdered my defenseless mother... and I didn't feel bad about it. At all. My mind didn't know how to process the enormous change. The significance of my actions was multifaceted. I'd have to face Vincenzo for killing his brother...I'd have to face Maria for killing her husband...I'd have to face Damon for killing his uncle. But none of that mattered because I'd avenged the best woman I'd ever known.

What frightened me was I didn't know who I was anymore.

CHAPTER TEN

Damon

or a moment after Jillian opened the door, I thought I was hallucinating. Maybe the concussion was actually a worse head injury than they realized. Maybe I had an allergic reaction to the medication. Maybe Leo had already shot me and I was dead. Because I specifically remembered telling her to leave—not to come inside the house. Then I remembered looking over my shoulder as she drove away, leaving me to finish the last of the family business I'd planned to be part of before she and I started our new life together.

The thunderous explosion of my .45 M&P firing dispelled any of those notions.

"Jilly, come over here and untie me, doll." I purposely kept my voice low and calm to draw her attention to me.

The weight of her actions hadn't sunk in yet. The blank expression on her face worried me. Was she in shock? How would she react when she realized what had happened? When that moment hit her, the last place I needed to be was tied to a fucking chair.

"How did you know, Damon?" The tone of her voice was bland. Lifeless.

"Jillian," I replied, my voice firm and commanding. Her eyes rose to meet mine, but my Jilly wasn't in there. She blinked a couple of times then seemed to come around somewhat. Her eyebrows drew downward, and the corners of her eyes crinkled in confusion. "Untie me, Jillian. Right now."

She nodded and robotically moved behind me. I heard her lay the gun on the wood floor, and she began working diligently on the knots in the rope tied around my hands.

"Jillian, grab the knife out of my back pocket and cut the rope." Marco looked over at me after he spoke to her and slowly raised his eyebrows.

The second she cut our bonds, I jumped out of the chair and gathered her into my arms. No physical pain I felt could match the pain I would've felt if Leo had shot her first. She melted into my embrace and laid her cheek against my chest. We lost ourselves in each other. Holding on *to* dear life and holding on *for* dear life became one and the same at that moment. She was my life—my reason for living, breathing, fighting, and loving.

"I killed your uncle, Damon." She didn't release me. She didn't even look up at me. She confessed to it with no emotion in her voice. "I'm sorry you lost your uncle."

"Jilly, I only care that you're not harmed. I told you to stay away from here for a reason. If you'd been hurt..." She swallowed hard, and I watched as she pulled her brave mask over her face to hide the uncertainty in her expression. She was so courageous, faking it until she made it.

"Damon, I feel the same way about you. If you thought I'd let you walk in here alone and already injured, you don't know me at all."

She was right. Deep down, I knew she'd find a way to follow me. I shouldn't have been surprised to see her standing in the doorway, though I still couldn't say I was pleased. The chances she took were too great. "I know you very well, doll."

"Then you know better than to tell me not to do something that'll help you." She gently pressed her cheek against my chest, still concerned with hurting me.

"I'll never admit to that."

When I felt her body shaking with laughter, I knew she'd be all right. Eventually. We'd have several nights of nightmares in the near future, whether she realized it or not. The mental pictures always returned, at first anyway.

"How did you know, Damon? What tipped you off that Leo and Geno were working together?"

"When Marco called, he said Leo told them that even Geno wanted Lorenzo killed to get him out of the picture. You and I knew that after the shootout at Geno's business, but Leo wasn't there when Geno's Underboss and Consigliere left Lorenzo in our hands. Leo didn't know what they'd said to us. There's only one way Leo could've known what Geno's plans were, and that's if Geno told Leo himself. And the only way he'd do that is if they were in on this scheme together."

"What happened when you got here? How did Leo get the upper hand on the two of you?"

"Fucking Geno ambushed us," Marco interjected. "Dad had already left, and I was about to leave with Leo in tow. But Geno and a couple of his guys came in just before Damon did, so they got the jump on both of us. Once Leo had control of the situation, Geno rushed out through the lower garage. I have a feeling he's on his way to Mom and Dad's house to finish what they've started. We need to move."

Jillian gave Marco the keys and told him where she'd parked my car. He rushed out ahead of us to pull the car around the front circular drive. I draped my arm around Jillian's shoulders, and we walked out together...slower. Marco was tapping the steering wheel impatiently when I opened the car door.

"Man, you need to sit this one out, Damon. You're moving like an old grandpa. Let the young studs handle the fight, and you watch from the sidelines."

"I'll show you 'old grandpa' when I kick your ass, Marco."

He laughed as he peeled out of the driveway, burning rubber in the race to stop Geno's plans. We met two teams of our men on the road headed for Leo's house.

"You already called in the cleaning crew?"

"Yep. I'm surprised they didn't already have the place cleaned in the time it took you to make it out the front door."

My brother was a smartass, spouting off with his typical digs at me. Still, there was no one I'd rather have on my side in an all-out war.

"Marco, one day when you're least suspecting it, you'll wake up to find me standing over you. You'll try to apologize for all these mean and hateful things you're saying to me right now, but your pleas will fall on deaf ears. Then I'll make your childhood nightmare come true when I throw you out of your apartment bare-ass naked and refuse to let you back in."

Marco threw his head back in laughter. "That would be a funny sight, little brother, if you could actually pull off something like that. I'm really not worried about it, though. But if it makes you feel better to dream about doing it, knock yourself out."

"I'll lock your ass out. Your naked ass. It'll be epic. That girl next door you're always panting over will finally get an up close and personal look at the disappointment she's dodged for months now."

"If you weren't already beaten to a pulp by an old, decrepit man, I'd kick your ass for that insult alone."

"Can you two finish this sibling rivalry argument later? I've had a very long and stressful day already, and I'd hate to have to remind you both who the real boss around here is."

Marco and I both chuckled, amused at how well Jillian fit into our family. She had that same air of her sweet personality from when I'd first met her, along with her Southern feistiness. But she'd also developed a definite edginess about her that wasn't there before. She was every bit as sexy and feminine, but now enhanced with a hint of danger and a splash of darkness.

"We'll settle that question later tonight. The first time you yell 'god,' I win." I murmured my reply against the shell of her ear then watched the goose bumps fan out across her arm. Every fucking time. I fucking loved physically seeing how much she wanted me.

"As much as I'd love to have that very long, drawn-out argument with you, I don't think either of us is in any shape to even think about it. I've been up over thirty hours now. As soon as my head hits the pillow, I'll be out for three days straight. Any chance we can wrap this whole family war up in the next fifteen minutes so I can get some sleep?"

"Let Geno show his face, and it won't even take that long, doll. If he runs off and hides somewhere, we don't have to find him today. His family is done and he knows it."

"In that case, I really hope he's on a flight headed for an island in the Caribbean to find a beachfront bachelor pad so you and I can go straight to bed instead of looking for him."

"If there's no sign of him at my parents' house, that's exactly what we'll do."

"When Dad sees you, he won't give you any other choice. You should've stayed in the hospital like Matteo said." Marco cut his eyes to the rearview mirror, shooting pointed looks at me as he spoke.

As my brother, he was just looking out for me, I knew that. But we both also knew why I couldn't appear weak—especially at that time. The other families were watching everything unfold and waiting to make their decision. Would they back us or the Sanfratellos? Would one of the smaller factions make a play of their own? Leo had already dealt us a deadly blow by betraying us the way he did, showing our house wasn't in order as it should've been. Division in our ranks couldn't be tolerated. A show of unity and force couldn't be delayed for even one day.

When we pulled into the driveway, I was relieved to see the gates closed and several of our best soldiers on active duty, vigilantly patrolling the yard. One glance at Marco and they waved us in. When my haggard appearance didn't shock any of them, I knew word had already spread of what had happened earlier. That was for the best, though, because they'd be even more alert and observant while they stood guard.

Inside the house, I heard the low murmur of voices coming from the kitchen. We stopped to listen briefly before entering the room. That was a habit I wasn't in any hurry to break. Knowing what I was walking in on had saved my life one too many times to ignore that instinct.

"That's Carrie," Marco whispered.

"Mama's in there too," I replied.

The three of us looked at each other, our eyes darting back and forth in surprise, when we heard the next voice.

"That was Lorenzo." Jillian walked into the kitchen ahead of Marco and me.

Just before I entered the room, I heard my father. "Carrie, you know I can't allow this. That's my final decision."

He stood to leave the table, his last words effectively ending their conversation. He took one look at me and froze in his tracks. "Damon, you look even worse than I heard. You need to rest—right now. The home health care nurse is already here and waiting for you upstairs. We gave her one of the guest bedrooms to stay in."

"Dad, there's a lot we need to discuss…there's something the three of us need to tell you."

"Damon, I know you're dedicated. But you have to take care of yourself right now. Marco can fill me in on everything while you rest. You and I will talk after you've recovered. Jillian looks dead on her feet—that's not good for her or the babies."

"Don't worry, little brother. I've got your back. Take Jillian to bed with you, or I'll be tempted to steal her away while you sleep." Marco winked at Jillian, and she giggled at his overt flirting.

"You know, I've killed men for less than that, Marco."

"You boys," Mama started. "Always picking on each other. It's good to see some things never change. Now, Damon and Jillian— off to bed, you two. Marco, you sit down in the den with your father and behave yourself."

"Yes, ma'am," Marco and I replied at the same time.

The nurse, Michelle, was waiting for me just as Dad said, but I convinced her to give me a few more minutes to bathe before she started her assessment. When I finished, Jillian jumped in the shower while Michelle thoroughly chastised me for my complete lack of self-preservation. By the time Jillian crawled into bed with me, Michelle had finished the paperwork and started a saline IV in my arm.

The medication Michelle injected into my IV hit my vein, and all the pain in my body melted away. Jillian's warm body was snuggled up to my side, her arm draped across my stomach and her cheek rested on my shoulder. My eyelids became too heavy to hold open. I vaguely remembered hearing her soft, rhythmic breathing before the deepest sleep I'd ever had pulled me under and wiped away all my cares.

Until I woke up.

Darkness had already settled in, making the bedroom pitch black with the curtains drawn. I reached for Jillian, but she wasn't there, only her cold, empty side of the bed. Concern and confusion propelled me from my slumbering position, making every muscle in my body revolt from the sudden movement. From how stiff I felt, I must have slept all day and into the night. If it was even still the same day, that was.

After I sat up on the side of the bed, I turned on the lamp and waited for my eyes to adjust to the sudden brightness. My eyes traced the IV tubing through the machine and up to the nearly full bag hanging beside my bed. Michelle must have changed it recently, and I must have slept straight through everything. After I pulled on my lounge pants, I stood, removed the bag from the pole, and made my way downstairs.

A very serious conversation was underway, so I stopped outside of the den to listen before making my presence known.

"Jillian, for the first time since I became the Boss of the Marchetti family, I don't know what I should do. Our law says Leo's betrayal couldn't go unpunished, and the only punishment we have for betrayal is death. I know this in my head. But in my heart, he's still my brother, so his death isn't an easy pill to swallow. The problem I'm facing, Jillian, is Leo had earned his place in our world. He was a made man. You understand what this term means?"

"Yes. It means he'd proven his worth and was protected by the family. He was untouchable."

"That's exactly right. A made man is only punished by another made man. As the Underboss of this family, Leo would've been punished by me and no one else. But that's not what happened, and my men may already know. How do you think that makes me look?"

"I understand your concern. But before I answer your question, I have to ask you a couple."

"Okay. Go ahead."

"Is there anything you wouldn't do for Lina?"

The pause in the conversation meant Dad was caught off guard by Jillian's question. That didn't happen with my father—except when Jillian was involved. She seemed to have that effect on the Marchetti men.

"No, there's nothing I wouldn't do for her. She is the best person I know, and I love her more every day."

"If Leo had killed Lina, would you have spared his life?"

"No. I wouldn't have thought twice about killing him. I would've watched the light leave his eyes without a single regret."

Dad usually reserved that gruff tone for the rare occasions he had to repeat himself to one of his men.

"My mother was the best person I knew, and I loved her more every day of my life. There wasn't anything I wouldn't have done for her. Leo taunted us when he described his plan to kill Damon and me. He couldn't wait to kill you and Lina to take your place. He took great pleasure in describing how he murdered my disabled mother in cold blood.

"So, I didn't think twice about killing him. I watched the light leave his eyes without a single regret for what I'd done. If I had it to do all over again, I wouldn't change a damn thing. Now I'll answer your question. If avenging my mother by killing the man who had an elaborate plan to overthrow you and kill your wife and your son means I can't be part of the family, then I think that makes *you* look weak."

"Weak? How does that make me look weak?"

"Because you're allowing lower-level men to dictate how you run your family. Because you reward tradition over loyalty. Because you don't have the courage to make your own rules when you know the archaic ones need to be changed. If you're so worried about your treacherous Underboss being killed by someone who isn't made, you can fix that by changing my status in the family. Induct me."

"Abso-fucking-lutely not." My deep voice carried through the den, startling Jillian and Dad with my abrupt intrusion. "That is not happening. We are not making her a capo."

CHAPTER ELEVEN

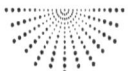

Jillian

"*I*t's time for you and the rest of the men in this family to join us in this century, Damon. Women can do more than stay home barefoot and pregnant. Haven't Carrie and I proved to you we are more than capable of contributing by now?"

"That's not what I meant, Jillian. At all. We all recognize how smart and strong-minded you are. You became part of this family even before you knew what that meant. But there are a few important decisions you and I need to talk about first, and we haven't had the time. We have some things to figure out together before you make this kind of commitment."

I weighed his words and his request against what Vincenzo and I were talking about—in a nutshell, whether I could ever truly be part of the family. Could Damon and I be together if I was never taken seriously in the family? Would I always feel uncomfortable around everyone else, knowing they thought less of me? My heart and mind agreed on the issue, but maybe Damon had other ideas I hadn't thought of yet. Then again, maybe he didn't realize what was truly at stake.

"All right, Damon. I'm willing to hear you out. But this conversation isn't over."

"For now, the conversation is over, *cara*. I've heard some of the newer families have women capos, but our family doesn't—and won't as long as I'm the Boss. None of my men want to see their women in the line of fire." Vincenzo rose, intending to have the last word.

"But their women *are* in the line of fire, whether the men want to see it or not. Look at Carrie and me, what we've been through. Do you honestly think your enemies care if we have a rank in your army? Do you think that'll stop them from killing us if our death furthers their cause? Times have changed, Vincenzo, but you haven't kept up."

He stopped in his tracks when my words sank in, making him consider possibilities he'd never entertained before. The odds were not in his favor in that equation.

Damon eased onto the couch beside me and laid his IV bag on the backrest as his dad left the room. I watched Damon try to get comfortable, but he couldn't find a suitable position. He was hurt worse than he showed the others. Probably more than he even realized while his adrenaline was freely flowing through his veins. After he'd had time to slow down then sleep, his injuries started catching up with him.

"Here, lie back." After I helped him turn, I leaned forward, pressed against him, and helped support his weight as he leaned backward. With his back against my chest, he settled between my legs, and I wrapped my arms around him. "How's that?"

"Perfect. I'm not too heavy on you and the babies, am I?"

"No, my love. Most of your weight is on my chest, not my stomach, but you're fine. Don't worry about us."

"I have no idea how long I've already slept, but I'm sure I could take another long nap right here."

"You slept for about fourteen hours, Damon. I'd say your body needed the downtime to start repairing itself. You should've stayed in the hospital."

"Maybe you're right. Or maybe I just needed you in the bed with me to feel better. For the record, I'll always vote for the latter."

"What did you want to talk about? I don't like cliffhangers, so let's hear it now."

Perfect timing, as usual, Mama Lina came rushing into the room.

"Damon, I know this isn't the best time, but you've been asleep all day, so I haven't had a chance to talk to you." Mama Lina patted his cheek.

"Now's fine, Mama. What's on your mind?"

"Jillian and I made funeral arrangements for Benny. Visitation is tomorrow afternoon, and his funeral is the next day. Maybe I should ask to postpone it a day or two until you're better."

"No, don't do that. I'm well enough to sit in the funeral home for a few hours. Thank you both for doing that for Benny."

"Of course. He was part of our family. It's getting late, so Vin and I are going to bed now. But you two need to eat all of this food now."

She put a tray with two plates piled with enough food for the whole family, two tall glasses, and a pitcher of iced tea on the coffee table beside us.

"My kids need to eat. You haven't eaten all day because you've been asleep the whole time. I made your plates, but there's plenty more where that came from if this isn't enough. Now, eat, eat!"

Funny thing, I didn't even realize I was hungry until the delicious aromas hit me, causing me to salivate uncontrollably. Pavlovian conditioning at its best—Italian-food style.

Damon's low grumble vibrated through his chest, groaning because he'd only settled against me moments before. Plates of heaping mounds of food meant he had to move again for both of us to eat. He started to sit up, but I tightened my grip on him and held him in place instead.

"Wait. I have an idea," I said to Damon. "Mama Lina, give me one of the plates and leave the other one on the coffee table. I'll feed us both off one plate at a time so Damon doesn't have to get up again."

A small smile played on her lips. Her expression, combined with the way she stole glances at our intimate but comfortable embrace, wordlessly conveyed how pleased she was with my idea.

"Good night, kids."

"Good night, Mama," we replied at the same time.

She started to leave but stopped to watch our joint feeding plan in action. With the plate in Damon's good hand and the fork in mine, I cut a hefty helping of stuffed shells with marinara sauce and offered the first bite to Damon. Only...I was behind him, leaning around his side to find his mouth...and I missed.

When I saw the long red streak of marinara sauce across his cheek, I started laughing and couldn't stop. The harder I tried to hide it, the funnier it became, until we were both shaking because of my giggles. Mama Lina drew her lips between her teeth, trying to control her mirth while I took the plate from his hand and she passed Damon a napkin.

His exaggerated wipes along his cheek while trying to clean off his face only made my laughter worse. His whole body was relaxed, not a single tensed muscle, as he tried to clean off the sauce that only smeared across his skin. My imagination ran wild as I pictured his expression while he also tried to hide his laughter.

"You did that on purpose." His tone was calm and casual, but I didn't miss the hint of playfulness. Or that he waited for his mom to leave the room first.

"No, I didn't, Damon." He probably couldn't even understand my broken words spoken through my continued fit of laughter.

"You'd deny it either way, doll. You're not fooling me. So just remember this moment and how you took advantage of me in my weakened condition. Remember how you laughed and picked on me when I'm virtually helpless and starving. I only have one good hand. I look like I went head-to-head with Iron Man. Not to mention, I still have an IV stuck in my arm. But that's all right, you go right ahead and have your fun."

I couldn't stop laughing throughout his entire mock tirade. Even though it was an accident, I wouldn't have changed it for anything. We needed a reminder that we'd laugh and be carefree again. That we had more to look forward to than a lifetime of fighting the world and seeing our loved ones die.

That we could choose to be normal, or at least, our version of it.

"Here, open your mouth and take this bite of food before it gets cold. You can't falsely accuse me anymore if your mouth is full." I successfully found his mouth that time.

"I can still talk." He made a point to prove me wrong, even if his words were muffled. "And, for the record, it's still warm. Had I gotten to eat it instead of having it smeared across my face, it would've been hot instead of warm. You gave me a hot marinara sauce facial."

"I'm cutting off a bigger bite for you next time. Big, hot, and delicious. Stuffing it right in your mouth." I sliced through the shell, making sure to coat my piece with extra sauce, and brought the fork to my mouth.

"I've got something big, hot, and delicious I'd like to stuff in your mouth right now."

A huge drop of sauce slid down the shell...and onto Damon's bare shoulder. I couldn't do anything but watch it happen in slow motion. With the plate in one hand and a fork in the other, there was no way for me to catch it midair. Damon's yelp of pain when the hot sauce landed on his shoulder probably should've made me feel bad for not being more careful.

But I burst out laughing again instead.

"Talk about adding insult to injury." He shook his head. "Want to grab some salt and just pour it directly into my wounds next?"

"You're such a baby." I lowered my mouth to his shoulder and licked the sauce off his skin. Taking my time, I lapped up every trace of it, noting the change in his breathing, the tensing of his muscles, and the low growl from his throat. "I licked it all up. It tastes too good to waste a single drop."

"Now I know you're trying to kill me. Count your blessings I'm not able to spank your ass right now."

"You never told me you were into that. Have you been holding out on me, Marchetti? I feel so betrayed right now. Maybe I should talk to Marco about this…get his opinion."

He turned his head to the side enough for me to see his arched eyebrow and the warning in his eyes. When he opened his mouth to counter, I quickly pushed another bite of food between his lips. He chuckled, knowing I was only teasing him, and I couldn't stop myself from leaning in to place a soft kiss on his cheek. Getting lost in him was so easy—too easy. He didn't know, but just being by his side helped me focus on the wonderful things in our life and forget about the terrible things. Or, at least, push them out of my mind for longer stretches of time.

He was a ruthless killer; I knew that. I justified his actions by separating the man from the job, since his targets weren't innocent bystanders by any means. But the lethal mafia capo was so far removed from the playful, affectionate man I loved, that most of the time I had a hard time seeing him as both. The man who I knew showered me with all his love, made me feel protected, desired, and fearless.

To my surprise, we finished every bite on both plates while talking, sharing memories, and laughing together. He held the plate in his good hand while I fed us. After he put the second empty plate on the coffee table, he slowly pushed himself up to a sitting position.

"Are you ready to go back to bed with me?"

"That depends. Are you going to be good in bed?"

"You and I both know I'm *always* good in bed."

"Let me rephrase that. Are you going to *behave*?"

"I have no plans to behave anywhere, least of all in bed with you."

"Marchetti, you are incorrigible."

"Take me upstairs, and I'll let you attempt to fix that. For you, maybe I'm corrigible and can be fully redeemed."

"I'm almost positive you're beyond the point of redemption by now, but I'm happy to give it my best shot."

He waggled his eyebrows, his gaze instantly changing to that sexy but lethal stare that slayed me every time. The hooded eyes. The unintentional swipe of his tongue across his lips when he looked at me, like I was his next meal he couldn't wait to taste.

My intention, however, was to have him for dessert.

WHEN WE WOKE THE NEXT MORNING, I FELT MORE RESTED THAN I had in months. Damon did too, because he called the nurse into the bedroom almost immediately to remove his IV. She protested at first but ultimately gave in to his demands. His main argument was directly related to Benny's funeral. Damon refused to carry a saline bag around in front of his men and anyone else who could be watching. Sickness was a sign of weakness, a trait that wasn't in his DNA, and he wouldn't allow anyone to question it. He compromised by agreeing to drink extra water throughout the day and stay off his feet as much as possible.

After I showered, fixed my hair, and applied a little makeup, I walked into the bedroom to find Damon. He stood in front of the full-length mirror, attempting to button his shirt with one hand in a cast. I stepped between him and the mirror and took over dressing him. Within a couple of minutes, I applied the finishing touches to his custom-fitted gray pinstripe Armani suit. The pink shirt and matching tie he chose only added to the suit's overall elegance—and to my libido. Merely the sight of him, dressed to kill with that inherently dangerous edge to his demeanor, made me weak in the knees, even with a bruised and battered face.

"You keep looking at me like that, doll, and we won't leave this room for a week."

"It's your fault. Look at that sexy man in the mirror. How can I look away?"

"You do wonders for my ego, doll. Keep talking."

I slipped my arms under his and around his waist, being extra careful with his still fresh injuries. "I'll stroke your ego anytime, babe. It'll be my pleasure."

"Block your calendar for two weeks. You'll be locked in the bedroom with me the whole time as soon as I'm back to one hundred percent."

He pressed his lips against mine, his kiss full of need and desire. There was no gentle swipe of the tongue. No waiting for permission to enter. He claimed my mouth as his. He invaded me in every sense of the word—mind, body, and soul. The kiss was both the most simplistic and most intimate I'd ever known. I felt the words he didn't say in his embrace. Love. Gratitude. Desire. Devotion.

"Wow, what did I do to deserve that kiss? I'll make sure I do it again."

"You deserve much more than that. I love you more than you know."

Before I could press him for more information, Vincenzo stepped into the room. "It's time to go. Are you two ready?"

"Yeah, we're ready, Dad. We'll be right behind you."

We walked hand in hand to the garage and slid into the back seat to ride with Damon's parents to the funeral home. The somber mood permeated the car and kept conversation to a minimum. That was fine with me, though. Damon pulled me to his side, wrapped his good arm around my shoulders, and kept his lips pressed against my temple.

The parking lot was already full of cars when we arrived, but the parking spot closest to the entrance was left vacant. When Vincenzo drove straight to it, I realized *the family* took care of even the smallest details for the Boss. Like saving the best parking spot for him.

The moment we stepped inside, the low roar of chatter stopped, and silence filled the room. The Boss had arrived, and everyone was well aware of his presence. After Vincenzo greeted a few of the men, everyone else took their cue and resumed conversations. Damon and I kept walking through the crowd. Several people spoke to him when we passed, but Damon didn't stop to engage with anyone.

The respect they had for Damon was apparent in their expressions, but I couldn't miss the way most of the family men sneered at me. Word that I shot Leo must have started working its way through the ranks. If they suspected the rumors were true, I wondered how long we had before they looked differently at Damon.

True to his word, Damon led us to a set of chairs close to the open coffin. People walked by and said their final goodbyes, and Damon kept his hand wrapped around mine the entire time. Blatant stares at our joined fingers became more uncomfortable for me, but Damon's resolve was unchanged. When a new wave of murmurs flowed through the room, I looked up just in time to see the crowd parting to give Carrie a clear path. A smile lit her face when she spotted me.

Vincenzo approached us on the other side of Damon. "Son, come sit with me for a few minutes, yes?"

"Sure, Dad." Damon turned to me. "I'll be back in a few minutes, doll."

"I'll keep her company." Carrie took his vacated seat and hugged me hello. "How's my preggie sister?"

"I'm okay. It feels like forever since we've talked, even though it's only been a couple of days. A couple of very long days. How are you holding up? What's going on with you?"

"I'm holding up okay, physically. Mentally, I'm trying to deal with everything that's happened. As for what's going on with my personal life—it's complicated. I'll tell you all about it when there aren't so many snooping ears eavesdropping on our conversation."

Carrie turned her head and looked directly at the man who was standing unusually close to us. With his motive exposed, he tried to move away nonchalantly, but his curiosity got the best of him. His gaze dropped to us briefly before he walked away.

"What's the deal? They've been giving me dirty looks too."

"They think we let Geno escape on purpose. They think I did it for Lorenzo, and you did it for me. These men are worse gossips than little old women, making up shit as they go."

I checked around us for anyone standing too close for comfort before asking about what had been on my mind. "So they don't know about what I did?"

"No. There were questions and speculations, but Marco squelched it quickly. He told them he did it, and if they had a problem with it, they could take it up with him personally. No one has been too keen on tangling with Marco."

Carrie and I chatted for a while longer, limiting our topics to only those we didn't mind the rest of the family overhearing. Every few minutes, I caught myself searching the room for Damon. He was in the far corner of the parlor, huddled around a table with a group of older men. His expression was impassive, his classic poker face when he was in business mode, but something was off in his body language. I couldn't put my finger on it, but I could tell he wasn't pleased with the conversation.

"Who are those men with Damon?" I shifted my eyes in their general direction but kept my face turned toward Carrie.

"That's the Marchetti Family Council. They're probably

talking about the chain of command with Leo's death, Dad's upcoming retirement, and Damon's imminent promotion. Or they could be plotting to take over the world. Either topic is just as likely as the other."

When Damon stood from the table, he walked straight back to Carrie and me. One of his men moved quickly to place another chair beside me then he stepped back, giving Damon a wide berth to claim the seat. Damon nodded at him as a thank-you but didn't speak. I recognized him as one of the two men from my fender bender with the dump truck that started me on this whole crazy journey.

Damon was unusually quiet the rest of the time we remained at the funeral home. He answered when spoken to, but with as few words as possible. He was cordial but aloof. He didn't make anyone feel as if they were intruding, but he wasn't warm and welcoming either. He was part of the family, but he was all business. Damon Marchetti was an enigma I still hadn't figured out completely.

We walked out of the funeral home with Carrie at the end of the evening. "I'll call you soon, and we'll go grab some coffee together. I'll fill you in on all the drama in my life."

"Sounds like a date to me. Just tell me when and where, and I'll be there." We said our goodbyes while hugging each other. I still felt eyes boring into us from every direction. Seeing us together probably started the rumor mill up again.

Vincenzo and Lina carried the majority of the conversation on the way back to their house. Damon and I chimed in when it was appropriate, but they mostly talked about wanting to return to Italy to see family and old friends who remained there. They wanted to stroll through the small village where they grew up and observe what changes the years had brought. Listening to them talk about doing the same things normal families would want was comforting, especially after the emotionally draining hours we spent listening to others recount memories of Benny.

He died while trying to save me. I supposed that also had something to do with the side glances from the family. Had I not gone to confront Lorenzo, I wouldn't have needed saving, and Benny would still be with them. That felt like a debt I could never repay.

"Do you want to have a nightcap with me before going to bed?" Vincenzo asked Damon when we walked into the house.

One side of Damon's mouth lifted in a half smile, but his eyes remained unaffected. "Better not. My nurse is waiting to shoot me up with pain medicine. I doubt she'd approve of mixing it with alcohol."

"You're absolutely correct. She would not approve at all." Michelle appeared out of nowhere from behind us, stealthy as a ninja. "No mixing pain meds and alcohol, unless you don't appreciate breathing on your own anymore."

"I guess that's settled, then." Damon pulled me with him toward the stairs. "We'll get ready for bed. Michelle, you can come up in a few minutes and knock me out."

"Just open your door when you're ready for me. There's no rush." Michelle smiled good-naturedly before returning to her temporary guest bedroom upstairs.

Inside our bedroom, I helped Damon remove his jacket and shirt, maneuvering the sleeve over his cast. "How did you manage to get this shirt on without me in the first place?"

He shrugged one shoulder in answer to my question. "I just shoved it through. Didn't care if it ripped the shirt or not."

Then I unbuttoned his pants, and he pushed them the rest of the way off. I didn't want to pressure him in his current state, but not being able to run my tongue over every inch of his muscular physique while he wore nothing but his boxer briefs was cruel and unusual punishment. Not that he would've stopped me, but after I'd insisted on pleasuring him the night before, there was no way he'd sit on the sidelines for a second time.

"What's going on up here?" I lightly tapped his head with my finger. He grabbed my hand and pressed my palm against his cheek. The warmth from his skin flowed through me, relaxing and exciting me at the same time.

"We make a pretty good team, don't we?" His voice was unusually soft, yet his expression was sincere.

"I think we do. We complement and balance each other well."

"For as long as I can remember, Mama has pushed all of us to get married and have kids. I'm convinced her only goal in life is to be a grandmother. When I was young, I'd daydream about what my life as an adult would be like. I'd placate Mama when she threw strong hints my way, telling her it would happen someday. Even though I knew nothing would make her happier, I couldn't see myself as a husband or a father.

"I couldn't stand the thought of settling down. I wanted freedom and adventure. Fortune and fame. For my name to make people tremble with fear. I worked hard to get where I'm at in the family. My men worked hard for me because I earned their respect. I'm even in line ahead of my older brother to be the next Boss. I've achieved everything I set out to do—and more. But now..."

Damon stopped speaking for several seconds while he stared at my slightly protruding stomach. Then he placed his hand over my baby bump. His Adam's apple bobbed up and down, the muscles in his throat tightening as he swallowed.

"And now?" I asked, prompting him to finish his thought.

"Now, reality has slapped me across the face. If I don't have you, I have nothing at all. Everything I've worked for and accomplished means nothing if you're not by my side. I would walk away from it all as long as you walked with me."

I was stunned speechless. So many questions raced through my mind, but I wasn't sure which one to ask first. The man had a habit of thoroughly shocking me—either with his brutality or his thoughtfulness. One extreme to the other, but never down the middle of the road.

"Damon…"

"This is part of why I interrupted your little talk with my dad earlier. When I heard you volunteering to be our first female capo, I nearly had a stroke. I realized, right at that moment, my heart already knew what I wanted. My mind just had to catch up and accept the truth."

"What do you want?"

"A safe home for our kids. A happy life with my wife. You know, I realized I've had a lot of 'firsts' with you. First time I got shot. First woman to hear me utter the words 'I love you.' First time I went against my dad's decree. First woman to carry my baby. And now, I'm about to admit something I've never felt or even thought about before meeting you."

He stroked my cheek with his knuckles while piercing me with the intensity of his eyes. When he stared at me like that, I had the distinct impression he was peering into my soul.

"Tell me."

"I've never needed anyone before. I've stood on my own two feet as long as I can remember. My men carry out my orders, but if one fails me, another is always waiting in the wings to take his place. Maybe I'd be mildly inconvenienced without most people in my life, but not you.

"Need isn't a strong enough word for how I feel about you. When I said I couldn't handle it if anything happened to you, I wasn't exaggerating. I need you more than my next breath. More than I need food or water to sustain me. The reason I get up in the morning and continue to wade through all the bullshit that's happened over the last few days is because I have to protect you. There's only one thing I can't live without, and that's you. Without you, I wouldn't have a reason to live."

"I'm not going anywhere, Damon. Why are you telling me this? Why do you think you'll have to live without me?"

CHAPTER TWELVE

Damon

"*D*eath is an inherent part of the business. There's no way around that, doll. I've known it my entire life, but I was never concerned about it before. Our love gives me strength, makes me feel invincible at times. Other times, it's the source of my greatest weakness and my worst fears."

I placed my hand on her slightly swollen belly, still amazed over the new life growing inside her. We stood there for several minutes, both of us staring at her stomach, but in my mind's eye, I saw our future. Before I could voice what I knew was coming at us next, I felt movement under her skin.

My eyes flew up to meet hers, my jaw slack and my heart racing. She covered my hand with hers and moved it toward the opposite side, and I felt it again. A beautiful, beaming smile covered her face before she released a giggle, amused over my reaction.

"Yes, that is our babies doing somersaults you feel. They're very active. Makes me wonder what you and I are in store for after they're born."

I dropped to my knees in front of her and pushed up her dress. Then I wrapped my arms around her and pressed my lips to her smooth skin. One taste wasn't enough. I'd never get enough of her.

"Take your dress off, doll."

"Damon, you're still injured, and your nurse is waiting to come in."

"She can wait longer, and I don't care about my injuries. I'd have to be dead not to want you. Take. It. Off."

She pulled her dress over her head and let it fall to the floor behind us. I slid my thumbs under her silky panties and dragged them down her legs. When I reached her ankles, I saw her bra land on top of her dress. I looked up at her perfect body from my kneeling position and couldn't wait another second to have her.

"Lie down on the bed."

Jillian sat on the edge and slid backward until she was in the center of the bed. I followed closely behind her, crawling up her legs until I reached the sweet spot. The rise and fall of her chest increased with each passing second, her anticipation building inside her along with her arousal. I planned to satisfy every single one of her carnal needs, even if it took all night. Especially if it took all night.

Slow and tame was never my preference, but thorough and meticulous had an enticing ring to it. I devoured every sound of ecstasy that escaped from Jillian's throat, her passion further fueling my desire while I greedily consumed her body. She writhed under the flick of my tongue, her back arching and her nails clawing the sheets as she reached the climax. When she first cried out, succumbing to the mounting intensity inside her, I slid my fingers into her warmth. The added sensation drove her further over the edge, leaving her body trembling and shuddering under my touch.

"Fuck, Jillian. I could watch you do that all fucking night long. In fact, that's the best idea I've had in a long time."

Even with one hand in a cast, I shed my briefs in record time and settled between her legs. I lowered my head to capture her mouth with mine, our tongues sensually gliding and tangling. Then I curled my hips forward, sliding inside her at an intentionally slow pace. The sharp pangs from my injured ribs dissolved into thin air the instant her body wrapped around mine. Pure fucking ecstasy was all I felt at that moment.

"You're exactly what I've needed. Fuck the medicine—you're the only painkiller I want from now on." I pulled her head to one side and slid my tongue down the erogenous column of her neck. Her inner walls gripped me tightly, and her heels pushed against me, urging me on.

The friction from my skin gliding across hers heated our bodies, causing beads of sweat to cover us. The moisture only heightened my senses, making my movements easier and faster. The thought crossed my mind that I'd pay for such vigorous exercise the following day, but the pure hedonistic bliss of having my cock buried deep inside her was more than worth any price it cost me.

Every wave brought us both closer to the edge, though I fought against mine to delay the inevitable as long as possible. I felt her climax building with each thrust, with me delving inside her over and over as far as she could take me. Soft moans and wanton sighs filled the room rather than the cries of pleasure she held at bay. Her velvety soft inner walls began to quiver, gripping and stroking me as if her hand was wrapped around me. She was on the verge, ready to crumble to pieces at any moment.

"Open your eyes, doll."

Her lids fluttered open and her ecstasy-laden eyes peered up at me, so much love in them that I could see and feel it without her saying a word.

"Now keep them on me. I fucking love watching you come."

She slightly lifted her hips to meet me each time I pushed into her. With my increased tempo and harder thrusts, she lingered on the cusp of her orgasm. Her fingernails digging into my skin only made me work harder. My eyes were locked on to hers, an invisible tether keeping either of us from looking away. Emotions swirled deep in her emerald green eyes, pulling me even more into her with every tick of the clock.

"Let go, doll. Scream as loud as you want. You know how much I love that fucking mouth of yours anyway."

Her entire body tensed at once for a split second when she reached the summit. The sexiest scream broke free from her lips as her body soaked me with warm gushes. The pure satisfaction in her eyes coupled with the constricting muscles around my cock made it impossible for me to hold out any longer. So I stopped resisting the urge and fell over the edge with her.

Stroking her cheek with my thumb, I kept my gaze fixed on hers. Sharing my deep feelings ran counter to my normal interactions, but there was something important I had to convey to her.

"Jilly, this isn't easy for me to say. I've never been big on explaining my feelings, so you'll have to cut me some slack. But it's important that I say this to you. It means a lot to me."

"Damon, you know you can tell me anything."

"You're a part of me now, one I can't and won't live without. Without you, any hope of me being a good man would be gone. You're the single light of my life, doll. I won't go back into the life of total darkness I lived in before I found you. I love you more than anything."

Tears welled up in her eyes before sliding out of the corners and down her temples, disappearing into her hairline. Tears of joy. Tears of love. I saw both emotions glistening in her watery eyes.

I gingerly rolled off of her, careful not to put my weight on her and the babies. I lay in bed beside her, stroking her bare skin with my fingertips while we talked.

"I love you too, Damon. More than anything in the world. You won't lose me—not now, not ever. I'll never leave you. Being without you those three months showed me there's no way I can be happy any other way than at your side. Now tell me what you're worried about. This isn't like you."

"It's not, is it? What was it you called me before? Oh, yeah. A cocky devil. I'm still all that and then some, but the stakes are higher than I'm willing to gamble against now. You were right when you said we needed to join the rest of the world in the current century, but maybe not in the ways you meant. As younger generations gain more leadership positions, they change the rules to fit what they want. The older Bosses expect everyone to follow the original laws, so they're more easily caught off guard when new rules are created. What Leo and Geno did was unheard of when they were our age.

"A Boss's wife has been known to run the entire family when her husband was in prison, but he picked right back up when he got out. Some families have had female capos, that's true. But those women were also the first to be taken out. Your own men are even more likely to turn on you. I love you, but I'll never agree to making you a capo. Sexist or not, no man in the family business wants a woman over him. When a rival family member uses that to taunt a made man, an all-out war is inevitable."

She was silent longer than usual. That wasn't the news she wanted to hear, I understood that. But there was so much she didn't understand. She was kind, thoughtful, and giving. She genuinely cared about others. Not quite the hallmarks of a cold-blooded killer. But a killer was exactly what she'd have to become to fit into that role.

"It sounds like you don't think I'm capable of doing whatever needed to be done. Even though Marco is taking the credit—or the blame, depending on how you look at it—for killing your uncle."

"When you shot Leo, that was different. In the heat of the moment and under extreme circumstances, you snapped. You had an especially personal reason for pulling the trigger. That act wouldn't come so easily if I ordered you to carry out a hit on a guy for not paying his weekly cut on time. Could you walk into his place of business, see the pictures of his wife and kids on his desk, and still pull the trigger when he didn't hand over fifty percent of his earnings on the spot?"

She didn't answer, but she didn't have to. "The horrified expression on your face tells me all I need to know, doll. You can't hesitate. You can't show weakness, because that flaw is the first one weeded out of the family. We're only as strong as our weakest link. That saying is old but true."

"Are you suggesting I just stay home and mind the kids? Take care of my man's every need and forget about my own? No job, no contributions to the family, no goals or aspirations to call my own?"

"Just the opposite, actually. I was thinking you could make all the money and I could stop shaking down the neighborhood businesses. That would go a long way in getting them on our side. We've ruled by fear for so long. Maybe it's time we change things up and get the jump on the other families."

"You just said I couldn't be a capo, and there's no way I can just walk into a building and kill someone who hasn't done anything to me. So, exactly how am I going to earn all the money?"

"We could create another segment of the family. We have capos, soldiers, associates, goons—all the muscle we need whenever we need to flex it. So, maybe I should pull Carrie's business into the family and create a new role for the two of you. That way, we could keep it secret and keep you both protected."

"Will you promise, on your family honor, not to keep secrets from me? Not to keep me in the dark about anything?"

"I will, but you have to do the same. No more approaching my father or anyone else with this kind of an idea before we've talked about it. No more setting up covert operations to take down a rival family member in the middle of the night."

"Hmm. You know, when you put it that way, you make me

sound very guilty of doing to you exactly what I've accused you of doing to me."

"Funny how it works out that way, isn't it?"

"Wait. How do you know about Carrie's business? I didn't think she'd told anyone about it."

"It was best to let her believe I didn't know what she'd been up to. Made it easier to protect her that way. She does the opposite of what anyone tells her to do. If I'd tried to strong-arm her, she would've done something really stupid and gotten herself killed."

"And you think she's changed?" Jillian laughed at the absurdity of her question.

"No, she hasn't exactly changed, but she does have a new perspective now. After everything that's happened with Lorenzo, Leo, and Geno, she realizes she's not invincible like she used to think. She wanted to prove she could run part of the family business on her own, and she's accomplished that. I believe she'll be ready to join us now."

"And if she isn't?" Jillian searched my eyes, already knowing what my answer would be.

"Then I'll shut her shit down and take it over the old-fashioned way. I won't be asking for her permission, Jillian. I'll tell her what her options are and let her choose which one she takes. Option A is she brings her schemes into the family, continues to run the operations, and expands the reach under our protection. Option B is she refuses to join us, and then I take it from her anyway and completely shut her out of all current and future operations. There is no Option C in this equation, though."

"Damon...you'd do that to your own sister?"

"Absolutely. And don't you dare think for one second that she wouldn't do it to me or you if the need arose. This is a dog-eat-dog world, doll, and we are the big dogs. And we're going to remain the big dogs one way or another, because I won't allow another family to move in and take mine away from me."

"Wow. Okay. I have to admit, you're right. I'm not cut out for this...to carry out the hard decisions you have to make. I have some experience with accounting systems, though. That secret, behind-the-scenes job you mentioned sounds great to me. I can even do that work from home."

"Perfect. I'd love to come home to eat lunch every day. Maybe we'll even have time for actual food now and then."

CHAPTER THIRTEEN

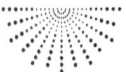

Jillian

"*I*t's too soon for you to go back to work, Damon."

"I'm fine, doll. I've had two weeks of nothing but rest since Benny's funeral. I love my parents, but I'm ready to get back to my place. But this time, you're not staying with my sister instead of me."

"Are you sure about that?" I couldn't help but tease him. With his cocky attitude, he deserved it.

His chocolate brown eyes slowly lifted to meet mine. The mischievous gleam I saw was both a warning and a dare. "I'm fucking positive about it. You want to see how much of my energy I have back? I'll show you...when I tie you to my bed and keep you there all to myself."

"Have I ever told you how sexy you are when you turn full-tilt alpha on me? It's so hot."

"Fuck. We'll never get out of their house if you don't quit talking to me like that. I can't even finish packing my clothes."

"You get Luigi to take our suitcases downstairs, and I'll finish packing for you. But for the record, you didn't just rest for two weeks. You worked the entire time, setting up the arrangement with your sister and searching for Geno. You haven't fooled me one bit, Mr. Marchetti."

The smile he flashed me was the same one that reeled me back in, every time. The charm of a little boy combined with the confidence of a gorgeous man. As usual, I was complete putty in his hands.

"If you don't mind putting the rest of my clothes in here, I'll go find Luigi. You'll be faster at it with two good hands anyway."

"I don't mind at all. It'll only take a minute."

Within minutes of Damon going downstairs, I had the rest of his clothes packed and both of our small suitcases sitting by the door. Carrie had brought items for both Damon and me from his apartment since her overprotective brother thought it was too dangerous for me to go alone. But I understood I could be collateral damage in Geno's lone war, or he could even use me against Damon, so I didn't press the issue. Carrie traveled with an entourage of armed muscle who were more than ready for an encounter.

But there hadn't been a sighting or rumor of Geno since that terrible day more than two weeks ago.

Speaking of that day, the nightmares had started almost right away and hadn't slowed down. I didn't want to change my actions, but I wasn't sure how to live with them either. I fought off panic attacks in the dark, scared that I'd be found out and arrested. I'd wake up and reach for Damon, clinging to him until the fears subsided. I'd started to dread falling asleep.

"You all right, doll?" Damon stood in the doorway watching me.

"I'm okay."

He narrowed his eyes, his keen instincts seeing right through me. "You were lost deep in thought. You left me. Where'd you go?"

"We both know I'll never leave you, Damon. I'm right here with you. Are we ready to leave?"

He nodded. "I'm ready to go if you are."

"Let's say goodbye to your parents. Your mom will probably be upset. I think she has enjoyed having you back home again."

"She'll be okay. It's not like we'll be far away. We'll still be here every Sunday for dinner. But I'll enjoy having you all to myself again."

"You'll be gone most of the time. It's more like I'll have me all to myself."

I should've kept my mouth shut because my knee-jerk response only raised his suspicions even more. His assessing stare intensified, and I felt my skin heating under the weight of his scrutiny. He had an uncanny ability to read my thoughts and feelings, sometimes before I'd even worked out what they meant. But being out of commission the past couple of weeks had only given him more time to perfect his skills, regardless of how hard I tried to deflect.

"Is there anything left for Luigi to put in the trunk?" Damon's question was innocent enough, but I knew better than to think he wouldn't press the issue later.

"No, we're all set."

In the back seat on the way to Damon's apartment in the city after saying our goodbyes, Damon and I were both quiet. Once we arrived at his place, he wrapped his hand around my arm and turned me to face him directly. The empathy and perception in his eyes were palpable, instantly reassuring me that I could trust him.

"When are you going to let me help you, doll?"

"Help me with what?"

"With all those bad dreams and restless nights. With the anxiety you try to fight off alone instead of talking to me about it."

"You've always been able to see straight through me. It's a little maddening sometimes." I slid my fingertips along his jaw.

"What's going on in that beautiful head of yours? Let me help."

"Damon, just the thought of being found out and going to prison nearly steals my breath away. Maria has to know by now. She has to wonder where he is. She'll eventually go to the police and file a missing person's report."

"First, going to prison isn't even a remote possibility for you. You'll never take the rap for Leo's death. If he somehow rose from the grave and fingered you for his death, I'd give a full confession and do the time before I'd let you serve one day. Second, he'll never be found, and arrangements have been made to explain his absence. Aunt Maria will be taken care of for the rest of her life, and she knows better than to go to the police. She knows what he did and the penalty he faced. Lastly, no matter what we come up against in the future, I'll be here to protect you."

"The other problem is I don't know how to deal with these feelings. It's not that I want to change it, but I don't know how to live with myself either."

"You saved my life, Jillian, and you saved Marco's life. You found the courage to stand up for your mom, and you saved two lives because of it. How do you live with yourself after that? With pride, knowing when most anyone else would've frozen in place, you had the guts to do what had to be done. When you look in the mirror, the reflection shows a beautiful, brave woman. I wouldn't even be here right now if it weren't for her. That's how you live with it, knowing the alternative would've been harder to accept."

After a heavy sigh to release all the tension I'd carried for far too long, I stepped into his embrace and wrapped my arms around his waist. "You put everything into perspective for me just now. With a simple explanation. Only a few words. But I already feel better and can breathe easier. Thank you, Damon. I know none of this has been easy for you, either, but you've taken such good care of me."

"I always will, doll." He leaned down and kissed me, soft and sweet but not lacking in the sweep-me-off-my-feet factor.

Since I moved from Louisiana to Carrie's to Mama Lina's to Damon's, everything I owned was in complete disarray. After a long day of unpacking all my belongings, I was more than ready to fall into the bed and stay for a week by the time night fell. Damon climbed into bed behind me, draped his arm over my waist, and nuzzled against the back of my neck.

Then his hand slid down to my stomach and protectively cradled our babies in his palm. I covered his hand with mine and guided it to the spot where one of them was extra active. "Before long, they'll both be using my bladder as a trampoline."

He chuckled, his lips brushing against the nape of my neck. "You have no idea how fucking sexy this is—your being pregnant with my babies. Your baby bump is still small, but I can't wait for that to change. I've done some reading up on it. They say one day, no one can really tell you're pregnant, but the next day you'll show all of a sudden."

"Every woman is different, Damon. Just because that happened to one doesn't mean it'll happen to me too."

"Twins, doll. Very good possibility of it. Could be tomorrow. Could be next week. Or even next month. But it'll happen."

"Remember when I said you take such good care of me?"

"Sure do."

"I take it back."

The silence only lasted for a couple of seconds before I burst out laughing uncontrollably.

"I'll have to think of creative and imaginative punishments as payback for that slight against me." Even the teasing tone in his voice was sexy.

"Think about them tomorrow. I need sleep tonight."

He pressed his front against my back, and we fell asleep, our arms and legs entwined and hands covering our babies. For the first time in two weeks, the nightmares didn't come when I closed my eyes. Memories didn't flood my senses. I slept soundly in Damon's arms without waking even once until morning.

When I rolled over, Damon's side of the bed was empty and cold. I padded into the bathroom but didn't find him, the scent of his cologne barely lingering in the air. He'd already showered and dressed, so I followed his lead before venturing toward the kitchen. I found him at the table, fully dressed in his suit and tie, drinking a cup of coffee while reading the newspaper. He looked like the quintessential tame businessman, only he was anything and everything except that.

"Good morning, beautiful. I was wondering when you'd finally get out of bed. The thought of waking you up with a special surprise crossed my mind more than a couple of times." He lifted his eyes over his coffee cup and winked. "But since you hadn't slept all night in weeks, I behaved and let you rest instead."

"I'll let you make up for depriving me later tonight."

"It'll be my pleasure." He lowered the cup to the table, keeping his eyes trained on mine. "And it'll definitely be *your* pleasure."

His innate confidence was an automatic aphrodisiac, but those bedroom eyes coupled with the seductive timbre of his deep voice were the real lady-killer. Not that I was complaining.

"Why are you all spiffy today?" I walked toward the coffee carafe, but he beat me to it and poured a cup for me.

"I've been out of commission far too long. I have a few loose ends to wrap up today before we're ready to go full throttle with Carrie. Not that I don't love my mom's cooking, but I'm ready to go out to eat at a nice restaurant. How does a seven o'clock reservation at The Fire sound?"

"That place has a yearlong waiting list, Damon. How can you get reservations for tonight?"

"You wound me, Jillian. How can you have so little faith in me?" He slowly lifted one eyebrow, waiting for my reply.

"How silly of me. I should've known better than to ask. That sounds perfect. I can't wait."

"What do you have planned today while I'm gone?"

"I plan to wander around your enormous apartment, snooping

through all your things, claiming one of the rooms as my personal office space, and some light online shopping for the babies."

The smirk in response was just as sexy as his full-on smile. "Snoop all you want. What's mine is yours. I'll leave my credit card so you can buy all you want for the babies. If you decide to go out shopping somewhere, call Luigi so he can drive you. I don't want you going out alone yet."

I took the business card from Damon with Luigi's contact information. "All right. I'll be so glad when this is over."

"You and me both, doll."

About an hour after Damon left, he called to say the security guard was on the way up to deliver a package for me. Whatever I imagined it could be, I was wrong. When I opened the door and found the guard there with a utility cart full of boxes, I was speechless. When I realized those boxes contained an iMac and all the possible peripherals, I squealed and showed him to the room I'd claimed as my office.

The top floor of Damon's penthouse was actually two, two-bedroom apartments connected. I'd decided one of those two apartments would serve as both my office and a nursery for the babies while I worked. The main floor was a huge three-bedroom apartment with over five thousand square feet in it alone, giving us enough room to have a permanent nursery close to our bedroom. The penthouse was gorgeous and the city views were to die for, but I found my thoughts drifting to that family home in the suburbs he'd talked about.

Someday.

While setting up my new computer network, I realized I didn't have the Wi-Fi password, so I set out on a snooping mission to find it. After checking all the usual places and not finding the modem, I started looking in the less likely spots. At my wit's end, I jerked open the closet door in the master bedroom...and spotted my old briefcase inside.

The hunt for the internet connection became an urgent

demand when I pulled my bag off the shelf and looked inside. The flash drive that contained all the data on the accounts tied to the Sanfratello embezzlement scheme was still hidden in an interior compartment.

CHAPTER FOURTEEN

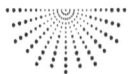

Damon

"Boss, Geno was spotted in a car near Dumbo, heading into Brooklyn. By the time our guys turned around, they lost sight of the car." Paulie stood in the doorway to my office, appearing uneasy after sharing the bad news with me.

"Get the car description out to all our guys. Everyone stays on the lookout for him. He'll probably go after Jillian first because he knows I'd walk through hell to get to her. Make sure the guys on her detail know I'll cut their fucking balls off and save them as a souvenir if they fuck up."

"You got it, Damon."

"I'll be back later. I have a few errands to take care of before heading home. Call me if you hear anything."

Someone was always gunning for my family and me. That was an unfortunate side effect of being on top—someone else was always waiting in the wings to take over that spot. Geno wasn't the brains or the muscle behind the attempted coup, so I wasn't overly concerned he'd suddenly grow a pair of balls—or a brain, for that matter. But then, I wouldn't give him an easy target to take out either. We'd keep our guard up while living normal lives. We'd go about our daily routines while growing eyes in the back of our heads. In short, we wouldn't change a thing.

However, what I had planned was anything but normal, especially for me. Everything had to be perfect and precisely match the picture I had in my mind. Going from store to store, overseeing every detail, and personally selecting every single item took hours. By the time I finished and was on my way home, I needed a fucking nap.

Until I walked through the door of my apartment and a small feminine body flew through the air and attached herself to me. I was suddenly very awake.

"Hello to you too, doll. Did you miss me today?" I chuckled as I wrapped my arms around her, holding her in place against me.

"I did miss you. And I'm happy to see you. But I also wanted to say thank you for the iMac and all the techie goodies you sent me today. You didn't have to do that, you know. You're spoiling me. But don't feel compelled to stop now."

"You're not spoiled yet, Jilly. I'm just getting started. Is this flimsy little robe what you're wearing for dinner tonight? If so, we'll both be arrested."

"Oh yeah? On what charges?"

"Definitely multiple counts of indecent exposure, when I can't keep my hands off you. Assault and battery, when I beat down the men who dare to look at you. Possibly murder, if anyone tries to touch you. We'll cause quite the scene."

"Considering I set up my office only a few hours ago and have the best idea for a nursery, maybe I should put my clothes on for this outing. I'm not exactly a fan of prison prenatal care—it'll cramp my style."

"Good call. You're welcome to be as indecent as you want when we get back home later."

"I'll take you up on that offer, Mr. Marchetti."

Her full, pink lips were too luscious to resist. I slanted my mouth over hers, caressing her tongue with long, slow laps. The temperature in the room began to climb—but not nearly as fast as the heat rose in my body. But with Jillian, all I needed was a simple touch, a passing glance, or a barely perceptible wisp of air.

"Mmm." Her hips surged, sliding against my cock, making it even harder...physically and figuratively...for me to stop.

"Doll, I'm about two seconds away from ripping off your panties and fucking you right here in the doorway. Once I start, I won't stop for the rest of the night."

"I'm not hearing a downside in this scenario."

"Fuck. I don't either. I'm sure I had a point, though."

She pressed her lips against mine again, determined to pick up where we left off. I was sorely tempted to let her, except for the warning in the back of my mind telling me to stop before it was too late. I kicked the door closed behind me and walked to our bedroom with her legs wrapped around my waist and her fingers threading through my hair.

"Jillian, doll, we have to get ready. We have reservations at The Fire tonight, remember?"

"That name sounds vaguely familiar. I can't say for sure though." She trailed her tongue down the side of my neck, tempting me to forget my own name.

Somehow, I managed to untangle her arms and legs from the death grip she held on me to lower her feet to the floor. With one last caress of her lips, I broke our embrace and held her at arm's length. "We have to get dressed for dinner, but I plan on eating dessert when we get home."

"All right, you win. We have kept you cooped up inside the house for the last couple of weeks, so you deserve a night out to let off some steam. Give me about an hour, and I'll be ready to go."

"I'll be waiting. Impatiently."

Everything was going according to my plan at first. Apparently, I was losing my touch, because I never saw it coming. There were no signs. No warning. No heads-up.

Just angry screams followed by desperate pleas.

"You've got to be kidding me!"

"Noooooo!"

"What in the actual fuck?"

I'd never been afraid of any man, but walking into that bedroom with an unstable pregnant woman was fucking terrifying. "What's the problem in here, doll?"

She stood facing away from me, wearing a tight black dress that scooped low in the back, revealing her beautiful skin all the way down to her ass. I had momentary second thoughts about staying in for the night. Then she whirled around to face me with a wild look in her eyes and a displeased expression on her face. That was when I realized the cause of her outbursts.

"You wished this on me, didn't you?" The accusation in her voice was clear—she meant every word she spat at me.

In my defense, I didn't *mean* to laugh out loud. Scout's honor. But that was exactly what I did.

Her hands curled into fists, and her eyes filled with rage.

"Hold up, doll. I didn't wish this on you. I only said I'd read this would probably happen. You're pregnant with twins. Of course you're going to show earlier. You're beautiful and sexy and the love of my life. You're also the mother of my children, and I'm proud to show that off. You should be too."

"You get points for that little speech because it was a good one. But it doesn't change the fact that my clothes don't fit now, Damon. My dresses are too tight to wear out anywhere." She turned toward the mirror, distraught and near tears.

We both knew it had only been a matter of time before her cute little bump became an unmistakable protruding belly. But a drastic change over the last eight hours? That was unexpected. I scraped my hand down my face, thinking my plans for the evening just blew up along with her baby bump. Then I remembered.

"Hold on a minute. I have something that may help."

"What?" Confusion and disbelief—I knew exactly how she felt.

I walked deep into my closet and moved boxes around until I found the one I needed. Without opening it, I handed it to Jillian and waited for her reaction.

She opened the box, pulled out the very brightly colored silk button-down shirt, and her bottom jaw fell open. She stared at it for several heartbeats, eyes wide and her head shaking in disbelief.

"Is this fuchsia shirt a gift from an old girlfriend, Damon?"

"No, doll. This shirt was a gift from my asshole sister. It's been in the far reaches of my closet for a few years now. I figure if anyone can pull off this color, it's you."

"Actually, this is perfect."

Within minutes, she'd arranged a full outfit out of my pink silk button-down shirt, a shiny black tank top, a black stretchy skirt, and a pair of sexy fuck-me heels.

"You look hot."

"I look like a hooker. A very pregnant hooker at that." She turned in the mirror, examining her handiwork. "But nothing else fits me, so this outfit will have to do for tonight."

With that crisis averted, we left the apartment and headed for the restaurant. She didn't believe me when I assured her everyone stared because of how beautiful and sexy she was. She said they stared because they wondered how much she made per hour. After we were seated, the obvious glances in our direction stopped.

"I've never been to a place like this. There's no menu?" she whispered to me over the tabletop candle, her eyes scanning the tables around us for eavesdroppers.

"No, doll. We get whatever ten-course meal the chef serves tonight. It'll be delicious. Trust me."

"Now I really do feel like a fish out of water. I've never been to a restaurant where the chef picks my meal for me. Or one that has a ten-course meal. I don't even know what all that would include."

"Relax and just enjoy it. We're in no hurry tonight."

A. D. JUSTICE

Course after course, the waiters delivered our plates, and Jillian devoured every bite. After each one, she said she couldn't eat anymore, but she couldn't resist the next serving. Watching her eat, hearing her make those little noises of pleasure, made me count down the minutes until dessert.

"For dessert, we have something very special tonight. The chef sends his best regards." The waiter set the covered plate down in front of Jillian first.

She grabbed her dessert fork off the table and could barely contain herself while she waited for the waiter to lower my plate. He removed both covers at the same time then took a step back from the table. Jillian froze when she looked down at her treat... and her fork slipped through her fingers, falling to the table with a loud *clang* against her plate.

Her cake was designed in the shape of a light blue Tiffany's box, complete with an open lid, a quilted pillow center, and held a round brilliant solitaire diamond engagement ring inside. When she finally looked up, she found me down on one knee beside her chair.

"Jillian, you changed my life from the first day I met you. Every day since then, you've made it infinitely better. Through the good and bad, my love for you has never wavered. For as long as I live, I only want to be with you. Will you marry me?"

I lifted the ring off the cake and slid it onto her outstretched hand.

"Is that a yes, doll?"

"Yes," she whispered, tears glistening in her eyes. "Every day for the rest of my life, my answer will be yes."

She met me when I stood, and I pulled her into my arms. She squeezed tightly around my neck as the onlookers in the restaurant clapped and cheered, sending their congratulations and well-wishes our way.

With a watery smile and a chuckle in her voice, Jillian said, "I can't believe you proposed on a night when I'm dressed like a hooker."

"If it makes you feel any better, I'll let you pretend to be one when we get home. Besides, you deserved a more romantic proposal than a hospital waiting room after we'd been awake for a hundred and ninety-six hours straight."

"You know I'll take you any way and anywhere I can get you, Damon."

The waitstaff descended on our table, bringing the other items I'd had delivered. Flowers arrangements were placed on every table—elegant bundles of lavender and ivory roses tied with matching ribbons. To my fiancée, they presented a special bouquet of three dozen lavender roses mixed with baby's breath and greenery.

"Now I know why you were so adamant to go out tonight. Very sly, Mr. Marchetti. The meal was delicious. This ring is exquisite—I can't stop staring at it. The flowers are absolutely gorgeous. Everything about tonight has been perfect, even with my wardrobe malfunction. You came through for me there too, finding me a shirt to wear to hide my too-tight clothes. Damon, you make me so happy."

"I love you, Jillian. There's nothing I wouldn't do for you. Let's finish our dessert, and I'll prove that to you soon enough."

On the car ride home, we passed a couple of mounted police officers that caught Jillian's eye. She slipped her hand into mine and laced our fingers together. "Did I tell you I used to ride horses back home?"

"No, doll. You've never mentioned that. How long did you ride?"

"Several years—from as young as I can remember through high school. Then college and work took up most of my time. I haven't ridden much in the last several years, but I always loved it. Watching you crossing the field to Leo's house reminded me of home and the farm where we boarded my horse."

"You miss it, don't you?"

"Riding horses or home?"

"Both. Either."

"Yes, I do. I miss both. But I don't have any family left down there, so you're home for me now."

"Home is where the heart is, Jillian."

"That cliché actually is true."

That was the moment when I knew exactly what I had to do, and I couldn't wait.

Something else I couldn't wait for was my extra helping of dessert. The moment we walked through the door to our apartment, I locked the door behind us and didn't let her out of the entryway before I dropped to my knees and feasted.

Best fucking meal of the day.

CHAPTER FIFTEEN

Jillian

"$\mathcal{H}$ere, take my credit card and go shopping with Carrie today. You'll have two teams of my men with you because Geno has been spotted in the area lately. I'm not taking any chances with your safety, but you need new clothes so you don't have another meltdown on me." Damon extended his hand toward me, offering his black American Express Centurion card.

"I didn't have a meltdown, Damon. It was just a temporary moment of panic because the clothes that fit the day before didn't fit yesterday. It was very a stressful event."

"I get it, doll. So go out for some retail therapy with my sister today so you'll feel better. Buy whatever you want, however much you want, and at any store you want. I only have one condition."

"And that is?"

"Don't buy anything for the nursery you're planning. I want to be with you for that shopping excursion. Deal?"

If I hadn't already been pregnant with twins, that request alone would've done the trick.

"Deal." My reply came out as a whisper, but my heart was

beating erratically against the inside of my chest. The man had such an overpowering effect on me.

He kissed me goodbye and slid out of the car. Luigi and Paulie remained in the front seats as my bodyguards for the day. Just as they pulled away from the curb, my cell phone rang.

"How's my favorite sister?" Carrie asked when I answered.

"I'm your only sister, and I'm fine, other than having already outgrown my clothes."

"So, you're naked today? This should be a fun outing."

"Ha. Ha. I'm wearing leggings and another one of Damon's shirts since his clothes actually do fit me."

"Another one of his shirts?"

"Yeah, it's a long story. I'll tell you all about it while we shop today. Are you already there?"

"Yes, I'm inside Saks Fifth Avenue, waiting for you to get here so we can spend all my brother's money."

When I walked into the store, Carrie had already secured a personal shopper to navigate us through the various departments. And we hit them all—clothes, shoes, makeup, and lingerie. I drew the line at buying any true maternity clothes. Instead, I bought the clothes I liked best in different sizes, hoping to delay the inevitable tent dress for as long as possible. But with how my stomach had already expanded so quickly, and with carrying twins, it was only a matter of time before nothing else would fit.

While we shopped, I took the opportunity to press Carrie for insider information on her relationship with Lorenzo.

"Spill it." I put my hands on my hips and stared at her, daring her to play coy with me.

She shrugged one shoulder and pretended to be overly interested in the clothes on the rack in front of us. Our bodyguards were just out of earshot, so I knew their presence wasn't keeping her from sharing with me.

"We decided it was best to put our relationship on hold until this whole mess is resolved. With Geno on the lam and still technically a threat, even though I doubt he'd made a move against us now, it's just best we wait. With tempers high, Lorenzo could easily get killed in a case of friendly fire."

"I'm so sorry, Carrie. I know how hard it is to be separated from the man you love. Is there anything I can do?"

"Short of drawing Geno out from under his rock so we can finish him? No, but I appreciate the offer. I know you would if you could."

"Actually..." I pulled my lower lip between my teeth and waited for her to meet my gaze. "I may be able to do just that."

"How?"

"Damon bought me a new iMac computer the other day. While searching for his Wi-Fi modem so I could get on the wireless network, I found my old briefcase in the closet. The flash drive I copied all the embezzlement documents onto was still in it, complete with account numbers. So I did some snooping on the accounts and found something very interesting.

"Someone is embezzling directly from Blaine Financial Services this time. Whoever is doing it is not smart enough to hide the transactions behind a shell company or run the money through a real company. From what you've told me about Geno, he fits the bill. He's old-school, so he's not tech-savvy enough to pull off something like this."

"Tell me everything."

"He knew Lorenzo had started the process, but he couldn't use Milo's name or MadTrich anymore. That would certainly alert the Marchetti family. He redirected the funds flow, sending it straight from Blaine Financial to a bank in the Bahamas. So, I thought maybe you and I could redirect his redirect, send the money to an account that's easy for him to identify. But impossible to mistake."

"What account would that be?"

"Leo Marchetti's. Then Maria could get the money, and we'd draw Geno out and end this feud once and for all."

"Did you clear this plan with Damon? Does he approve?" She

eyed me suspiciously, obviously not keen on running another operation without her brother's help.

"I haven't yet, but I will. I needed to know if this is even possible. You're the expert in this, so I wanted to run it by you first. If you can do it, then we can present it to Damon together."

"Of course I can do it. And I can find Geno's IP address and track him down. I can even get into his network and turn on his laptop camera so we can make sure it's actually Geno before we make a move. I do believe it's him, though. He would've lost everything when his takeover attempt fell through. Without the muscle behind him, no one would pay him for anything anymore. When do you want to talk to Damon about it?"

"Talk to Damon about what?" That familiar masculine voice appeared out of thin air from behind me. "Do I have to chaperone you two at all times? One day of shopping and you're already devising some plan I'm sure I'll hate."

I turned to face Damon. "What are you doing here?"

"Thought you two might want to have lunch with me. Seems I arrived just in time to save you both from yourselves."

I couldn't help but laugh because he did have a point. "No, my love. We weren't going to do anything without you. You heard Carrie ask when we'd talk to you about it. Your timing is perfect—but not for saving us this time. Maybe for saving your men from more shopping, though."

Damon smiled before leaning down to kiss me hello. "I'm glad to hear I get to be part of the planning process this time. For the record, I am not checking up on you. Your doctor's office called my cell number by mistake to remind us of your appointment tomorrow. Naturally, I wanted to deliver the message in person, and it just happened to be time to eat."

"I have nothing to hide. Feel free to check up on me whenever you'd like."

"Oh my God. Could you two be more in love? You're so sweet

it makes me sick." Carrie feigned disgust, but I caught the smile that broke free before she turned her face away from us.

"I would say, no, we *couldn't* be more in love. But every time I think I can't possibly love Jilly more than I do now, I'm proven wrong."

"You just had to make it worse, didn't you?" Carrie shook her head and rolled her eyes while Damon and I laughed.

Over lunch, I explained every detail of the changes I'd found in the embezzlement accounts from Blaine Financial and why I thought Geno was behind it. Damon understandably didn't want to wait until Carrie had accessed Geno's computer to verify it was him. He suggested we talk to Lorenzo face-to-face first. If Lorenzo had revived his original ploy, Damon didn't want to interfere in it. However, he was interested in reviewing all the information firsthand before we brought Lorenzo in, so we agreed to meet at Carrie's the following evening to finish our discussion.

"If you ladies are done shopping, there's somewhere I want to take Jillian." Damon's gaze shifted between Carrie and me, waiting for one of us to end our spree.

"You two go ahead," Carrie replied. "Jillian and I can spend the rest of your money another day. I'll start doing some preliminary digging into Geno Sanfratello for our planning session tomorrow night."

"Thanks for spending the day with me and helping so much, Carrie." I hugged her goodbye before she left with her security team and I left with my overprotective brute.

When we drove away, Damon cut his eyes over at me. "That was some impressive research you did on those transactions, doll. How did you get into their system to find the recent movement?"

"I may have learned a trick or two from Carrie while I lived with her." I looked over at Damon, unable to hide my smile. "Or maybe I checked my remote login credentials through Morgan and Bartholomew and found my access is still active. I guess in the aftermath of Lorenzo abruptly leaving Blaine Financial, they forgot about me since I wasn't an employee of theirs. My boss approved a month of personal leave of absence so I could move up here, but my time off work doesn't revoke my access."

"Brilliant. I love your brain as much as I love your body. What if someone figured out what you were doing and tracked you?"

"Not possible. I routed the IP address through several other countries and had it terminate in the middle of nowhere. My tracks are very well covered. Even you couldn't find me if I wanted to hide from you now."

"I think my sister has been a bad influence on you, Jilly. Maybe I should chaperone you two more closely."

He thought he hid the ghost of a smile, but I caught it nonetheless. He wanted to rile me up—he liked feisty Jillian. Or my feisty mouth, anyway.

"Be my guest. We'll just talk in code all night long and leave you in the dark. Then we'll laugh at your confused expressions and disgusted sighs. It'll be entertaining—for us. No skin off my back."

"That fucking mouth of yours." He shook his head, letting his gorgeous smile finally show. "No skin off your back, huh? How about some skin off your ass after I spank it?"

"Hmm. We've done that, though, so it's lost that new car smell. How about skin off my wrists after you tie me up? You've threatened to do it before but never came through. I'm starting to think those were only empty words. Warnings without real consequences."

"You know, it's no fucking wonder why you're the only woman who has ever held my attention and affection. They say opposites attract, and I believe it. You are the opposite of me in almost every way. But then we have conversations like this, and I'd swear you're the female version of me. It's a little scary sometimes."

"I have to keep you on your toes, Damon. Keep you guessing

which personality you'll get from day to day. Variety is the spice of life, after all."

"In all seriousness, I'm thrilled to see you laughing and joking again. We've been through a lot over the last several months, and I've had plenty of reasons to worry about your long-term mental health. But you've proved to me time and again that we're meant to be together."

"Damn skippy, we are." For the first time since getting in the car with Damon, I checked our surroundings and realized we were headed away from the apartment. "Where are you taking me?"

"It's a surprise. I'm not giving you any hints because I don't want to spoil it by letting you guess."

"That's really not fair, Damon. You can read my mind just by looking at me. I can't do that with you. Yet."

"Yet is right. You've gotten way too close to being able to read my every thought. We'll start communicating telepathically before long."

About thirty minutes outside of Manhattan, I would've sworn we were in a completely different world. Damon pulled off the highway onto a winding two-lane road that disappeared into the trees. With a forest all around us, the sights and sounds of the big city were only a memory. Then he slowed and turned onto a driveway—a very long driveway—that ended at the most beautiful house I'd ever seen.

House? No.

Palace? Definitely.

The English manor-inspired four-story stone mansion sat on top of a hill, surrounded by open pastures dotted with giant oak trees for shade, a flowing river, and a state forest behind it. It was love at first sight for me, and I hadn't even seen the inside yet.

"You have some very fortunate friends." When the car stopped, I jerked the door open and jumped out, unable to take my eyes off the palatial estate in front of me. "This place is so gorgeous—it's breathtaking. And that barn is huge. How many horses do they have? I can't believe this place."

"I take it you like it here, then?"

I could hear his smile in his voice. "I love it here. I can't believe we're so close to the city. You'd never know it from how serene this country setting is. Whose house is this?"

"Ours, if you want it."

I whirled around on my heel and openly gaped at him. "What?"

His usual smug, confident expression was nowhere to be found. Instead, I found a hopeful yet somewhat shy one in its place. He wanted to impress me, and he wanted me to love the surprise.

"If you want it, it's ours. I'll call the real estate agent in the morning and have her finalize the offer and set our closing date. When you told me about your horse and missing home, I set out to find our family a new home. It had to be one that somewhat reminded you of home. The horses, the barn, the forest, the water —this one has it all. All you have to do is say the word."

"Damon, I absolutely love it here. This place is amazing, and I'd love to live here with you. But I'd also live in a one-room shack with you. I don't need a twenty-thousand-square-foot house to have a home with you and our babies. You know that, right?"

"Of course I do. But I want only the best for you and our children. All twelve of them. So, what do you say? Should we go inside and look around, or have you already made up your mind?"

"My mind is made up, but I still want to see inside."

He took my hand, and we strolled through all four floors and so many rooms I lost count. The outdoor pool and hot tub were every bit as exquisite as their indoor counterparts. Then we walked the grounds, thoroughly inspected the barn, and peeked into the smaller houses on the property that served as housing for the servants.

"Well?" He asked the question even though he already knew the answer.

"I seem to say this to you a lot, but yes. Yes!" I jumped into his arms and crushed my lips to his. "I love you, Damon. Not because of this extravagant house that's way too big for the two of us, but because you do everything in your power to protect me, and provide for me, and make me feel special. You always put me first. Is this where you want to live? Would you rather stay in the city? Or move closer to your parents?"

"I'm right where I want to be, doll. In your arms. My favorite place on earth. Wherever we happen to live doesn't matter to me. We're close to the city, we're close to my parents, and this is a very nice area for our kids to grow up in. And for you and me to grow old together in."

"How can I argue with that? I'm ready to move in when you are."

"Perfect. We'll need new furniture, of course. Guess we'll give my credit card another workout soon."

When he finally convinced me to get back in the car and leave our new home-to-be, he let me in on the other plans he had.

"Are you ready to go tell my mom the official good news before she hears it from someone else? We're only about thirty minutes from her house."

"Yes, I guess we'd better. Carrie noticed the large rock on my finger while we were shopping today. She didn't ask for any details, but she held my hand up and made a point of looking at my ring then at me."

"Carrie knows Mama hasn't been told yet, so she's letting her be the first person we officially tell. If Mama knew, the whole family would already know. I don't know how you feel about wedding planning, but my mom has waited her whole life to plan a huge wedding. She'll probably take over. Let me apologize now if you feel like you've been pushed out of your own wedding. She means well."

"Your mom planning our wedding doesn't hurt my feelings at

all, Damon. I would be honored. Maybe I'll ask her to help me pick out my wedding dress, too."

"Don't be surprised by the waterworks when you ask her. She'll be so excited, doll. You'll make her entire *century*."

"When she starts, I'll be crying right along with her. Some coldhearted, badass hit man I am, huh?"

"Mamas have that effect on the best of us, doll."

1 6

CHAPTER SIXTEEN

Damon

The usual clamor echoed from the kitchen when we stepped into my parents' house. Mama was cooking. Dad was hungry and trying to grab bites of food before Mama was ready to serve it, and my brothers and sister were intentionally making the situation worse. All the teasing and arguing were tempered with even more love.

Sounded like home to me.

"What's going on in here?" I bellowed with an extra dose of bass in my voice.

All eyes flew up to meet mine in a stunned silence for a heartbeat, then they went back to their teasing and play-fighting. Mama, as usual, was the referee, while Dad encouraged his kids to win by any means necessary. They only stopped long enough to rub Jillian's pregnant belly as if it were a fucking magic lamp and they were waiting for the genie to emerge. Then they resumed aggravating each other. Through all the gouging and threats and name-calling, there was laughter and love and the knowledge that no one outside this room would ever get away doing the same. We were a family through and through.

Mama grabbed Jillian first and kissed her cheeks before turning to me. "Back so soon? You just can't stay away, can you?"

"You know I can't. You'd hurt me if I tried."

"That's right. Are you two hungry?"

"Famished."

"Carrie, set two more places at the table, please. Dinner is almost ready."

"Sure, Mama." Carrie looked at me, smiling from ear to ear like the Cheshire cat. She knew exactly why we were there again so soon. "Always glad to see my big brother and his...girlfriend."

The pause in her statement was barely perceptible. Had Mama not been distracted by Dad and my brothers, she would've caught on and grilled me for answers I wasn't ready to give. For Carrie's sake, I was glad Mama didn't hear it. After the food had been placed on the table and everyone was seated, I stood and waited for a lull in the conversation.

"Something to say, son?" Dad asked.

"Yes. I believe Jillian has an announcement she'd like to make. I realize it's hard for most of the people around this table, but we'd appreciate a moment of silence so she doesn't have to repeat herself."

Crumpled napkins flew at my head while my brothers booed me, but they became instantly quiet when Jillian stood. The glare in her eyes was betrayed by the smile on her face.

"Thank you, Damon. I do have an announcement to make. Mama Lina, I need help planning a wedding." She intentionally paused—long enough for it to be noticed and to capture Mama's undivided attention. "And, if it's not too much trouble, I also need help picking out my wedding dress. Would you mind going with me?"

The squealing and screaming that followed was nothing short of the loudest ear-piercing alarm. Mama flew up from her seat and grabbed Jillian in a full embrace. Happy tears flowed from her eyes, and a huge smile was plastered on her face. "Of course I'll go with you, *bellissima regazza*. And don't you worry about a thing with the wedding. I would be so happy to oversee every detail so you don't have to stress over anything."

"There is one detail I've already settled on."

Mama leaned back to look at Jillian. "Whatever you want, *bella*, you will have. Just tell me, and I'll make it happen."

Jillian kissed Mama's cheek then moved her gaze to meet mine. "Damon took me to look at a house today. I want us to become husband and wife in our new home."

"That is a great idea, doll."

"I agree, Jillian. That is a perfect idea. Where is the house? What does it look like?" Mana grilled me for answers, wanting all the details of our soon-to-be new home.

To satisfy her curiosity, I grabbed my phone and pulled up the real estate office website. We scrolled through the pictures they had online, giving her time to examine each one. She was thrilled for us, and I could see the wheels turning in her mind as she planned the shower, wedding, and reception in the enormous house and grounds. That was fine with me, though. I wanted to fill the property with love, laughter, and the best memories when we moved in, from the very first second.

Mama, Carrie, and Jillian spent the rest of the evening talking about the wedding and making plans to go furniture shopping together. Dad took advantage of their distraction and asked me to join him in his home office for our own discussion.

"Son, I've given this a lot of thought. My mind was mostly made up before we found out about Leo's betrayal, but that just solidified my decision. It's time for me to retire and enjoy my remaining years with your mother while we're still healthy and young enough to do what we want.

"We've talked about returning to Italy for an extended trip for a long time now. After the babies are born, I won't be able to drag your mom away from them long enough to go on a trip. So, after your wedding and honeymoon are over, I'm retiring and handing the reins over to you. You'll be the official Boss of the Marchetti family. Have you thought about who your next-in-command will be?"

"I have, and I've decided to ask Marco. He's had my back my whole life, and I couldn't imagine anyone else running the family with me than him."

A pained expression crossed Dad's face, an unusual show of emotion for him. "I once thought the same of Leo. But he and I were not close as children as you and Marco were. This family is much closer. Plus, Marco knows he'd answer to all of us if he stepped out of line."

"Marco has never been jealous of me, Dad. He probably doesn't even want to be the Underboss, but he'll do it because of his allegiance to me."

"You're right—he's never been too interested in creating the rules, but he's good at enforcing them. He'll serve the family well in that role. Good choice, son."

We spent the hours following that conversation poring over every business transaction Dad had set up during his time as Boss. Maybe that was an exaggeration, but not by much. Going through the list with him was more eye-opening in a different way. Dad had taught me everything he knew—but he hadn't kept up with the times and technological advances. Carrie was right when she said our family had to join the current century or our rivals would get the upper hand on us before we even knew what happened.

She deserved credit for that, but I couldn't give her a high-ranking position and put her in an automatic line of fire. But I could make her a lieutenant on the business side, separated from the enforcers. Her expertise would be acknowledged at least, and she would gain the respect of the men in that aspect. If they admired her, they'd also protect her, knowing she was an asset to the family but not a threat to their standing. My mind was made up, and I planned to share the idea with Carrie when Jillian and I went to her house the following day.

After my training session in the antiquated methods Dad used was over, he locked his desk and the office door behind us. "Let's find the women and see if we have any money left after they've been shopping on the computer all evening."

My brothers were in the den, watching a reality TV show and mocking the people who believed the hype. We found Mama, Jillian, and Carrie in the formal living room. All three of them were glued to the computer screen, oohing and ahhing over whatever had captured their attention.

"Have you three set the wedding date, closed on the house, and finalized the wedding plans yet?" I walked straight to Jillian and leaned down to kiss her.

Carrie quickly clicked the mouse, changing the screen before I could even get a glimpse of what was there. I cut my eyes at her, unconsciously narrowing the corners while I read her expression.

"We're looking at wedding dresses, babe. You can't see any of them before the wedding, or you'll ruin the surprise and the fun of it. I want the one I choose to be a complete surprise."

Funny how just a few words from Jillian cooled my flaming temper and set my mind at ease. And just the opposite was also true. Just a few words from her could set my whole body on fire and push my mind to the limits. I fucking loved the hold she had on every part of me.

"Fair enough, doll. That's one secret I don't mind you keeping since I'm the one who gets all the benefits from it."

"As for the date, we've decided when the wedding will be. Jillian is four and a half months pregnant now, so you'll get married when she's around six months. That'll still give us time to arrange everything after you move in to your new house, and Jillian will still feel good before the third trimester begins." Mama wasn't asking if I approved of the timing; she was telling me I approved.

Jillian looked down and ran her hand across her protruding stomach. "In six weeks, I'll be *huge*."

"Don't worry about it, doll. In six weeks, you'll still be just as beautiful as you are now. Probably even more so with the pregnancy glow."

"Maybe I should wait until closer to the time to pick out a wedding dress. If I wake up the day of our wedding and it doesn't fit, I don't know what I'll do."

"You'll walk down whatever aisle at the new house you three have picked and marry me wearing your pajamas for all I care. Our vows are what I care about the most. Putting the ring on your finger and changing your last name are tied for a close second."

"Oh yeah, that reminds me." Jillian stood and walked over to my father. I could tell she was nervous by the slight shake in her hand before she laced her fingers together. "Dad?"

My father looked up at her, his eyes wide, his eyebrows reaching for his hairline, and his bottom jaw hanging open. She'd called him Dad for the first time, and my usually stoic father forgot all about keeping his poker face intact.

"Yes, *cara?*"

"I wanted to ask you for a favor, but I don't want you to feel obligated. If you'd rather not, just tell me and it'll be fine."

"For you, I will do whatever you ask of me. What is the favor, *cara?*"

"Will you walk me down the aisle? I don't have anyone left in my family to do it, but now I can't imagine it being anyone but you."

Dad stood and pulled Jillian into a bear-sized embrace. He would deny it until his dying breath, but I heard the quiver in his voice when he answered. "I would be honored to walk you down the aisle, *bella*. But I can't guarantee that I'll give you away now that I have you. You and Carrie will always be my little girls."

"You might be able to convince me to share her from time to time for odd jobs around the house, as a loaner. But I have to insist you give her to me on our wedding day. You have no idea how badly I need her to take my last name so I can say I have papers on her."

"Is this really what I have to look forward to for the rest of my life?" Jillian's deadpan expression was a ruse. She couldn't hide the teasing glimmer in her eyes any more than I could.

"You know it, doll. Till death do us part."

17

CHAPTER SEVENTEEN

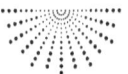

Jillian

Our prenatal visit with Dr. Bowers went as expected, with one minor point. He was very old-school, and though I insisted I felt fine, he insisted on treating me as a high-risk pregnancy. That meant more frequent office visits—and more of Damon watching my every move like a hawk zoned in on its prey.

Good thing I enjoyed being my man's prey.

When the doctor announced I'd need more frequent sonograms to monitor the twins' growth, the extra visits suddenly didn't seem all that bad.

"But everything's okay with Jillian and the babies, right?" Damon instinctively slid his hand across my stomach, cupping the ever-growing bulge in a protective move.

"Everything's just fine. This is more precautionary since twins tend to come prematurely. The extra sonograms let us measure growth rates from month to month. I prefer to get ahead of any potential problems if at all possible. We'll do the next one when you come back in two weeks. Do you want to know what you're having?"

"No, we don't want to know until the moment they're born. It'll kill me to wait from now until then, but I love the thought of being surprised."

"Technically, Doc, *she* doesn't want to know until they're born. I want to know right now, but I'm going along with this plan because I love her. And because she's the one who has to go through the pregnancy and delivery, so I figure she deserves to make this call."

Dr. Bowers laughed with us and nodded. "With her small frame, carrying twins may be a little rough on her toward the end. She'll be beyond ready to get this over with. But we'll take good care of her, don't you worry."

Of course, that only made Damon even more hypervigilant about my comfort and safety. Had I been the type to take advantage of someone, I could've milked the situation for everything I wanted. But since I still enjoyed being moderately independent, I wasn't ready to give in to being a kept woman. Even if my quote-unquote prison was a beautiful mansion.

"Seriously, Damon, I'm fine. Dr. Bowers just told you not to worry. That doesn't mean you should worry more than you already do." We walked out of the doctor's office, Damon's hand on my lower back, and headed toward the car.

"He said twins are considered high-risk. That means we have to be more careful with everything you do. More rest. Less stress. Definitely no more shootouts in the middle of the night."

"Well, I'll agree to the last part. I'm not staying in bed all the time, though. Your mom is doing all the heavy lifting for the wedding, but I plan to be intimately involved. Put your caveman tendencies away, and realize women have been giving birth to babies for centuries upon centuries now. I'm sure we can manage with all the high-tech care we have today."

"So, I guess dropping you off at home before I go to Carrie's to discuss the embezzlement scheme is out of the question, then?"

"That is absolutely out of the question. I'm the one who found every bit of that information. You're not cutting me out now."

Later that evening, we pulled into Carrie's driveway for our working session, but Damon grabbed my arm when I started to reach for the car door handle.

"Babe, seriously, I can open the door for myself. I'm pregnant —not helpless."

One side of his mouth quirked up in the sexiest smirk. He tilted his head to the side and arched one eyebrow. "Believe me, I know how capable you are, doll. But something is off, I can feel it. Indulge me for a minute and sit right here while I check it out. When I'm sure the coast is clear, I'll let you know."

"Okay. We'll wait right here until you signal it's safe." I patted my stomach then watched him exit the car.

The truth was I didn't like Damon being in the line of fire any more than he liked the idea of me being a target. But since he had more experience in that area than I did, I heeded his warning while I held my breath. He walked around the car, appearing nonchalant when he approached my side, but I knew better. His keen eyes scanned our surroundings, homing in on any potential danger with pinpoint accuracy.

When he opened my door, I knew he'd spotted what had raised his hackles.

"Want to fill me in on what you know, Damon?"

"It seems Lorenzo has volunteered as Carrie's personal security detail. I wonder if she knows."

"What do you mean?"

"He's sitting in his car over there." Without moving his head, Damon indicated the direction with his eyes. "From the look of him, he's been there for a while. I'd almost think he was on a stakeout if I didn't already know he's not a Fed."

"He worries about Carrie the same way you worry about me. You should cut them some slack, you know. I don't even know him, and I can tell he's crazy about her. If he makes her happy, where's the harm in supporting their relationship?"

"Maybe you're right, I don't know. All I know is I was the last one to find out about it, and that didn't sit well with me. We'll see. I'm not the Boss yet."

I laughed out loud before I caught myself. "Damon, you may not have the official title yet, but that doesn't mean you accept anything less. I mean, your approval of Carrie's boyfriend holds more weight than anyone else's."

"You have a solid argument there, doll. But there's a reason why they look to me for the final say-so. That's because my reputation proceeds me, and they're more afraid to cross me than anyone else."

"Thank you for further making my point, Damon."

Carrie met us at the door, and we followed her into the command center in her basement. True to her word, she'd been doing her homework on the accounts and money transfers we believed Geno had made.

"This whole plot just took a new twist." The excitement in her voice immediately conjured a vision of her rubbing her hands together in an evil madman fashion. "I may have broken in to the offshore account where the money is being deposited and found other deposits. I also may have backtracked those funds to their origins...and found the money that has been trickling out of Lorenzo's account—the Ponzi scheme account."

"So, who is behind this—Lorenzo or Geno?" Damon's expression hardened, and I knew exactly where his thoughts went. If Lorenzo was behind the scheme, his presence outside Carrie's house might not be benevolent, after all.

"My opinion is this has Geno written all over it. The funds transfers started before the showdown at his garbage station. He wanted his son to take the fall for the money and for Jillian's mother. He wanted you to kill Lorenzo that night, then while a war raged between the families, he'd take the money for himself and run." Carrie clicked between screens, showing us the dates and amounts deposited into the offshore account.

"But you don't know that for sure, right?"

"No, I don't know for sure, Damon, but I can make an educated guess."

"You know I don't work off guesses. I want confirmation."

"Well, let's just call up Geno and ask him ourselves. I'm sure he'll be forthcoming with us about all of his plans."

"Smartass. I have a better idea. Stay here, I'll be right back."

Carrie looked at me with raised eyebrows when Damon rushed out of the room. That was one battle I wasn't interested in getting caught in the middle of, so I shrugged my shoulders. "You know how your brother is. Give him a minute, and you'll have more questions than answers."

"You just summed up my life with him in one sentence."

The front door slammed shut just before we heard the sound of heavy footfalls on the stairs—from more than one set of feet. I didn't have to turn around to see what had so completely caught Carrie's attention. Or, more accurately, *who* caught her attention.

"Lorenzo." She scrunched her eyebrows together while her eyes darted between the two men. "What are you doing here?"

"So you didn't know, after all." Damon took his seat next to me and pointed to an empty chair. "Have a seat, Lorenzo."

"I didn't know what?" Carrie was still trying to catch up.

"Lorenzo has been parked outside your house for what appears to be a while now. I wasn't sure if you didn't know or if you'd hired him as your new security detail."

"Why have you been sitting outside my house? Has something happened?"

"I don't trust my dad. He's still around here somewhere, moving frequently so he doesn't get caught in one place too long. He's still in the area for a reason. I don't want that reason to be you."

"As it turns out, your presence outside my sister's house today is very fortunate. If you're the one running this scheme, we'll back off and let you have at it. If not, we have other plans for the money. I just need you to be upfront with me either way. Are you running money through the Blaine Financial accounts into an offshore bank?"

"No. I stopped everything when I quit working there soon after Jillian went back to Louisiana. I left my offshore account in place, but that's the extent of my activities right now. My mind has been otherwise preoccupied." Lorenzo cut his eyes to Carrie for a split second before meeting Damon's gaze again. "Who do you think is behind it?"

"We're almost one hundred percent sure it's Geno's operation. You should also know it's set up to trickle money out of your offshore account. Looks like your father plans to bleed you dry." Damon kept his eyes locked on to Lorenzo's, gauging his reaction to the news. Deciding if Lorenzo was telling the truth or not.

When Damon realized Lorenzo honestly didn't know anything about it, Damon's facial features relaxed and a shadow of empathy passed across his eyes. He understood how a close family member's betrayal shook the very core of a man.

"Carrie, can you put Lorenzo's money back and stop any future transfers?"

"Sure. It'll take a little time to make the money route through different accounts and different countries before it deposits into his account so nothing can be traced back to me. But I can stop the future transfers right now with no problem."

Damon nodded, giving Carrie the green light, and she turned back to her computer, her fingers began flying across the keyboard while she worked her hacker coding magic.

"Listen, Lorenzo. After we put your money back, we're taking the rest of the money Geno stole and giving it to Maria. She hasn't been around since Leo died, but we're not going to leave her out in the cold for something she didn't know was happening. The thing is, I want Geno to know it was me. I want him to come after me so I can end this once and for all. Any suggestions how I can accomplish that?"

"Cryptic clues are always an option, but I prefer the direct approach. I'll be glad to give you his cell number. Text him and tell him. Send him a picture of his account balance. Sign your name. He'll eventually figure it out." The grin on Lorenzo's face left no doubt he liked the idea of helping plot revenge against his father.

"Great idea. That could give you away too, though. He'll assume you gave me his number."

"Let him assume whatever he wants. I don't give a fuck what he thinks. I'm ready for him if he wants to come after me, too."

We talked while Carrie worked for several hours straight, routing money transfers through several shell corporations, across oceans, and finally back into Lorenzo's account. When it came time to transfer the money from Geno to Maria, she wasn't as careful. She found his IP address and cloned it so it appeared the money was transferred directly from him. When the transaction was complete, she took a screenshot of Geno's zero balance and sent it to Damon.

"The Marchetti Family would like to thank you for your generous donation to Maria Marchetti in her hour of need. She will live comfortably for the rest of her years on the millions you gifted her. From my family to you, thank you. –Damon"

He hit send with a smile and waited for the message to be delivered.

"Did you hear that? It's funny, but I swear I just heard my name being cursed all the way from Brooklyn."

Funny wasn't the word I'd use to describe it. I felt the same sensation, only it felt more like a warning of what was to come.

18

CHAPTER SIXTEEN

Damon

*A*fter sending the text to Geno, I sent an update to Dad and my brothers so they weren't blindsided by any sudden move from the opposition. After all the shit Geno had caused my family, I wanted him to bring the fight to me. The time to end all the bullshit passed long ago. He'd already taken way too much of my time and energy as it stood.

He didn't reply to my text, but then, I didn't think he would. Texting wasn't really his thing. But he'd make a move soon enough. He'd verify the screenshot I sent him was accurate, then he'd be out for blood. In the meantime, I just had to make sure Jillian was far out of his line of sight.

Surprisingly, weeks went by without a word from Geno or even a sighting of him. Our men had their ears to the ground, but there weren't even any rumors floating around about him. I would've liked to have believed he'd vanished into thin air, but the warning in the back of my mind told me to remain on guard. I'd humiliated him and bankrupted him in one fatal swoop. We were cut from similar cloths, and there was no way I would ever let something like that go unanswered.

The contract on the house Jillian and I wanted was accepted as soon as we submitted it. The previous owners had already moved out and were anxious to close. As soon as we were given a set of keys to the place, Jillian dragged me out shopping for furniture on a daily basis despite my best attempts to pawn that task off on my mother and sister. Not that I didn't want to spend every waking minute with my fiancée, but I'd rather that time be when we were naked and writhing in the bed or against the wall or the floor behind the couch. Shopping for one room at a time was killing me.

We'd been to Mama's every weekend for our standing family dinner, and every weekend Mama and Jillian spent more time planning our wedding. Watching Jillian get so excited over every little detail thrilled me more than I let show. My chest swelled with pride knowing she wanted to be mine for all eternity. Truth was, I didn't care how big or small the wedding was. All I cared was that it happened and that it happened soon.

The fourth week after taunting Geno, we walked into Mama's dining room and found Aunt Maria sitting in her usual spot at the table. I thought my eyes were playing tricks on me for a minute until she spoke. I could hear a smile in her thick Italian accent, though it was still mixed with a hint of sadness. She was happy to be back in the fold, even if she was without Leo for the first time since they were teenagers.

Beside me, I felt Jillian's entire body tense when she saw Maria. Even if my aunt didn't know the truth of what happened, facing her again would be hard for Jillian. Her soft heart and tender nature just didn't lend to the characteristics of a hardened hit man. Even though she saved my life and avenged her mother, Jillian would look at Maria and only think about what she'd taken from her.

"Who have we here?" I asked loudly when we entered the room. "Have we met?"

Aunt Maria jumped from her chair and rushed toward me with tears in her eyes and a small smile on her face. She wrapped her arms around my waist and squeezed me tightly. "Damon, thank you so much for what you did. Lina told me the money came from you, Jillian, and Carrie."

"It was actually Jillian's idea. She found all the accounts, she came up with the plan to redirect the money to you, and she worked with Carrie to make sure it could be done. I'm not taking any credit for this plan. My only part was to sanction it."

She turned to Jillian and only held eye contact with her for a couple of seconds before Maria's eyes dropped to the floor. "Jillian, you helped me after what my Leo did to you and your mother?"

Jillian's eyes flew up to Marco's, looking for direction on what she should say. He shook his head from side to side then she looked at me for confirmation. When she saw I agreed with Marco, she closed her eyes for a second and steadied her breath.

"I don't blame you for what Leo did, Maria. None of this is your fault, and you shouldn't be punished for someone else's crimes."

After Maria and Jillian finished their reconciliation hug, and Maria spent a few minutes rubbing Jillian's growing belly, we all took our seats at the table for dinner. Any remaining discomfort dissipated when the platters of food were passed from person to person. Soon the clatter of silverware and the chatter of multiple conversations filled the room, and we fell back into our old comfortable routine.

"Jillian, *cara*." Mama's voice cut through the clamor of the multiple conversations, getting everyone's attention at once. "Since we only have four weeks until the wedding, we're having your bridal shower here tomorrow at four. Damon, you make sure she's here on time."

"I have a great idea. You two could go furniture shopping tomorrow morning, then she can come back here with you tomorrow afternoon for the shower."

If looks could kill, I would've been dead at that moment.

"I would love to go shopping with my *cara*, but I'll be very busy tomorrow getting everything ready for the shower. We'll go one day this week, yes?"

"Sure, Mama Lina. I'd love that."

After dinner, the ladies moved to the den while the men went into Dad's office. The topic of Geno's location was always first on the list.

"We've gone weeks without hearing anything about Geno. All of a sudden, a rumor surfaced last night. After losing all his money and his alliances, he has left the Tri-State area and moved to Las Vegas. While it's true he has family there, I think this story was concocted to throw us off. Keep your eyes and ears open— he'll resurface somewhere nearby, mark my words. He's trying to catch us off guard." Dad didn't normally share rumors, even with his top tiers. He thought rumors were nothing more than made-up tales meant to scare people, and he didn't scare easily. For him to share a rumor with us meant his gut was strongly warning him.

"Do you have an extra burner phone here, Dad?" My gut said to follow my dad's instincts.

"I'm fairly certain I do." He rifled through his desk drawers until he found it. I took it from his outstretched hand and slipped it into my pocket. "What's on your mind, son?"

"Just a bad feeling. Rather be safe than sorry."

Mama cracked the door open wide enough to stick her head inside. "You boys come have some dessert and coffee with us. We're testing wedding cake flavors and want to use your taste buds."

"Cake? You don't have to ask me twice." Marco jumped up and rushed out of the office, my other brothers close on his heels.

Carrie was standing at the dining table, slicing the different types of cake for the taste test. I slid up next to her and took one of the prepared plates. "Can you pinpoint the location of a burner phone if it's on?"

"Sure. It won't be as precise as a smartphone location, but it'll still ping off the two closest towers. Why do you ask?"

"Checking for security reasons."

She didn't buy my excuse, but she didn't have to. All I needed to know was if she'd be able to find it in case of an emergency.

After we'd devoured all the cake and drank all the coffee, I finally convinced Jillian it was time to drive home. After two full weeks in our new house, we still hadn't christened all the rooms, and I had big plans to rectify that oversight. When we pulled into the garage, I glanced over at her and was immediately enraptured with her beauty. The most peaceful, contented expression covered her face. She seemed to glow with happiness.

As the automatic garage door lowered, I turned off the car and remained in my seat, staring at her. "I love you, Jillian."

My words jarred her from her inner thoughts. She jerked her head to the side, meeting my stare, and searched my eyes. "I love you too, babe. What's on your mind?"

"You mesmerized me. You looked so happy just now, I couldn't resist watching your expressions."

"I'm incredibly happy, Damon. I love our home—that's why I'm taking my time and finishing one room at a time. I want everything to be perfect for you and our babies. I love our life together. I love planning our wedding and knowing we'll be official very soon. I love being pregnant and feeling these two little lives growing inside me. And, most of all, I love you. I couldn't wish for a better husband-to-be."

She certainly knew how to make me feel ten feet tall. After I got out of the car, I walked around to her side and opened her door. That small act had been the source of many discussions between the two of us. She reminded me she was fully capable of opening her own door, and I assured her I was well aware of that fact, but that didn't stop me from wanting to spoil her, so she should let me do the little things.

She usually gave in to my request—except the times when the twins jumped up and down on her bladder, causing her to make a mad dash for the bathroom.

"I don't want to lose my title as *the best husband ever to have lived throughout all of history*, but there is something I want to ask you about. Something you don't talk about." With my extended hand, I helped her out of the car.

We walked into the house—me first, as usual, in case someone waited inside—but she remained quiet. After I checked the alarm and was satisfied we were alone, I walked back to my love and tipped up her face with my finger under her chin. "Look at me, doll."

Tears glistened in her eyes, though she visibly worked to hold them at bay. "I know what you're thinking, Damon. Yes, I miss my mother *so much*. Sometimes I can barely breathe when I think about how much I wish she were here with us. She'll miss our wedding and the birth of our babies. But I don't blame you for her death anymore. I can't hold the actions of your uncle against you. Had you been able to prevent it, I know you would have."

For the mere fact that Leo hurt Jillian so badly, I wished he were alive again. So I could kill him. The pain of losing her mother would never subside. Time would not lessen it, because all the firsts our children experienced would serve as reminders of what she couldn't share with her mother. She would learn to live with the constant ache, but she was right. If I could've changed it, I would have, without a doubt.

She stepped into my waiting arms, wrapping hers around my neck and stretching up on her toes to reach my lips. "I'm getting better at reading your mind. You were just thinking about going back in time to fix everything for me, weren't you?"

"Something like that."

"For the record, I miss Daddy too, and wish he were here to

walk me down the aisle. I want him to be a grandfather to our children and to come visit us so often you start dreading his arrival. But he died long before I met you, so you can't take the blame for his absence either. This is the hand we were dealt, Damon. We're doing the best we can with it. Your parents have been wonderful surrogates to me. I'm grateful to have them in our lives. And I'm very thankful to have *the best husband ever to have lived throughout all of history.*"

"Maybe we should trademark that title. Have a special font created for it, put it on a plaque, and hang it over the fireplace."

"Yeah, I'll get right on that for you."

"There's the feisty mouth I love so much. Pick a spare bedroom and let's see what else you can use that mouth for, doll."

"We haven't made it up to the top floor yet. We'll work our way through those rooms tonight."

She turned to walk away, leaving her clothes where they dropped on the floor as she went. By the time she reached the right side of the dual curved stairs, she was fully naked—and I was fully trotting after her. When I caught up with her and my hands touched her supple skin, I decided I couldn't wait long enough to reach the top floor.

The stairs needed breaking in too.

I lowered my head and took her lips, forcefully and without a second thought. My tongue dipped inside her mouth and curled around hers with smooth, gliding passes. Her unique taste drove me wild. The scent of her arousal tested my restraint. The soft moans and purrs that escaped from her throat spurred me on.

My fingers moved over the softness of her skin, over her swollen stomach, to the apex of her thighs. I moved my mouth down the side of her neck, nibbling on the sensitive skin that made her knees weak and her heart race. Her fingers dug into my arms and she held me tightly, on the verge of succumbing to her desires. When shudders overcame her body, my name fell from her lips in such sweet surrender.

405

Then she surprised me when she slid down my body, taking a seat in front of me on the stairs. The sight of her plump lips wrapped around me nearly unhinged me, but when I felt the back of her throat tighten around me while her tongue curled around me, I thought I'd died and gone to heaven. On the edge but not ready to dive headfirst off the cliff just yet, I begrudgingly stopped her vigorous attention.

I sat beside her and pulled her onto my lap. "Ride me, doll. Ride me hard and put me up wet."

She straddled me, taking every inch inside her, tortuously slow on purpose, until I was at the hilt. Her hips rocked back and forth while mine surged up and down, creating perfect synergy—the same way our personalities complemented and completed each other. Beads of sweat covered our skin, gasps and cries of pleasure echoed in the vaulted entryway, and we tumbled over the edge of ecstasy together, arms and legs entangled, completely wrapped in our love.

I wanted to take my time and make our love last all night, claiming every room in the house as ours. I wanted her to know, without a single doubt, that she was my world and there was nothing I wouldn't do for her. I wanted to show her, tell her, and make her feel it with my every caress, every kiss, every thrust of my hips and arch of my back. But everything about her made it hard for me to hold back.

She made it so fucking hard.

CHAPTER NINETEEN

Jillian

"Damon, I can't believe we're getting married in less than three weeks. Time is flying by. Before we know it, these two little munchkins will be running around the house, getting into everything."

"Speaking of our wedding…you'll be close to the cutoff time to travel while pregnant, especially with twins. Would you rather go somewhere close for our honeymoon? Or wait until after they're born and go to Maui? Or do you have a better idea?" Damon was driving us to Mama Lina's, his eyes continually scanning the road for potential threats. The wedding shower would begin soon, and his entire family would be there.

"We were going to have a quick wedding in the Bahamas then a long honeymoon in Maui later, weren't we? That conversation seems like so long ago now. So much has changed since then."

"If you still want to go to Maui, I'll be glad to take you, doll. But you'll have to promise you'll rest a lot while we're there. You did say Hawaii is your dream vacation spot, and I'm all about making your dreams come true."

"You are the sweetest hit man I know."

"Hawaii it is, then. But we're staying there for two weeks, then you're taking it easy for another two weeks after we get home. Deal?"

"Deal! Deal! Deal!" I bounced in my seat, overcome by my excitement with our honeymoon destination.

"We'll charter a midsize jet that can fly nonstop to LA before refueling, and it will have plenty of space for us to stretch out. You can put your feet up on the way there. It'll still be a long trip, doll."

"We can lie on the beach and wade in the water. We can rent a car for our own sightseeing tours. I'll take it easy, I promise. You know, I don't *want* to be admitted to the hospital on our honeymoon."

"Okay, you convinced me. We're going."

I leaned across the center console and kissed his cheek. "Thank you, Damon. You're spoiling me, and I love every minute of it. You're the best."

"Maybe I should've told you I have some business to take care of while you're at the wedding shower first. But you can't take that back now."

"That's fine, babe. I didn't expect you to stay for the wedding shower. It's usually all women, bows, packages, and punch. They're not exactly your scene. Are you coming back to pick me up?"

"I won't be back anytime soon, doll. I've arranged for Luigi to load all the gifts into the car and drive you back home. Let him do all the lifting—he knows to take them inside the house for you then stand guard outside until I get home. Be sure to lock up and set the house alarm anyway.

"I'm going with Dad to a Council meeting where he'll announce his retirement and succession. They have a ceremony after the meeting to name me as the new Boss. The smaller families aligned with us will be there as witnesses. Only the made men are allowed to attend, and it's all very boring. I'd probably rather stay at the shower with you, to be honest. But this is one tradition I can't shake."

"I understand they have rules that say I can't go with you, but I would like to be there when you officially get your promotion. You'll have to tell me all about it when you get home."

"You know, I used to think the same thing when I was a kid and Dad was promoted at these meetings. I couldn't attend them either before I had my official rank in the family. I had built it up in my mind as some elaborate gathering, with all the finest foods and adult libations on silver platters, offered by waiters dressed in tuxedoes with tails.

"Then I went to my first one and realized nothing about it matched what I'd envisioned. Nothing, doll. Stale cigar smoke fills the room, and not even the good cigars. We're talking cheap imitations. No waiters in tuxes with hot hors d'oeuvres. We had cold deli sandwiches wrapped in wax paper and small bags of chips. The adult libations—no flutes of champagne anywhere to be found, but we do have a lot of beer in longneck bottles. Old guys sit around, shooting the shit about 'the good ol' days' and how hard they had it compared to now, then they make the official announcement to the same people we've talked to all fucking night. You're not missing anything, I promise you."

"Maybe I'll just stick to the shower your mom has coordinated for me. No flutes of champagne for me, but the food will definitely be better than cold deli sandwiches. I can bring you a plate home with me if you want."

"That'd be perfect, doll. Just so you know, you're spoiling me too. But don't stop. Ever."

"Wouldn't dream of it."

"So that means you won't be too busy having fun with the ladies and forget about feeding your man tonight?"

"I promise, I won't forget your supper."

I leaned over and kissed him again, then smoothed the hem of my short black dress. I'd found it during my shopping excursion with Carrie. It was a pullover and the hem hit at mid-thigh, but the fabric was soft and loose, giving me plenty of room to grow into it. And growing into it I definitely was. The main reason I chose it for the shower, though, was because it turned out to be the most comfortable outfit I bought that day.

Every day, the babies were stealing my ability to breathe. Not in a bad way, just in a they're-growing-and-pushing-on-my-lungs way. My handy book of what to expect predicted this would happen. Being vertically challenged also didn't help the situation of the ever-expanding babies. Despite my increased energy, had I mentioned how easily I became winded to Damon, he would've nixed the trip to Maui and used restraints to keep me bedridden all the time.

We turned into Mama Lina's driveway, and my mouth gaped open at the number of cars parked in front of the garages and along the front circular drive. "Damon, I've never seen this many cars here. Who are all these people?"

"All my cousins and aunts, I'm sure. I doubt my grandmother and great aunts made the trip from Italy for the shower, but I could be wrong. I'm sure some of Mama's friends and neighbors are in there too. We may need to get Paulie to bring the van over for the gifts if everyone bought us something. They won't fit in Luigi's car." Damon chuckled and shook his head before getting out of the car.

I sat in stunned silence, picturing enough presents to fill a utility van, while he rounded the front of the car, headed for my car door. The size of the family struck me once again, just as it did the first time Damon brought me to meet them. The large family I'd always wanted waited inside—for me. They'd arrived at Mama Lina's bidding, but they were here for me.

Having no family left, not even in Louisiana, had presented a dilemma when we first started planning the wedding. Mama Lina pictured a huge, elaborate wedding, with at least ten bridesmaids and ten groomsmen. When I pointed out I only had Carrie to be my maid of honor, tears sprang to her eyes, and I immediately thought I'd killed her dreams of coordinating the perfect ceremony for her son.

Then she hugged me and apologized.

"I'm so sorry, *cara*, for being so inconsiderate. I should've thought about that from the very beginning."

"Inconsiderate? You're the most considerate person I know. Look how much you've already done for our wedding. Mama Lina, I didn't want to let you down. Damon told me how much you've wanted your kids to marry." I grasped her hands and held them in mine.

She laughed and shook her head. "No, *bella*, Damon misunderstood. I've always wanted my kids to find a love like Vin and I have. I want them to be as happy as they can possibly be. Of course I want grandkids—every parent does. But only if my kids are with the person made for them."

With the arrival of the wedding shower, the actual ceremony wouldn't be far behind. And everyone inside the house would be there to watch our nuptials and celebrate our special day with us.

"Doll, are you getting out of the car?"

Damon's hand appeared inside the car in front of me, so I took it, and he helped me to stand. Though I didn't admit it, I appreciated his help. Getting out of his low-profile car was getting harder and harder to do gracefully.

"I can't believe so many people came, Damon. This is a little overwhelming."

"They're family, Jilly. Mine—and yours. They'll treat you like family from the moment they meet you. Trust me. And you'd better get used to all this. Whatever mountain of wedding presents you see in there will pale in comparison to the baby shower Mama's planning."

"Oh. My. God. I hadn't even thought about that yet."

"No time to think about it now. Focus on this shower first. Mama's food awaits you."

"That actually helps. A lot. Thank you."

Damon was absolutely right, of course. The moment I stepped into the room, I was surrounded by multiple Marchetti-related women. Cousins, cousins of cousins, aunts, sisters, friends, neighbors, sisters-in-law. There were so many, I lost track of names and how they were related or not related. The love in the room had a hum of its own, though, and I was completely surrounded and enveloped by it.

We played games, we ate, and we laughed for hours. Some gave practical gifts such as cookbooks, sets of pots and pans, and Italian kitchen how-to manuals. Others gave naughty gifts, including edible panties, sexy lingerie, and assorted flavors of warming lube. I lost count of how many times my face flushed deep red and I hid behind the package while laughing along with all the new women in my life. But I wouldn't trade one minute of the elaborate celebration for anything in the world. The new friends I made, the new family I attained, the new bonds I sensed —my lifelong dream of being in a huge family was finally realized.

Damon was also right about another thing. There was no way all the presents would fit in Luigi's car, even with me sitting in the front seat and packing the back seat and trunk. When Paulie arrived with the van, the two men loaded it with all the packages while I said my goodbyes and thanks to everyone. Paulie drove on ahead of us to the house while I fixed Damon's to-go dinner plate, then Luigi and I left in his car.

"Thanks for driving me home, Luigi. The shower ran longer than I thought it would, but I had so much fun with Damon's family. They're the best."

"It's my pleasure, Jillian. You know, I wasn't sure about you at first, what with you and Damon being from completely different walks of life and all. But now I get it. Miss Lina was right—you are the one for him. No doubt about it. True story, this is the first wedding I'm actually glad to attend, because I know the couple truly means it when they say until death."

"Thank you, Luigi. That's so sweet of you to say. I appreciate your—"

Screeching tires interrupted my sentence, turning my words into screams instead. Cars came at us from all four directions, boxing us in so the men inside could jump out with guns drawn. Then I saw him. He approached our car in a leisurely stroll and with a satisfied smirk on his face.

Luigi grabbed his gun and jumped out of the car.

"Luigi, no!" I yelled for him to stop, but he didn't.

Shots rang out so I crouched down with my stomach to the back of the seat. One arm covered my babies and one covered my head. When the gunfire stopped, the car door opened and the devil himself spoke.

"Get out of the car, Jillian. You can come on your own, or my men can drag you out by your hair. Personally, I prefer the latter, but it's up to you." Geno Sanfratello had made his move.

When I sat up, his men had the car surrounded and were all leering at me. In that moment, the reason I couldn't breathe had very little to do with the position of my babies. Somehow, I managed to slide across the seat and climb out of the car. Someone behind me grabbed my arms and tied them behind my back. Geno took a wide piece of black tape from his soldier's hand and slapped it over my mouth. On reflex, I pulled my head away from him and took a step backward. When I did, I saw Luigi lying on the road, the blood from multiple bullet holes in his body quickly covering his clothes.

With a violent jerk of my arm, Geno pulled me toward one of the cars. One of the soldiers popped the trunk open, and my legs suddenly refused to move on their own. Geno yanked again, causing me to stumble behind him. I was barely able to regain my balance and avoid eating the pavement. When we reached the trunk, I fought being put inside, but I was no match for the two goons who picked me up and tossed me inside anyway.

Another man walked up to Geno and handed him my purse.

413

Geno rummaged through it until he found my phone. With an evil grin, he spiked it on the pavement like a football, before throwing my purse on top of me. Then he closed the lid while laughing.

"Damon." All I could do was cry his name, hoping he found me in time.

CHAPTER TWENTY

Damon

"What the fuck do you mean, they aren't there? Where are they?"

"Boss, I've been calling Luigi's phone for the past twenty minutes, but he's not answering. I even tried Jillian's phone, but she's not answering either. Miss Lina said they left her house in plenty of time to be here by now. I'm headed back to Fort Lee now, backtracking the whole way to try to find them."

"I'm leaving the Council building right now. I'll do the same from this end. Keep your eyes open, Paulie."

"Don't worry, Boss. If there's a hair from her head out here, I won't miss it."

We disconnected, and I immediately called Marco to alert him to Jillian's disappearance. He assured me he'd be on my tail within minutes to help find her. Though part of me didn't want to accept it, I knew there was only one explanation for why neither Jillian nor Luigi answered their phones after repeated calls. My gut feeling was spot-on once again.

Geno had never left town. He'd simply bided his time. Probably made a few new friends. Or worse, he hired several thugs to be his new friends.

Piecing together everything I knew up to that point, the wedding shower had run way over the expected time. That wasn't unusual, though. Once the Marchetti women got together, they enjoyed the company too much to give it up early. As I predicted, there were too many gifts to fit in Luigi's car, so Paulie took them in the van. He said he'd left Mama's house before Jillian was ready to go. She'd mentioned she had to make a plate of food for me—because she'd promised she wouldn't forget it. Mama said Jillian and Luigi left about twenty minutes after Paulie did.

"So Geno made his move after she left Mama's house and before she reached our house. Well, that narrows it down to about a twenty-five-mile stretch. Real fucking helpful."

Speeding through red lights and stop signs, weaving through traffic moving way too slow for the panic rising in my throat, and cursing Geno with every breath should've been Olympic events. I would've won triple gold.

When my phone pinged with a message, I felt my blood boil in my veins. The attached video showed Jillian with her hands bound and black tape covering her mouth. Rivers of tears created streaks down her beautiful face. Black mascara had run underneath her eyes and dried there, only to be smeared even more when her tears resumed. But when I realized she was calling my name, the fiancé in me faded to black and the notorious hit man fully emerged.

I'd have Geno's fat, ugly head on a spike before the night was over. That much was for fucking sure.

And I'd have Jillian back in my arms, safe and sound.

"Carrie. Track the burner phone and Geno's phone. He has Jillian."

"Oh my God. I'm on it, Damon. Give me two minutes to get the program running. What are you going to do?"

"I'm going to kill him and anyone with him." First, I brought my sister up to speed on what I knew so far. Then I rattled off the burner cell phone number when her computer finished booting up.

"Okay, Geno's phone isn't pinging anywhere near the burner phone, so he must have turned it off after he grabbed her. The burner phone shows they're in Ridgewood. I'll text you the address of the approximate location. You'll have to search the entire area around the address I send you, Damon. I can't pinpoint it exactly with this phone."

"Just get me close, Carrie. By the time I'm finished with that neighborhood, they'll welcome a hurricane."

The text with the address came through as soon as we hung up, so I forwarded it to Paulie and told him to meet me there. Marco was already behind me, and Carrie was alerting the rest of the family. Geno wanted to start a family war? He had one hell of a fight coming his way, but he had no idea what he'd started or the way his life would soon end.

The only outcome I'd accept was one that included a happily ever after for Jillian and me.

When I arrived in the area where the burner phone signaled, my gut said we were on top of them regardless of the shitty location services a prepaid phone provided. The abandoned farm had a "For Sale" sign at the driveway. The chain link gate across the drive had a brand-new padlock keeping the two panels closed. The house was set back off the road, secluded by a cluster of trees and a bend in the long driveway.

I continued past the driveway and parked on the side of the road, close enough to the next house on the road that it appeared I was visiting there. If Geno's goons patrolled the area, they were more likely to dismiss my vehicle. Marco took my lead and pulled off the road next to another driveway.

Dad called just as I got out of my car. "Son, we're on our way. You'll have backup there in less than five minutes."

"Just follow Geno's screams begging for his life."

"You two be careful and watch each other's backs."

"Always."

A large white utility van approached us, and I flagged Paulie down. Before he'd stopped the van, I jerked the door open and told him to get in the back and be ready for a firefight. Marco read my mind and jumped into the passenger seat.

I turned the van around and floored the gas pedal. We burst through the gate like it wasn't there and barreled down the bumpy dirt driveway until the structures came into sight—a dilapidated house, a barn, and a two-story cinder block garage. Using the van to block the only way out, I angled it between two trees. No way around it. No way through it.

Complete darkness in the house ruled it out immediately. The barn and the garage were both closed up tight, and she could've been in either, but I closed my eyes and replayed the images of her tied up again. They were as clear as if I'd watched it on the big screen. Cinder blocks.

"She's in the garage. His men could be anywhere, though. Leave no one alive."

"Got it, Boss." Paulie screwed the suppressor on the end of his gun before moving silently through the night in front of us, headed toward the garage but watching all around him as he went.

"Keep your head on straight, brother. We don't know what we'll see when we bust the door down." Marco's concern was valid but not one I could fathom at that moment.

"I hear you, Marco. But I can't make any promises."

His lips formed a thin line and he nodded, understanding I wouldn't be in control if Jillian was dead. The level of savagery I would resort to in that case had never been seen before, and likely never would be again.

We started for the garage with our silenced guns at the ready, taking opposite sides of the drive and checking behind every large rock, tree, and bush along the way. Paulie waited for us with his back against the building, ready to engage anyone who dared to step out of the shadows and into the moonlight.

"And just where do you think you're going?" The cool metal of a semiautomatic handgun pressed against the back of my head. If he thought I was intimidated, he was fatally mistaken.

When I turned my head to look at him, he took a step away from me. No doubt the deadly intent shone in my eyes, even in the darkness. He opened his mouth to issue another threat, but I raised my gun and silenced him forever. The crackle of his two-way radio caught my attention, so I pulled the cord to his earpiece out and grabbed the handset from his belt.

"Curtis! Answer me! What do you see? Is Damon here?" A panicked voice asked repeatedly in a whispered shout.

I lowered the earpiece and strained to locate where the other soldier hid. Then he made the mistake of leaving his post and moving closer to Curtis, and I had him dead in my sights. Literally.

The muffled sound of gunfire from my right meant Marco had taken another man down. Hearing the shot, another man stepped out and leveled his gun on me, but that didn't break my stride. A double tap later, and even dental records wouldn't identify him. The bastards were dropping like flies around us, but I was still looking for one specific fucker.

When Marco and I reached the door, I realized why Geno had chosen this structure. The metal door was impossible to kick in and could only be locked from the inside. With no locking mechanism on the exterior, we couldn't pick the lock to get inside. But he only thought he had outsmarted me. I had other news for him that could only be delivered in person.

Keeping in line with the rest of the structures, the outside of the garage was littered with discarded items and pieces of plastic or metal that used to be useful tools. I grabbed part of an old metal file and a thick rock and removed the pins from the door hinges. Within seconds, I'd removed the last barrier between

Jillian and me. The men inside that room didn't count because they were already dead, they just didn't know it yet.

Two of Geno's goons were positioned on either side of Jillian, their guns aimed at my chest as I stood in the doorway. Geno stood behind Jillian with his gun pressed firmly against her temple. But I wouldn't be intimidated by that motherfucker, so I walked straight at him without acknowledging his bodyguards. The experienced hit man in me surfaced without a hitch. The terror in her eyes would've swayed my approach if I allowed myself to think about it. So I couldn't. I had to push it aside. If I showed a millisecond of weakness, Geno would exploit it and tear my world to pieces.

"Dad and the rest of the family just pulled up. This is over, Geno. There's no way you walk out of here alive if she's hurt. Let her go right now." Marco stepped into the room and moved to my side.

"If she didn't want to be a target, she shouldn't have tracked my money. Your fucking sister shouldn't have stolen it from my account. The Marchetti family ruined my life, so I'll take your world away while you watch. Now, say goodbye to your girl and your baby, Damon."

"Babies." With an even and calm voice, I corrected him.

"What?" He scrunched up his face and drew his brows downward.

"Not baby, you fucking moron. Babies, plural. She's pregnant with twins."

"What the fuck does that matter?"

When he asked the question, he raised both hands up in front of him. Some stereotypes were accurate. As with any typical Italian, he talked with his hands, making big gestures to amplify his point. In the split second the gun was away from Jillian's head, I aimed and fired at his head, putting an end to the pseudo-threat that was Geno Sanfratello. Marco and Paulie fired immediately after me, taking out the two extra dead weights.

"It matters a lot."

In two strides, I knelt in front of Jillian and pulled the tape off her mouth while Marco cut the ties off her wrists. As soon as her hands were freed, she threw her arms around my neck in a death grip and cried into my neck.

"Are you hurt anywhere, doll?"

She shook her head, and I barely discerned a muffled "no" coming from the general area where her face was still pressed against me. I slid one arm under her knees and the other around her back then stood while cradling her.

"We're going to the hospital to have her and the babies checked out." I didn't bother to stop and talk to my father as we passed him.

"Go. We've got this covered, son. Call me when you know something."

Despite my near sprint all the way from the farmhouse back to my car, I didn't feel like I'd exerted any effort at all. The adrenaline that flowed through my veins was more than enough fuel to keep me going for days on end. If we got an all-clear from the doctor, then I'd slow down. Until then, I couldn't and wouldn't rest.

When we reached Columbia Medical Center, I was so relieved to find Dr. Bowers was on call and already in the hospital. He met us in the labor and delivery triage area and gave Jillian a thorough examination.

"Everything looks and sounds fine, but I'd like to keep you here the rest of the night for observation. I don't know exactly what all has happened to you, but I can tell you've been under a lot of stress, my dear. I'd feel better if we put a fetal monitor on you for the night and just kept tabs on the babies' heartbeats and movements." Dr. Bowers moved close to Jillian on the rolling seat, studying her features and committing every sign and symptom to memory.

He wasn't Matteo, I got it. But his scrutiny made me uncomfortable.

"Observation sounds great to me, Dr. Bowers. I just want to make sure my babies are healthy. I'm fine, physically. Just a little shaken up."

"I'll have them put you in one of the delivery rooms for the next several hours to monitor all three of you. These nurses are great—they've worked with countless pregnant women. Sometimes I think they know more than I do." He laughed good-naturedly, taking their expertise in stride and putting Jillian at ease. "And I'll be around if you should need me for anything. I'll put the order in now, and one of the nurses will move you out of the triage area and into your room in just a few minutes."

We thanked him as he left the room, and I released a long, tired sigh. The events of the day and night were catching up with me, but until we had the answers we needed about the health of our twins, I'd remain on guard.

"Jilly."

When she met my gaze, tears immediately filled her eyes. "Damon, I was so scared."

"I know you were, doll. I'm sorry I wasn't there to protect you when you needed me. I wish I could take that fear away from you. If I could bear it for you, I gladly would."

"Geno said he'd set up an ambush to kill you here when he realized you weren't in the car with me. He bragged about how his goons were the best and you'd be too busy hunting for me to realize you were the one being hunted. I was so afraid he was right, because I knew you wouldn't stop until you found me. He knew you'd come for me. He even said you'd find me within minutes of realizing I was missing. He picked a place that would be fast and easy to find so he could get to you. How did you find me anyway? Geno trashed my phone."

"Dad had heard a rumor about Geno moving to Vegas, but we knew better than to believe it at face value. I hid a burner phone under the liner in your purse this morning. Call it a sixth sense or intuition, whatever, but I knew something was coming. Anyone who grabbed you would get rid of your smartphone, but they wouldn't take time to look under the lining. Carrie was able to track the burner phone to a general area. From that location, I knew exactly where you were from the video text Geno sent to me."

"Geno must have counted on me having some sort of tracking device other than my phone. You saved me again, Damon. You're always rushing into dangerous situations to help me out of them."

"And I always will—no matter what the situation is. Remember that warning I gave you a long time ago? That still stands. You go, I go. Simple as that."

"Would you think less of me if I told you I've had enough scrapes with death over the past year, and I'm okay with waiting until my nineties for the next one?"

"No, doll, I wouldn't think less of you at all. I'd be so fucking relieved, you wouldn't believe it. If you'll put that in writing right now, I'll let you be the boss at home for the rest of our lives."

The sound of her laughter was music to my ears. "Damon, I don't want to be the boss at home."

"Oh? So you *want* me to be the boss at home and at work?"

"No. You can be the boss at work. But at home, we're a team. Deal?"

"Deal, my love. That is the deal of a lifetime, and I'll take you up on that starting right now."

21

CHAPTER TWENTY-ONE

Jillian

or the first two weeks after I was released from the overnight observation, Damon barely left my side. Knowing that the only remaining threat had been eliminated didn't console him in the least. The video Geno sent to Damon's phone struck a chord deep inside him, ringing a bell that wouldn't easily be un-rung. Even when I went with Mama Lina and Carrie to pick out my wedding gown, he insisted on going with us. But he knew how important keeping the dress a surprise was to me, so he agreed to stand guard outside the enormous dressing room without peeking.

Choosing the one dress I'd wear for my one and only wedding was more than a little daunting. Besides finding the perfect gown, I also had to find one that would fit my ever-growing midsection and still look halfway decent on me. Damon claimed I was overreacting, but he only said that to placate me. The reality was, I could tell a difference in the size of my belly every morning when I woke. Our wedding day seemed so close yet still so far away. At that rate, I wasn't even sure the dress would still fit when the day finally arrived and it was time to wear it, yet I didn't want to get a size so big it swallowed me whole either.

There was no one-size-fits-all dress or solution to my conundrum.

"Good morning, gorgeous. Did you have trouble sleeping last night?"

"Good morning, my love. I slept like the dead between the fifty times I had to get up to pee in the middle of the night. Did I wake you?"

"I'm naturally a light sleeper, doll. Comes from years of sleeping with one eye open."

"Good to know. I'll try not to disturb the eye that's asleep in the future." With a smile for my fiancé, I slid into my seat and began devouring the scrumptious breakfast he cooked.

"By the way, I have a pre-wedding gift for you." The words rolled off his tongue so nonchalantly, but I sensed the undertone of excitement he tried to hide from me.

"What is it?" I was intrigued. There weren't many material possessions that excited him.

He smirked at me for a moment, considering his extortion options. What could he get from me in exchange for information? How much should he hold out for? All the old negotiation tactics I'd seen in contractors over my years of professional experience. But I was good at negotiating for what I wanted too. With my fork held in midair for added emphasis, I arched one brow and pursed my lips, waiting for him to make a decision and daring him to make the wrong one.

He reached into his breast pocket, pulled out a key fob, and held it out in the palm of his hand. "I'm sorry it took me so long to do this."

I took the key fob attached to a leather keychain from him and ran my finger across the four connected circles at the bottom. "An Audi?"

"Yes, ma'am. A dark blue Audi RS7, to be exact. It's a luxury sedan—sporty but still very safe for you and the twins."

"I would jump into your lap and cover your face with kisses right now if I could fit between you and the table."

Without hesitation, he pushed back from the table using his legs then patted his lap. "Problem solved."

After I'd smothered him with kisses for several minutes, we walked to the garage together where my new car waited. After I'd checked out all the buttons, knobs, bells, and whistles, I wrapped my arms around Damon's neck and kissed him again.

"I love this car. It's perfect. Thank you, babe."

"My pleasure. I should've done that a long time ago. It finally occurred to my thick head that you may want to drive yourself somewhere instead of relying on me or one of the guys. Luigi won't be able to drive for a while. He's lucky even to be alive. As much as I want to keep you safe, I don't want to keep you prisoner."

"I don't feel like your prisoner, but I do appreciate not depending on someone else for everything I want or need."

"Yeah, I get that. I'm the same way. The car made me realize I should've already given you this, too." He pulled an envelope from his jacket's inside pocket. "We'll update the name after we're married, but these will work until then."

I opened the envelope and pulled out lots of plastic. "You added me to your bank and credit card accounts?"

"What's mine is yours, doll. Maybe you've noticed the lack of any lawyer involvement or requests to sign prenuptial agreements. I told you before, once we're married, it'll be forever. You're the only one for me for the rest of my life, doll."

"No keeping secrets or leaving me in the dark about anything?"

He shook his head. "No way. Two heads are better than one. Besides, I want you by my side in everything I do. Sometimes figuratively, sometimes literally—but always with me just the same."

"That's where I'll be—always with you. But I have a warning of my own."

"Oh yeah? Let's hear it."

"If you double-cross me, I'll make sure your enemies know you're secretly a huge romantic."

He threw his head back in laughter. "Trust me, doll. None of my enemies would ever believe I have a single nice bone in my body, much less a romantic one. That side of me is reserved for your eyes only."

He kissed me goodbye and walked to his car. "You should take your new toy for a spin while I'm out today. Make sure you like it."

"I'll do that—if I can fit behind the wheel and still reach the pedals."

He laughed, amused by my self-deprecating humor. "I'll be home late, doll. We're meeting with some of the smaller factions that aligned with the Sanfratellos a few months ago. They want to play nice with us now."

"Please be careful, Damon. You're a bad influence on me—I don't trust anyone now, and I definitely don't trust someone who used to be your enemy."

"Don't worry about me, doll. I'll be fine. If we can use them, we will. If they don't prove their loyalty soon enough, we'll get rid of them. I consider everyone a potential enemy until they give me concrete proof showing they're not. I'll call you later and check in." He blew me a kiss as he climbed into his car. I watched him drive away, wondering if I'd ever get used to the danger he faced in his line of work.

I grabbed my purse from inside the house and took Damon's advice on taking my new car for a spin. As with every other high-end item, Damon also had impeccable taste in cars. I'd racked my brain trying to come up with a wedding gift for a man who had the world at his fingertips. He, on the other hand, had no problem coming up with extravagant gifts for me.

Driving through our township, I saw a sign in the window of a women's boutique, of all places, that gave me an idea. Something he didn't already have and wasn't likely to initiate for himself. Something that could be completed within a day, with Mama Lina and Carrie's help. After a brief phone call and quick explanation to each, they were both on board to make my idea a reality.

Our basement was finished, but it was initially slated to be the last room on the list for furniture shopping. But I changed my mind when I saw the "Babe Cave" sign. Damon deserved a true Man Cave where he could unwind and de-stress after a long day. A playroom for adults, where problems didn't exist and troubles took a back seat.

When I reached Mama Lina's, she'd already assembled a small army of Vincenzo's men to be at our beck and call.

"Tell me, *bella*. What do you want to get first?"

"I want to get the biggest flat-screen TV we can find and hang it on one end of the room, with rows of recliners like his own theater, and a sectional sofa on the opposite end of the room. We need a fully stocked bar with stools along one of the side walls, a pool table in the middle of the room, and a card table off to the other side. Can we make all this happen today?"

"No sweat, Miss Jillian. We'll make sure it's finished well before he gets home." I recognized the man as one of Vincenzo's most trusted lieutenants. If they trusted him, I knew I could trust him too.

"Thank you, Joseph. You're such a good man. We need to find you a good wife, no?" Mama Lina patted his cheek, and I could've sworn he blushed from her attention.

Carrie pulled up just as Mama Lina and I were getting into my new car. She jumped out of hers and into the back seat of mine. "Where to first? This is exciting. I love spending my brother's money."

We laughed and took off on our shopping spree with the day's work crew behind us. From one store to the next, I picked out every item to accomplish the room's exact look and feel I had pictured in my mind. The men stayed with us, doing all the heavy lifting and immediately taking the items available to carry out of the store to my house.

I learned a few new negotiation tactics from Mama Lina to get the bigger delivery items dropped off within the same business day—mainly dropping the Marchetti name in the store and watching them scramble to make it happen. The furniture store was more than willing to take the sectional sofa and leather recliners right away, considering I'd already spent a small fortune there and they knew I'd be back for more.

With all the big-ticket items being assembled and secured by the family men, Mama Lina, Carrie, and I spent most of the day shopping for decorations to add the finishing touches. When we finished and returned to my house, I was beyond thrilled with the progress the guys had made. They unloaded the pictures, lamps, and throw rugs from my trunk and made quick work of getting those items into place.

I couldn't wait for Damon to get home. His late night at work would mean a long night of anticipation for me.

"You guys did such a great job today—and you were so fast! I couldn't have pulled this off without you. Thank you so much for all your help." I made sure to make eye contact with each man while I spoke, letting them know their hard work didn't go unnoticed. Their mumbled replies and uneasy glances left little doubt they weren't used to receiving accolades.

"I'll drive Miss Lina and Miss Carrie back so you don't have to make the trip, if you'd like."

"That would be great, Joseph. Thank you."

Joseph gave one quick nod of his head, but I didn't miss the appreciative smile that flashed across his face just before he turned away. After a hug and kiss goodbye from Mama Lina and

Carrie, I was alone in the enormous house, impatiently waiting for Damon to walk in so I could surprise him. To help pass the time, I decided to tackle the bags of nursery decorations Damon and I picked out together. When I finally heard the garage door opening, I rushed out to greet him.

Damon looked tired, with his unkempt clothes, disheveled hair, and heavy eyes. When he looked up at me, standing in the doorway waiting for him to reach me, his expression brightened. "You've been up to something. What have you done?"

"Stop reading my mind!"

"Doll, I don't have to read your mind to know you have something to confess. It's written all over your face."

"I actually don't have anything to confess. But I do have a surprise for you. I've been waiting for you to get home for days now."

"For days? Really now?"

"It felt like days anyway. Now, come with me. I can't wait any longer."

"That's exactly what you said to me last night." That mischievous grin covered his handsome face, making me instantly quiver inside from the simple reminder alone.

"Follow. Me." I tried to maintain my stern tone and face, but that was impossible when he smiled at me that way.

"Yes, ma'am. Lead the way. I'm all yours, wherever it is you're taking me."

When we reached the door to the basement, I glanced over my shoulder at Damon, intentionally keeping my face passive as I turned the doorknob.

"Now, this is what I'm talking about. You can meet me at the car every day so we can finish initiating every room in the house. The basement is a great idea for tonight, doll."

"I'm glad you think so." The stairs were lit with scattered night-lights. When we reached the bottom stair, I flipped on the overhead lights and closely watched his reaction.

He was speechless as he slowly walked through the room, checking out all the new additions and décor. When he finally turned back toward me, I held up a sign that read *My Cave, My Rules. My Wife Said So.*

He threw his head back in laughter before covering the ground between us in two long strides. "You did all this for me?"

"Of course. You've done so much for me, I wanted to surprise you with something I knew you wouldn't do for yourself. It's my turn to spoil you, and you deserve it. Do you like it?"

"Like it? I fucking love it. This is awesome, doll. It'll be put to good use, believe me."

"I was thinking, as you start to take over from your dad, your brothers and your men could come here for the family meetings. They could even bring their wives or girlfriends so I'd have more friends than just your mom and sister. This room is isolated enough from the rest of the house that you wouldn't be bothered by us upstairs, and then you wouldn't have to stay gone so much."

"You wouldn't mind all of them coming over every week?"

"Not at all."

"You know, doll. I have no idea how I ever lived without you before, but I know without a shadow of a doubt, I can't do it now. You're the absolute best, and I love you more than I love my next breath. Come here."

He placed his palms on my cheeks before he slanted his mouth over mine, teasing my lips open with a seductive slide of his tongue. Then he delved deep inside, and the rest of the world faded away. It was a soft and slow kiss, unhurried yet commanding as he melted me from the inside out. My heart raced and my chest heaved as my need for him increased. With every pass of his lips, the tingles inside me increased until I was certain my body would detonate from his simple touch.

"You're absolutely perfect," he murmured against my lips, his masculine voice sending goose bumps fanning out across my skin in response. "And right now, I want to fuck you on that pool table more than I've ever wanted anything in my entire life."

"How do you want me? On my back or on all fours?"

The sexiest growl rumbled through his chest and worked its way up his throat. I loved when I made him lose control—no matter how brief it was.

"Both. Fucking both. Right now."

CHAPTER TWENTY-TWO

Jillian

"*A*re you nervous? Are you getting cold feet? Do I need to put on my running shoes so I can catch you when you take off?"

Damon stood in the hall outside the door of one of our guest bedrooms while I attempted to get dressed. For our wedding ceremony. While he was trying to be funny with the barrage of questions, I wasn't feeling the humor.

My dress didn't fit.

I knew it. I'd predicted this would happen, even waiting until a week before the wedding to pick up my dress. Even though I had extra room around the waist just seven days ago, the twins had filled in the gap and then some. To add insult to injury, my boobs decided all on their own to pass *Go* a few times, collecting more volume with each go-round. My dress wouldn't zip past halfway up my back, but it wouldn't have mattered even if I could suck it in enough to make the zipper move more. My fucking boobs were spilling out over the top of my strapless dress.

There was sure to be a nipple incident if I pushed my luck.

"I'm way past the running stage now. It's more of a fast wobble. Like Weebles."

His quick burst of laughter quickly covered up by an exaggerated cough didn't go unnoticed. "Doll, I told you before. I don't care what you wear, as long as you marry me. You can say the vows in maternity shorts and an oversized T-shirt. I don't care. Honest to God, it wouldn't bother me. I'll go change out of this monkey suit and match you."

"Damon, I'm not getting married in maternity shorts."

I heard a thud on the other side of the door and knew without asking the noise came from his forehead hitting it.

"Jilllllll-eeeeee-annnnn." He drew my name out in long syllables, pouring on the charm and keeping his voice reassuring. "You know I love you, right?"

"Yes, I know you do. You know I love you too."

"Then you know I mean this with all the love in my heart." He paused for dramatic emphasis. "Get your ass out here and marry me right now."

"Nope."

"I've got it! I exchanged her dress for one almost exactly the same pattern. She'll be dressed in just a few minutes. Damon, get downstairs to your spot where you're supposed to be and stop harassing my sister-in-law before she crawls out the window and shimmies down the drainpipe out of desperation." Carrie always did have a way with her brother.

"If that dress doesn't work, wrap a white sheet around her and call it a designer gown, Carrie. Get her down the aisle and in front of the altar." After his demand, the hard footfall of his steps diminished, so he'd at least followed her instructions.

Carrie rushed into the room, breathing heavily while carrying an extra-large garment bag. "Here, sis. This is just like the original dress, only better. The waistline is much higher, right under your boobs, so it'll give your stomach plenty of room."

She hung up the bag on the coat rack and unzipped it. I held my breath until she stepped out from in front of it. "Oh, Carrie, it's perfect. I love it even more than the original."

She was right—the bodice design of the original dress was way too tight all the way down to where I used to have a waist. But the replacement was exquisite—a strapless white dress with champagne gold applique that started on the breasts and flowed down the skirt. When I stepped into it, the zipper slid all the way to the top without a problem. My fuller breasts filled the strapless bodice with ease, keeping it snug but not too tight. With my veil in place, I was ready to walk down the aisle.

Barefoot. Because my feet were too swollen to fit into my shoes.

Carrie handed me the bouquet of flowers—deep purple Chapeau de Napoléon roses mixed with lighter purple morning glories and white calla lilies. Carrie was my gorgeous maid of honor. She slipped into her dress that was the same deep purple as the roses, with a halter top neckline and a high waist. Then she picked up her bouquet and flashed a nervous smile.

"It's time, Jillian. Are you ready?"

"I've never been more ready for anything in my life, Carrie. I'm walking toward the rest of my life—happier than I've ever been. The crazy hit man I fell so desperately in love with is waiting at the end of the aisle for me. We're getting married inside our home, filling it with so many happy memories and promises and declarations of our commitment to each other. Before we know it, our home will be filled with the sounds of our babies. This is more than I've ever even dreamed of having, and I can't wait to start this beautiful new life as married partners."

"Married partners in crime."

"That too."

We laughed together like young schoolgirls until we heard a quick rap on the door.

"Damon, she's coming out now. Cool your jets."

The door slowly opened, and there stood my soon-to-be

father-in-law, dressed to kill in his black tuxedo and white shirt. He didn't even try to hide the mist in his eyes after he took a good look at me in my wedding gown.

"*Cara*, you're so beautiful. I'm honored to have you on my arm and present you to marry my son. Come with me, *bella*. He's waiting—very impatiently, I should add."

I slipped my hand around his proffered elbow and gave it a squeeze. "You look very handsome yourself, Dad. Let's take a stroll and see if we can find your son."

The music started when Carrie and Marco stepped into the double doorway of the great room. When they'd taken their places on either side of the aisle, the wedding march began.

"Here we go, *cara*. I'm so proud to call you my daughter. Damon couldn't have picked a better woman than you. I love you, Jillian."

"I love you too, Dad."

The room was full of people—all of them were my new family. Blood or water, it didn't matter. We'd stick together through the good times and the bad times. The man of my dreams watched me with a heated gaze, his eyes traveling up and down my body several times on my approach. When we finally reached him, I read his lips when he mouthed the words to me.

"You are stunning. I love you so much."

Vincenzo announced he was presenting me to his son, but he refused to acknowledge he was giving me away. The crowd laughed along with us, and it felt so right in my soul. Our wedding was a celebration of our love, and that included all the laughter that came with it. Uptight and formal was never my style anyway. Vincenzo joined my hands with Damon's, then used his big hands to cover ours.

"There's something I'd like to say. I'll make it brief. Jillian, when I first met you, I knew you were different. I had a very strong feeling you'd change my son for the better, that you'd bring the light and love and laughter to him that had been missing for most of his adult life. You've done more than that. You've made him a better man, and I didn't even think that was possible. Lina and I are ecstatic to call you our daughter, now and forever. I could never fill your father's shoes, and I don't even want to try because he had to be a very good man to raise such a wonderful daughter as you. But I hope you've saved a small place in your heart for me to be your new dad."

Wiping the tears from my cheeks, I rose up on my toes and kissed Vincenzo's cheeks. "I love you, Dad. You have a very special place in my heart, and you always will. Thank you for everything you said. Words can't express how much it means to me."

When Vincenzo took his seat next to Mama Lina, Damon and I turned to face the priest. The vows were a blur because all I could think about was how happy I was, how happy he still made me after everything we'd been through. A family bigger than I ever could've hoped to have. Our twin babies that would join us in only a few months. The sister I never had. But most of all, I was marrying a sexy as hell, dangerous bad boy, secret romantic, protective alpha man who showered me with love and spoiled me to no end.

"You may now kiss the bride."

In true Damon Marchetti fashion, he broke tradition when he circled his arms around me, dipped me with a sudden lurch to the side, and turned me into putty in his hands with his obscenely inappropriate but insanely hot and sensual kiss. Public display of affection? No. Had a cop been present, we'd have been arrested for having public mouth sex.

The priest presented us to our guests as Mr. and Mrs. Damon Marchetti, and we were greeted by loud cheers and thunderous applause. Damon leaned over to me, kissing me on the cheek before whispering in my ear.

"You're all mine now, doll. I have papers on you to prove it."

"What a coincidence. You're all mine too, and I have the same papers to prove it."

"Abso-fucking-lutely. Speaking of fucking, can we tell everyone to get out now? We need to consummate our marriage as soon as possible."

"No. We have too much cake to eat for everyone to leave just yet. But I'm sure I need help with my zipper or something."

"Fuck the zipper. I have a better idea."

We walked back up the aisle arm in arm and with smiles so big I thought our faces might permanently freeze that way. The family began filing out of the great room and moving outside onto the covered terrace, where the cake and finger foods were laid out for our reception. But Damon steered us in the opposite direction, toward the library on the opposite side of the house.

"What are you doing, Damon?"

"I wasn't kidding, doll." He closed and locked the door behind us. "Now, this may seem a little familiar, but since we still have to take a bazillion pictures, this position will have to do for now. Bend over the back of the couch and hold on to something. Tight."

He lifted the back of my dress and hissed when he saw I wasn't wearing any panties. I heard his zipper lower. A hand gripped the back of my neck before he positioned his cock at my entrance, sliding it up and down me, teasing and driving me out of my mind. Then with a sudden thrust, he filled me so fully I felt my delicate skin stretch. The hand on the back of my neck squeezed, and then he placed his other hand on my hip. His deep lunges at that angle hit the sweet spot every time, making my body crave him more with every movement.

Though it was the same thrilling sensation he'd always given me, our union was also different that time. We were literally one person, our bodies so connected it was impossible to tell where one ended and the other began. Our love and our life together felt the same way—only whole and complete when we were together. Mad with love and insane with need that only intensified when he was inside me. The feeling of being so *completely* loved and worshiped while also feeling so *completely* satiated by the one man who was capable of taking me to the highest highs.

Unquestionable. Unstoppable. Unyielding.

Passionate. Consuming. Relentless.

Our love for one another matched the ferocity of our love-making in every way. The words he spoke, the pleasure he gave, and his fingers digging into my skin created the perfect storm of hedonism and decadence. I was unable to hold back any longer. The free-falling sensation began low in my abdomen and quickly spread until I couldn't stop the shudders and shakes that tore through me. Feeling my violent and forceful release, Damon followed close behind me before his upper body collapsed onto my back while supporting his weight with his arms on either side of me.

"Mrs. Marchetti, I think you're already trying to kill me. That was so fucking hot."

"Mr. Marchetti, if I were trying to kill you, it would be with a knife at your throat while you slept. Not while you're making me scream your name in ecstasy."

He chuckled and kissed the back of my neck, where I was sure the light bruises from his hold on me would begin to show within the hour. Not that I minded, but I did hope our wedding guests were well on their way out the door by that time.

After cleaning up, we rejoined the festivities on the terrace. Cutting the cake, feeding each other, throwing the bouquet and garter—all the traditional wedding activities. We also took more pictures than should be allowed, but I knew once I saw them, I'd cherish them all. Then a slow song came over the speakers, drowning out the multitude of conversations and making everyone pause to watch as Damon and I had our first dance as husband and wife.

After several lines of the familiar love song, I glanced away from Damon for a split second—long enough to see Carrie step into Lorenzo's arms, and their bodies began to sway as one.

"You invited Lorenzo." I jerked my eyes back to Damon, his knowing smirk squarely in place. "Are you turning soft, Damon?"

"I've already shown you once today exactly how hard I am. Sounds like I need to prove it to you again."

"Don't play dumb with me, husband." I chuckled at the mere thought. "Thank you for doing that. You made your sister very happy."

"As long as he's good to her, I'm okay with it. What I care about most is that you're happy, wifey."

"I have you. How could I not be?'

When the wedding party left and the house was finally quiet, we changed into our comfortable pajamas, settled on the over-stuffed sectional sofa in his newly decorated man cave, and relived the entire day through each other's eyes.

The next day, we'd leave for Maui to enjoy our two-week honeymoon before my ban on travel started. But for that night, we were lost in each other and the miracle of love that brought and kept us together.

"When we get back from Maui, Mama and Dad are taking an extended trip to Italy. They'll be back before the babies are born, but Dad will hand over the keys to the kingdom to me before they leave. So, for the two weeks we're away, we'll simply be Damon and Jillian—madly in love newlyweds with no other cares in the world. Sun, sand, sea, and sight-seeing like two normal tourists."

"You won't hear any complaining from me. I get you all to myself for two solid weeks. No sharing you with anyone else for any reason. No cell phones. No computers. No communication with the outside world at all. If there's an emergency, they'll have to call the hotel. Deal?"

"I completely agree. Totally alone. We can even stay in the room naked the whole time and leave the phone off the hook. That's a fucking deal right there."

CHAPTER TWENTY-THREE

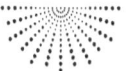

Damon

"$\mathcal{D}$oll, it'll be fine. Trust me."

Famous last words of a fool.

Our honeymoon was two weeks of pure bliss on some of the most beautiful beaches in the world. The crystal-clear water, the beautiful flowers, the lush vegetation, the perfect weather—we couldn't have custom-ordered a better vacation than the time we spent in Hawaii, lounging in the sand, soaking up the sun, and playing in the surf. But then we had to return to reality. And...

"You're not the one being put on modified bed rest with almost three months left before your due date." The forlorn expression on her face wasn't an exaggeration. My high-energy wife was suddenly told to sit down and stay put.

"I tried to tell you—"

"If you dare to say *I told you so* right now, so help me God, you'll see me become deranged right before your eyes." She cut her tense gaze up at me and waited for me to amend my original statement.

"I strongly suggested we wait until after the babies were born to make the trip to Maui. I'm afraid the extensive flight time may have been a contributing factor. You know, it's still possible the doctor could lift the restrictions after a couple of weeks—if you can behave until your next appointment."

"Well, I really don't have a choice except to behave, do I? All my furniture shopping will have to be finished online, or with your mom walking around the store while talking to me on Face-Time. I'll have to bring someone in to decorate the nursery because I can't do it myself now. All my plans just went down the drain.

"And he won't change his mind after a couple of weeks, but I don't think this has anything to do with our trip. Dr. Bowers had already warned me that this would probably happen around the seventh month."

She'd hit an energy spurt when we got back from our vacation. She suddenly wanted to clean, organize, and finish every room in the house. Immediately. The extended shopping sprees came to a screeching halt after our prenatal appointment one morning a week after we arrived back home. The doctor said she was only allowed on her feet no longer than the time it took to shower because of the weight of the babies and the increased chances of pre-term labor. Thankfully, our bedroom and the nursery were on the main level of our new home, because she also wasn't allowed to climb stairs.

"Now I'm regretting quitting my job just after we moved Geno's money to Maria. I could have at least worked at home, kicked back on the couch, and kept myself busy. I'm afraid my brain will turn to mush watching TV all day." She clicked the remote, changing the channel for the hundredth time in the last five minutes.

"Maybe Carrie could use some help with her business activities."

"Damon, that's a great idea. At least that would be interesting work. I can't infiltrate system security programs like she can, but I can handle the accounting from right here. I'll give her a call, and see what she has in the works."

"Tell her to get her ass over here. She's probably going a little stir-crazy from all the hours she's been working in her basement. Do you need anything before I head upstairs and handle some work, doll?"

"No, I'm good. Thanks for checking though, babe. Try not to worry about me while you're all the way upstairs today."

"You'll be down here with my sister all day. How can I not worry?"

"Good point. Love you."

Yeah, that made me feel so much better. I jogged to my office upstairs, grabbed my laptop, and returned to the great room. Jillian's eyes were glued to her watch when I walked back into the room.

"Forty-three, forty-four—you're late. You should've been able to make that trip in thirty seconds or less. You're already slipping and you've only been the Boss for a couple of days. What would Dad and Mama Lina say if they saw you now?"

"Wiseass. I'm not slipping—I didn't even know I was being timed. And Mama and Dad are already in Italy, enjoying their retirement. When will Carrie be here to entertain you?"

"She replied to my text and said she'll be here in about thirty minutes."

"Good. While I have your undivided attention, let's talk about the what we want to name our babies. We should pick out two of each so we're prepared, especially if they unexpectedly arrive early."

"I've been tossing a couple of names around in my mind, seeing how they fit. You know I adore you, so don't be upset over this, but I think every child should have his or her own name. No junior or Damon the second. Same goes for me."

"Fine with me. By the same token, there's be no naming them after our parents either. Deal?"

"Deal. Do you want to use my baby names book to help pick out names you like?"

I shook my head. "No, doll. I have a couple of ideas of my own, too. How do you suggest we proceed with finalizing the names?"

"I suggest...we write down our top picks, swap papers, and we'll use the ones I like best." She grinned from ear to ear, thoroughly enjoying her idea.

"How about...we wrestle for it, and whoever wins gets to pick the names?"

"Fine. We'll compromise, since you agreed to wait until they're born to find out if we're having girls or boys. When you have your list ready, we'll go through them together, cross out the ones we don't like, and then we'll figure out what to do with the names left."

"Why do I get the feeling you'll be running an extortion game on me?"

"Hmm. I'm not sure why you think that." She picked up a magazine and began thumbing through it, pretending not to notice my unconvinced expression.

"You're not fooling anyone, little missy. You're becoming more and more corrupt every day." I shook my head and folded my arms across my chest in a mock threat. But she knew I wouldn't lay a hand on her in anger, as proved by the giggle she unsuccessfully tried to suppress behind her magazine.

The alarm at the gate sounded, letting us know someone had keyed in the code and entered the property. Jillian perked up, dropped her magazine on the coffee table, and rushed to the front door as fast a woman pregnant with twins could move. Within a few minutes, my sister walked through the front door after giving Jillian a hello hug.

She had Lorenzo Sanfratello with her.

Even though I'd invited him to my wedding, I wasn't sure I'd ever get used to seeing him with my sister. A lifetime of disliking someone was hard to overcome within a matter of weeks.

Forgiveness never did come easy to me. Then I watched Jillian welcome him into our home without even a hint of a grudge on her part. Maybe I could give him a chance, after all.

"Come on in. Can I get either of you something to drink or anything?" Jillian used any reason she could find to get up and move around.

"No, you can't. I'll make myself at home and get our drinks. You three go sit outside by the pool, and I'll join you in a few minutes. Kick back in the sun and get off your feet before my brother has a stroke. That vein in his forehead is already popping out."

Jillian looked up at me then ran her finger over said vein. "Huh. Look at that. Imagine how protective he'll be of our kids."

"I'm glad you're amused. I've just added finding a housekeeper to my to-do list for today. She'll double as *your* babysitter when I'm away." I scooped Jillian up in my arms and started walking toward the patio with her. "Follow us, Lorenzo."

He chuckled under his breath from behind me. "Looks like married life suits you, Damon."

To the outside world, I was the same man I'd always been— fearless, in charge, and focused on the business side of the family. While he was inside my home, Lorenzo saw a side of me very few had experienced—and none of those people was outside of my immediate family. Watching me in the role of doting husband and concerned father must have been a culture shock for Lorenzo to witness.

"There's no doubt about that. You know, had I not met the most perfect woman in the world, I never would've known the first thing about marriage. Never wanted it, never even considered it until Jillian came along. She just had to run into one of my trucks on the expressway."

"Hey! Your truck sideswiped me—not the other way around. I'm an excellent driver. It's a good thing your guys were terrible drivers, though. Otherwise, we never would've met."

I sat her down on the lounge chair beside the pool before taking the one next to her, the large umbrella providing enough shade to keep us cool and comfortable in the late morning sun. Lorenzo sat at the table beside us and stared at the ground, his mind clearly preoccupied with something important.

"Let's hear it, Lorenzo. What is it you don't want to tell me?"

"What do you mean?" A classic deer-in-the-headlights expression covered his face, his eyes wide and unblinking and his jaw slack.

"Come on. Being able to read people when they're hiding something is why I'm so good at what I do. But you're not even trying to hide that you have something weighing on your shoulders. It's written all over you—from your face to your body language. Spit it out."

He leaned forward, putting his elbows on his thighs and looking me directly in the eyes. I had to give him credit for that, at least. "I want to talk to you about Carrie getting out of the family business. She and I have talked about it extensively, and we're both ready for a major change in our lives. If you can manage your business without her, we'd like to start our own legal business."

My genuine reaction was surprise—Carrie hadn't mentioned a word of this new plan to me. Jillian stared at Lorenzo for a moment as he waited for a reply before turning her gaze to me. She searched my eyes, looking for a clue of which direction I'd take, while not interfering with the family business decisions.

"She's my little sister, Lorenzo." I paused, noting the determination in his eyes didn't waver. "If that's what makes her happy, I'll fully support her. What business are you two going into?"

"Real estate—mostly commercial and high-end residential. I already have my broker license and Carrie wants to get her agent license, so we're starting our own agency. Of course, she'll also design and update our website. It's not like I need the money, but it's something I enjoy doing."

"Are you two getting married, Lorenzo?" Jillian asked, not bothering to hide the hope in her voice.

"No, nothing like that. We haven't moved past the friend zone yet. Vincenzo hasn't given us his blessing, so she won't risk more than just friendship right now."

"Why does everyone look so serious? What are you talking about?" Carrie joined us on the patio, carrying a tray with a pitcher of lemonade and four glasses of ice. She already looked like Suzy Homemaker, concealing any trace of the badass lurking just beneath the surface.

"We were talking about your new business venture. That sounds so exciting, Carrie! If there's anything I can do from here to help you get established, I'll be happy to do it. I'll be bored out of my mind being on bed rest for almost three months before the babies get here." Jillian stood long enough to pour our drinks while offering to lend her expertise, not missing a single opportunity to defy her doctor's orders.

Made me realize how she felt when I did the same to Matteo.

But I'd never admit that.

Carrie shot Lorenzo an irritated glance. "Damon, I wanted to talk to you about this myself, to explain why. I'm sorry you found out this way."

"It's fine, Carrie. As usual, I pushed the issue, not really giving him an option but to answer me. I'll tell you just like I told him—if that makes you happy, I'll support you. I'm not mad about it at all."

"Then you won't mind if I take your wife up on her offer to help me fill out all the legal paperwork, accounting, and human resources protocols?" Carrie purposely smiled, knowing Jillian wouldn't even give me a chance to reply before she jumped in.

"He won't mind if you use his wife in that capacity at all. Will you, babe?" Jillian turned to look at me with that daring gleam in her eye.

"No, I don't mind at all, as long as it keeps her off her feet so my babies can continue cooking in her little oven."

"Okay, I have to agree with my brother on this one. When you draw up your employment contract, please be sure to include a section on your punishments for putting my nieces or nephews in danger." Carrie sat beside Jillian on the lounge chair. "Tell me honestly, sis. Will helping us put too much pressure on you? I can hire someone else."

"Don't you dare. I need this distraction over the next couple of months, especially when Damon isn't here with me all day. I promise, I can do it all from my computer without a problem. Damon can move my office and everything I'll need to the main floor. I'll prop my feet up two hours in the morning and two hours in the afternoon. I won't take any unnecessary chances with my babies."

Carrie leaned in and hugged Jillian, the first fully contented smile that I'd seen in way too long covering her face. "I'm so excited for this, Jillian. I'll come over here and work with you when Damon's gone so you won't be bored alone. We'll keep each other company while you're on bed rest."

"Maybe I should reconsider this arrangement," I deadpanned.

"Not a chance, babe. We're already thick as thieves."

"That's exactly what I'm worried about, doll."

After having a good laugh, we settled into friendly conversation about anything and everything. The camaraderie between Lorenzo and me grew naturally over the course of the day, and I realized Carrie's feelings ran deeper than she showed. The way she looked at him, the occasional brushes of her fingers on his arm, the frequent references to things they'd done together.

I had a feeling we'd have a family meeting as soon as Mama and Dad returned from Italy. My little sister would be seeking Dad's approval sooner rather than later.

24

CHAPTER TWENTY-FOUR

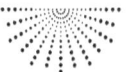

Jillian

J'd been counting down the minutes over the past couple of months, and the time had finally arrived. "Damon, wake up."

I lightly ran my fingers along his jaw, but he barely stirred. The scruff of his faded beard felt a little like sandpaper, only it was the sexiest sandpaper imaginable. If I could manufacture and sell it, women everywhere would suddenly become polishing enthusiasts.

"Babe, you need to wake up now." I called his name a little louder.

He was sleeping so soundly, I was trying not to startle him awake. Just a gentle nudge. But he'd stayed up all night putting two baby cribs together and making sure they were safe and sound. Something about the big, bad Marchetti Family Boss fighting with random crib parts and unclear directions made me feel all warm and fuzzy inside. He wouldn't accept help, and he wouldn't admit defeat.

I may have videotaped him in the act without his knowledge.

But I'd never confirm the existence of such a recording since I was supposed to be off my feet at the time.

Unable to resist his plump lips, I leaned down and pressed mine against them. A smile spread across my face when his hands reached for me and his lips responded. No matter how tired he was or how little sleep he had, there was one thing he was always ready to do. Maybe he had the right idea, considering what we were in store for later and how long we'd already had to wait. But I'd become more than uncomfortable with two small humans cohabitating inside my body, so I quickly pushed that thought away.

He pulled me closer to him, his touch gentle but still firm in his hold. He slid his hands across my body, and his eyebrows drew down in confusion.

"Why are you wearing clothes, doll? You know we always sleep in the nude."

"Yes, I do know that. But I'm dressed right now because it's almost time to meet our babies."

That made him open his eyes.

"It's time?" That panic mode I'd tried to avoid hit without warning. His eyes were wide, and he was already getting out of bed before I could answer.

"We have about an hour before we need to leave. You were in such a deep sleep, but I wanted to give you enough time to dress so we aren't rushed."

"I'll shower and be ready in record time. Are you okay? Is there anything I need to do for you first?"

"No, babe. Everything is packed and ready to go. I've been nesting like crazy for the last few months with the help of our housekeeper, even from the confines of the couch. The cribs were the final missing pieces that were driving me crazy because they were not ready until last night."

"I know, I know. Lesson learned—don't special order cribs from another country and expect them to be delivered on time. I won't do that for the next set of twins."

"That's not funny, Damon. We're not even joking about this happening again."

That mischievous smile of his flashed across his face, pulling me right back under his spell. Keeping me exactly where he wanted me. Good thing that was also where I wanted to be.

"I wouldn't be disappointed if we had another set of twins. How about triplets?"

"Get in the shower before I leave for the hospital without you." My threat was empty words, and we both knew it. There was no way I'd go through the delivery without him by my side.

At the strong suggestion of my obstetrician, we'd opted for a Caesarean section delivery. The twins were a good size and weight, but with my small stature, neither of them had turned. Dr. Bowers wasn't convinced they even had enough room for one of them to turn head-down.

Damon kissed my cheek before disappearing into the bathroom. Twenty minutes later, I was waiting in the den when he emerged, dressed and ready to go. He could barely contain his excitement. But me? I had a sudden and severe strike of terror and panic in the car on the way to the hospital.

"Let's go back home. I'm not ready for this." His fingers were laced with mine, and I squeezed them as I spoke. "How about two more weeks in Maui first?"

He glanced over his shoulder at me as he drove, confidence oozing from his every pore, and he squeezed back. "You got this, doll. *We* got this. In a few hours, we'll hold our babies, and you'll forget all about this moment of panic. You'll do great, you'll see."

We walked onto the labor and delivery floor together to check in, his hand on my lower back and his strength rolling off him and into me. My heart beat wildly, pounding against my rib cage. My pulse matched the rhythm, with the swishing of my blood echoing in my ears. I rubbed my enormous belly and felt the jab of feet or elbows against my hand. We would soon cradle two beautiful miracles in our arms.

We were only in my room for a few minutes before the obstetrician breezed in with a friendly smile. "Good morning. How's my favorite patient today?"

"I'm *extremely* pregnant, Doc. Like, uncomfortably pregnant. More pregnant than any other woman in history. Think you can do something about that?"

"Not to brag or anything, but I'm the only doctor in this room who can do something about that." Dr. Bowers turned his attention to Damon. "Come with me, Dad. Let's get you ready for surgery."

Damon hesitated for a moment, conflicted as to what he should do. Go with the doctor's command or stay by his wife's side? When his eyes met mine, I smiled reassuringly at him. "I love that you want to stay with me, but you have to go with the doctor, babe. We're going into the operating room, so you have to take off your street clothes, put on your scrubs, and sterilize your hands first."

"She'll be right behind us, Damon. We'll take good care of her. The nurses will prep her for surgery while you put on sterile scrubs. Then you'll have a first-row seat waiting for you when we walk into the OR."

Damon moved to my side, a sea of uncertainty in his chocolate brown eyes, and placed his palms on my cheeks. He kissed my lips so sweetly then dropped his forehead against mine. "My life is about to change for the better yet again because of you. I love you, doll. More than life itself, I love you."

He wiped the tears from my cheeks with the pad of his thumb. "I love you, Damon. We're about to be parents. We're about to meet our babies for the first time. Oh my God, I think I'm about to hyperventilate."

Damon chuckled as he stood upright again. "What'd I tell you? You'll do great. I'll see you in a couple of minutes. If you're not there when I walk into the room, I'm coming to find you. Don't think you can run off with my babies."

"Wouldn't dream of it. I can't run. You know the best I can do is a semi-fast waddle."

That moment of humor was just what we needed. Damon left with Dr. Bowers, and my nurse came in to wheel me down the hall and through the secure double doors of the operating suite. After I was prepped and given a spinal epidural, the nurse placed a rolling chair beside my head. Damon's front-row seat, right beside my head.

Dr. Bowers walked in first, with Damon close on his heels. My husband searched my face and picked up his pace until he was beside me again. His hands automatically clasped mine, holding on with a firm grip. The staff went over where Damon could and couldn't put his hands to keep a sterile environment, but he didn't seem to be listening. His eyes never left mine, and he didn't release my hand.

"Don't worry about me. I'm staying right here with Jillian until you're ready to hand me a baby."

"You're going to be a good dad. I can already tell. Did you bring a small digital camera with you? I can take a couple of snapshots of you two real quick." My nurse had obviously been in a lot of deliveries.

Damon pulled the small camera from his pocket and handed it to her. Then he put his face next to mine, and she snapped pictures of us wearing the sterile hats over our hair and huge smiles on our faces.

"Okay, Dad, put the camera away until the surgery is over. You'll have plenty of time to take baby pictures after we're finished here." She gave the camera back to him and went back to what she was doing.

"Do you have any family waiting in the hospital?" Dr. Bowers moved to the side opposite Damon. I could only see his head and neck over the sterile drape, but I had a good idea of what he was about to do.

"No, we asked them to wait until this evening to come visit. Jillian needs recovery time, and we need time alone with the babies before they get passed between my parents and siblings."

The time alone with the twins was important to both of us, but we also couldn't wait to show them off to Damon's family. Over the past few months, Carrie had become more like a sister to me than ever. We spent so much time together, setting up her company, talking about her refusal to admit her feelings for Lorenzo, and her excitement over finally being an aunt. Mama Lina and Dad returned home from their extended stay in Italy just in time for the big event.

In the operating room, a flurry of activity seemed to occur all at once, but Damon kept my attention on him. My lifeline. The man who held my heart and love captive in every way possible. He distracted me from the active surgery happening on the other side of that curtain. He talked to me about bringing our babies home to our still-new house, to their new nursery, to sleep in their new baby beds.

"They'll probably never get to sleep in those shiny new beds you spent all night putting together. You probably won't let them out of your arms long enough to put them down." I squeezed his hand tighter when a strange sensation hit my midsection. It wasn't painful, but it was obvious pressure.

He glanced away only for a second then his gaze swung back to mine. "You may be partially right about that, doll. But I don't think I'll be the only one who refuses to put them down."

The pressure I felt stopped momentarily, and I saw one nurse briskly walk away from us, toward the workstation she'd set up before surgery. Then I couldn't tear my eyes away, because when she stepped to the side to write something down, I saw a perfect little baby lying under the heating lamp. Another doctor stood by the nurse, cleaning the baby and completing the initial assessment.

"Damon." I could barely force his name out on a whisper. My breath had seized in my chest while my heart picked up speed.

"I know, doll. Eyes on me. You're cheating." He rolled in his seat to block my view with his gorgeous face. "We meet them together. Remember?"

I nodded, still unable to speak with the emotions overtaking my senses.

Then the pressure returned, and I realized what had caused the first sensation. The doctor had put his hands under the baby during delivery before the nurse took over to complete the assessment. I caught a glimpse of a second nurse walking quickly in the same direction as the first, only toward the second baby station where the pediatrician stood ready.

Our babies were waiting for us.

For Mommy and Daddy.

Tears flowed freely, but I didn't care. They were the best tears I'd ever cried. They held more happiness and love than I ever imagined, and I hadn't even held the first baby yet.

Two figures approached us, walking up behind Damon. With his sixth sense, he already knew, but he waited until they were close enough to us before moving his chair again.

"Mom and Dad, we'd like to introduce you to your son," the first nurse said.

"And to your daughter," the second added. They laid both babies in my arms, their heads resting on my chest, and Damon safely cradled all three of us in his arms.

"You're both so perfect." My voice was shaky and my eyes were watery, but the moment was flawless. Somewhere in the distance, I heard a camera snapping pictures, but I was too mesmerized by our two bundles of joy to think twice about it.

"Jillian." Damon whispered my name with a strained voice.

When I lifted my eyes to his, my breath was stolen yet again.

There, in my dangerous hit man's eyes, were tears of joy. I'd never seen him even close to tears before. Not when his best friend died. Not when his uncle betrayed him.

"Babe." One whispered word conveyed my complete understanding of how he felt.

"Mamas have that effect on the best of us."

"Do you have any names picked out for them yet?" Dr. Bowers peered over the drape as he continued to work on me.

"Madison and Mason." My reply answered the doctor's question, but I was addressing our beautiful babies.

"Dad, you come with the babies and me. It'll be a little while before Dr. Bowers is finished with Mom. You can stand guard over them while we finish the preventative measures. Mom will be in recovery for about an hour. If all goes as planned, you'll be back together very soon."

Before the nurse took Madison and Mason from my arms, I kissed their sweet baby cheeks. Even though I knew it would be only minutes apart, letting her take my newborns away was harder than I'd ever imagined. Damon left with them, close on the nurse's heels, so I knew they were safe.

"Relax, Jillian. They're in good hands, and so are you." Dr. Bowers winked, his eyes crinkling in the corners from his smile. "Rest now while you can. You'll have your hands full soon enough."

After my time in recovery, I was moved to a private room where Damon waited for me. He tried to convince me to take more time to rest before having the twins brought into the room with us, but I couldn't do it. I couldn't wait another minute to hold them, kiss their cheeks, and inhale their sweet baby scents. When the nurse finally arrived with two clear plastic bassinets, I was *almost* ready to jump out of the bed to get to them. However, my pesky incision kept me from moving too fast. That, and the pain medicine that was pumped into my IV every fifteen minutes or so.

Damon picked up Mason and handed him to me, taking extra care to help me hold him comfortably. Then he settled into the chair next to my bed with Madison, snuggling her close to his heart while she slept. My heart was full, overflowing with love for my perfect little family and all the adventures we had yet to come.

"Before you, I thought my life was complete. Then, without warning, life turned everything I thought I knew upside down. I realized my life had no real purpose or meaning before I met you. But you opened my eyes, Jillian. And my heart. You've made me a better man than I ever thought I could be. It's funny how life can turn on a dime, isn't it?"

While watching my husband, the notorious hit man and Marchetti Family Boss, cradle his swaddled newborn to his chest, I realized how right he was. Nothing about my life was as I'd originally planned or even remotely how I thought anything would be, but I wouldn't change places with anyone even if they offered me the world. Everything that happened brought us to the happiest moment of our lives. By Damon's side was exactly where I always wanted to be.

EPILOGUE

DAMON

"*H*ey." My whisper was intentionally extra low. I couldn't stop the smile that covered my face.

With the long feather firmly held between my finger and thumb, I lightly grazed it over his face while he slept. His eyes remained closed at first in a deep sleep, but that would soon change. I swept the tip of the feather across his nose, back and forth, until he began to rouse.

When he tried to lift his hand to swat the foreign object away, his whole body jerked from the effort. But he was tied up. With extra rope. And extra knots. So he couldn't move his arm.

That was when his eyes flew open.

"Hello, Marco. Did I wake you?"

"Damon? What the hell are you doing in my apartment? And why the fuck is this rope wrapped around me? How did you do this?"

"You're my brother, and you know I love you. But there is a certain slight against me you have to atone for now. You know I can't let it go—it's a matter of pride and fairness. I've told you for years you sleep too hard, Marco. That's dangerous in our line of work. Thankfully, it fits perfectly with my idea."

"Damon. I swear to God. If you do what I think you're planning..."

He didn't have a threat strong enough to finish his thought. No matter. He could think about it later. He'd have plenty of time and nothing else to do.

"Let's go, big brother."

I stood him up, his arms tied together from his wrists to his elbows and his legs tied together from his ankles to his knees, and secured a gag over his mouth. My other brothers stepped out of the shadows, ready to help. We picked him up, carried him to the door, and set him in the hallway of his apartment building—naked —then locked the door to his apartment behind us. One of my brothers pounded on the neighbor's door several times, leaving no doubt that someone waited in the hall.

We rushed down the stairs far enough to barely see over the landing. He ranted and raved behind the gag, jumping with both feet and hitting his door with all his weight, while we laughed our asses off. When we heard the click of lock opening on the apartment next door, we shushed each other and waited for the door to creak open.

At first, there was only a slit of an opening, barely ajar enough to look out. Then she caught a glimpse of his bare ass and miles of rope, and curiosity got the best of her. She stepped into the hallway, and we all held our breath. Marco hadn't lied—she was gorgeous. And she couldn't keep a straight face to save her life. She started laughing even harder than my brothers and I were.

"That must've been one hell of a party. My invitation must have gotten lost between your door and mine." She leaned against the wall, not even attempting to untie Marco without an explanation.

He pushed his hands down in front of his junk as far as the

ropes would allow and shook his head. The muffled sounds behind his muzzle amused her even more, but she stepped forward and removed it from his mouth.

"What was that?"

"There was no party, except the one my asshole brothers had at my expense."

"Ah, siblings. Aren't they great?" She cut her eyes over to the stairwell and caught us watching. Her smile widened, then she gave a conspiratorial wink. "Maybe you deserved this punishment. What'd you do to them?"

"Nothing compared to what I'm going to do when I get ahold of them. Uh, do you think you can untie me now?"

She hesitated for a moment, contemplating if she was ready for the joke to be over. He arched one eyebrow at her and she returned the gesture. No wonder he'd been so hot for this girl—she'd not only take his shit in stride, she'd serve it right back to him with a smile.

Game on, brother. Game on.

⁊⧉

SNEAK PEEK OF FINE LINE

PROLOGUE

A Terrible Idea
Nick

"FOR THE RECORD, THIS IS A TERRIBLE IDEA."

My director, Calvin Montgomery, locks his angry eyes on me while speaking to the handler who will be assigned to me—if Calvin approves the operation, that is.

"Sir, Special Agent Nick Tucker has repeatedly proved what a valuable asset he is in the field. He's one of our best. He has

463

outscored most of his peers in both field and psychological profile tests—even those who have previous undercover experience. We can't deny the man has the skills we need on this assignment. He deserves this chance."

"Yes, I can read the reports as well as you can, Jack. But Nick doesn't have any true undercover experience—not even on short-term cases, and the others do. Maybe they didn't score as well on the psych tests because they're already accustomed to living among the criminal element and acting as one of them. Did that ever occur to you? We both know how hard this life is even for a few months, but the case you're asking me to put Nick on is potentially a multiyear mission."

Calvin turns his penetrating gaze to me, constantly assessing my every reaction, looking for a weakness and a reason to deny my involvement. I've been in hectic firefights before and kept my cool, though. My time in the military, working for Steele Security, and providing private security for billionaire Dominic Powers before joining the DEA prepared me for most every perilous situation they can throw at me. Drawing on my inner strength, I keep my expression passive, my breathing regular, and my instinct to remind him he's driven a desk for too many years to remember what working in the field is actually like under wraps.

"You'll be cut off from everyone you know, Nick. You'll essentially divorce your entire life—for years. Your friends, your family, wife, girlfriend, boyfriend. *Everyone.* You hear me? And that's the easy part of the job. Even contact with Jack will be sparse, especially due to the group you'll infiltrate, so you'll be making decisions on the fly. Any outside affiliation will be scrutinized—and these guys won't ask questions first. They'll shoot you in the head and replace you with the next guy in line. I'm not convinced you truly understand what you'll have to do to be one of them."

"I can assure you, I do understand."

"Is that right? This UC op has been issued special permission to break the very laws you've sworn to uphold. Your psych profile shows a strong sense of duty and a penchant for following the rules to the letter. So, you'd be fine if they order you to force some young kid to sell drugs on the street corner and bring you every penny of the money he made? Then rough him up if he doesn't bring you enough?"

The visual that pops into my brain before I can stop it makes my heart rate increase instantly, the artery in my neck jerking and giving away my reaction.

"Or maybe it's not a him. Maybe it's a her. You'd willingly force a young woman into prostitution, selling her to any Joe Blow off the street, who'll do whatever the fuck he wants to do to her? You can make them believe you don't care about her at all, just how much money she brings in for getting her John's rocks off? What if that means her customer gets to beat the shit out of her just because he has mommy issues? I mean, as long as he doesn't kill her and she can perform for her next trick, what the fuck does it matter, right?"

My stomach churns with disgust, and the room around me turns red with my rage. But I tamp down those feelings inside my chest until they form a mangled ball full of drive and determination to see this through to the end.

"I'll do whatever the fuck I have to do to stop these bastards. The longer we sit here repeatedly arguing the same points and imagining hypothetical situations, the more time they have to commit those very crimes. Sir."

"I'm sure I don't have to remind you we're after the major charges to shut them down for good. Small-time hoods are a dime a dozen. We want the source—their suppliers. Local reports say this group is using a prescription drug that hasn't even cleared the FDA yet. It's highly effective and lethal in the wrong hands. That's in addition to the influx of opioids and other controlled substances from their Mexican drug cartel affiliation. We can't blow the entire operation because you feel the need to feed your savior complex over every sob story you hear.

Most of those women asked for it anyway—they probably even enjoy it."

"I'm well aware of what we're after and how to do my job." Inside, I'm seething; outside, I display a calm demeanor.

He's testing me, that much I know. His last comment was to gauge my knee-jerk reaction because that's exactly how this gang thinks. If Calvin approves my request for undercover work, the group I'll join will say and do a lot worse to me than my director has ever even thought about. If I can't handle my boss yanking my chain inside the comfort of his office in our secure, air-conditioned building, I have no business being an undercover agent where anything and everything can go wrong.

Will go wrong.

Something always does.

To stay alive, I have to think fast on my feet, improvise, and give an award-winning performance.

No time like the present to start earning a few of those golden statuettes.

"Sir, I can handle anything they throw at me. I've been in intense situations in my career, starting in the Army, through private details, and in my time with the DEA. I'm ready to take my career to the next level, and I need undercover experience to do that. This wasn't Jack's idea—I requested to be assigned to this case."

The muscles around Calvin's eyes contract, crinkling the skin until only small slits remain. He draws a slow circle around his mouth with his thumb and forefinger before resting his chin on his hand. With my gaze locked on to his, I wait for him to make his decision. The first one to blink will be Calvin, because I am all in.

"All right, Special Agent Tucker, you've convinced me to give you a chance. On one condition."

"What condition is that?"

"If at any time you suspect your cover is blown, or your gut warns you that something is off and they've turned on you, get out of there. To hell with the case and the charges. Call Jack, get to the safe house, do whatever it takes to extract yourself from the situation."

"I appreciate your concern, sir, but it won't come to that. I'll see this through till the end."

"All right. We'll get your name, background, and criminal history established. Congratulations, Nick. You have the distinct honor of pledging to one of the most notorious motorcycle gangs in the world. The Devil's Dominion rules their LA territory with an iron fist. I only hope they don't turn that fist on you."

"Thank you, sir. I won't let you down."

Six Months Later

"ARE YOU SURE YOU'RE READY TO APPROACH THEM, NICK? NO NEED to rush things." Jack paces in his kitchen while I sit at the table and finish my coffee.

Jack Collins fits the bill for a retired biker. He is a handler, but he's curated his entire life around the motorcycle club lifestyle to avoid arousing any suspicions. He hasn't pledged to any outfit, but he is known by enough bikers that no one questions his presence, and no one crosses him. He has the don't-fuck-with-me air down pat.

His long black and gray hair is pulled back in a low ponytail. His sun-weathered skin bears the ravages of years on the open road—the deep-set wrinkles, the sunspots, the year-round dark tan. His brown eyes are keen, assessing a man and his intentions with a quick glance. The skin on his hands matches his face, but his grip is as strong as a man half his age. The long span of his career gives him advantages others could only hope to attain one day.

"It's time, Jack. You're my handler, you know I'm ready, and you know that shit is escalating out there. My hair has grown out, along with my beard. All my ink is finished—nothing overly distinguishable but still believable. My criminal background is airtight, and my stints in San Quentin and Pelican Bay legitimize my badass felon status."

"You can't use words like *legitimize* around these guys, Nick." Jack scrubs his hand down his face.

"I can talk real dumb too, Jack. Like I ain't got no schooling or nothing."

"Make fun of this all you want, Nick. But I'm telling you, these guys have a grittiness about them, a certain way they talk, a language all their own. It's a combination of the motorcycle gang lingo and prison slang."

"Trust me, I got this. I've mastered how they speak, the motorcycle gang terms, and the prison slang. I've memorized my background and rehearsed how I became a badass ex-convict, looking to join the baddest MC club around. One point that is pure genius on your part is showing I was part of a Tijuana-based gang before I was sent to prison. Thanks for that."

"Anything I can do to keep you from having to murder someone as part of your initiation. Because that's what they usually require—and could still order you to do it. But we'll cross that bridge when we have to. If you can patch in, you won't have to do the lowly probie bullshit. That'll at least give you a leg up in earning their trust and working your way up the chain faster than most.

"If you have to improvise and add anything to your history, don't forget to tell me immediately. We can build your experience around whatever you need, but it could take a little time to get it on paper. And don't say gang. You know how one-percenters feel about that word."

"Striking the word gang from my vocabulary now. And I'll try to keep the improvisation to a minimum, but I'm sure it'll come up. My documented history is solid, but that doesn't account for the things I never got caught doing. If you happen to have any former gang members in your back pocket, that would be useful too."

"I'll see what I can do. You never know, this old dog may still have a few tricks you don't know about."

One thing about Jack Collins, he always has another trick up his sleeve no one else knows about. How he stayed one step ahead of the agents under his charge when he went weeks without hearing from them is a mystery in our world. He takes his job home with him every night, and the safety of his agents is his first priority. I know I am in good hands.

"Thanks for the coffee. I'm heading back to my dinky little apartment to get into character. They're having a party at their clubhouse tomorrow night, so I'll use that opportunity to make my presence known."

"Good luck, kid. Don't die."

"That's the nicest thing you've ever said to me, Jack." I smile over my shoulder as I leave his bachelor pad and climb onto my bike.

My new life waits for me, in the gritty, dirty underbelly of the criminal world. Getting the approval for this level of undercover work is a boost to my ego and a rush to my senses. The heightened danger, constantly surveilling my surroundings, and testing my ability to decipher friend from foe within a matter of seconds will take my career to the next level.

I feel as if I've found my purpose in life. Finally.

Major Mistakes
Savannah

THE WOMAN STARING AT ME LOOKS FAMILIAR, BUT I DON'T KNOW

her. Not anymore anyway. Her red hair is longer than when she was younger. Her deep green eyes hold so many secrets, ones she'll never tell. She's also much thinner than she used to be—a telltale sign of stress and depression settling in over the long haul. The sad fact is, I used to know her very well. But now she's only the outer shell of the vibrant, bubbly personality I remember from just a couple of years ago. The light in her eyes is dim now, barely perceptible even when I'm searching for it.

"When did this happen, exactly? How did I become *this* woman?" I stare into the hollow green eyes reflected in the mirror, talking to myself. Again.

A loud bang on my apartment door abruptly ends my one-sided conversation. My heart drops, and a groan escapes from my throat. Dread covers me like a lead blanket. There's only one person that can be...the one person I really don't want to see, much less spend the evening around. But I don't have a choice. I'm trapped, like a frightened, timid animal in a cage.

After removing the door chain and unlocking the multiple bolts I had installed, the door swings open before I can even grab the knob.

"Why the fuck do you have the door locked like that? Who are you hiding in here?" Butch pushes past me, moving from one room to the next through my apartment as he searches for the invisible man.

"There's no one here except me. Just like last time. And the time before that. You know I always keep all the door locks in place when I'm here alone."

It's a phobia I have—an intense fear that drives me to check the locks several times before going to bed every night. He knows this about me, because he's complained about it every time he's stayed at my apartment. Thankfully, that hasn't happened in a very long time.

He stomps toward me in his heavy leather boots, the ones he wears every day because they best protect his feet and ankles while he's riding his motorcycle. It's strange how what I initially thought was intriguing, dangerous, and sexy about him when we met are the very traits that make me want to run away and start a new life somewhere else today.

I just haven't figured out how to get away from him yet.

"Pack all your shit. We're leaving."

"What?" I whirl around on my heel and stare at him, completely dumbfounded.

"We're moving. Prez is sending me and a couple of other guys to DC to induct a smaller club into ours. We have to try them out, see if they're worthy enough to wear the Devil's Dominion colors. This is my chance to show him I'm officer material and get on the voting ballot to move up in the club. I've been waiting years for this day."

The only thought in my mind is that my opportunity to get away from him is finally here. The day I've been waiting to come for far too long. There's no way I can move from LA to DC—they're at completely opposite ends of the country. Literally from one coast to the other. My entire life is here in LA, including my job and the few friends I had before I started seeing Butch.

Maybe my friends will take me back when I get rid of him.

"That's great news for you, Butch. I'm glad the president finally sees your potential in the club, and I hope they make you an officer soon. But I can't just up and move across country with you. My job is here—my entire career I've worked years to establish. I also have a lease on this apartment I can't just break."

I'm listing every logical reason I can think of, no matter how lame it will inevitably sound to him. He doesn't care about excuses—he only cares about results. More specifically, he only cares about the results he wants to see.

"Wouldn't that just fucking thrill you? Wouldn't you just love for me to go across the fucking country for the next six months and leave you here alone so you can fuck every swinging dick that crosses your path? Of course you're going with me, you stupid

471

bitch. Who the fuck do you think is gonna drive the truck behind us and haul our shit across the country? All our stuff won't fit on our fucking bikes, you moron. Now, pack your shit like I said."

With his final command, he shoves me and slams my head into the wall, catching the edge of the doorframe with the full blunt force of the impact. Even with my eyes closed, I can feel the room spinning. Nausea settles into my gut and the bile churns, threatening to work its way up my throat. The pain in my skull makes me whimper. His only reply is a disgusted huff.

"Now, rent the fucking moving truck, pack your shit, and let's go to DC before I'm too old to ride my damn bike anymore."

After I hear the door open, he hurls one last threat at me. "If you even think of trying to get out of this, I'll kill every single person you love. All your fucking friends from the hospital. Your mom. Your sister. Try me, bitch. I dare you."

He stomps out, the chains on his boots and belt clinking with every step, growing fainter until I hear the engine of his bike roar to life. Funny, or not funny, how it reminds me so much of his own terrible roar. After he rides away, I open my eyes and gingerly move off the wall where he left me.

The door to my apartment is standing wide open.

He knows my paralyzing fear of leaving the door unlocked. Irrational or not, it's still there.

I want to rush to lock every bolt, but the first step in that direction reminds me of my head injury. The disorientation, nausea, and I are not new friends. With slow movements, I lift my hand to feel the goose egg forming behind my ear. I'm not even surprised to find blood on my fingers when I lower my arm again.

My walk to the door is slow as I calculate each step and how much farther I have to go. My chest is heaving from the building anxiety. When the door is finally locked—every bolt is secured and every chain is in place, my pounding heart slows enough so I can breathe normally again.

After I put a cold compress on the back of my head, I slide

onto the couch and carefully lie back on the throw pillows. I waste a few minutes daydreaming about never leaving my apartment again, never unlocking the door again, while waiting for the throbbing in my head to subside. As often as I dream about this, I should've already found the master plan for leaving Butch in my dust.

Since nothing else I've tried so far has worked, I pick up my laptop and rent the moving van as the asshole commanded. A one-way trip to Washington, DC coming up, sans the excitement a cross-country trip should elicit. The only way I can describe how I feel about what I just did is I'm positive I've just signed my own death certificate.

In fact, the longer I'm around Butch, the more I realize that outcome is inevitable—it's only a matter of time. The odds there will come a day when it's him or me increase with our every encounter. I let my eyes drift up to the ceiling, staring at nothing in particular while thinking about my situation. My job as an emergency room nurse is stressful and adrenaline-filled, but it pales in comparison to a single interaction with Butch. In an ironic twist, I would be required by law to report potential domestic abuse if one of my patients presented with the same signs I bear.

He wasn't always like this. When I first met him, the tall, muscular, brooding man was much sexier. His brown hair was longer than other men I'd dated before, but it gave him an edgier appearance. Eyes so brown they're almost black sparkled with playfulness and teasing. But it was all a charade—he was pretending to be someone he wasn't. And he was so good at it for so long—long enough to ensure I fell for him. Long enough to ensure I was caught in his trap. When I look at him now, all I see is the ugliness inside. Any desire that once burned for him has long been doused.

Thankfully, those nights with him have dwindled to an occasional visit—and only when he needs me to do something for him.

He disappeared for a couple of weeks one time, and I thought he'd found someone else to prey upon. Selfishly, I hoped he had—but then I immediately felt bad for wishing him on anyone else. Unfortunately, one day, he simply walked back into my apartment as if he'd been here all along. No explanation. No questions.

His visits have been sporadic since that day. Usually when he's drunk and looking for somewhere to crash after a night out with his friends. He passes out in my bed, and I sleep on the couch, unable to stand being in the same room with him any longer than absolutely necessary. His insane jealousy makes no sense to me whatsoever. We are not a couple and haven't been for a very long time, yet he calls me every name in the book when he accuses me of seeing other men.

Not that I'm the least bit interested in even trying to date. I still can't get rid of the last mistake I made.

Now he shows up and demands I move across the country with him. I'm having a hard time wrapping my head around this one. It's not like either of us wants to be with the other. That much is clear. But I believe he'll make good on his threat to kill everyone I love. In fact, I have no doubt he will.

One problem at a time, though. Before we even reach the East Coast, I have to survive the actual 3,000-mile trip with him and his buddies. That should be fun—waiting for them to pass out on the bed from the abundance of drugs and alcohol so I can grab the extra linens and sleep on the nasty floor. But I prefer the floor over touching any of them. Maybe I'll sleep in the truck...with the doors locked...under the guise of protecting our belongings.

A few hours later when I walk into the hospital for the night shift, my heart is heavy, and all my feelings show on my face. My coworker takes one look at me, and her face falls.

"What has Butch done now?" Stella puts her hands on her hips and draws in a deep breath. She already knows she won't like the answer.

After explaining the series of events and the commandment

Butch issued, I watch her face for the disappointment I know will come. On one hand, I completely understand it, and I was even the same way...before I became the abused and battered victim. Life is now divided into two sections: BB and AB. Before Butch and After Butch.

Before Butch, I said no man would ever lay a hand on me and live to tell about it.

No man would ever abuse me in any way—physically, mentally, or verbally. I would leave him in a heartbeat.

No man would replace my job, my dreams, or my friends—the sacred relationships I'd always held so dear.

After Butch, I withdrew from my friends.

My dreams took a back seat.

Self-esteem was what others had, but not me.

I miss the Before Butch version of myself. But now I feel as if I'm in too deep and can't claw my way out. One thing I've realized after looking back over the past eighteen months is none of this happened suddenly. He chipped away at the very core of me little by little, bit by bit, day by day. Until the very spark that made me *me* disappeared. And I allowed him to do it.

It's my fault.

If I'd been stronger, smarter, faster...maybe I would've seen the warning signs for what they really were.

Huge signs that flashed "Bridge Out Ahead."

But his apologies were so sincere at first. So heartfelt. He was remorseful and promised those bad things would never happen again.

He'd drunk too much. He always liked to fight when he drank. Such a man's man.

He was under too much stress. Work was a constant sore spot. His coworkers or his boss never liked him. They always made up a reason to get rid of him.

Of course, that was before I found out the truth about him. Before I understood what being in a one-percenter motorcycle club really meant. When I made the mistake of calling his club a gang during a heated argument, I saw stars after he backhanded me for disrespecting his brothers.

That was the day the apologies stopped and the real threats began. Old ladies didn't leave bona fide club members. Ever. It wasn't the woman's decision whether to stay or go. She just did what she was told and lived with what she got. He warned me to be glad I wasn't a sheep—one of the women they pass around to each other indiscriminately, using at will for any hedonistic pleasure they wanted to indulge in at the moment.

Ignoring the pleas and concern in Stella's eyes, I continue updating her on my plans. "I'm turning in my two-week notice tonight. That date was the earliest I could get a moving truck big enough for my stuff plus theirs anyway. I'm so glad it has a towing hitch for my car too."

I leave Stella, disappointed expression and all, to start my rounds and focus on the emergency cases. I wish I could stop time so my shift would never end. But working in busy emergency rooms always makes the time go by faster than the slower pace, comparatively, on the medical-surgical floors. Before I know it, the sun rises and a new day dawns, and I have to face the unpleasantness of packing all my belongings.

Two weeks will pass in the blink of an eye.

࿔

The Initiation
Nick

"You ready for tonight?" Jack's serious expression gives away his thoughts. Unusual for him after the years of handling undercover officers.

"I'm as ready as I'll ever be." I slide my arm into my cut and complete the persona of Renegade.

Turns out, the idea to convince them I was part of a Tijuana-based club was a stroke of genius on Jack's part. The Devils' ties to the Mexican cartel are already in place, but with my joining them, the full backing of the cartel is implied, giving them more muscle than they already have. An ATF agent has been working a few members of that gang over the last several years, so interagency cooperation kicked in, and my alibi was instantly airtight. With my background in prison and ties to the Mexican cartel-sanctioned motorcycle club firmly in place, I approached the Devils with an offer they couldn't refuse.

The Devils' already long reach just increased with no effort on their part. At least as far as their reputation with rival clubs is concerned. Keeping those other clubs at arm's length while the Devils conduct business is vital to maintaining their dominance in the territory. When the club president realized the possibilities I could bring, the dollar signs in his eyes were so bright, they rivaled the neon signs of the Vegas strip.

Headbanger, also known as Bobby Blalock, is the club president. He has a rap sheet longer than my leg, along with countless other crimes he's never been charged with committing. Or ordering. His officers and many other members are all too eager to carry out plans on his behalf. They're brothers in colors, but they're also all vying for the attention of one man. The one who can make or break them in the club.

Tonight is initiation for a few new prospects who are on their way to becoming full patch members. The ceremony to patch in is a big deal to these guys—it seals their identity and their place in the family.

I've been riding with the Devils for the past two weeks. Hanging out with them in the clubhouse provides a completely unique perspective on the inner workings of a notorious outlaw gang. Some of the guys have done hard time, and it's a miracle most aren't still in prison. I've had to bite my tongue way too many times already—something my director knew about me before he approved the assignment.

My moral compass always points due north. Always.

Their skewed sense of right and wrong doesn't mesh well with me. In fact, we're like oil and water at the very core. The only peace I have is when we're on the open road, the wind whipping around me, and the road rushing by under my wheels. The sense of freedom on a motorcycle is the sole only thing I have in common with these guys. It's the only time we're even remotely on the same page.

The long ride to the initiation grounds in the hot, arid desert of Southern California gives me time to get myself back into character. Jack stressed over and over how I have to be part of the group to avoid suspicion. Because of the high stakes, I've been given special clearance to break the laws I've sworn to uphold. But there are oaths I've taken, and I have no intention of reneging on them.

There are lines I refuse to cross.

There are rules I refuse to break—even for the greater good and the thrill of closing the case.

But I have to act like there are no lines I won't cross. To be convincing, I have to put Nick Tucker away and be Renegade to the bone. In my mind, I have to think of Renegade as a completely different person. It's the only way I can pull this off.

He's an ex-con, fresh out of a maximum-security prison, and that has to be my persona. As a convicted felon on parole, I can't legally cross the border to ride with my old club because the pigs will nab Renegade immediately. I can't exactly drive my motorcycle through the underground tunnels to cross the border. Of course, as Renegade, I have the contacts, so I could find an illegal way, like a fake passport or hidden in a caravan. But I'd take that risk only for a golden opportunity, a sure thing.

Renegade has talked a good game in his two weeks with the Devils. Tonight, Prez will present me with the final piece of my colors—the top rocker panel for my cut—because I scored the largest shipment of meth and negotiated the best deal for the club he's ever seen. Compliments of my DEA and ATF friends.

When I finally roll up to their private hideaway in the desert, my Renegade character is in full swing. After grabbing a couple of beers from the cooler, I stroll over to where the officers are hanging out with a few of the lifers—the men who have been part of the club for so long, they aren't required to attend all church meetings and outings anymore, but they're every bit a part of the club as any other member. They can come and go as they please, though most stay more than they leave. This is the only life they know.

"Good of you to bring me a beer, Renegade." Axle reaches for one of the longneck bottles I'm carrying, so I hand it over without a fuss. He's one of the most respected lifers in the group. His experience combined with his naturally level head makes for a powerful ally in a group of trigger-happy thugs. Despite Axle's advanced age and lack of officer status, no man in this group wants to tangle with him.

"You know I always got your back, Ax."

"Back atcha, kid." He takes a long pull from the bottle but keeps his eyes locked on mine. "Heard about that big score you got for us. I'm impressed—and I don't impress easily. Good job."

"Appreciate it, man. Just glad I could help out."

"Well, well, look who's coming our way. The new prospects are here, and they brought their offerings to the Devils with them." Nutcrusher, the club vice president, stands and rubs his hands together, eager to get down to business.

When I glance over my shoulder at the approaching prospects, my stomach drops to my knees and my empty hand curls into a tight fist.

Their "offerings" are new sheep, women being shoved into the midst of the already rowdy scene. The three prospects are each forcing a woman to walk in front of them. The women alternate from stumbling ahead a few steps to digging their heels in to try to stop, only to be shoved from behind and start the process all over again. Their eyes are wide and full of fear. Their faces are tear-stained and their hair is disheveled—and not from the ride here since they arrived in the club van.

I'm positive these three women have already been used as offerings before the new patches ever brought them to meet the brothers. Before I consciously realize I'm moving, my feet develop a mind of their own and take a step forward. Then I feel a hand on my shoulder, holding me back.

"What you see tonight will test your mettle, boy. You've never been around anything like this, I can already tell. But I guarantee, if you blow your cover now, you'll never see anything at all, ever again."

Shocked by his words, I whip my head around and meet Axle's knowing gaze.

"Use it, kid. Use everything you have to see and do as a member to take them down. As shitty as it sounds, you can't save these women and do what you came here to do at the same time. Keep your eyes on the end goal, son, and make them pay for their crimes when it's all said and done."

"What are you talking about, Axle?" He knows. We both know he knows. But I'll be damned if I'll blow my own cover.

"I'm CIA, Nick Tucker from the DEA family. I've been on this case for a long time, waiting for my foreign target to make his move so I can take him down. I told you, I got your back."

"The CIA can't operate on US soil, Ax. Everyone knows that."

His grin resembles one connected to an inside joke. Everyone else is clueless, and one person holds all the aces in his hand. "Sure we don't. I'm on loan to whichever agency wants to take the credit for the bust when it goes down. If you're still here when it happens, maybe that'll be the DEA."

Before I can reply, the shrill shriek of a woman's scream combined with ripping fabric fills the air, making my guts churn with disgust. Any man who would lay a hand on a woman in anger or abuse is no man at all. He's a pussy who knows he couldn't stand toe-to-toe with a real man.

The crowd that gathers around the three women—to watch, to encourage, or to participate—are the worst of the underworld. Preying on the defenseless and taking advantage of those who are hanging on by a thread as it is.

"Come with me, Renegade. This is as good as this scene gets. It's all downhill from here, and I don't think you can stop yourself from intervening yet." Axle guides me away from the ruckus.

I can still hear their pleas to stop. Their screams that echo through the desert air. Their cries for someone to please help them...to make it stop.

But I do nothing.

What kind of man does that make me?

"When they finish with the girls, they'll take them back to the clubhouse, and the club doctor will patch them up. They'll use them as sheep, or they'll cycle them into the prostitution ring and run them on the streets. They're not easy on them, but they don't permanently damage them either. Headbanger has a strict rule on that part since it affects his cash flow."

"Axle, your explanation doesn't help me one fucking bit. Do you even hear yourself? Of course they're permanently damaged now. Maybe not in the way you meant, but they still are." He nods in understanding, and he knows he can't say much more to justify what we've witnessed. "Where did they get those girls? Did they kidnap them?"

"No. They pick up hitchhikers or strays. Bring them into the family. Give them food, a place to sleep, and the protection of a notorious motorcycle club. But they expect the girls to earn their keep one way or another. This may be the first time you've ever seen this, but it won't be the last. It won't even be the worst thing you've seen by the time your undercover operation ends."

The silence between us only seems to amplify the mixture of screams and catcalls behind us.

"Talk to me, Axle. Tell me about life in the CIA. Were you in the service? Anything, man. Talk about the fucking weather. I don't care."

"This gets easier, kid. You'll learn to compartmentalize shit like this. Picture those assholes in prison orange, enduring the same fate they're subjecting those girls to right now at the hands of a big, angry brute in their cell, where they have nowhere else to run. Then make that your end goal and sole mission in life. Find what gets you through the rough spots one day at a time. Your assignment will be over before you know it. Then you can put all this bullshit behind you."

I don't see that happening.

Read the rest of FINE LINE free with KU!

ACKNOWLEDGMENTS

This part is the hardest part of the book to write because I don't want to leave anyone out or make anyone feel unappreciated. I am so grateful for everyone who supports me in this endeavor. Singling people out for their specific support is my way of saying an extra special THANK YOU for their unwavering help.

First and foremost, I want to thank my Lord and Savior for His continued forgiveness of a sinner.

To my husband – I love you. Thank you standing beside me and helping me every step of the way.

Readers – I am so grateful for each and every single one of you! Without your constant support and willingness to shout from the rooftops about your favorite books, none of these characters would have a chance to live, even for a moment, in this fictional world we love so much. From the bottom of my heart, thank you for everything!

Bloggers – I know how much work goes into what you do for free, to support others, to share the word of new releases and books you love. I just want you to know I appreciate you so much!

Special friends – Michelle Dare, T.K. Leigh, & Gina Whitney, I'd be lost without your friendship!

My beta team – You yell, cry, and threaten me with almost every book—and I love you for it!!! Thank you for your time, your input, and your loyalty. Beth, Dana, Becca, Cheryl, Chelle, Meghan, Kelly, Rachel, Heather, Crystal, Christy, Brittani, & Tabitha—all my love to you!!!

Tabitha – thank you for always standing by my side, helping in any and every way, and giving your honest opinions. I know I can always count on you!

Lisa Hollett, with Silently Correcting Your Grammar – my editor and my friend, thank you for all your help, the last minute penciling me in, the witty messages that always make me laugh, and your honest feedback as a reader and a professional.

Deena Rae, with EBook Builders, thank you for making my baby gorgeous…always on short notice!

Dana Leah, with Designs by Dana, thank you for the making my covers gorgeous, being so patient with everything you do, and being such a wonderful person!

ABOUT THE AUTHOR

A.D. Justice is the award-winning USA Today bestselling author of the Steele Security Series (Wicked Games, Wicked Ties, Wicked Nights, Wicked Intentions, Wicked Shadows), the Crazy Series (Crazy Maybe, Crazy Baby), the Dominic Powers series (Her Dom, Her Dom's Lesson), the Immortal Obsessions series (Immortal Envy), and a few stand-alone romance novels, such as Saving Grace, Completely Captivated, Just One Summer, Envy, and Intent.

When she's not writing, she's spending time with her own alpha male character in their North Georgia mountain home. She is also an avid reader of romance novels, a master at procrastination, a chocolate sommelier, a twister of words, and speaks fluent sarcasm. An avid animal lover, A.D. Justice has two horses, two dogs, and three cats.

While the primary focus of her books has been romantic suspense, she has expanded into different sub-genres of romance. Stay tuned to read what she has in store for you!

Connect with her online!
Newsletter
Facebook Reader Group
Website

facebook.com/adjusticeauthor

instagram.com/adjbooks

bookbub.com/authors/a-d-justice

BOOKS BY A.D. JUSTICE

Steele Security Series

Wicked Games (Book 1)

Wicked Ties (Book 2)

Wicked Nights (Book 3)

Wicked Intentions (Book 4)

Wicked Shadows (Book 5)

Crossing Lines Series

Fine Line (Book 1)

The Crazy Series

Crazy Maybe (Book 1)

Crazy Baby (Book 2)

Crazy Love (FREE Short Story)

Dominic Powers Series

Her Dom (Book 1)

Her Dom's Lesson (Book 2)

The Vault

Warning, Part One

Warning, Part Two

Warning, Part Three

Immortal Obsession

Immortal Envy (Book 1)